DAMAGED

A REBIRTH NOVEL

BECCA VINCENZA

Copyright © 2016 Becca Vincenza

Cover done by: Airicka Mystical Creations
Editing by: Onica Editing
Beta Read: Dawn Yacovetta
Proof Read by: Melanie Williams

THE REBIRTH SERIES:

Damaged

Healed

Stolen

STANDALONES:

Hexed Hearts

MERCENARIES FOR HIRE:

Freelance

Hired

Dedication:

To my family and friends - my friends who are more family than anything else.

Acknowledgements

I have to be frank, this is going to be hardest part of the whole damn book. There are a ton of people that I have to thank. And I don't want to offend anyone if you aren't part of this but felt like you were a huge part of it. So sorry if I forgot you.

First and foremost I have to thank Anthony Onica for taking on this huge hurtle of re-editing this beast for me. I have never felt more proud of this book. And for that I will be forever in your debt.

I have to thank both Andrea and Anna for being my friends, being my support in person, and helping me through the very beginning stages of this book. Well, actually they were there when I was writing in high school, reading my stuff, and even editing me then. You ladies are my friends from home, and my life-preservers.

I have to send a special—so very special—thank you to Stephanie Constante. A friend that I met and emailed for a month or two until we moved over to Facebook and chat at least once a day. You, my dear, are one of the biggest reasons I decided to do this. And I can never thank you enough for being there during the beginning of Damaged, when I would message you giving you only bits and pieces, but helped me all the same.

To Hannah Pole, my love, who I instantly clicked with, though you weren't there for the very beginning, you supported me the moment you found out and have gone over and beyond with keeping me sane.

My beta readers: Melissa Haag—I cannot thank you enough, you really went over and beyond what I was ever expecting. Nanette Del Valle Bradford, Crystal Allmon, Janelle Stalder, Nellysa, and Jaime Radalyac which all of you ladies contributed so much to Damaged, and so much support to me. A special thanks to Dawn to read this after the re-re-re-edits, and is my personal rock star. Thank you all, you are all my personal heroes, and I love you so much.

My awesome support system, my girls. I am more than certain you know who you are; I can't thank you ladies enough. Airicka Phoenix, Kimberly Schaaf, Terri Dion, Kathy Pegg Eccleston, Mary Unterstab, and there are so many I could make a book of people I want to thank.

A really special thanks goes to Jennifer Burkhalter, Ethan Gregory, and Stacey Rourke who both loved this book before its major re-edit and have been unwavering in their support. Who have helped me keep my sanity, which is much appreciated, during this process. Also supplied me rum ... Stacey.

And lastly, thank you. Yup, you who is reading this right now. Thank you for picking up this book and thinking to yourself, this sounds kind of awesome, so yes I do want to read this. I hope for you this does what reading does for me. I hope this takes you away from the world for just a bit, and lets you experience something truly unique.

Damaged

Prologue

Ruled by a council of Elder Races, the paranormal world existed in a state of peace. At this time, true love was a gift given freely from the gods to the paranormals, who found their true matches because of it. But when the Elder Races decided it was time for the paranormal races to take their place in a largely human world, to emerge from the shadows and live side by side with the humans, the other races disagreed. They turned against the wisdom of the Elders, broke into five main clans, each competing for influence and power, with the humans not-so-innocently caught in the middle.

The resulting uprising attempted to wipe out the Elder Races. To usurp their rule completely. And when the Elder Races were finally believed to be destroyed, there was no one left to stand up to the families that ruled the paranormal clans. Where there is power and desire, rivalries become poisoned by desperation and violence. The paranormal world has been in perpetual unrest since creation of the clans, but soon the scales will be tipped.

Soon everything will change.

Chapter 1

AUDREY

Three hundred and sixty-five days in a year.

Multiply that by four.

Add by one—the leap year.

One thousand four hundred and sixty-one days.

In four minutes, minus thirty seconds, it will be one thousand four hundred and sixty-two.

I did not sigh. I did not cry. I was only mystified at how something I never had ever missed before was like a hole in my heart.

The first year, I craved touch like food. The second year was blinded with a hunger so fierce that I knew only one thing: I would die without touch, surely as I would without water. Another year passed. In the third year I had disentangled myself from the madness that had infected me the year before. I convinced myself that a touch, that any form of contact, really, wasn't worth it. By the fourth year I accepted those lies. It wasn't easy. Not with hunger gnawing at my sunken gut and my body wasting away. My new form unsettled me.

This year, I wouldn't cave. I wouldn't close my eyes and pretend that different arms held me close. Held me together. I wouldn't do it. I peeked through the matted and tangled mess of my hair. The clock on the wall, the only decorative piece in my room, moved slowly. The red second arm dragged its way around the clock face.

Ten seconds left … *I'm fine* … Nine … *I don't need comfort* …

Eight. *Another year* … That red arm hesitated … Seven. *Another year.*

Six … *My hands have a will of their own* … Five. *No, they don't* … Four. *I am fi—*

A wailing noise pierced the air. My hands went to my ears. It was unceasing. Were they playing with me now? Was my fifth year to begin so cruelly? Maybe this year I *would* surrender. It might be worth it for a lingering touch, a simple brush of another's arm against my own. At this point, I'd even take a lingering stare.

No, the thought occurred like a reflex. *Not a stare. Not that. Anything but a stare.*

The piercing noise continued. I twisted my torso as a whimper escaped my lips. The sound was painful in my ears. It was overwhelming. I clawed, clutched, and plugged—anything to escape the sound. My wrists brushed my cheek. There were tears there. I'd thought those had long dried up.

I shrieked as the door burst open, cowering, pushing myself closer to the white walls surrounding me. Making myself smaller meant there was less area for them to hurt. Less places they could leer.

My torn hands twined deeper into my hair, muffling the sound. My elbows blocked my view as I tucked them in. Breathing heavily, I lowered my right elbow a bit to search for the source of the new sound.

He had already invaded *the white*. That's how I thought of it. The room I had been kept in all this time was blank of color. Blank of life. Blank of anything and everything. He brought color with him from the outside, and he certainly was alive.

Color. I felt myself yearning for it in the face of his black attire, which covered him completely. His face was expressionless, the mirrored black plastic of his helmet only interrupted by reflections from the overhanging lights.

"Holy shit."

I wasn't sure who said it—me or the helmeted being.

"Jacobs, I got something."

Definitely him this time. He spoke into a small device clipped close to his neck. I watched him warily, not sure what he intended. He stepped closer and I flinched. His eyes were hidden, but I sensed a curious gaze. I didn't think he could fully see me. If he had, he'd be scared. But maybe if I

18

didn't move, he'd touch me without seeing what I knew would eventually turn him away.

What would his touch feel like? If only I could feel another living thing, I could live off that touch for years to come. I had made it this far with only memories and violent touches. A neutral touch might help me survive for the rest of my life. I could have hoped for a kind one, but that kind of foolish thinking ended years ago.

I saw another man rush by and then backtrack to the door to my room. He was wrapped in the same clothing. The first man turned and looked at the other man. The new man was bigger in the shoulders. He stood about the same height as the first, but there was something unsettling about him.

The first one though … my mouth went dry. Fear and a strange, fleeting feeling of attraction shivered through me as he made himself more comfortable in my space. He shrugged his shoulders at the other. I jerked my head to watch both of them as my suspicion grew. The fear I felt started to overwhelm me. Who were these men? Certainly not guards who lived here. The guards who worked here knew me. They didn't hide their faces.

They didn't hide their eyes.

"What? Um … what should …" the first one said. He sounded distracted. His neck rotated slowly, his helmet reflecting me. In that quicksilver glimpse I saw a distorted figure, huddled close to the wall, with his partner nearby.

His voice traveled through my ears and made my body hum with pleasure. I closed my eyes, savoring it. Another human's voice. How long had it been? I sighed, hating how much I savored his voice. I winced in response to the screaming of the alarm, but I kept my eyes on the men. They both turned toward the doorway. Cold fear pitted in my stomach. It wasn't that I was scared for myself. I was scared for these men. They didn't know. Death would be a gift for me, but these two strangers had obviously never known hell. I, on the other hand, had lived it for years.

"You should go," I whispered, my vocal cords grating as I stumbled over the words. Years of silence had roughened my voice, and I wasn't sure I'd be able to tell them to save themselves without begging for them to save *me*. What little hope I had would disappear with them. The first stranger tilted his head. The second let out a small snort, coughing quietly covering up his quiet laugh. A laugh! I would treasure that memory till the end of days.

"What's your name?" I sensed calm from the first one as he spoke. I retreated even further. I knew the scene that was to come. The steps stopped. The siren continued blaring, but in between, for a precious second, the silence hung thick.

He moved a step closer and I pulled away, hiding in the corner. I didn't know him, but I knew his fate. I knew what would happen once the men—the ones whose faces I knew—would come. The guards. The ones with the hateful stares and the snarls of disgust. The second one edged forward.

"Back off," his partner said. Above the noise of the siren: his voice. It imprinted itself perfectly on my mind. Even though his voice held an edge, it was pleasing. His steps came closer. It was funny how sensitive I had become to his movements.

I tried to force myself into the wall, to become part of it, which was funny since another part of me still craved the touch of another human. And that touch was getting closer. I tucked myself away in the farthest corner of my square cell. Last I had seen he had stood near the doorway. Far, far from me. But now, fabric rustled close. It sounded like he was next to me. Still I didn't move. He must have been inches away.

My breathing became haggard at the thought of him touching me. Equal parts of fear, excitement, and curiosity made my blood run faster than it had in years. I could feel my heart pounding against my ribs. I had to see, though I was terrified. I needed to know.

I turned my head toward him, my whole face now exposed. I was still all curled up and closed off. He must have removed his helmet while I was turned away. His eyes took in my face, and I could see it. I could see the disgust starting to form there. The downward tug of his lips. His nose wrinkled distastefully, and from there I looked directly into his eyes. His brow was furrowed. He crouched down low. He was so tall, I never thought he would be able to reach my level. But he drew close, studying me carefully until something stole his attention away. He twisted his head to look behind us.

I knew why. I had been so engrossed in him, in seeing a new face, that I completely forgot about the other man.

I looked that way. Five other helmet clad men stood in the doorway. I saw them with an enhanced kind of focus. It was a sense of sharpness, a razor focus that became disorienting. The only color I had lived with all these years was white. Their hands were so pink and full of life. I could hear a few irregular heartbeats. Most drummed, betraying the presence of adrenaline.

The first man still kneeling before inched closer. Hesitantly, I twisted my body to face him again. He was the first man I had seen in four years and about ten minutes who didn't look at me with pure hatred. He was handsome. He had a flawless, tanned face with a clean cut jaw and dark, black hair void of any color. My legs, moments before, had been pulled tightly to my chest and were too close to my shuddering heart. It pumped like it was trying to beat out of my skin. I kept my arms braced around my stomach. I couldn't meet his eyes. I turned away pulling into the fetal position. My tangled hair hid one side of my face, the side that made him look at me like I was a monster.

"What's your name?" he asked again, his perfect, full lips no longer muffled.

"Stone, grab her and let's go. We don't have time," the second man spoke up again.

I tucked every limb as close as I could to my wasted torso, trying to escape their words. I was pressed close to the corner of the room. Clutching at it. Scrabbling with my fingers. My knees and legs were tucked away from the open, my arms sandwiched between my stomach and my knees. I kept my eyes on the others in the room from my bent forward position. Out of the corner of my eye I saw his movements. His arms were outstretched. I was unfazed by the whimper that escaped my lips. It had to be mine, even though I had no memory of the sound.

"Hey, I'm not going to hurt you," he whispered.

It's not you I'm scared of, I thought to myself. He reached for me. My clothes got in the way, denying me the skin to skin contact that I craved. I hated that I wanted it. Hungered for it. My back tightened. I tried to move. Escaping by becoming part of the wall seemed more plausible than these men helping me.

"I promise you are safe now."

His hand moved excruciatingly slow to my cheek. I felt the tips of his fingers brush away my hair so that he could see my face. My breathing became hollow, I felt my own catch in my throat as he pressed forward. His smooth fingers were feather light as they brushed against my cheek. Then he took his hand away from my face. I watched as he gently placed it on my arm. The motion was natural for him. It seemed instinctive. He hadn't thought twice about it. I could see this clearly in his movements. To him this was nothing. To me it was everything.

Four years and over ten minutes without touching another human. The closer he moved, the thicker the fear became in me. My movements were wooden. My terror became suffocating, like a woolen blanket in summer. Stifling. My heart raced. This had to be wrong. It wasn't possible. Terror filled me, pumped right to my heart. It took over and pulled me into darkness.

***

"Stone's got the fucking magic touch!" someone joked loudly, jarring me awake. I flinched but kept my eyes closed. I felt scrunched up and I was rocking. There was something under my legs, around my back. Something I hadn't felt in years.

Arms.

"Watch your mouth," a new voice shouted. It was gruff and slightly pained. Everything felt disjointed; the voice had sounded out from a void. "What's happened now? What have you discovered, aside from the girl, who we will be waltzing away with in just a moment—what else have we learned from this excursion?" The voice sounded almost triumphant.

While he spoke, I felt the muscles in the arms under my head twitch and roll, but I didn't open my eyes. The hand was soft and smooth. It brushed aside the hair hanging in front of the left side of my face. I tried to hold still, even though my reflex was to escape his touch. Then his hand stopped. I could feel his warmth close to the surface of my skin.

"Jacobs, I think she might be waking up."

The voice was close, so close.

"Blindfold and gag her," the gruff voice ordered.

"But—"

"Do it. We don't know what she knows. We don't know if we can trust her."

"They kept her captive. You saw her face."

His voice, the man they called Stone—the one who carried me—it was strained. I knew what he was thinking. Same thing everyone who saw me thought. *Monster.*

"I don't care. Do it."

I tried to remain calm, but fear won out. I felt panic take over when the light was extinguished. The fabric was coarse. I tried to pull it away, but someone grabbed my wrist painfully. I whimpered, again unable to speak. Terror clawed at my stomach. I felt screams creeping up my throat. But soon after they covered my eyes, a gag was pulled into place.

"Please," my voice came out wet and muffled around the gag. Tears slipped down my face. Cold metal closed over my wrist. I didn't know which way was up, but I wanted to be right-side up. Freedom had been a vain dream; at least I still had freedom through death. An end to it all. I didn't think—even after these scant few moments of contact—that anything could make me want to go back to solitude. It wouldn't be fair with their voices and words rolling around my head. Taking the place of old memories.

"Don't cry. You're safe," he whispered. His breath, tickling my cheek, was a sweet thing of agony. He was so close.

"How can she be scared? She can't see your face, Stone," another voice jeered from somewhere to the right.

I recoiled and, in doing so, touched someone new. An arm brushed against mine. I pulled away, but not quickly enough to escape. The arms holding me tightened. Stone's heat seeped into my body. I was trying to force myself to be small, untouchable. Why would they torture me like this? And then his hand was on my shoulder.

I screamed, pulling away. It was part of their plan. Part of how they were punishing me. I couldn't stand the thought of having it being ripped away. That would be in the end. Distant, old memories ghosted to the forefront of my mind, callused hands that were rough. Pinching, biting against my soft skin. *Not now.* I wanted to be touched so desperately, but at the same time it created a need in me. A hunger for another human being. Touch was a poison that could destroy me. Or whatever was left of me.

"I'm sorry," Stone said quietly, pulling his hand away. The loss of his heat, and his words left me hollow. The damage was done.

Chapter 2

STONE

Her long legs were crossed at the ankles. She pulled them close to her chest, where her arms were wrapped around her stomach. She looked too small, especially in that position. It reminded me of when I found her moments before. I had no idea why the Vedenin Clan had her. Jacobs seemed to believe that she was some sort of secret weapon. But that didn't make any sense to me. Not that he believed me. He never believes anyone. As I tried to make her more comfortable, I felt a sickness in my stomach. Unbelievable. A single touch on her shoulder was enough to cause her to scream.

When Jacobs, our team leader, said they were hiding something in their facility, I assumed he meant files or maybe data we would have to pull off a computer. Someone had tripped the alarm as we took down their patrols. It had been quick. Clean, save for the tripped alarm. There weren't many to resist us, which made me wonder. Just how valuable could this "thing" be, with so few men guarding it?

I had been opening every door I passed. I was looking for servers, an IT room, an administrative suite—anything that might hold the information Jacobs had sent us in for. Hers was the only door locked. It didn't take much to break through. A glance left no doubt in my mind. It was some kind of holding cell. The walls were barren, there was a metal frame bed, much like others I had seen in raids on the Vedenin Clan. That's where I had found her. Her long, maroon hair had been thickly tangled around her slim shoulders. It was a stunning color, yet the matted, greasy state left me disgusted. Not with her, but with the clan that had let her get this way. Gods, she was too tiny.

I knew what it meant. Her unwashed body. The way she cowered into the corner. Her malnourished frame. She hadn't been there of her own free will. A prisoner, then.

Dallas ran up behind me after I called it in to Jacobs. Who was this woman and where was the data? Had Jacobs known about her all along? I turned to him, wondering if he knew anything about this. Dallas was Jacobs' son, after all. But what could I say? Would this turn into a hit mission? Would I be asked to kill her? Would we take her with us? I couldn't fathom either. She was terrified. She moved further into the farthest corner of the room. I watched her through the visor of my helmet, locking away any emotions. Willing my body to deaden its scent. Who knew what she was. I didn't want to give her any advantages. But whoever she was, she didn't seem to be a threat. It was strange how when I spoke to her, her tense body relaxed just a little. That put me back on guard. Was this some kind of trick?

"You should go," her voice cracked and wavered. She even flinched at the sound of her own voice. Dallas stifled a grunt. I've seen some bad things, but nothing could have prepared me for this girl. She was purposefully hiding her face from us. She tilted it away, holding it on an angle. She took great care to only expose as little of herself as she could. Yet she was trying to get *us* to leave?

"What's your name?" my voice was muffled. A shiver wracked through her body. A pang of guilt stabbed my gut. It had been so long since I had felt anything closely resembling guilt that it almost forced me a step back. Maybe she sensed this, maybe it was some other noise that startled her, but somehow she pressed herself even closer to the wall. Dallas moved in and was followed in by two more of our men. Who was she? How was it we knew nothing about her?

"Back off," I growled as Dallas stepped closer. Instinct forced the words from my throat in a primal, protective sound. We didn't even know what kind of paranormal she was – she could be something dangerous. But seeing her as she was, curled up in the corner, her filthy hair

26

cascading down her back, I couldn't believe in my heart that she was a threat.

I moved closer, taking my helmet off. She kept one eye on my movements. I crouched down, hoping that doing so would calm her somewhat. Her muscles were tense. They were like bands of iron firmly locked into position. I leaned in until I was inches away when she finally turned to face me.

I had held my composure until that point. I had expected, much like a frightened animal, that she would keep both eyes on danger. But she had kept half her face hidden. Until now.

Jagged, destroyed skin deformed her face. Three distinct claw marks puckered the skin in the middle of her forehead, running past a dead eye on the left side of her face, ending at her jawline. The skin was permanently damaged. These were old scars. Her vacant, scared eyes lingered on me. But not for long.

I stared at the rest of her face. Her skin was unnaturally pale from lack of sun. Her other eye, the one that wasn't clouded, was a stunning, almost unnaturally transparent blue. I had never seen someone who looked so wild, yet so utterly and completely sad. I asked her name again. She didn't say anything. Dallas was getting impatient, and rightfully so. We only had a small window of time here. And it was closing, fast.

A radio crackled to life somewhere. Even with my senses strained, I couldn't tell anything about her, aside from the obvious. She was like a black-hole. I couldn't focus on anything but her. The voice speaking over the coms was garbled and without meaning. Dallas relayed the command to me. It was time to go. Some other members of our ops team were waiting around the entrance to the room, ready to go back to the extraction point. I moved to snatch her waist, but I wasn't prepared for her reaction when my hand made contact.

The fear in her eyes before she passed out was indescribable. I could *feel* her heart beating—practically beating out of her chest. Her pupils dilated, and her breath came out rushed and panicked. I knew I shouldn't be concerned. This wasn't my first time out on a mission, and I knew physically she would be okay. Mentally, though … that was another story.

She wasn't the first, nor would she be the last person I would see pass out. But there was a different sort of worry that accompanied her unconsciousness. I found myself nervous for no reason. She'd be fine. Still, I wanted to see her eyes open.

I wanted to see in her eyes that she was going to be okay.

I had no idea why, but something inside me told me I had to save this girl. Demanded it. The image of her pressed against the wall, her eyes wide with fear, had burned into my memory. I wasn't repulsed by her appearance, not in the way most probably were. But at first sight I knew this was someone worth saving. And I was the one that had to save her.

We exited the compound swiftly. The cops would still be miles away, but we were cutting it close. Jacobs had said New Year's Eve was the best night to do this. He had been right. Everyone was out getting drunk and having a good time. Cops were on high alert, but not for special operatives raiding what appeared to be a laboratory. There were only the four of us on Jacobs' normal special ops team. The rest of the team tonight was comprised of guards unlucky enough to piss him off around the time of a mission. They had complained about not being able to be home having drinks with everyone else. Personally, I had a bottle of Jack squirrelled away in my room away from the festivities. I would need it.

She barely weighed anything in my arms. The van and Humvee idled quietly outside the rear entrance of the building. The parking lot was still and empty. The sounds of New Year's Eve celebrations were distant and mingled with the barest droning that could only be police sirens.

Jacobs heaved the van's rear passenger side door open and his eyes went to the girl in my arms. When he looked at her, an expression flickered across his face too quickly for me to distinguish. But it gave me an apprehensive feeling. My instincts prickled. A warning rushed through my veins. Adrenaline surged. But just as quickly—it dissipated. Must be leftover adrenaline from the mission. Another job well done.

He looked me right in the eye and silently motioned toward the backseat with a nudge. The others were already in the car and had already taken off their helmets. Dallas was in the process of pulling his off as well and shook his head when finally free. The other two in the vehicle, Marcus and Elijah sat in the front. Dallas climbed into the farthest back

28

seat. I followed with the woman in my arms. Jacobs was the last one to get in and settled into the middle seat as he hauled the door closed.

And then we were on the move.

***

I could see her shaking. I had hoped that she would fall back to sleep. She needed rest. She needed *food*. I didn't know what would happen when we arrived, and for some reason that worried me. I gritted my teeth and shifted in my seat slightly. We'd been on the road for almost seven hours and had about five more to go. I leaned next to her. She sat between me and Dallas. She moved away, clearly attempting to avoid touching anyone.

"You should sleep. You're safe." I paused. *For now,* I finished in my head. I had no idea what the future held for this girl. She cringed and tears slipped first from her right eye and then the left. I swallowed. She was whimpering again. Gods, she was so *broken*.

"We havin' a party here?" Dallas's loud voice boomed as he bent closer to us.

The girl shrieked through her gag and started squirming. A headache bloomed behind my eyes. Dallas could be a little socially inept. And while he might have been trying to cheer her up, he was only scaring her.

"Hey … ease up, Dallas," I said as I moved to touch her shoulder. I instantly corrected the reassuring gesture. Since she didn't seem to want to be touched, I'd give her what space I could. But there was this strange feeling inside me. A part of me that wanted very much to comfort her. To do something for her.

I gestured to Dallas. His light blond hair was a mess from the helmet. His brown eyes bored down on the girl for a moment longer before he turned my way. I could tell by his look that he was thinking the same thing I was.

Who the hell was she?

Chapter 3

AUDREY

Stone and the loud one moved away from me. I could hear their secretive murmurs, but I didn't care enough to listen in. I instead used their distraction to shield my ruined face. I had convinced myself long ago that facing death would be easier than living as I was. Death would offer my only escape.

Just shut your eyes and let it happen. That's what I told myself whenever some new torture came into my life. This was anything but the escape I had hoped for. This was a new prison. A new hell.

Part of me wanted to face it head on. The men beside me held hushed conversations. They were distracted, so I cautiously slipped off the corner of my blindfold and looked around. Though the left side of my face would be forever disfigured, my dead eye saw more than anyone knew. There were no windows in the back of the van where they had sandwiched me between Stone and the loud one. I synced my movements to match those of the car. I didn't want them to know I was eavesdropping.

But what was I even looking for? For approximately four years, thirty days, and ten hours before I arrived in that room, the only hands I could remember were harsh and uncaring. Touches resulting in pain. At the time, I'd wished for it to end. For the pain to be taken away. A year without human contact changed that, and at this new torture I found myself longing for even a violent touch. For even harsh words. And the cruel stares that accompanied them. Anything would have been better than nothing. Now I had it all. Sight, sound, touch …

I waited for the right moment to execute a well-planned jarring bump. After a few minutes of the vehicle gently rocking back and forth, it finally happened. Suddenly the van started to lose speed. Were we already there? At the new prison? Did I still have my chance to lunge forward? To throw myself out the door and into the sunlight? That would be my way out. I felt the desire for freedom in every fiber of my being. Still, the car kept slowing.

"Traffic," a new voice grunted from up front.

Maybe if I made a run for it, they would kill me. Probably wishful thinking, but it was enough to start my hands and legs moving. Fear returned quickly as the reality that, yes, I was being taken to some new prison, started to sink in. Fear had kept me frozen, but hope had begun to thaw me. I kept thinking of the sun. It had been so very long since I felt it on my skin. So long since I had felt the wind rush past me. I wanted it. I needed it. The desperation clawed at my insides demanding I make a move.

I pulled down the gag and ripped the blindfold off, no longer caring about stealth.

I threw myself into the loud man on my right. Shock flashed over his face, and even though my weight was nothing compared to his size, the element of surprise caused him to fall back. The van jerked, aiding my last ditch effort. He smacked into the metal side of the van with a loud smack. I pushed off the bench seat and leapt forward for the door. The van was double doored, two on either side. My full attention was on the handle in front of me. I managed to grip it before heavy arms wrapped themselves around my waist.

It was violent touch, but a touch nonetheless. I found myself conflicted again, not wanting to squirm away, but still terrified, still twisting from his grasp. Part of me so wished that I could stay here, suspended between one prison and the next. Something deep inside of me cried out for contact, for anything. My heart stuttered in my throat. A wracking desperation shook me, but I didn't know what I was searching for. I pulled the handle, but it wouldn't move. A new sound pierced their noises of alarm.

An ominous click.

I froze and turned, so only my left eye, the eye that looked dead, could see in painstaking detail the gun pointed at me. Not at my heart or head, but my shoulder. He was aiming to wound.

I could finally see this new man holding the gun. He was older and had been sitting on the middle bench on the other side of the van. At a glance I could tell he was hard and unyielding. There was an air of authority around him. He had to be the leader. He obviously wasn't worried about causing pain, and I didn't want that. I had enough of that in my life already. Death was what I wanted. Pure release. An end to torment. But this? I would survive this wound, should he shoot.

My breathing grew shaky. I withdrew my hand from the handle.

"Ah, so you *can* see with your left eye. I thought about as much. Sit down. Right here is fine." As he spoke, I recognized the voice as the older, gruffer voice I had heard from before.

He was still holding his gun at the ready. His hair was mostly grey, but I could tell it had been blond. His eyes were deep brown. I sat with my chained hands still up in surrender. My weak body already felt the effects of the adrenaline fading. I swallowed hard, trying to catch my breath.

"Don't fear death, do you, child?"

I didn't speak or breathe.

"Dallas, move her hands behind her back," he said without looking away.

I didn't want turn away from those empty eyes; those were eyes that could do anything. But I didn't want to lose the ability to move my arms. If they were behind me, it would hinder my movements. I would have to work at it if I wanted to get them to kill me. I would have to provoke them.

Dallas was the loud one from before that I had pushed into the wall. He was large and intimidating, much like their leader in front of me. Dallas had the same blond hair and brown eyes as their leader as well. He unclasped the handcuffs and grabbed my wrists, pulling them behind my back roughly. I wondered briefly if it was payback for shoving him into the van wall. His hand left behind searing pain, a pain that was disturbingly similar to pain once felt, memories I worked hard to forget.

"Now, will you speak?" the leader pulled my chin in his direction. I gritted my teeth and forced back a hiss of pain. The tension in his grip, the hard edge in his eyes—he wasn't a man to defy. Yet I still I didn't answer.

The one called Stone—the one I warned to save himself—tensed in the corner of my vision. He wasn't looking in our direction, but the way his body straightened and his fists tightened, he seemed upset at how Jacobs was acting. I dropped my gaze immediately. I saw a hand move toward my face. I backed away, heart slamming in my chest in the unnatural rhythm of fear.

"Interesting. Do you know how you got those scars?"

I shook my head ever so slightly.

Liar, liar. No matter. I couldn't tell them.

"You don't remember anything but that room, do you?"

Again, I shook my head. A sliver of truth in the agreement.

Liar, liar pants on fire.

"Hm. Well, I'm sorry about this."

I felt a prick on my neck and the world went black.

Chapter 4

STONE

Jacobs held her by the shoulders as she slumped forward. While Jacobs had been speaking, I had gauged her reaction. She had remained silent even though we already knew she could speak. When she had first spoken, it had been to give a warning. Yet when Jacobs blatantly threatened to kill her with the gun, her reaction was less drastic. She didn't like to be touched, but had no problem knocking Dallas into the wall. He had been glaring at her the entire time Jacobs spoke to her.

"Dallas, you all right?"

His breathing had become labored. His hands were curled tight. She hadn't hurt him. It took a lot more to hurt a werewolf, but it was likely he was pissed and there was no way in hell I wanted to be in the same car as him if he started to shift.

Everyone knows uncontrolled shifts are nasty to be around. The idea of sharing a car with an overgrown wolf was not one I enjoyed imagining. Considering his age, Dallas should be in better control, not that werewolves were my kin. But even level-headed wolves had difficulty controlling themselves when startled or angry.

"Yeah."

It was more a grunt than an actual answer. His nose had been subtly lengthening. A telltale sign of his paranormal side starting to take control. My own muscles started to contract and shift. Power filled the car. The air was charged around Dallas as his hands unclutched. Sharp, black claws protruded from the tips of his fingertips. I rolled my shoulders in preparation of dealing with the unruly wolf.

Noticing the charged feeling that preceded a shift saturating the air, Jacobs sharply turned to his son. Jacobs' eyes flashed, the golden color of his wolf eyes coming to the fore. His teeth bared to reveal long canines. Dallas kept his eyes on his father, not breaking contact. I sat tight and watched them closely. The rest of us on the team had no trouble ignoring Jacobs' commands if we wanted to. Dallas was different though. All pack members obeyed the commands of their Alpha.

No one dared to breathe as the two werewolves growled at each other. Their fight for dominance had never lasted quite this long before. One day, Dallas wouldn't bow to his father, who was currently the Alpha. But until that day came, listening to Jacobs, his Alpha, wouldn't be a choice. The compulsion to obey the pack leader was ingrained in them. Finally, Dallas turned away from his father. He shook his head, his nose returning to human proportions.

The van was silent. The woman who now sat on the middle bench with Jacobs was silent. I couldn't see her face, her hair draping over her shoulder blocking her face from view. The way her body swayed with the hair and the way her head hung forward, it looked like she sleeping.

I looked forward to the windshield trying to get a sense of where we were. Unfortunately, from my position I could barely see the street signs before we were already passing them. Marcus, the red-headed fey who was driving, turned and looked over his shoulder at her. His lips pressed together before he returned his eyes back to the road.

"What is she?" Marcus called from the front, his tone at odds with the look he had just given. He sounded curious, but his gaze was too causal, like he already knew the answer. He was fey, so he couldn't read her scent like the rest of us. Not that I could smell her, either. But that was partially Dallas' and Jacobs' fault. The shifting of a werewolf had a distinct scent, and their shift-scent overpowered anything I might have picked up. Dallas, still getting his shift back under control, ignored the question.

Jacobs' nostrils flared as he pulled in her scent. I'd never seen Jacobs lose his poker face, but in that moment his expression changed. Puzzlement. It slipped off his face seconds after.

"She will have to tell us," Jacobs whispered. He kept his head forward, only occasionally glancing at the girl.

"What should we call 'er?" Marcus asked again. All fey had an unnatural fascination with names. Some of their power stemmed from knowing and using a person's real name to work their magic. "Scars," Dallas grunted next to me. He had his eyes shut. A small bump caused him to sway, but still he kept his eyes shut. His skin had a flushed, sweaty look to it. I considered myself lucky that I would never have to feel a shift take over like that.

He was probably trying to lighten the mood with that nickname, but I didn't like it. That didn't stop Marcus from testing it out. And once he got an idea in his head, he usually ran with it. Jacobs said nothing to deter him. I glared at the back of Marcus's head when movement next to him drew my attention to Elijah.

Looking at him always sent a shiver running down my spine.

Elijah sat beside Marcus. He finally turned to the girl after Marcus' name comment. I couldn't read any emotion on his face or in his black eyes, which always scared the shit out of me. But that's how it was with wraiths.

Even though Elijah was one of our best, one of the *good* guys, wraiths could be unsettling. It was a part of their essence. Part of their nature. With eyes completely black and bodies empty of human warmth and emotion, these nightmare creatures were difficult to spend time with. They were almost impossible to be around for an extended period of time. It wasn't healthy for a living person to look into the void like that. I was happy as hell when he turned away.

"Ye jist wan' tae call her that because she caught ye off guard, mongrel."

There were moments, especially when he was excited, when Marcus reverted to his thick, Scottish accent. Fey were a secretive race, and Marcus was like the rest of his kind. I knew little about him. It was impossible to know how old he might be simply by looking at him. Not that I had ever tried. If a fey wanted you to know something, you would know it.

"Marcus, how long?" Jacobs called out, obviously done dealing with us younger folk. He had to be about as old as Marcus himself. The major difference between them was that Jacobs acted his age. Then again, who really knew? Werewolves lived, on average, twice the time a long lived human did. But even werewolf vitality had its limits. Unlike the fey who claims immortality.

"Less than an hour."

Jacobs mumbled *good* to himself about three times.

"So, who's watching Scars? I thought we could celebrate New Year's tonight," Dallas said, apparently unwilling to let the nickname go. I ignored them and instead watched her. The scars were not from a werewolf or any animal I had ever encountered. They were more than an inch wide. The claw that made them would have been pointed to a sharp tip. And they were too small and clean for a large cat or wolf. A bird's talons would have left a hooked trail at the end. The skin wasn't newly healed, but time wouldn't do anything for those scars. They were the kind that would remain for the rest of her life. How old had she been when it happened? Was that part of the reason why she warned me?

"Stone? You all right?" Dallas looked at me, concerned. I realized I was clutching the edge of the seat, and I nodded my head to reassure him I was fine.

"Yeah, can't wait for tonight. Who's taking first shift?" my voice sounded gruff, tinged as it was with my lie. I was too caught up in my own thoughts.

"Elijah has generously offered to take over our duties," Jacobs answered. The wraith turned around, not to acknowledge his name, but so his black eyes could take in the girl. There was no reason for the nervous twinge in my stomach. Elijah didn't even bat an eye at her. He just stared. It was unnerving. He was so still and silent. His face was a blank slate, but there had to be more going on in his mind.

I shouldn't go out or drink tonight. The thought came out of nowhere as we pulled into the hotel that was our home. The idea of Elijah watching over the woman didn't sit right with me. His cold, unwavering stare burned in my mind.

Even arriving home didn't shake off the weight that laid heavily on my shoulders. I looked up to the concrete blocked building. It was almost ten stories tall. The hotel was a building that had been renovated as one of the headquarters for our clan. Different floors contained a range of different things, from training rooms to apartments, from single person rooms to family suites. The outside was plain and misleading, thanks to spells casted by witches and wizards. From the outside, a slightly falling apart building was all that would be seen. But inside we lived comfortably.

"Marcus and Dallas, you're going to debrief. Elijah, Stone, you're going to take her to room 640."

Room 640? Damn.

Dallas opened his side of the van and stepped out. He took his time in front of the door, stretching his tense muscles. His skin shuddered in the moonlight. A soft, irritated growl escaped the back of my throat.

Annoyance gripped me and my teeth lengthened. I was certain he was taking longer than necessary just to annoy me. I pushed him out of the way. Marcus was already headed toward the building with the keys twirling on his finger. He didn't look the least concerned about what was happening behind him. Dallas, on the other hand, seemed reluctant to go into the building. His head kept turning toward the nearby woods. The hotel had been built originally at a time when the town had bustled with tourism. But that industry had failed, and it had been abandoned years ago, until we arrived, that is.

Elijah drifted to our side of the car. He was eerily silent as he moved. He wasn't like the rest of us. We moved with practiced stealth, silent and light on our feet. I could watch Elijah move, see the movement, and still not hear him. He was heard only when he wanted to be.

Our prisoner looked past me. Her eyes were huge as she took in the building behind us. I wondered what she saw, especially with her one eye. I had overheard what Jacobs had said.

I reached in to help her maneuver out of the van. It was difficult for her without the assistance of her hands. It would have been kinder to unclasp her handcuffs before getting her out of the van, but I resisted the temptation to touch her again. Touching her sent a sweet sizzle through my blood that confused me. Was it related to the kind of paranormal she was? Was there some kind of magic at play? No, I'd have noticed something like that.

Elijah didn't look like he was going to help her at all, which suited me just fine. I wasn't ready to give her up. I unlocked her handcuffs as gently as possible. I wrapped my fingers tightly around her upper arm. She eyed my hand and drew her lips downward while her throat convulsed with her rapid swallowing motion. Her eyes traveled up my arm to my shoulder, but never went farther. Never made eye contact with me. I kept my line of sight high and ignored her.

At this point we were already headed inside, going in the back so there wouldn't be a scene. She was taller than average. Not quite as tall as me, though. Her unbelievably skinny frame was something of a problem. It was the kind of skinny that would draw eyes.

I felt her trembling in my hands. Something in me was drawn to her. She magnetized me in a way that made it hard to ignore her. I released my grip on her bicep and moved my hand to her shoulder. I pressed down lightly to remind her who was in control, though I tried to do it in a friendly way. I didn't want to scare her any more than she already was. But she didn't seem fearful; she actually moved a little closer.

Instinct moved my arm before my mind knew what I was doing. I stood with the disfigured side of her face close to my chest. She didn't warp her arms around my waist like a part of me wanted. For the next few steps, I hoped that people would assume she was a special someone I had found for New Year's Eve. Jacobs wouldn't want us to cause a scene, and the less people who knew about her, the better.

Elijah and I took the elevator up. I've never spent much time with Elijah. No one really did. He was quiet and observant, like most of his kind, and unlike the others on our team.

"She's stronger than she realizes," Elijah said without looking at me or her. Still, I could feel his attention.

"She's probably scared," I said, regretting it instantly. God, I was a dumbass. Of course she was scared.

"Yes."

Was Elijah ...? Could his empty eyes see the thoughts in my head? He didn't say anything more as the doors opened.

The doors chimed and parted as the elevator came to a halt. This floor was meant for special guests and was barely used, but I knew from a prior visit that 640 was the most spacious and reinforced of the rooms. And in this case, "special guest" was not the usual euphemism for a prisoner. It's a dangerous world out there. Some allies of our clan have, in the past, needed protection. Which, I guess was what we were pretending we were doing.

Elijah opened the door. The room was set up like every other. Entering through the door led down a narrow hallway that ended in a small kitchen and living room area. Off to the immediate right was a bathroom. To the left was a bedroom. The room had black leather couches and a love seat. The coffee table had a cast-iron frame with a glass top. All the wood work was rich mahogany. The scent of wood polish stung my nose and memories flashed behind my eyes. I pushed them away, as usual.

There was a huge plasma TV, which would have excited the others on my team. We took care of our guests well. But Elijah and I barely glanced its way. He was simply uninterested, and I was too concerned with the woman in my arms.

I headed to lay the girl down on the bed. For some reason I felt my hand move to brush away the hair covering her scars, but held back. I didn't want to leave, but I had other things that needed to be done.

I left her alone with Elijah standing outside the door.

Chapter 5

AUDREY

I dreamt of hands. I had longed for contact, but somehow this was wrong. Hands questing where they shouldn't without permission. Cruel hands. Hands that touched and pulled, tore me apart. Dissected me. But suddenly, it all stopped.

"Don't you wish for solitude?"

Quickly following the voice was a dark laugh. It sounded far away, yet echoed to an overwhelming crescendo.

And then I was alone again. Alone in a room of mirrors. Only, in place of my face, I saw my eight-year-old self, staring back at me. A me from before the scars. Flawless. Until a monster came and marked me. I screamed until my lungs felt like they were bleeding. Screamed until my voice was like glass scraping its way out my throat. I watched in the mirrors as it happened over and over again. I was trapped there, on the cusp between waking and sleeping, confronting a day that I remembered all too well.

I screamed myself awake.

I usually didn't remember my dreams. And waking up scared—that was just a part of life. But this was different. Why? I looked at the pale white walls of my room. There were no sharp edges or tight corners. The bed was uncomfortably soft. I rapped my knuckles against the wood of the headboard. My heart was thundering in my chest. This wasn't right. I moved to the edge of the bed and stood shifting my weight. My eyes darted around the bed, to the floor. My exposed feet touched and it was the softest ground I ever felt. The feeling was alien and left me uneasy.

This wasn't my room.

It was too open. I was too open. My breathing became short. It jerked from my lungs. My hands shook. It was open. So very ... *open*.

My mind was racing. My breath got caught in my frozen throat.

I needed a room with a door. I ran to the bathroom. I didn't look inside. I just shoved the door shut and locked it. The cold hard tile was more familiar. It felt safe.

I couldn't trust the softness. I wouldn't. I wouldn't fall for their trap.

I stared at the door for a long time after I had this thought. When I turned, a mirror confronted me. Staring back at me was a gaunt-faced girl. Scars had mended the torn skin and muscles. I cringed at the memory of the pain. I moved my eyes to the reflection standing before me. One eye was the beautiful pale color. It was the color I had been born with. I began to probe at it with my fingers. I had to make sure it was real. To make sure it was really me. When the prodding became too much, I snatched my hand away. The girl in the mirror's eyes had widened. Her body was shaking. *My* body was shaking.

I grabbed blindly for the first thing I could lay hands on. The mirror couldn't remain. I couldn't stand the gaze of the figure confronting me there. I would shatter the mirror to chase it away. A ceramic dish clattered as my questing hands came into contact with it. Suddenly, it was in my hand, my eyes still transfixed by the pale face in the mirror. Fear was painted thick upon the face. My face. A sickness was in my stomach. The dish felt light. Lighter than anything. I raised my arm and the mirror girl followed.

The crash of glass was music to my ears. It resounded so deeply. The shards tinkled as they crashed together. As the glass exploded outwards, I brought my arms up defensively to protect my face. But as I stepped, the shards stabbed my feet. I tried to swallow the scream working its way out of my mouth.

My back slammed into the wall as I tried to dance painfully backward. I sunk to the ground, feet bleeding, sore, scared, and utterly overwhelmed.

A door slammed open. Footsteps followed. I held in my whimpers, hoping the newcomer would leave. That they wouldn't find me.

"What the hell was that?"

I knew that voice … Stone. That's what they called him.

"I smell blood. Bathroom."

That voice, too. Dallas—the loud one. I pressed my hands over my ears. The footsteps came closer. There was a gentle knock.

"Are you okay?" Stone asked.

I liked his voice, but I knew he didn't actually care. This was a trick. It was always a trick. Lies were the only constant these past few years. I remained silent. I scooted back and my hand grazed against a sharp mirror fragment. I sucked air through my teeth in pain. My blood was leaving a smear on the floor with every move I made.

A more insistent knock riveted my gaze back to the door.

"Open up!"

He was angry now—I knew that tone—so I folded into myself. I cradled my hand as blood pooled in my palm. I brought my knees closer, but kept my bleeding feet pointed away. Shivers chased their way up and down my body.

I was safe here. I was safe here. I was safe here.

"You want to do the honors?"

I looked at the door for a moment, not understanding. Who was this new voice? It was musical and calming. It was unnerving. The fear kept me sharp. Everything had been taken from me but the fear, and I wasn't about to allow that to disappear, too. But the voice got beyond my defensive instincts, it touched me on the inside. It was a light caress. It made me shudder.

"My pleasure. Hey in there! Scars! You should back away from the door," Dallas said. And seconds later, the door exploded inward. I swallowed my startled shriek and ducked my head. Through the strands of my hair and my uninjured arm, I could make out a large figure that stood in the doorway, staring at the mirror. Dallas. He shook his dirty blond hair and shifted his gaze from me to the shattered glass. I curled even more tightly into myself.

Don't notice me. Please don't touch me. Don't torture me. Please.

"Whit the hell happened?" the lilting voice said, closer than before. I was too scared to look back up. "Did ya do this, ya idiot?"

"Move," I heard Stone say.

I didn't look anywhere; my small, safe room was quickly becoming crowded and dangerous. It was infected. My eyes squeezed shut so hard that bright dots started to float behind my eyelids.

I felt Stone's eyes on me as he moved toward me. His footsteps were different from the light steps that accompanied the musical voice, and different from Dallas's slightly heavier gait, too. They stopped before me and I hid my eyes. I could sense him before me, and then his warm breath breezed across the crown of my head.

"Will you tell me where you're hurt?" His voice was quiet, coaxing me to answer. I pried my eyes open. I wanted to shake my head. Tell him no.

"We at least have to get the glass out. If you don't tell me, I'll have to look," his voice had taken on an edge now. I couldn't identify it. But the thought of being touched again brought memories to the surface.

Hands, touching everywhere. Fear ran my blood cold.

"Why?" I whispered.

"We only want to help you," he paused as he spoke, halting like the words were hard to say. Like they weren't natural. But finally it was proven. No one ever wanted to help. No one ever came to save me. The only guarantee was more suffering. The silence hung, waiting for something yet unsaid to be spoken, but he wouldn't go on. There was a tremor in his voice. I wouldn't have noticed it if I hadn't known the feeling so well. I placed it instantly.

Fear.

"Feet. Hand," I whispered, not looking at him. I made no attempt to look away from the comforting whiteness of the floor tiles. A detached calm took hold of me.

"Can ..." he cleared his throat, "may I touch you?"

His voice held an unsure tone. Was it my scars? What could possibly be scaring him? When he asked to inspect my wounds, my heart skipped a couple beats. Part of me was revolted by the idea of being touched. Each and every touch held some fragment of those old memories. Dark memories. But something buried deep inside of me needed it, longed for the contact that had been lost so long ago.

I nodded, tears falling. I shut my eyes. Hopefully the memories could eventually be shut out. He touched me gently, trying his best to avoid skin to skin contact as he lifted me. His arms were cords of muscle beneath my knees and back.

"Move."

Feet shuffled against the ground in front of us. He set me on the soft bed that cradled my body. I tried to move, but his hand held me fast at the shoulder. And that's when I finally opened my eyes.

"Don't move."

I hadn't noticed his eyes before. They were a wet red color mixed with clay. They reminded me of the Earth I longed to see. They were beautiful. He didn't take his eyes off of me as he spoke to his friends.

"Dallas, Marcus, go find a doctor and Jacobs."

"Why?"

My voice was unbelievably quiet. Stone's back tensed, slowly he rolled his neck until he faced me.

"What?" His eyes now burned crimson red. I swallowed hard. This ... wasn't possible. His eyes had changed. Now they burned a deep red, displaying his anger. The brown of a moment before was gone completely. Tears slipped down my face. I couldn't stand the waiting. Eventually, the ax would fall. The kindness would end and new torments begin. *They* always did.

I just wanted it to end. The pain of this kindness was too much. A false seed of hope could be more damaging than anything else. The shards of glass in my feet may as well have been stabbing my heart. Stone continued to glare, the muscles in his jaw clenched. I cringed.

"She thinks we are toying with her. Pain is all she knows. You're torturing her without meaning to."

This was another new voice. It was flat and unemotional, but his words rang true deep within me.

I curled up so that there was less of me to see. This sterile voice was what I needed. I wanted to retreat far away so I wouldn't be spread out for all to see. It felt like Stone was pulling me apart from the inside, with his touches and soft stares.

"Elijah, leave."

Stone's voice was quiet but demanding.

"As you wish," the last word came out in a hiss, and I physically recoiled. Too close ... too close to past memories.

"Hey, it's okay. He's gone now. I know wraiths are hard to be around at first, but you get used to it."

Was he trying to be conversational?

"What is—"

Before I could ask, the door was wrenched open. Heavy footsteps sounded, crashing against the floor, getting closer and closer and *closer*. I flinched. All the sounds demanded to be heard. But it was too much, far too much. After silence for so long, I couldn't bear it. I wrapped my arms around my head painfully tight, whimpering against the pain. Suddenly, an unfamiliar hand touched me. Heat radiated from the skin. I screamed. Pulled away. Heat, I remembered. Could never forget. Heat burned. Heat ...

"I told you not to touch her," Stone's voice rang through the fog in my head, somehow the clearest. I tried to hold onto his voice. Footsteps retreated, and then came forward again.

"Hey, we need you to show us your feet."

His voice again.

"Audrey," I said, my name leaving my lips so quietly I couldn't believe that he heard it.

"Audrey," he said slowly as if savoring it on his tongue, "please, show us your feet."

I passed out when they took out the first shard.

Chapter 6

STONE

I was startled by the fact that she told me her name. Or, more accurately, I was startled by how knowing her name made me *feel*. I should have passed the information on to Jacobs immediately. But I didn't. I kept it a secret. I savored it when I spoke it the first time, much like the fey do. One of the doctors attended to her. I watched as he sedated her again when she started to stir.

Since we didn't know what species of paranormal she was, we didn't want to take any risks. Some doctors used herbal anesthesia, which was more effective for certain paranormals, but they could be dangerous. In extreme cases, they could be poisonous. But damn, it was better than seeing her in pain.

"What did she say tae you?" Marcus, the tall, red-headed fey asked. I wouldn't—couldn't—tell him her name.

"Not much. She kept asking 'Why?' over and over again. Elijah seems to think she's so abused that our *kindness* is torture to her."

I could still see the pleading in her eyes. The fear.

"Maybe th' wraith is right," Marcus said, watching her closely. "Damn shame about those scars. Probably what fucked 'er up so much."

He leaned closer.

"Looks like 'er skin healed alright. Ugly scars, tho'," Marcus paused, his iridescent yellow eyes studying her.

"What's yer name, sweetheart?"

I alone had the satisfaction of knowing her name. I was the only one that she trusted enough to share it with. And I savored that exclusive knowledge.

"Stone," Jacobs barked my name, breaking my attention away from Marcus and Audrey. "What the hell happened?" Each word came out clipped.

"I came to relieve Elijah when we heard a crash. We came in to find the bathroom door locked. She smashed the mirror, no idea why."

Jacobs looked at his son and Elijah before turning to the doctor.

"Doc, how long will she be out?"

"Maybe another hour or two."

"We need to move her somewhere more secure," Jacobs paced as he spoke. It was a werewolf trait to pace restlessly, especially when under stress, but Jacobs was something else. He strode back and forth rapidly. The air around him grew thick with tension. He glared at Audrey and ran his hand through the light strands of his hair. He kept muttering to himself. I heard him list off open rooms, unsatisfied with the options.

"The cells," Elijah was motionless, watching her with dark, pitiless eyes as he said this. I felt a pang of opposition, but I didn't show it. Jacobs stopped at the sound of the wraith's voice.

"No."

There was finality in it. Still, Elijah made his case.

"That's where she'd be most at ease. And she wouldn't be able to harm herself there."

And she would feel like a prisoner again! I thought for a moment Elijah was giving in to his darker side. That he wanted to taste her fear and feast on her pain. The contract he'd formed with the Braden Clan—our clan—said he would abstain from unchecked feeding. After all, it could become an addiction for wraiths.

When Marcus laid his hand on my shoulder, I realized how close I had been to unconsciously attacking Elijah. That primal instinct was kicking in again. Protect.

"I said no."

Jacobs wasn't a true Alpha, though he still acted like it. Alpha's had packs. Jacobs only had us. Dallas flinched. Damn, I was glad I had no ties to Jacobs like he did. No one had that sort of power over me.

"We could put her in one of the overnight rooms," Dallas suggested from where he stood off to the side. He'd spent time among other wolves last night, and I could tell he was itching to be on a team with more werewolves. They were social creatures. They liked to be around their own kind.

Jacobs was different. He was a beta wolf who yearned to be Alpha. He was the leader of our team not because of his status as beta but because he fought hard for his position. He was well-liked by the higher ups, and I knew that he was close to Cain who ruled our clan. Jacobs had earned our respect, as well. As a team, we couldn't ask for a better leader.

Jacobs stopped pacing as he considered Dallas' idea. The overnight rooms were small. They contained a bed and a small dresser, nothing more. There was one problem with those rooms, though. They didn't lock.

The overnight rooms were only intended for people passing through. Friends of the clan, that sort of thing. Most would stay for a single night, as the name implied, or sometimes only a handful of hours before leaving. Some would stay for a week, but that was a rare exception.

Jacobs was pacing again, probably thinking about the lockless rooms. She jerked her head to the side, her brow scrunched together. The sedative that the doctor gave her must be wearing off. As the drug loosened its grip on her, her dreams must have returned.

"Stone," Marcus said, nudging me.

"What?" I pulled my gaze away from her.

"I asked if you still had that padlock and chain from when you were so damn concerned about Dallas taking your motorcycle out," Jacobs growled.

I was briefly consumed by an urge to laugh. The lock had been Jacobs' idea; he didn't want his son driving my motorcycle any more than I did. I nodded.

"Dallas, you and Marcus go install the lock."

My brows pressed together. A silent question was poised on my lips, yet I hesitated. Why did he need both Marcus and Dallas to install the lock? Perhaps he noticed his son start to twitch. A single night out with the other wolves wouldn't sate Dallas' paranormal side. His wolf still itched to be with its kind.

"Stone, you and Elijah take her to the room. Don't leave until the lock is installed."

I picked her up, again hating how light she felt in my arms. It was a dark reminder of her sunken cheeks, her prominent ribs. We headed down the elevator to the main floor. Which reminded me of another flaw in using the overnight room, but I figured Jacobs had already considered it.

They were easy to escape. The elevators would take her right to the entrance. And though the main floor tended to be busy with people coming and going, if she got that far she would stand out, to say the least. We'd have to keep a guard posted just in case she somehow managed to escape her room. If we were careful, she wouldn't.

We moved through the hallway taking the stairways down two floors. The visiting rooms were on the lower levels, close to the dining hall and visitors' gym. Elijah lead, probably to scare off anyone before they got too close. He stopped when we arrived and opened the farthest door.

With her held in my arms, I shifted her closer to me so she wouldn't touch Elijah as I slipped past. I walked into the small apartment and set her on the bed. As I moved away, her eyes started to flutter open. I guess the sedative that the doctor used wouldn't last as long as he had thought.

Not for the first time today, I was left wondering—what was she?

Chapter 7

AUDREY

My face was in agony. Ripping. Tearing. A shadowy attacker, faceless, nameless. But I knew him. I would always know him. And so I didn't scream. That was before the forgotten memories came. Before I returned to that awful place again.

The light was bright and my eyes squinted as they opened.

Stone stood over me. Why had I told him my name? That was the first time I had said it out loud in five years and … I'd lost days, hours … how long had it been? And where was I? This room was different. Smaller and safer though, it felt entirely too small with two strange people in it with me. I tried to pull my feet in, but stopped abruptly. I struggled to shake off the dream and grasp what was happening. I remembered the sound of glass breaking. A door smashed to smithereens. A cold needle and the flush of strange drugs in my system. I was shivering again. Panic seized control.

"Hey, you're okay now. Your feet didn't need any stitches. It wasn't that bad."

Stone's voice was the same as before. Utterly calm, informative … masculine. His features were as I remembered, except for his eyes, which had again changed. A calming blue replaced the red that I must have imagined before. Or maybe he was a monster, like the one they called a wraith.

The wraith. Elijah. He was sickly pale. He didn't quite reach Stone's height, and he wasn't as broad as Stone, but I could clearly see his musculature beneath his clothing. He had black, black hair that flopped over his eyebrows. I dropped my eyes to his and felt my stomach drop. Vortexes of darkness. I had never seen anything so void of color. It didn't just seem cold, it looked cold. It was a silky, inky black that swallowed any light that dared enter. My breath caught. I couldn't look away from those eyes.

"Hey," Stone said moving closer. "Audrey? Are you okay? Like I told you before, Elijah is a wraith, but you're safe. He's one of us."

There was that word again. *Safe.* I shook my head. Elijah tilted his head as a small, knowing smile appeared on his lips. It was barely noticeable. I tried to breathe, but I couldn't. I should have been able to see something, anything in his eyes. I didn't understand how this could be possible.

"You won't find any color there," his emotionless voice stated flatly, as if he knew what I thought.

Stone glanced at the wraith and the color from his face drained a little.

"She knows more than she thinks. She can read the colors in the eyes of any paranormal. But of course, you haven't used that skill in years, have you?"

"Elijah," Stone's voice warned.

I turned to him. His eyes were an amber-red color again. I was overwhelmed. I still couldn't breathe right. I wanted my cell back. I wanted my white walls. I started to mumble, pulling my limbs in tight. I hadn't held on this desperately to hope in years. The hope for comfort. The hope for an end to the pain. The one with the dead voice and black eyes watched me uncaringly. I couldn't look at the other one. He offered me *too much* hope.

"Are you enjoying her pain?" Stone asked. A snarl lifted his top lip.

"What's a wraith?"

I couldn't believe my mouth betrayed me, giving words of my deep thoughts. When Stone turned toward me, his eyes were bright and expressive. I winced at the emotion held there. It was too much to process. He turned back to Elijah, who still had a tiny, knowing smirk.

I knew that smile. The nameless men who had come for me four years ago had the same one on their faces.

"Elijah."

I could hear the warning in Stone's voice. Something about his friend was making him ill at ease.

Stone stood fast and I scrambled backwards, thinking his fury would find me as its target. His eyes softened for a moment, but he quickly wiped his face clean of emotion. Still, he didn't seem happy as he stormed over to Elijah and pulled the wraith out of the room.

I peeked around the corner to see a lean, tall, red-haired man with glowing yellow eyes. Dallas was there too, his mussed dirty-blond hair sticking up at odd angles as he stood outside the door watching Stone and the dead-eyed one or me.

I was alone again. It should have been a relief, but I felt instead a sudden pain of loneliness. Was this what they were planning all along? To tease me with their voices, their touches, and then abandon me again?

I had known this was coming. Yes, I had known. Still, I silently yearned for their unfamiliar presence. I took in shaky, uneven breaths. Tears fell.

Cruelty, as always, was their specialty.

Chapter 8

STONE

Audrey kept glancing over at Elijah. She looked somehow comfortable in her fear.

"What's a wraith?"

By the look in her eyes, she couldn't believe she had actually spoken. She flickered her gaze uncertainly between to me back to Elijah. The look, while bound up with tentativeness and fright, also held a quality that was quizzical. Like she was trying to figure him out. At times she would cock her head toward the noises made by Marcus and Dallas who were fixing the lock. I stared at Elijah for a moment before it finally dawned on me that he wasn't savoring her fear. He spoke to her as if he knew her, or knew something about her. That pissed me off to no end. My possessiveness flared. I could barely control myself. My skin itching, I could feel my muscles expand.

"Elijah."

I wanted his attention off of her so badly, my voice all but came out in a bark. We passed by Marcus and Dallas when I couldn't take it anymore and forced Elijah out of the room.

Pushing past them, I called out, "Marcus! Dallas! One of you get in there, now."

As Dallas moved past us, his shoulder bumped mine. His face was impassive, but in between blinks, I caught his wolf eyes staring out. Marcus stayed in position in front of the door, finishing installing the lock.

There was a hint of interest in his eyes. He watched me, but he kept most his attention on the lock. My gaze moved to the wraith in front of me. He wasn't looking toward the door, only at me.

"You don't know, do you?"

Elijah was a man who rarely smiled. But when he did, without fail, my skin crawled. It was one of the few things that I didn't mind admitting scared the hell out of me.

I was used to Elijah's cryptic words, but this game he was playing was starting to piss me off. If he had caught something from her mind, why didn't he tell us? Why didn't he tell *me*? My knuckles drained of blood as my fists tightened. I bared my teeth as another growl rumbled through me. Marcus noticed and stood up. A fierce fey, brimming with power … for once appearing his actual age.

"What's goin' on?" His musical voice held no warmth.

I was losing control. The growl still lingered in my voice. I was trying hard to keep my muscles under control, but I could sense the beginnings of a shift, my bones expanding, my cells stirring with excitement. I needed to calm down. Anger and frustration excited further my already expanding muscles. I clenched my jaw. Confronting Elijah would do no good. There was still much about his kind we didn't know.

"She doesn't know what a wraith is."

"Well, I would call 'er lucky," Marcus' eyes pinched in around the edges. They darkened with his rising anger.

"No, Marcus. She doesn't know anything."

His words had felt like a snake coiling around us. Her lack of knowledge of our world lead me to ugly conclusions. *How long have they had her?* Marcus became utterly still.

"Is she human?" Marcus asked.

"Jacobs and Dallas would have been able to tell if she was human."

Not only that, but Jacobs hadn't sounded surprised when I had reported my find. He knew something. We were silent for a moment before Dallas came out.

"What? I couldn't hear you over the drill. What doesn't she know?" he asked as the door shut behind him, the lock finally installed.

"Anything. This is why I ordered you not to talk to her."

Jacobs strode down the hall in one of his many suits. He enjoyed the refined elegance of suits when not on missions. Personally, I figured it was posturing. That he wanted to show his dominance with his expensive taste. It did nothing for me. Most paranormals respected power. And Jacobs wasn't a born Alpha, at least not in a werewolf pack. Packs existed under clans' names and rarely elsewhere. Still, all of us came to attention except Elijah, who simply turned to face the door. The small smile, however, slipped from his face. Even Elijah made sure to show Jacobs the proper respect.

"She is curious."

Elijah concentrated on the door as if he could see through it. Wraiths were a strange sort. Who knew? Maybe he could see through that door or sense somehow beyond it.

"The best of the best, my ass. Get out of here, all of you, before you ruin everything." It was obvious that Jacobs was restless again. "Elijah, stay."

Fear held me back, but my anger boiled in my gut. It was an instinctual reaction that I didn't understand. The higher-ups wouldn't command Jacobs to use a wraith on her.

Would they?

Chapter 9

AUDREY

Elijah and Stone walked out of the room and Dallas took their place. My fear spiked. The need to hide was overwhelming. I didn't know these people, and I didn't know what they might do. Without putting much thought into it, I tipped the bed as Dallas entered the room. It was a comforting barrier between him and me. Sure, it was soft to lie on, but I felt safer this way. Behind its protection, I could curl against the wall. Not that any of them had tried to hurt me yet. But I was waiting, expecting that eventuality.

Jacobs walked in with the heels of his shoes thumping a crescendo as he got closer. I peeked through my hair, keeping my head down. Elijah watched a few paces behind Jacobs with his pitiless eyes.

Jacobs, however, looked at me with sad brown eyes. They were the same amber I saw in Dallas. And there was much to see there. These eyes were older than the body they lived in. In his copper flecks I could read his loose control. The way he stood though, tall, regal—I felt like he was completely in control. Fear shivered down my spine. Men that like this were dangerous.

"Will you say your name?" Jacobs asked. I shook my head once. "Audrey, right?"

My head shot up. A sense of betrayal, something I hadn't felt in years, soured my stomach. Fear that had been my constant companion, my only companion, but now ran my blood cold. Names could be dangerous. So very dangerous. And Stone had told them. I shouldn't have trusted him, even though I didn't even know why I told him at the time. It had to have been him. No one else knew, no one else had muttered my name in years. I had been referred to as the "little monster," "creature," or "it" since I first arrived. Disembodied faces jeering with disembodied voices.

A sad smile spread across Jacob's face to match the sad expression in his eyes.

"Yes, that's what we thought."

I wanted to ask if they knew. They must. How could they not know I was a monster? Instead of that question, unbidden words came.

"When am I going to die?"

Jacobs barked out a small laugh. It rang through the room and echoed in my ears. There was something wrong with that laugh. My muscles tightened and my instincts urged me closer. Smaller.

"You are a rarity, my dear. We would never kill someone like you."

My greatest fear. My body quaked. My very core trembled at the prospect. He continued.

"Audrey, we won't hurt you. We promise. You have nothing to fear from us, even if you do have a lot to learn about the world we live in."

I wouldn't meet his eyes. He was a liar. All of them were. The other men had used those words so many years ago. It's always the same at first. *We're here for you. We won't harm you.* Lies. Lies. Lies.

"What was the one pleasure they gave you?" Elijah asked out of nowhere. His voice was utterly flat. How could he know? How could anyone know that? I found myself willing to answer.

"... a shower."

My cheeks reddened as I said this. Once a month, they came and took me blindfolded to a place I could clean myself. They always kept my eyes covered. The men knew about me, knew about what I could see. Once in the room, I would wash, dry, and comb through the tangles in my hair.

Elijah stepped closer to me. He wasn't even looking at me.

"How?" My voice quavered with uneasiness.

He turned to me and smiled, revealing his dangerously sharp teeth. Each tooth was filed into a sharp point. The cruel points of those teeth—I knew those from nightmares long ago.

"Magic."

It was the first time I heard any semblance of emotion in his voice. And I had almost forgotten about Jacobs, who restlessly patrolled the room.

"You're Dallas' father," I said quietly, watching him. He stopped pacing and looked at me.

"Yes, he is my son. My name is Jacobs." There was a hint of a lie in his eyes. Not that that bothered me; I was comfortable with lies. "If we allowed you to shower, would you try to hurt yourself?"

Which was the answer he was searching for?

"No?"

Another smile lifted Elijah's lips. I wanted to keep them happy, but I had nothing to hide. Lies resulted in punishments when discovered. And they were always discovered.

The idea of being clean, though, was tantalizing. And to be left on my own, to do it myself, that was a luxury I hadn't had in a long time. It made me cautious. I didn't like this. It felt like a trap.

Jacobs was stunned by my words and stared openly at me. Then he motioned to Elijah and the wraith glided forward.

"I need to read your intentions. The best way is physical contact."

Elijah held his hand out, this time facing me. It was a great temptation, this simple trade off. If it was being offered, how could I possibly refuse? To be clean and to receive a nonviolent touch?

When I touched Stone, I could also feel a sense of anticipation. Whereas when others touched me, I felt their fear. Not that I could trust any of them. They might do anything. Yet the offer was too great to resist. So I slipped my hand into Elijah's. He didn't scare me, at least not like the others. Once his hand gripped mine, a flutter went through my stomach. His was a strong, cold grip. He grasped my hand with an unspoken purpose. There was no emotion. It was empty, and for once, I wasn't scared of someone's touch.

He closed his eyes. His hand was cold, but it was real. It made me feel alive. And then, quick and unexpected, images flashed in my mind. I gasped.

I saw myself from Elijah's point of view. A tall, gangly woman, her body coiled. Gaunt cheeks, dark soul, endless amounts of fear. He could see that I was saturated in it. Lived in it. Knew nothing aside from fear.

Then the image changed. I was in the hallway with Stone, and his eyes kept changing colors. Flickering the whole range of the spectrum, his irises moved from light to dark and back again.

Again, the scene before my eyes shifted. I was in the darkness with Elijah. We weren't alone. He was speaking, but I couldn't hear him. Even so, somehow I could understand. And I felt a strange new presence. It wasn't scary, not like before. This presence offered a sense of security.

Again, the images before my eyes changed. This time another person stood in front of me. They spoke, though their words didn't mean anything to me. Something about a deal registered in my head. But these were foreign memories. These weren't my own, could they be ... Elijah's memories?

It all faded away when Elijah pulled his hand from mine. I could *feel* pain. His pain. I could feel it prickling through my skin, causing warm tracks of fresh tears down my face.

"How did you do that?" His words held anger I didn't understand and his face twisted into a scowl.

"Do what?"

I had never experienced anything like that before. I recalled the touches from Dallas and Stone, slight as they were. They had been abrasive, but nothing out of the ordinary had happened. I could feel his black eyes on me as I stared at the ground. I waited for his next question. It was coming. Soon he would ask me what kind of *thing* I was.

The only answer I knew anymore was that I was a monster.

"Jacobs, she won't hurt herself if you allow her to shower."

With that, Elijah stood and left.

"I'm sorry I had to have him do that. It's never pleasant having your thoughts invaded. But I needed to be certain you wouldn't harm yourself. I'll send down one of the girls. She'll help you."

60

And then Jacobs left as well.

I could tell he felt uncomfortable, but my mind remained on what had transpired. Maybe I'd somehow done the same to Elijah as he did to me? But I pushed those thoughts aside at Jacobs' words. He was sending someone new. I didn't know if I could bear it. Even the thought of someone new made me cringe and pull my limbs closer to my torso, and I closed my eyes. I just wanted a moment's peace.

***

I don't know how long I slept in my corner, but I awoke to the feeling of eyes on me. I jerked my eyes open and scooted to the wall. Dallas leaned casually on the door, a bored look on his face. His eyes were faraway. He hadn't yet noticed I was awake. I felt a slight tremor of fear, but stifled it. So far I hadn't been harmed by them. I still didn't trust them. Not one bit. Even so, a small, nagging feeling of trust had started to form.

Sitting beside me on the bed was an unnaturally beautiful girl with hair green as seaweed. Her eyes were like coral and her skin itself had a hint of green in its pallor. I swallowed, uncomfortable with her closeness. Only two feet away, but her long legs were almost touching me. I was afraid what happened earlier might happen again. I wanted to keep my distance, just in case. But … there was something odd about her legs when I looked at them—the air around them wavered. It was like a ripple of water in the air. But as soon as she saw I was awake, she clapped her hands and startled me. I jumped, swallowing hard.

"Hello!"

Everything about her was aqueous, even her voice sounded liquid. It was haunting. Exquisite.

"I love, *love* meeting new people! I'm Nixie. What's your name?"

She practically squirmed in her seat. She made me uncomfortable.

"She doesn't talk much," Dallas called in from the hallway. "We've been calling her Scars."

I reached up to my scars, turning away slightly. Was I really so ugly?

"Dallas you are such a … a … a blowfish!" Nixie turned her strange eyes to him.

"Call me an ass, Nixie. That's how we talk here on land," he said, a playful note carried in his voice. Before I read more into it or saw too much, I turned my left eye away.

"Dallas, leave!" Nixie's voice was now shrill, like she was really hurt by his words. She turned away from him.

"I'll be back later."

With that, he slipped through the door. Silence followed the click of the door closing.

"Now, what's your name?"

I felt tight with the weight of her stare, though her deep voice soothed me. There was a slight wavering in her voice. Try as she might to sound upbeat and calming, I could tell she was shocked at my appearance. Even her chipper personality wouldn't change what I was.

"Audrey."

It felt so strange coming from my lips. The green haired girl—Nixie—made an excited noise at this one-word answer. I cringed. I wasn't sure how much of her I'd be able to take. The noise made me want to run and hide.

She barely even noticed.

"Your voice is so pretty! I wouldn't be shocked if you were a cousin of mine. Now come on. Shower time! I love the water."

I sat back, trying to catch my breath. As I tried to pull air into my lungs she had already grabbed me. And she was incredibly strong … or maybe it was that I was weaker than I realized. I tried to reclaim the hand she had taken, but she held tight, either ignoring my pull or not noticing it. I fought her, albeit weakly. I had to admit that I relished the softness of her silky hold on me. This lasted only for a moment before the fear I knew so well swallowed all other feeling.

They wanted something. That had to be it. But I didn't have anything. I'd been locked away so long, I didn't even have information, should they ask for it. And once they realized that, they would lock me away, alone forever. Again.

She pulled me down a narrow hallway lined with doors. I didn't want to know what was hiding behind them. Were there more scarred, broken people? Were they beautiful people like Nixie? I could feel the memories trying to surface. I closed them out by focusing on my feet now slapping against wood floor. *Wood that was* not *spattered with blood.* Sometimes, they came no matter what—memories.

I whimpered and closed my eyes, willing the dream not to manifest. Slowly I peeled my eyelids open and the memory blurred. Oblivious, Nixie continued to pull me along.

We stopped. In front of us the metal doors had opened. It had been a very long time since I had taken an elevator. I might have once before, when they had blindfolded me and moved me from my cell. But I wasn't sure, though I remembered them from when I was a kid. Usually I was pushed into them. The movement of the floor, that instant of weightlessness, it was a dead giveaway. Nixie took a step forward, my hand tightly gripped in hers. The walls of the elevator were a dark wood and a gold railing went around its perimeter at waist height. Nixie stood in the middle, letting go of my hand after the doors closed, and hummed along with music coming from above. Usually enclosed spaces gave me a sense of comfort, but another person invading that space added a tinge of fear.

The floor hitched and jerked and then we were moving without moving. I lifted my head, Nixie watching me closely. Her eyes ran along the lines of my scars to my ruined eye. Held in her eyes were a million shades of coral, each wavering and dancing. It was like looking through the clear shimmering waters of the ocean at a forest of coral, different pinks glinting, drawing my eye. She had no idea the way in which I scrutinized those hues. In them I found all manner of things. For instance, I could see deep sympathy in the darker shades at the outside of her iris. There was something lamentable in those eyes. I could only look for so long. She wanted to cry for me, for the pain I had suffered, for my scarred and ruined appearance, but kept up the bubbly appearance anyway. And then the elevator we were in stopped and dinged.

"Come on."

She pulled me along. The halls were dimly lit, the walls painted beige, the bottoms trimmed in white. The doors to either side of the hallway were spread out, but there were many that lined our way. The carpet was an unappealing design of small geographic shapes in bad color choices.

Nixie lead me through the halls, turning one way then another. My heart stammered more and more as we moved.

Nixie started to slow her pace at last. She stopped in front of a door with the same heavy wood as the rest. The gold numbers 39 on the front. She leaned over and pulled out a key.

"Sorry, my room is a complete mess. But when I heard there was a fellow sister in need of a shower, I practically jumped up and down volunteering. I didn't have time for any cleaning."

Nixie opened the door to reveal a small apartment. From the door I could see a living room decorated with a seafoam colored couch that looked worn and well loved. The couch looked maybe as old and beat up as I felt. Opposite it was a small TV, with a small coffee table in between. There were clothes on the couch, a dress hung from a lamp that was pushed into the corner. Another step into the room revealed a plush rug, into which I sunk my toes.

Looking back up, the kitchen caught my eye. It was attached to the living room, a little space with narrow counters. She had a moderately sized refrigerator and an oven with a stove on top. Dirty dishes sat in the sink and a few on the countertops. The fridge was decorated with magnets that looked like they were in the shape of mermaids.

Unlike the beige in the hallway, the walls of Nixie's room were painted a soft blue color. Photos and paintings were scattered across the room, full of scenes and places and people I couldn't possibly know. The walls were filled with pictures and art. I took it all in. It was overwhelming. My left eye enhanced every color in the pictures, adding nuance and depth. Each picture held a memory, a thought, an emotion. Some dredged up old, old memories. I turned my head downward. Sometimes, all you could do was hide.

"I'll show you to the bathroom, then we'll work on finding you something to wear. I bet you want out of that outfit. I know I would!" Nixie's voice was sympathetic, but her nose crinkled a little. She noticed me shift my weight, bent her head forward a little, and tucked a piece of hair behind her ear while red crept up her neck. I had never once felt uncomfortable in front of the men who held me captive, but with her it was different. I had a choice, it seemed. And somehow, that made it feel like it mattered. She had called me a sister. Dragging me toward the bathroom, she paused at the door.

"One second."

She ran in and I was left alone. I twisted my hands together, shifting my weight from foot to foot. My teeth scraped my bottom lip. Memories crept up my spine, a dark chill against the bones. Those phantom eyes. The door suddenly opened wide. Nixie appeared wearing another bright smile.

"Well, come in!"

I stepped into the bathroom. It was much bigger than the one I had been allowed to use. The tiles beneath my feet were pristine white, making my pale skin look grey against it. To the right was a large tub that looked more like a small swimming pool. It was made of the same delicate, white porcelain. My shoulders relaxed a little at the familiar color. Gold trim and accents shined brightly under the lights. Adjacent to the tub was a glass shower stall, its dark rock contrasting starkly the white of the room.

Out of the corner of my eye I saw a tic of movement. I swallowed hard and turned away quickly, looking to the white for comfort. A tight fist formed in my stomach as I thought about how I would look in the mirror. How long had it been? Would I look different from the child I was when I was taken?

"Sorry, time for awkwardness. I know about your circumstances, but don't worry. Only the members of Jacobs' team know about your true background. Jacobs is telling everyone you are a random pick up. Anyways, do you um … well isn't this awkward? Fine, okay. I can do this! Do you know how this works?" Nixie asked motioning to the simple shower.

"I was put in there when I was 16 years old. Yes."

Thank you, though. It was on the tip of my tongue. But I wasn't sure if it was the right thing to say. Those words were as foreign to me as the magic they spoke of earlier. It cost me more than I liked to say the few words that I did.

"Oh! Good! I kinda feel like I shoved my fin right into my mouth, but I had to ask! So, I'll find you some clothes! All the shampoos, conditioners, and soaps you'll ever need are in there. I left a brush out for you to use. Take all the time you need."

She said it all with a smile, but that didn't keep me from retreating farther and farther back into the room. She closed the door with a friendly wave goodbye. As the door closed my eye fell upon the doorknob. No lock. I guess that would have been too much to ask for.

I stripped down, feeling exposed. Scars seamed my body. While I might be allowed to shower, I would never look at my monstrous self. Showering blindly was easy, you just needed to find a spot on the wall and not *ever* look away. That was how I had done it for years. I remembered those instances I had showered in captivity. How it made me feel human afterwards, but during … it was a nightmare come to life. Their eyes fell upon my naked skin hungrily and pricked my shame like razor blades. Memory overtook reality. I squeezed my eyes shut. It was like being dissected. Tongues would paint their lips with moisture. My chest staggered with short breaths.

As the years went on, new scars added one after another. Blood loss would frequently take me to a blissful world of nothingness. But I was always brought back to the waking world. My traitorous body simply would not give up. Unwilling to give up a life not worth living. Freedom was not so easily won. And with the spreading of my scars, so too did my hatred of my skin.

But I could pretend my skin didn't exist, for just a few minutes, under the spray of water. I would pretend the water would sweep me away. I'd be lost in the liquid. The freedom I could have, to flow away and keep moving. The luxury of that idea allowed me to emerge from my haven.

I could ignore the map of horrors upon my skin. I bore a set of three on my right ribs and another set on my left thigh. Three claw marks ran from the top of my right shoulder to the back part of my left hip. My body had been more fragile then, when I received the scars. It looked foreign to me. The scars grew with me, misshaping my body as an adult. I was afraid to look at myself.

I walked into the shower, not even looking down at my body for fear of what I might see. As I entered, I was engulfed in a naturally soothing fog. This was a place of warmth, where the memories of poorly healed wounds were hidden. I didn't want to spend any more time there than I had to. I averted my eyes from my skin as I scrubbed myself clean. I didn't want to be alone with my nakedness. I wanted so badly to crawl out of my own skin and belong to something, to someone, to be less … me. I don't know how long I stood frozen, the water drumming warmly, before Nixie knocked. I came out to find a towel on the tub's lip with a note on top.

"Get dry, sweetie-pie!"

I wrapped myself in the towel, trying to cover as much as possible, but the scars on my thigh peeked out a little. I attacked my hair, brushing it ruthlessly. I loved and hated every moment.

"Hey! Can I come in?" Nixie's muffled voice called through the door. I nodded my head only to realize she couldn't hear me. The door opened a crack.

"Audrey?" Nixie's voice slipped through the crack, sounding worried. I made a quiet noise not sure how to answer. She took it as an okay and opened the door a little wider. She had her hand over her eyes at first, but pulled it away. "Oh wow! You look so much better."

She looked me up and down with a satisfied smile until she saw my scars. She stepped closer and pulled the towel up to look at the scar on my thigh. Then she looked up at me.

"Oh my gods. How many more do you have?" her voice was quiet, less than a whisper.

I swallowed.

"Four more."

Her face held a deep softness, and her eyes glistened with sympathy. The scar on my thigh was probably the worst. It reached the entire way around. Nixie took a moment to compose herself as my fingers fidgeted with the top of the towel.

"I-I'm so sorry. Let me blow dry your hair, then we'll get you some clothes."

I stood as she blew the hot air machine at the ends of my hair. I kept my eyes lowered, not wanting to look into her coral eyes as she moved around me. I knew what I would see, flecks of undeniable sadness, hints of remorse, and what they tried to hide … gratefulness. It was something that flickered for a moment before it passed as that instinctual thought comes through. Though she didn't say it, some part of her was thinking, *Thank you, God, it wasn't me.*

When I peeked up, the mirror was covered. She had draped dark, heavy material over it while I was in the shower and I was grateful. My hair was much longer than I had thought, and it reached halfway down my back. When Nixie had finished with it, it was in loose curls.

"Time for clothes! You're shorter and smaller than me, so you'll have to deal with a limited number of styles ..."

Nixie led me out of the bathroom, but before we got too far away, I stopped and waited for her. I didn't feel comfortable in the towel that I was standing in. She snatched up the pile of neatly folded clothes. When she turned back to me, she was smiling brightly.

"Sorry about the personal items. The best I can do is a sports bra. And I got undies more your size from a friend of mine."

She winked.

"Anyways, go ahead and put these on."

She placed the clothes in my hands. I took them back inside the safety of the bathroom. The top, a slightly over-sized t-shirt, had a lacy back. My stomach dropped at the thought of people looking at my exposed back. I tasted bile in the back of my throat as I started to tug on the bra she had given me. The fabric covered me and pressed down. Among the clothes, there were black skinny jeans. I pulled them on. They were a little big at the waist, but they covered the entire length of my legs. The fabric felt stiff compared to the clothes I used to wear, and heavier, too. They covered more. I was still uncomfortable with the shirt. The dark lace allowed the air to brush against my skin.

"Oh! You look good!"

She grabbed my hand and pulled us out of the bathroom before she stopped. Her compliment brought red to my cheeks. I ducked my head to avoid her seeing the reaction. There was a slapping noise and I looked up. Nixie had smacked herself on the forehead lightly.

"Stupid me. You need shoes."

She turned her tall, curved frame around and strode through another door. She walked with her head held high and a sway to her hips. Her green hair flowed like silk with her movements. She was absolutely stunning. It brought me a small sense of comfort. People wouldn't dare to stare at me with a beauty like her around. She returned a few moments later, her coral eyes twinkling.

"Here, this is the best I can do. I doubt you want to be wearing high heels."

She plopped down some shoes by my feet. It took me a moment before the name came back to me. Sandals. She was wearing a similar style. The kind where the fabric of the shoe slips into the space of the big toe and the one next to it. I slipped them on. The fabric wedged into place. It felt foreign and uncomfortable.

I took a tentative step forward to get used to the shoe on my foot. It snapped up and hit my heel as I walked. They weren't terribly uncomfortable, but I would have preferred to walk bare-foot. The wounds where my feet had been cut barely stung. The bandages had come off while I had showered and I had tossed them into a small trash bin in the bathroom.

"Well, I'm absolutely starving! Let's go get some food."

She pulled me along to the elevator again. I was afraid of these things, which is why I had blocked them from memory. Or, was it ...? No, not me, someone else. Memories from before my white room were nonexistent. Names. Faces. People swirled together.

New sounds pulled me from the deep place I had disappeared into. Nixie had her arm wrapped around mine. My heart started to pound against my chest as the noises grew louder. My sensitive ears, that had only known silence for so long, began to ache. My teeth chattered together. My hands shook. The hallway we walked down now was similar in color as the ones earlier, but it was missing the doors lined down the sides. In this hallway, they were sporadically placed, and not all looked the same. Some had no handles at all and swung upon their hinges.

"We're just going to the cafeteria; gotta head there to eat. I didn't expect company, so I didn't have food. Sorry!"

I shook my head. That much noise meant there were people. A lot of them. My knees started to lock.

"They won't bite. Well, most of them won't." She laughed a little at her joke trying to lighten the mood, but the lines around her mouth never deepened into a full smile. She was cautious, but her grip on me remained strong.

This was a brand new hell for me.

"No, please."

But I was too quiet, and Nixie pulled me in. The noise didn't stop, but it decreased. I didn't look up. I couldn't. Fear swarmed my gut, souring it.

Chapter 10

Stone

I had to find out more about Audrey. The rest of the team split to do their own things. Charlie wasn't in his room, as expected, so I went to search for him in the cafeteria. I'd just entered the cafeteria when Dallas came in behind me.

"Hey, she's with Nixie, before you ask. Elijah's watching them," Dallas was quiet as he spoke.

Nixie was still ignoring him. It was a little surprising to me that Nixie took his rejection so personally. She was usually okay with little flings, as far as I understood. But in the end, Dallas would probably leave to be part of a pack, so I couldn't blame him for wanting to be with his own kind. It was in his nature. Their fling really didn't concern me in the first place, but since they were both part of my team, I needed to know where their heads were at.

"Stone!"

Charlie jumped up from the table as we made our way toward him. Charlie was lean and stood a few inches shorter than me with dirty-blond hair. His eyes lit up yellow when he saw me—a normal occurrence for our kind. Our eye color changed with our emotions.

"You missed our New Year's party."

We clasped hands.

"Had better things to do."

"You mean you got a top secret job."

"Sort of."

Charlie led Dallas and me back to the table where more of us sat. They were discussing who had done what at the party, but my head was elsewhere. The others knew that Dallas and I were on Jacobs' team. What we did on those missions, though, was kept quiet from the rest of the clan. This was only one branch of the clan.

Before I had come down here, I had stopped by my small room. I had wanted to get a shower and change my clothes. I thought back to the bare walls and tidy apartment. The furniture had been given to me when I took my position on the team. I had trained for years to reach this position. To better protect the clan.

Charlie was smiling as he and the others talked about their night. I had been protecting them. And even though Charlie was a bit younger than me, it felt like we were separated by decades, not a few years.

Then the clatter of the room started to die down. Past anxieties made me leery of such lulls. I lifted my head and my shoulders stiffened as I searched the room. My hand went instinctively to where I kept my gun. I preferred to fight hand to hand, but sometimes that simply wasn't possible. My eyes shot straight to the doors.

Nixie stood there, regal, her coral eyes taking in the room. She might act easygoing, but the woman was trained and deadly. Her arm had wound around Audrey's slouched shoulders, her frame looked small, her hair covering the left side of her face. The breath in my lungs was stolen for an instant before my heartbeat stuttered to life again.

Audrey.

Audrey looked completely different, yet the same. The shower had returned some life to her. Her hair, no longer a tangled, matted mess, was long and flowing. She had a wild sort of beauty that was, at once, as dangerous as a wolf and as elegant as a dancing ballerina. Before I realized what I was doing, I was walking toward them.

Elijah followed Audrey, but I couldn't focus on him. Audrey was all I cared about at the moment. The feeling was unnatural in its intensity, and I felt a twinge of anxiety in me at it, yet I couldn't look away. She looked nervous. I convinced myself that I only wanted to comfort her, but there was something more there. Nixie smiled at me, but her eyes were full of sadness. Had Audrey revealed something about herself to Nixie?

"Stone-boy!"

Nixie threw herself at me in an uncharacteristic hug. I stiffened under her touch. It wasn't a secret that she was affectionate, but she didn't normally hug me. I made no move to wrap my arms around her, either. Instead I waited for her to release me. A foreign feeling of wrongness filled me with her arms around me.

"We need to chat later," she whispered in my ear then pulled away with that smile still plastered on her face. I resisted the urge to curl my lip at her touching my shoulders. I only nodded in response. Nixie wouldn't have done that under normal circumstances. I turned my attention back to Audrey.

She fidgeted as she stood alone. Her hair draped over the left side of her face so her scars couldn't be seen. Her eyes kept moving across the room, skittish and afraid. She flinched every so often.

I couldn't take my eyes off her hair, knowing as I did the secret that it hid beneath. I touched my right arm. Her emaciated form slumped over slightly, her body shaking with her obvious fear.

"Audrey?"

She finally looked at me, a small smile lit up her face.

"Oh! You already know her name! Maybe she'll even be willing to tell you—" I cut Nixie off with a warning glance. I didn't want to push Audrey to talk until she was ready.

The woman who stood before me was scared—I could practically feel her fear. If there was one thing I knew, you didn't push someone so timid and fearful.

Nixie dropped the subject.

"I'm going to get us food. Audrey, why don't you go with Stone to find a table?"

And then she glided away, whistling.

"Do you want go somewhere a little quieter?" I asked.

Audrey nodded then opened her mouth hesitantly to speak.

"Please."

I nodded. We headed toward a corner in the back. Nixie was particular about her own food, and hopefully she would put together an assorted plate for Audrey. I wasn't sure where that thought came from, but the idea of Audrey eating well made me feel better.

"Are you feeling better?" I leaned in toward her, unable to stop myself. She let out a shaky breath.

"I don't know what you want."

She kept her gaze averted from me.

"Have you considered that we are actually just trying to help you?" I asked, trying to look her in the eye. She shook her head, avoiding eye contact.

"Why would you?"

Finally she lifted her head. Her eyes, dark, were colored by her troubled past. Tears glistened there, and the sight invoked deep, protective instincts. It took all my strength not to pull her close and cradle her to my body. I suddenly found myself imagining her tentative touches on my back as imaginary arms wrapped around me.

I clenched my jaw in response. I wanted to give her a reassuring answer. The need to comfort her was strong, but I had no reason to. I knew nothing about her, save for what I could surmise from her rescue. I slowly rolled my neck and felt it pop and crack. I didn't trust Jacobs to be honest with her in front of him. But I didn't think saving her was a happy accident. Before I could say anything, Nixie appeared carrying trays piled with food.

"Here!"

She shoved a tray toward Audrey, but I intercepted it and set it more gently in front of her. Nixie's tray was filled with seafood, which made me scoot farther from her and closer to Audrey. I had always hated the smell of seafood, and since Nixie ate most things raw, I wanted to be as far away as possible.

"Eat. We need to put weight back on you, little guppy!" Nixie announced loudly.

Silently, I waited for her to eat, but Audrey just stared at the food. I couldn't understand her hesitation. She was clearly underfed. But as she regarded the food hesitantly, I considered a few possibilities. It only took

74

me a moment to come to a conclusion. Her food had to have been drugged before. And from her scars it was obvious that she had little experience of kindness and trust.

"Mind if I have some?"

I had bent close to her as I said this, and my lips brushed the rim of her ear as I spoke. As close as I was, it was impossible for me to miss her scent. It was sweet—like incense. In the way that only some scents can, hers chased the tension from my shoulders. I curled my fingers into fists to remove the temptation of touching her. She must have sensed the impulse in me, or seen the errant twitch of my hands, because she jerked away. Her eyes stared at me wide. Her chest heaved.

"Unless you want it all?"

She gave an uneasy smile.

"This is ... too much," she was hesitant in her response.

I grabbed a grape, popped it in my mouth. Audrey watched my movements closely. Her brows bunched as I swallowed. But then they loosened. The tight line of her lips relaxed. After I swallowed, exaggerating the motion for her benefit, I leaned in toward her once more, still refraining from touch.

"If you don't eat it, I will. Or we'll just have to throw it out."

She shifted in her seat, her eyes inching along the room, seeking out the trash bins. I hoped my comment about wasting food would encourage her to eat, but it was a shot in the dark. Being starved, perhaps the threat of wasted food would encourage more possessive instincts. I plucked another grape from her tray and rolled it between my fingers and held it out to her. I was struck by a vivid image of her wrapping those full lips around my fingers. It came completely out of nowhere, but the simple action of offering the grape spurred an undesired reaction.

"They're really good," my voice was tight as I tried to erase the image.

Her lips turned upwards a little. Slowly she unfolded her hands from her lap and grabbed the grape from my waiting fingers. She imitated me, popping it in her mouth. She closed her eyes and chewed slowly, looking like she never wanted to stop.

"There's more," I whispered. It seemed to bring her out of her daze. She opened her eyes and gave me a shy smile.

"Thank you."

It came out hesitantly and unsure. The way she said it made me think that it was the first time she had said thank you.

"Gods! Eat already! Protein!" Nixie's voice sounded from across the table. I internally scolded myself for being so unaware of my surroundings, even for a moment.

I looked at her with confusion, wondering how long she had been sitting there, watching us. That was when I noticed Charlie heading over. I moved away, feeling a spark of irritation, like he would somehow know what I was thinking. Like he knew I couldn't get the image of her out of my mind. Even for a moment.

As I thought this, Audrey started to pick at a few items on her plate, not really eating anything. Only the grapes.

"Maybe it's best if Charlie doesn't come over here," Nixie said with a glance at Audrey.

She was right. No one but the team knew how we found Audrey. The rest thought she was a lonely, lost paranormal. They didn't know she was a prisoner from Vedenin Clan, liberated into our own.

"Right. One sec. I'll be back."

I stood and I felt Audrey's eyes on me. Though I wanted to, I didn't look back.

Chapter 11

Audrey

There was far too much food, more than I'd seen in years. Food in the white room was sparse, and the times before that were hazy, lost to me. It overwhelmed me, but when Stone started to eat, I felt as though I could trust the plate that had been made for me. He didn't seem drugged. Even so, my breath was tight in my chest as I waited for any signs or symptoms. The constant fear was making my head light. But it wasn't just fear for myself. I found myself fearing for him, too. There was a twinge of regret inside me for allowing him to eat first. He had been so kind to me.

Stone's throat moved as he swallowed. And then he smiled, his eyes now bright yellow. There was a slight hint of worry there that made me turn away. I made sure to move slowly to keep my hair covering the ruined left side of my face and what that eye might see. Hiding that eye was the only way to save me from knowing exactly what he felt.

I picked up another grape, bit down, but still didn't swallow. The taste was incredible. I hadn't had food like this in years. Before it was mystery slop, the best of which were unidentifiable meats. This was something whole, something real, something I could recognize. I was afraid I would start to cry.

When Stone spoke to me again, my head was light and my stomach all fluttery. Nixie said something, but I didn't hear what.

"Right. I'll be back."

Stone got up and didn't look back. The half of grape I was about to eat was suddenly less appetizing. I set the grape down and stared at the table, feeling exposed without Stone's tall form blocking everyone's eyes. The sounds of the room were no longer muffled by his presence. Suddenly there were too many eyes. Too many words thrown around. It was too much. Too much.

Too much.

I pulled my knees to my chest when I felt a hand on my back.

"Are you okay, Audrey?" Nixie's singsong voice wrapped around me along with her arms. An unusual sense of calm filled me. My hands, which had been shaking, were finally still. The panic that I felt was stifled. It was there, but buried. Though, deep down, I could feel it clawing to be free. But the peace overwhelmed it. A sense of calm permeated. Relaxed. A soothing tide washed over me. My lungs released a breath that I felt like I had been holding for years. Nixie didn't make me feel as safe in the same way Stone did, though she, too, had a reassuring effect. Somehow she quieted the noise. Her touch was already warm with friendship. But when she let go, the loss would burn. And that loss was something I knew intimately. It injected a cold feeling of dread into my veins. If only she wouldn't torture me so. She didn't understand.

When I didn't reply, she removed her hand. I tried to hold back the whimper so close to my lips, but I only managed to muffle the cry.

It was unnaturally cold where her hand had been. Illogical thoughts consumed my mind. *I'll never be touched again. No one would want to touch a creature like me. She knows, she knows, she knows. Enjoy the warmth of human companionship for now, lonely monster. Soon it will be no more.*

My need to be touched, to be comforted, was almost animalistic. At the loss of it, I shrank away from Nixie. Their kindness was a farce. None of it was real. Fakes. Liars. Torturers. A new voice drifted in, but the world was closing around me.

Dark, dark, dark. The world was so dark.

"Nixie! What the hell did you do?" Stone's words were abrupt, his tone angry.

I tried to retreat from his voice, but he was already moving around the table back to me. The bench was small, but I sat on it length wise. Those harsh whispers came back from that dark and damaged place inside me.

Why would anyone want a monster like you? They're not here to help you. Every touch should be like fire on your scar-ridden body. Hate. That is all you are worth. Pain. That is all you deserve.

"Step away."

The voice came out of nowhere as Elijah appeared. He bypassed Nixie, ignoring her completely. I felt his cold fingers under my chin as he forced me to look at him.

"Well, isn't that … interesting."

I wanted to pull away. His icy touch made me whimper. Inwardly, I pleaded for him to let go.

"Elijah, I'm warning you. Get away from her."

Elijah looked toward Stone.

"Calm down." His voice held an arctic edge. He looked back at me.

"Please—" I begged. *Let go.* But he kept his hand on my chin. I wanted to look away. I wanted his hands off of me.

"Interesting …"

Finally he released me, and I pulled my legs close to my torso, wrapping my arms around them.

"Don't touch her!" Stone warned.

Nixie stepped forward and touched my shoulder. His warning came too late.

It felt like a thousand volts of lightning went through my veins. The world went dark.

Chapter 12

STONE

"Don't touch her!"

The warning came too late. Nixie's hand touched Audrey's shoulder. Audrey slumped suddenly and Nixie somehow managed to hold her up.

"Sorry," Nixie looked over her shoulder regretfully. I felt Charlie behind me, looking at Audrey, whose face was now hidden completely behind her hair.

"No need to apologize, Siren. She was going to pass out anyway," Elijah said, still regarding Audrey with interest. Nixie ground her teeth and shot him a warning glance.

"Elijah," my voice was low with a warning.

He was keeping something from us. While I knew it was in his nature to be secretive, this would only be problematic to us.

"Yes, Stone?"

I ground my teeth and my skin stretched tight against my muscles. My agitation grew in the face of his rather blasé response to what was happening to Audrey.

"What aren't you telling us?"

Those simple words were both demanding and dangerous. We had a right to know. I had the right to know.

"I saw something. The Vedenins. They put a wraith in her as a failsafe. It will take time, but I will be able to remove it."

With that, Elijah turned and left.

The Vedenin Clan was the rival clan we had stolen Audrey from, a fact we wanted kept quiet. But now, everyone in the cafeteria was openly looking at the mystery girl who had passed out. I moved over to her and Nixie. Nixie was holding onto her, keeping her on the bench, trying to comfort her by petting her hair. She sighed quietly and looked up at me as I made my way to them.

"I need to take her back. And *you* need to report to Jacobs."

Nixie flinched at the coldness in my voice. I had to remind myself every moment. Audrey wasn't a guest here. She wasn't a friend. She had been a prisoner of another clan. Until we knew more about her, there would be little trust about her.

Someone had to inform Jacobs what happened. And Nixie was already getting too close, too attached. She looked at me with wet coral eyes.

"It's the way it has to be," I said almost regretfully. Whatever Jacobs decided to do, we would have to follow orders.

She nodded. I gently removed Audrey from Nixie's arms, and I reminded myself yet again that we knew nothing about this girl. Even though I knew nothing about her, I couldn't help holding her tenderly.

I wanted to tell Nixie to visit because it was obvious that in their short time together she and Audrey had formed a type of bond. I could see it. Nixie, like most sirens far from water, tended to become possessive. Water-based paranormals needed a life-line here on dry land. It made long periods of time without a body of water bearable. Dallas had made the mistake of breaking that bond. As I started toward Audrey's room, Charlie moved out of the way and headed back to the table with our other friends.

***

I set Audrey down on her bed. The trip to her room had been quick and uneventful. Her hair still covered the scarred half of her face. I wanted to brush it away. The shirt Nixie had given her was too big for her.

It had slipped off her right shoulder to reveal three claw marks—jagged, uneven tears in her flesh.

Anger, hot and fiery, engulfed me. I shut the door, barely remembering to lock it. Down the hall I saw Marcus approaching.

"Ye all right?" he asked, watching me closely.

"She's got a wraith in her, so be careful what you say around her," I explained as I blew past him. My muscles were tight with frustration. How many more scars did Audrey have? I hadn't been able to bring myself to look, but someone else might know.

I knew who I had to find.

I had left Nixie in the cafeteria, only when I got there, I realized that I had told her to report to Jacobs. My head had been so consumed with anger at seeing those scars that it was seared into my mind. The corners of my vision were tinged with red. My breathing was ragged. I had been so wrapped up Audrey's problems I had forgotten that I sent Nixie away. I wanted to vent, to punch something. Instead, I switched directions and headed to Jacobs's office.

Jacobs' office was on the next level up. I took the stairs, hoping to save precious moments on the way. As I reasoned with myself, the anger began to dissipate. I didn't know this woman. She wasn't a clan member in need of protection. Obviously she was a prisoner, there was no disputing that, but she could belong to the York Clan or the Long Clan. If so, she was their business. Wasn't she? Our clan, the Bradens, didn't have many allies.

I exited the stairwell. This floor had been renovated, within the last few years, for the offices of upper clan members. The ugly carpet had been ripped up and replaced with hardwood floors. The doors had been replaced with heavy oak. Behind the double doors at the end of the hallway was my goal—Jacobs' office, though it was more of a suite than an office.

I didn't even knock when I pushed the doors open. The front room was supposed to be a waiting room, but our team had used it as a briefing area many times. It didn't feel much like a waiting room anymore. My step faltered a little as I burst in on unforeseen company.

Dallas stood stoic leaning against the farthest wall from Nixie, trying to keep his focus off of her. He kept his head held high, but his gaze obviously averted from her. She was sitting on the small, plain couch. While she had a carefree smile plastered on her face, she kept glancing in the direction of the door as if she wanted to leave. Elijah stood rigid next to the inner door of Jacobs' office.

Cole, a dawon were-tiger, was present as well. The Asian descent were-tigers were larger in size and almost always albino. Cole, however, was different. His mother had been a witch and he had inherited some of her powers. Marcus was missing. I moved toward Nixie as Dallas bent down to talk to Cole.

"Why isn't Marcus here?"

"Where do you think he is? Guarding Scars," Dallas answered, but at the mention of Audrey, I began to fixate again. Audrey. I was reminded of the scars I had seen. The ones on her shoulder. My stomach turned violently and my anger spiked at the thought of the pain she must have gone through. I turned to Nixie.

"How many scars does she have besides her face?"

"Which one was it?" Nixie's voice was unusually timid.

"What do you mean?" I was taken aback by her question.

"Which one did you see?"

"On her shoulder." My voice came through clenched teeth.

"I didn't see them all, but there is another bad one on her thigh."

We were silent while the others whispered. My body shook. I wanted to roar. I had to calm down. I tried to breathe.

"I can't … how young was she when she got them?"

No, I didn't want to think about that. I didn't want to think about how old the scars looked. How familiar she seemed with them. As if it were natural. I knew I would lose control if I found out that information now.

But I was saved by the door to Jacobs' office. The man himself stepped out, standing tall with his head held high. He looked over the room, his gaze finally landing on his son.

"Marcus is with her?"

"Yes, sir."

"Good. Elijah already informed me of our *guest's* situation," he paused. "And I know I wasn't clear about the reason for our mission. Cole, you told me yourself there was something very important there. It just so happens the purpose, though I could not disclose it at the time, was the girl."

I noticed Cole's jaw tense. I wasn't sure why he reacted that way, and I felt irritation flash through me. What was going on with me? I shook my head at myself and focused back on Jacobs.

"Elijah has just informed me of the wraith trapped in her mind. The Vedenins must have implanted one in her. It's likely it was commanded to hide inside her while she was with them. Its influence could push her to do things she doesn't want to do. Elijah doesn't think the wraith will be able to take over completely. He and I have decided that he will extricate the creature from her, but it's important that, while Elijah removes it, we be cautious of what we say around her. What's more, it seems her memory has been warped by the presence of the wraith inside her. She seems to have little to no idea about any of the supernatural world—our world."

"So, she's human?" Nixie asked. She sat a little straighter now. Jacobs was watching our reactions, but most of us were well trained enough to keep them to ourselves.

"No. We don't know what she is. And as expected, the Vedenins are now looking for her." Dallas twisted his shoulders as he stood straighter, his gaze flickering to Nixie for a moment before his brows bunched deeply to overhang his eyes. Nixie's lips twisted, but otherwise she remained still. Cole's gaze cut around the room, a low rumble rattled his chest.

It wasn't surprising Jacobs already knew this. Our clan had many spies, and they would have told us immediately had our liberation activities been discovered.

"Our sources say they are furious. Not only did we hit their pride and hit it hard, but apparently this woman was more important than we realized. The Vedenin Clan isn't ready to spill blood yet, but they will be on high alert and likely on the search. We need to keep her hidden."

Jacobs' voice was tense. He trusted our team. We were hand-picked by him, but it would be impossible to know whether there were any spies in our own clan. If the Vedenins caught wind that she was here, they might strike hard and fast.

"Apparently they fell for our distraction and thought our target had been something less significant, thanks to the mess Dallas made on the other side of the building. They hadn't bothered to do a full sweep until well after we left. But the wraith inside her sent out a signal when it awakened. They not only realized she is gone, but they have information. Not much, our barrier here protects us, for the most part. But they've been able to surmise that she's in the care of another clan. Elijah, how long will it take to extract the wraith?"

"Well, if I could extract my way, five hours. Your way could take up to five days."

A chill went through the room. The members of this team didn't fear much, we had spent years training and had faced dangerous foes. But we could all sense Elijah's thinly veiled threat. Wraiths, especially one of his power and skill, could frighten the bravest of men.

"Five days it is," Jacobs said, looking at no one.

The meeting was over. We all knew it. Still, none of us moved.

"Why would the Vedenins want her in the first place?" Dallas mused, not looking at anyone, simply speaking aloud what was on all of our minds. I saw Cole straighten his back.

If there was a reply, I didn't want to hear it. Elijah left abruptly, and I followed. When he arrived at Audrey's room, I was steps away. His hand on the doorknob, he stated that he had to work alone and in silence.

The sound of the door closing behind him filled me with dread.

Chapter 13

Audrey

The dream was always the same, yet different from reality. We were in the kitchen. No, not *the kitchen*, a kitchen. He was mad. Really mad. I was—no—I *am* wrong. Or had done something wrong? Dark, dark eyes and a face deep set in a scowl. I whimpered. I could feel myself as a child, confused and naïve. A ten-year-old. I only wanted to trust him—my father. No, not my father. Something was strange about him. He was shrouded in darkness. All but his claws, which he raked through the air toward my face. Lines of fire, and a distant voice—my own?—screaming.

I shouldn't have cried out. I knew better.

It was a familiar dream, though no less hellish for its familiarity. I woke quietly, as I always did. I wasn't in the whiteness of my cell. No, I wasn't there anymore. They had come. Taken me. A new prison. At least the vicious details of the dream had lessened. It was growing dimmer with every day. White and black were all I had. The white of the walls. The black uniforms of the guards. Tears slipped down my face silently.

A foot shifted weight against carpet somewhere close by, drawing my attention to the fact I wasn't alone. The unearthly beautiful one with unsettling yellow eyes, the one who talked strangely and who usually watched over me, was there. There were no blemishes on his face. It was perfectly symmetrical and looked like it was carved from marble. His skin was a silky pale, his hair was all types of different shades of red, some so bright I wasn't sure it was natural. The colors in his eyes were different from the others. They had a basic appearance, even when I viewed them with my other eye. But the range of the colors held in his was overwhelming. There were so many things there I had never seen before. He made me uncomfortable. His eyes scared me. They were so old, far older than he appeared.

"What's got ye cryin'?" He paused waiting for an answer that wouldn't come. "Oh, nae talkin' again. Awright, I'll respect that. I'll try tae ask ye yay or nae questions."

He winked at me, which was alarming in its own way. I moved as far from him as I could and avoided looking at him.

"Dae ye know how ye got those?"

He pointed at my scars. I didn't move my head to answer his question.

"Nae answer? Okay. Dae ye enjoy futbol?"

My eyebrows pinched together for a moment in my confusion as my mouth settled into a grim line. My eyes narrowed slightly. The term was familiar, but not entirely. Vague memories swam before my eyes. There was a small TV that flickered. Large men ran at each other. They clashed and tackled. They were faint memories.

The white was void of everything but the memories. Horrible, painful memories that screamed at me, even now. Flashes of a life before it flickered through my mind. Small houses. Smaller rooms. A brief moment of happiness. Claws. A tearing sensation crawling along my skin.

"Ach, Scars! Ye don't even know what that is? I would nae min' takin' a peek at those memories of yours."

"You may think you have seen it all, Marcus, but you would not want to see into her memories."

Elijah's cold, flat voice slipped into the small room from the beyond the doorway.

"Aye, I suppose ye might be right."

He paused, stroking his chin.

"But I fear nary a thing could scare me. Nae in 'er bonnie wee head nor outside it."

"You would not be able to handle the horrors that invade her mind. That I promise."

I looked at Elijah as he spoke. His face was blank as if this were a normal conversation, but somehow he knew. He knew my pain. His pitiless, black eyes held mine. I didn't react as they came closer, pinning me where I stood. It made me uneasy.

Do you know what hides in the deepest corners of your mind?

The question was directed at me, but not really. It was almost as if he was airing his curious thoughts, and I, somehow, had heard them.

Before I realized what he was doing, he grabbed my head in his large hands roughly. His hold was too tight, his touch icy. I could feel him apply pressure. It wasn't especially painful, but it wasn't comforting either.

"Hmm, it's been there for years. More of a residue, but dangerous all the same."

Then a buzzing started. An instinct to react shot through my body. But … no, that wasn't quite right. My body wasn't under my control. My head looked up at the man named Elijah, but his face was blank, unsurprised. He raised an eyebrow ever so slightly. I could see an amused look cross his typically blank face.

"You stupid fool. You're out of your league, wraith. I wouldn't mess with her fragile mind."

The voice came from my mouth, but I hadn't said anything. I didn't understand. Desperation had wrapped its way around my throat. I had gone years without screaming, it wasn't worth the breath, but I had been in control then. Now all I wanted to do was scream. I was, for the first time, a prisoner inside my own body.

Then Elijah did the scariest thing he'd done since I had met him. He smiled. His teeth were sharp and pointed. His tongue ran over them, black and unsettling.

"Apparently you don't realize who you are dealing with."

Elijah looked at me with an air of calm. I was shaking.

I tried to move, to speak, but I could not. I remembered a similar instance, only that time … that time had been fear. This was different.

"Oh yes, the great, Elijah, child of the oldest reaper. I know who you are. *You are nothing,*" I heard myself sneer at him. My voice was different now. Deeper. It scared me.

"This will be a fun few days," Elijah hissed before he touched his other hand to mine.

Pain blinded me to the point that I knew nothing but darkness.

Chapter 14

STONE

The next few days were torture. Elijah was at her side most of the time. Both of them deathly silent except for intermittent screams and whimpers. Audrey spent most of the time unconscious, and watching her like that tormented me. The protectiveness that I felt for her had only increased during the time Elijah worked with her. I didn't understand it, but it was impossible to ignore. Audrey was just another prisoner. But the third day was the worst. I was stretched to my limit. My skin strained tight with impatience, pinching and burning.

I had been staying right outside the door. Elijah had informed me that the chances of the wraith jumping bodies would be higher if another body were nearby. It had pained me to think she was in there enduring more torture in addition to what she had already suffered. My desire to her protect was palpable, and those instincts only seemed to be growing stronger. Nixie would join me sometimes, but I could tell Elijah made her uncomfortable.

I looked over at the siren. Nixie was biting at her thumbnail. Audrey had somehow worked her way into the hearts of the siren and myself. Who wouldn't feel at least something for someone so obviously mistreated? She kept pacing in front of the door. She would stare at it, as if willing it to open. My muscles tightened, strained, and burned under my skin, begging for something to do. Muscles shifted underneath. Without my conscious choice or direction, my body was changing. It was instinctual for shifters. Strong emotions forced a corresponding change in our cells.

Time moved slowly in the hallway. The days stretched on in unending minutes. At one point, Nixie told me that she would be back and headed toward the elevators. I didn't ask where she was going. I found that I didn't care much. My concern was for the woman behind those doors. The one that I shouldn't care for at all. There was something about her.

"You need to go for a run," Charlie said. I couldn't stop pacing; I felt so restless. My head was full of the possibilities of what might be happening in there. No one really knew the secrets wraiths had learned before emerging from the darkness, but I had seen paranormals after coming out of a torture session with Elijah. Those thoughts still made icy fear run down my spine. An irrational reaction shivered through me at Charlie's words.

I turned and snarled, feeling my eyes swirl with the deep red color of my rising anger in the way that only a shifter can. Charlie responded in kind—wolves responded reflexively to any display of dominance. But what I was asserting myself for, I wasn't even sure. I had been a master at controlling my emotions. It was one of the reasons I was on Jacobs' team. Charlie's teeth had lengthened in response to my aggression. He snarled right back at me, his own eyes flashing red.

"Don't take your anger out on me."

I needed space. That was all. I felt bad for the girl and I needed space.

"Back off, Charlie."

I replied with the same amount of venom in my voice. My body buzzed with energy, like I was waiting for him to make the wrong move, though I knew he was a friend. My stomach twisted, the muscles in my shoulders and calves were tight. I released a breath, trying to let go of the anxiety that was shaking me.

"Fuck!" I slid my hands through my hair, pulling back on the strands in my frustration. *What the fuck is wrong with me?*

"You need to get out of this hallway. You haven't really left in *days.* I know, poor her, but you just got back from a mission, right? Don't you need a rest, buddy?"

Charlie had already calmed, but I was still heated. His previously livid red eyes began to fade to a more mellow blue. His pre-shift muscles started to deflate, which is when I realized I had shifted my shape a little without realizing it. I closed my eyes and breathed in. I released a strangled breath. He was right. I needed it. Freedom. I needed to get out of this building.

"Call me if anything changes, Charlie. Anything."

He nodded, waving me off.

Instead of swinging to the left where the elevators waited for me at the end of the hallway, I took the shorter route to the stairs. My feet ate up the distance like it was nothing, falling heavily against the old, tattered carpet. This floor was only used for overnight stays or guests who planned to be here a few days. So the clan hadn't spent the time or effort renovating it like we had the other floors. And though this particular base was fairly new and there were always upgrades going on, different floors were being repurposed. Cain Braden, the head of our Clan, had bought this resort in the middle of the woods as a getaway from the city life. In winters prior to our ownership, it had been used as a ski resort, though that had been almost a decade ago.

I pushed through the heavy door leading to the stairs and made my way down the concrete steps of the stairwell. The movement was already helping to loosen me up, and the more I moved, the better I started to feel.

Tension had straightened my spine unnaturally, stiffening my posture and resulting in discomfort that a shift would surely help. As I walked through the hallway, I rubbed the back of my neck while ignoring stares of other clan members as I hurried past them on the first floor. I glanced briefly at the other doors, considering a more roundabout, more discreet way out of the hotel, but this would take me directly to the woods that ran alongside. It was an old forest, full of strong trees. Some areas were thickly wooded and choked with brambles, while others thinned to clearings. Nestled at the edge of the property line there was a small pond. And best of all, the closest city was a good distance away. No need to worry about human interference.

The city itself had once been a thriving, bustling place, but it had never recovered after the recession. The owners of the hotel had been desperate to get rid of the land, and Cain had jumped at the chance to expand his holdings. Other than that, there wasn't another town within twenty miles.

That left plenty of room for us to roam. I shed my clothes at the edge of the forest in preparation for my run. A dryad had created cubby holes in the trees for this exact purpose, into which I placed my garments. I let down my guard and the transformation began.

First came the stretching as the cells shifted, bones extending. The feeling was exuberant, muscles that hadn't been stretched in days started to loosen. I rolled my shoulders as I let the image of the animal I was shifting into flood my senses. My hands came down with a loud slap on the ground. My forearms bulged, growing in width and length. My hands turned inwards, rounding in a distinctly inhuman shape. Hair sprouted from my pores. My back lengthened, my hips widened, and a shiver went through my body as I finished the transition. My cells and muscles rejoiced. My body was built for this sort of change. Finally, in the form of a black leopard, I entered the woods.

It was rare for me to take large cat forms. The sensitivity of the whiskers was hell when it wasn't necessary. But my legs felt stronger with every stride. I could feel my raw power increasing. In this form, I could get the run I needed without going too far.

Pushing off with my hind legs and keeping my tail low, I darted into the woods. My mind kept going back to Audrey. I pushed myself harder trying to keep my mind from her. Out here I wanted to be free from those thoughts. I needed to get things back into perspective.

I lifted my nose and drew in a scent. Frustration bored down on me and I snorted it out and shook my head. Wolves. I didn't know the werewolves were out running today. I would have chosen a different form, if I had. Branches snapped from behind me, as the scent of a wolf got stronger.

The werewolves wouldn't attack when they knew in advance about other shifters, but caught off guard, their animal instincts could be dangerous. A massive blond wolf with yellow eyes leapt from the brush suddenly, running beside me. His lips peeled away from his teeth in a canine warning as he kept pace with me. More would follow, so I focused my mind. I imagined long eyes, a shorter torso, a tail, and pointed ears. My body responded immediately. Once the transformation was complete I knew my eyes had changed to an ugly shade of brown to mirror my annoyance. The blond wolf howled and turned away, to him the threat had disappeared.

The wolf and my own unplanned change had distracted me until I was farther than I had planned on coming. I noticed the cabins not too far off. These were built for larger families in our clan who wanted or needed space of their own. Some of the cabins were built for creatures that couldn't live too far from nature. There were also some paranormal creatures that could read minds, and those who weren't practiced in building mental walls or couldn't control their powers found refuge from the noisy thoughts of other paranormals out here. I couldn't blame them, and I sure as hell didn't enjoy people getting into my mind and hearing my thoughts. The houses were at least five miles out, which all but guaranteed they were out of range. I shook my lengthened snout and turned back toward the hotel.

As I ran, I tried to reason out why I felt this undeniable need to protect Audrey. It wasn't a shape-shifter thing. We didn't have quite the same instincts as the *weres* did. They were part animal down to their core. Shape-shifters were not. We didn't react the same way they did. Their protective instincts weren't as ingrained in us. We fell in love much like humans and many other paranormal creatures. I didn't know Audrey. It wasn't a familial connection I felt, but I felt something. I just had to figure out what that was.

"Stone! Stone-y boy! Stone!"

I let out a low annoyed huff when I heard Nixie call out to me. Her voice managed to carry through the forest. But I didn't want to deal with the six foot, green-haired siren at the moment. My body, and mind, were still restless. I was agitated for reasons I couldn't understand.

And then, there she was, looking so out of place in her high heels and short skirt. All sirens had problems with hiding their legs. They claimed pants were too constricting.

"Hey! Stooone!"

Now she was dragging my name out. Adding syllables. Her voice started to lilt into a song, and if that happened, I knew she would not be denied. Nixie wasn't part of Jacobs' special ops team because she was an average siren. She was anything but that.

I broke through the woods into the clearing, shifting as I walked toward my clothes. Her eyes trailed down my body slowly, with one eyebrow cocked. She pushed a hip out and placed a hand on it. I wasn't an easily embarrassed person; no shifter was. We were used to shifting and wearing different forms, and I was proud of my usual human form. It was thickly built, with solid thighs and a strong torso, corded with muscle. But for some reason, this felt different. I felt a sense of wrongness so I turned, presenting my backside to her instead. Rooting through the cubby in which I had placed my clothes, I pulled out my boxer-briefs.

"What do you want, Nixie?" I asked as I put them on.

I looked over my shoulder when she didn't answer. Her eyes boring holes in my ass. I pulled myself up to my full six-foot-five-inches and stared her down.

"Are you finished?" I asked, getting more annoyed.

She shook her head.

"Sorry, what was I saying?"

Usually sirens were much more composed than she was. After all, they had called sailors onto the rocks long ago for the sake of their own perverse sense of fun or to mate. Sirens these days were a lot more civilized, even if I was still of the opinion that the lucky ones were the ones that were killed.

I resisted the urge to roll my eyes at her.

"I don't know, Nixie. You were going to tell me."

"Oh right, I want to see Audrey."

I was silent, raising a brow.

"And you called me back here why?"

"They won't let me and I demand that you help me." She set her legs shoulder width apart and jutted out her jaw defiantly.

"Nixie, you know I have no control over that. Elijah hasn't let anyone into that room since he entered it three days ago. You know why we can't go in there."

I pulled my black shirt over my head as I spoke. When my head poked through, Nixie was looking at the ground defeated. This reminded me how sirens easily formed strong bonds with people, especially when they have spent long time away from the water.

"Nix, when was the last time you went to the lake?"

"I don't know ... a week. Maybe a month and half ..." she whispered the last part, but she knew I could hear her.

I slanted my head, raising my brows. It was her decision to do what she wanted, but she could put the team in danger by being so careless. Sirens needed to commune with a large body of water at least every two weeks in order to remain healthy.

"Look, going back to that lake is not an option. I spend a little extra time in the bath or in the pool. I'm fine!" Her coral eyes flashed. I countered with a glare. We were at a stalemate for some moments. Her determination flared in response to my suggestion, but it leaked away after only a few moments more. She knew I was right. She started to squirm where she stood looking decidedly uncomfortable.

"Fine! I'll go to the lake."

This must have been how Charlie felt when he had been dealing with me earlier. The more we got wound up over a woman we barely knew, one that was a prisoner here, the more danger we were putting ourselves into.

"You don't understand!" Nixie screamed at me. She was losing her temper. Normally, I could deal with the shorter-tempered creatures, but at the moment, I was on edge myself. The run had only helped so much.

"Don't you dare yell at me, siren," my voice came out strangled and distorted. I knew at this point my fangs were out, my eyes already shifting to a deep red color.

Nixie dragged her hands down her face.

"Whatever. This is getting out of hand. Look, I'll go to the fucking lake. Call me if anything changes with her."

She flipped her deep green hair and headed toward the lake. I headed back upstairs.

When I arrived on Audrey's floor, her screams were even louder than before. I tore through the hallways without a thought. I tried to push her door open, but it was locked. Charlie, who I had barely noticed, regarded the door with wide eyes. I shot him a glance that demanded an answer, but he just shrugged.

"Elijah! Let me in!" I slammed my hands on the door. "Audrey!"

Chapter 15

Audrey

White surrounded me. It was safe. It was home. The only home I really remembered. Someone was calling my name.

No, that wasn't right. This wasn't home. The whiteness melted, drained away from my vision, and a forgotten home took its place. My old home. A worn-down, one-story, three-bedroom house. A living room with a stained, hole-ridden couch, the stuffing overflowing. A small, broken TV. There was a kitchen with broken tiles, everything vaguely stained by age and poor upkeep. A closet had been converted into a bedroom by the simple act of tossing in a mattress, a comforter, and an old pile of clothes. And his room. My father's room.

I never went in there.

I stood in the kitchen, not moving as he added new scars to join the others. I was being punished. What I had done this time? I didn't remember, but these were the last scars I would receive. The set that wrapped around my thigh.

"You belong to me. You understand? I am branding you, as is the right of our kind. If anyone else tries to possess you, I will kill them. Or demand the same of you. There are few of us left, little one. We must stick together. And beyond all things, you must always obey me. You understand?"

His voice had a slight hiss to it. His pupils were slits.

I nodded as I cried and screamed on the inside. He took his time, letting his claws do their bloody work. I could hear it. The sound of skin parting at the knifepoint edge of those insistent claws. Blood ran down my leg. Muscle, too, offered no resistance. I shifted my weight. I didn't want to fall and make it worse.

Make it stop, make it stop, please make it stop. My only relief was when he finished. He carefully wrapped my leg in gauze and set me down in my bed. I wasn't to move for several days, until the wound was fully healed. He would bring food to me. He wasn't a horrible father all the time. It's just, his instincts ran deep. He was fond of telling me that *no one* stole property from our kind. And I was his property. By marking me with his claws, he was sending a signal to the world. A fearsome beast had claimed me as its own. The only exception was the time he scarred my face. That had been a punishment. He had meant to hurt me.

I was thrown into my next memory without transition. Without warning.

My legs were drawn tight to my chest and I was on my side, trying to make myself small. The smaller my body, the less they could attack. Attacks from every side—punches, kicks, unwanted touches. All of it, never ending. I cried for them to stop. They demanded things I couldn't give them. They demanded that I do things I would never do. I'd rather claw out my own eyes than use them for these people. I wanted to … something. I couldn't remember what. It was hidden deep inside me, an instinctual impulse. But it remained elusive. I could never remember.

And the attacks continued.

"Audrey!"

I knew that voice, and it gave me a small sense of comfort. Like a vast ocean finally breaching the final barrier, I felt myself pulled deeper into my memory.

"Audrey, the wraith is weakening. You must awaken now."

This voice was colder, cut off from any emotion. It was a voice unconnected to my painful memories, but somehow inside them as well.

My head throbbed. My mouth was dry, but somehow I managed to strangle out a *no*. I wanted the peace of the white room, the safety it had offered.

"It's safer here," a voice whispered in my head. The voice hissed, tickling my ear. It was a promise of what I wanted, what I needed. Safety. Safety in my room.

I shut my eyes tighter to block out what I was not ready to confront. I forced my brain to blankness. I pushed away every thought, silencing their pestering voices. The sounds that filtered into my awareness were ignored. I shut my eyes to keep the light out. To keep my head focused only on the white that had for so long been my only solace. White walls. White bed. White. White. White. My head began to hurt. Were those cracks forming in the walls of my safe place?

"Please, please, please."

The mattress was beneath me. Eyes watched, waited patiently.

"You must not listen to the wraith in your head. If you wake now, you will break his hold. The safety you feel is false. Let go."

The unemotional voice was back. But he was asking the impossible. How could anything be safer than the evil I knew? I was safe here. At least this was familiar.

"Audrey!" came the other voice, again. I liked it. Something in its tone. I savored how it made me feel. For a second, I felt … safe? This voice promised me things. This voice belonged to someone who'd … saved me.

"Audrey!" it roared again. I twitched.

"Wake, Audrey," Elijah urged once more.

I was scared to open my eyes. Something held me back. In here was safety. Out there was the unknown.

"The wraith is influencing your thoughts. Safety is not in sleep, but in waking. It is there that you can break free from his hold. Now, wake."

The voice sounded almost angry. I had learned much about anger in my life. I knew how to react to it. I obeyed. My eyes cracked open. The light was dazzling. The shapes bleary and indistinct, but taking shape with every blink of my eyes. The walls here weren't white. I was scared. I wanted to shut them against the pale blue walls confronting me now.

Not in sleeping, but in waking. The words made sense. I took a shaky breath. My eyes opened again. The walls really weren't that bad. They were pretty, actually, and the mattress comfortable. Even the blankets were unbelievably soft.

And there, right before me, cold black eyes. I could not avert my eyes from those pitiless depths. I clung to those as if I would fall out of existence otherwise. And they watched back. I could stare forever and I knew those eyes would stay the same. I would never see flecks of different color reflecting the emotion in his eyes. He was unnatural. It should have been unnerving, but I found it calming. It was safe. Though opposite to the white I had treasured, his eyes were as safe as those walls in my old prison.

"Wh—" Oh, that hurt. My throat was bone dry, and suddenly it was hard to breathe.

"Here."

Elijah handed me a cup with a straw.

I wanted to throw the straw aside and gulp down the water, but the last time I had done that while in prison I had drank too quickly and coughed it back up. The water was room temperature, but offered sweet relief. I stared at the strange creature next to me as I drank. His emotionless eyes and voice clashed with his actions. I didn't do well with conflicting personalities.

"A wraith had a trap door of sorts in your mind. If you were ever taken, the wraith was spelled to awaken. The Vedenins have realized you were taken. We had to remove it or they would have used the wraith to collect the information they needed to take you back."

And with that, Elijah stood abruptly and headed out the door to the small living room.

There was a loud crash followed by a voice growling. I knew that noise well. It meant to hide. I tried to pull myself up, but I could barely move. Instead, I rolled myself off the bed. I took the blanket with me and pulled myself into a ball in the farthest corner from the noise. All the while, there was screaming in the other room. Too much noise, too much anger. I counted to distract myself.

One, two, three. I am safe. Four, five, six. Safe.

"What the hell were you doing to her?"

Stone. It was Stone's voice, though distorted and rough ... *twenty, twenty-one ...*

"I did as I was ordered. Remove your hand."

Elijah's voice was different, now. Darker. The air around me was cold with dread, and I pulled my limbs tighter to my body. There was another crashing sort of noise, followed by feet stomping into my room.

"Audrey."

His voice was quiet now, as if he were coaxing a small frightened animal. I suppose that was what I was. A small, frightened animal.

"Audrey..."

"She is wraith-free now."

Elijah's words came through the door as he retreated. I wasn't sure if I wanted to look up. There would be nothing for me to hold onto. There would be no solid safety. Nothing familiar remained.

"Audrey," he whispered my name again. I couldn't look, not even for a second. Stone smelled different. Like things I could barely remember. Things I associated with open spaces and growing things. His hair was a tangled mess and his eyes were a strange yellowish color. He let out a long breath when I looked into his eyes. In the color of his eyes I could see his worry. It was a particular sort. One that was somewhat relieved, but also unsure.

I wanted to hide, but leaned forward tentatively. I felt his fingers brush against mine as the soft fabric was tugged gently away from my face. My heart raced in my chest. His movements were subtle, calm, and by all means should have calmed me.

Squinting against the bright light, my eyes met his. They were in a state of flux, a mixture of turbulent blue and lightly amused flecks of yellow. His lips twitched, apparently undecided whether to go up or down. He was carefully searching my face, trying to decipher how I felt.

His hand stroked my cheek in the briefest of touches. My eyes closed involuntarily, the act shaking me. How easily I trusted him. A long breath slipped from my lips at the delight I felt at his touch. Something touched them, but when I opened my eyes, although Stone was frighteningly close, he was also painfully far from me. I had never felt like this before. What did it mean? I could see him searching my eyes as he pushed my hair away from my face. His hand grazed my scars. I flinched.

"Don't," Stone pleaded. I looked at him, not understanding. "Please don't flinch when I touch you."

102

"But …"

"These are beautiful."

He glanced at the scars. His words were sincere, but held a weight to them.

I didn't understand. They were a brand, a punishment. They were meant to keep others away. They were meant to make me belong only to my father.

Stone cleared his throat and pulled away.

"Elijah says the wraith is gone. Can I take you down to the cafeteria or bring you food? Or if you want, I can get Nixie. She can give you a hand in the shower."

As he said this, Stone held out his hand to me.

I looked up at him. His eyes had turned to a deep blue color. Before I could read anymore, I shifted my eyes back to the hand he offered me. I raised my shaky hand to his and he pulled me up. He tucked me under his arm and guided me out of the pale blue room.

Chapter 16

STONE

Gods, she looked like a fragile bird. I didn't know whether to touch her or let her remain where she was. I was afraid that if I so much as breathed on her, she would crack into a million pieces and I would never be able to put her back together. But those thoughts confused me. When did I decide it was my job to make sure she wouldn't break? When did I decide that I would be the one to put her back together? Probably when her eyes fluttered shut, she sighed at my touch, and I brushed ever so softly against the deformed side of her mouth. A moment that I would relive for the next few nights. I couldn't help but remember how even though the right side of her mouth was slightly rigid and malformed from her scars, it was soft and inviting.

She looked at me like I was an oddity she could never understand. I knew that she was wondering how I was able to touch her scars without a hint of disgust or pity. I understood the scars that littered her skin, and I hoped one day that she would allow me to show her my own. That thought made me recompose myself. A shape-shifter like me would never show off their true form, not to anyone. So why did I suddenly have the urge to show myself to the magnificent creature in front of me?

"Don't," I whispered. "Don't flinch when I touch you."

"But ..." She tried to urge me away, but I couldn't.

"These are beautiful." I traced her scars with my eyes. "Elijah says the wraith is gone. Can I take you down to the cafeteria or bring you food? Or if you want, I can get Nixie. She can give you a hand in the shower."

She took my hand and stood. In this form, I always chose to be taller, but not excessively so. I didn't want to draw too much attention to myself. Six feet three inches worked well for me. Her head reached my collarbone and I realized that she was not a tiny little thing at all. I thought that maybe in a different life, in a different place, she would have been a fierce warrior.

We didn't make it far before Nixie came rushing toward us. I wondered if the wraith had erased some of Audrey's memories because she hid behind me as Nixie approached. Nixie took it in stride and continued forward with a smile still plastered on her face.

"Audrey!"

I felt Audrey jump and flinch at her name, but then she edged out around me and moved a little closer to Nixie. Nixie threw her arms around Audrey and hugged her enthusiastically. I wanted to shout at Nixie not to be so rough with Audrey, since somehow the girl looked even more frail than when she had first arrived. Nixie turned around and glared at me.

"I told you to call me. Now you don't get to come with us. You may trail behind, but you are not with us." Nixie stuck out her green tongue at me.

I just rolled my eyes, hating the fact that I wasn't the one holding Audrey. Nixie started to talk to Audrey about random things, but my thoughts drowned out their conversation.

I wondered where Elijah went. After I had busted through the door, I'd caught Elijah by the throat. Still in a blind rage, I'd ignored the instinct against treating him that way. He had snarled in response, his sharp teeth clenched. I had never seen him so angry, and the fear that should have been overpowering me was surprisingly absent. My instinct to challenge him wasn't though. Thankfully, common sense had pierced my rage before it had gotten worse. I had pulled away from him before I could say anything, and he had left the room looking distracted.

We headed toward the cafeteria, and I started wondering if maybe we should have allowed Audrey to eat in private. But the cafeteria was mostly deserted. A few people lingered, but not many. I let out the breath I didn't realize I was holding as Nixie led Audrey to the back in a dark corner. I stayed with Audrey while Nixie left to grab food.

"I hope you told her that you didn't want seafood." I tried to make my voice light, but I knew that tense, stiff muscles, fisted hands, and rapidly changing eye color betrayed my mood. Audrey looked up at me with worry in her eyes. "I was trying to make a joke. I didn't realize I was that bad at making them." I tried again to give her a smile, but she shrunk into herself some more.

"Here we go, sweetie." The plate was filled with a mixture of food, small portions of pretty much everything. Nixie had her own tray of seafood. I about gagged when I looked at it, so I focused on Audrey. My heart broke looking at her because she just stared at the food as if it would eat her instead of the other way around.

"Eat!" I rumbled before I realized how that word came out of my mouth. Audrey's eyes shot up to me, and I could see the fear there. She would eat, but only because she was afraid of what would happen if she didn't. I needed to leave. I needed to give her space, yet I couldn't move. I couldn't force myself to even look away from her. She looked like she was about to grab some of the fruit, but I knew she needed protein. She needed meat. Goddammit, if she got any skinner she would be pushed over by a gust of wind. I controlled the growl that wanted to force its way out of my throat. I didn't like to think about how weak she really was, how the Vedenins made her that way.

"Hey, Stone, how about you go find out where Elijah went?" Nixie muttered through clenched teeth.

I knew she was mad, but at this point, I didn't care. I wanted to force the food down Audrey's throat.

"Hey, Stone, look at me."

I finally turned and made the stupid mistake of looking her in the eyes. They glowed a bright coral color. Her green hair seemed darker, turning an almost purple color.

"Can you go find Elijah for me?" Her voice was a song. A song that I would never be able to resist. It was like something digging in my brain, trying to get me to focus, but all I could feel was the silky feel of her hand touching mine. I leaned closer. A song played in my head, all piano, starting out low and moving to an easy beat. I closed my eyes to hear the song better, to let it wrap around me. I started to move. I had no care in the world other than to find where the song originated.

When the song ended, I was at the doorway of Jacobs's office and I knew Nixie had used her siren song on me. She was too attached to what was mine. Wait. I meant she was just too attached to my charge. To our team's charge. Nixie wasn't a real fighter. She was a seductress, a torturer of the mind, body, and soul, and she was part of our team. But Audrey was mine to protect. Ours to protect.

I didn't bother knocking on Jacobs' door since I knew he caught my scent in the hall. When I entered, Elijah, Dallas, and Marcus were already there. Marcus was draped over the couch, looking relaxed as always, but Dallas was pacing. Wolves could never seem to stay still for long. Even Jacobs looked like he wanted to join his son. Elijah remained motionless next to Jacobs's desk. Instead of watching our team leader, he was watching my progress into the room. I felt unnerved by his attention. No one really wanted a wraith's attention on them and that included me.

"We need to get her informed and quickly. If what Elijah tells me is true, then we have a bigger issue on our hands here." All of us looked Elijah's way. I wanted to know what Jacobs wasn't telling us.

"Are ye going to elaborate there?" Marcus called casually from the couch. He looked at the walls with a blasé amusement.

"First, all you need to know is that Elijah seems to believe that she can read emotions through your eyes. Not aura readings, something different. You need to be careful around her. We can't trust her not to play on your emotions. When the whole team is here, I will tell you the rest. I don't like to repeat myself. Cole left late last night on a mission. They should be back in a couple hours. Until then, try to get her situated, make her feel comfortable amongst our clan. Marcus, you and Stone go. Dallas, stay here. I need to talk to you. Is Nixie still with her?" Jacobs watched us with eyes that slowly faded to yellow.

Apparently, whatever Elijah had told him was making him stressed. I didn't care. I wanted to get back to Audrey, and I was pissed off that that Nixie had used her song on me.

"Come along, pal. Wouldn't want tae leave the bonnie lasses unattended." Marcus wasn't looking at me. He glared at Dallas. Dallas growled. Apparently, more had happened before I had arrived.

Honestly, I didn't care. Shape shifters tended to stick with our own. We tried not to get too involved. Many paranormals did in fact. Even though we were in mixed clans, we didn't trust easily.

By the time we arrived back to the cafeteria, my skin itched. I felt restless like I needed to change forms, as if an animal had taken over. I didn't realize that my pace increased until I noticed Marcus was no longer next to me.

In his glamour as a human, Marcus wasn't short by any means, he was about six-foot-tall, a slightly broader build than most fey. They, as a race, tended to be slender and tall. Marcus had a head of deep red hair and scruff that lined his jaw, which annoyed all the other fey to no end; they considered themselves to be a classier breed of paranormal. I had always felt they had their noses a little too high in the air for my taste. The fey acted as if they were better than other paranormals and lived in their veil. Marcus wasn't like normal fey most of the time.

"Mate! The lassie isn't leavin'. Nae need tae run to get to 'er," Marcus called out, laughing slightly. His darker mood had vanished.

"I wasn't running," I muttered as I tried to control my pace. That made Marcus laugh all the more. When I walked in, Charlie and some other shifters surrounded Audrey and Nixie and one of the younger shifters touched Audrey's arm. Shit. I saw red. I felt possessed. I couldn't control what happened next.

Chapter 17

AUDREY

Stone's intense gaze made me uncomfortable. My eyes kept flickering over to him, then back to nothing at all. I shifted in my seat, squirming restlessly. A mixture of nerves and something I couldn't really name swam through the waters of my heart. It felt light. Tingly. Apprehensive. My mind was so distracted by him being close.

When Stone left, I relaxed a little. The sour feeling in my stomach wouldn't go away completely, though. It had morphed into something else. Something I couldn't identify. But it was hard to focus on anything for too long. Nixie was constantly chattering and encouraging me to eat.

She was nice enough about it, but I could tell that she was worried. Instead of looking into her strange coral eyes, I looked at the plate. Eight grapes. Three pieces of broccoli ... The food looked good, but I was scared. At any moment, it could be taken from me. And eating it might prove another cruel trap.

There was meat on my plate. I tucked my hands in my lap as they began to shake. My head was light, my fingers felt disconnected from my body. Meat ... the meat in my father's kitchen. Glinting silver. Scars yet to form. Stained tiles. I bit the inside of my cheek at these memories. At their promise of pain ... of pain and blood.

His eyes.

"Calm down. Breathe, guppy, breathe," Nixie's tone had turned soft and pacifying, unlike her natural upbeat voice. She was calming a cornered beast. She was calming me.

But I could immediately sense that the calm now invading my body with her voice was unnatural. I responded to it the only way I knew how: with panic. Not that I suspected she was doing anything to harm me. It was just overwhelming, like being emotionally smothered. Fidgeting in my seat did nothing to break the spell.

"Hey, easy."

A sing-song voice. Music filled my head. The tune was unrecognizable. It was subtle, quiet. A sweet sultry tune that meant to encourage calmness. I remember long, long ago, someone used to hum to me. To calm me.

"You're okay. I promise nothing will hurt you here. You're safe."

Nixie was rubbing her hand up and down my arm. And for once, the need to shove it away—to shy away from her touch—was still there, but muted. My body had been hijacked by the calm. My eyelids started to droop. Though they were heavy, I was still awake.

Nixie and I sat together that way for a while. She coaxed me into eating. More people filtered into the cafeteria. Nixie said hello to a man named Charlie. His eyes changed colors much like Stone's did. It unnerved me. The eyes of the people with him shifted colors as well, but theirs were limited to one or two colors.

They talked and I shrank away. I was uncomfortable with the crowd forming around us. The calm that had taken control before was dull now. One of the men who had joined us moved alongside me and his arm brushed against mine. My heart raced, began to beat as though it would burst free of my chest, to escape the unexpected touch. I recoiled.

It was like a gust of wind. Barely even noticeable. The result of rapid motion. Stone stood between me and the other man, now. He grew bigger with every breath I took, until he stood towering over the stranger. His eyes were a horrible red color. I could see the rage there. But then he was in front of me, and all I could see was his back. His voice was a deep rumble. I couldn't understand, couldn't hear what he was saying.

"Right, lads, time tae head off!"

Marcus came over to Nixie and me. He rested his hand on the small of Nixie's back, but he made no move to touch me. My lungs deflated, my shoulders drooped, loosening from their tense position.

The crowd dispersed. The one that had touched me looked scared and practically ran for the door. And when Stone turned back around, I ducked my head to hide from those terrible eyes. I couldn't stand the idea of upsetting him. And punishment was sure to follow. Stone had been a shield for me all this time. He had been kind to me, even if he was a little scary. I feared the repercussions.

I squeezed my eyelids together and waited with my breath caught in my throat. I had learned how to control my screams. I always imagined a metal clamp on my vocal cords. In my experience, screaming made things worse. And the moments preceding, those spent anticipating a strike, anticipating flesh to hit flesh, those were the worst part of punishment. The anticipation made my heart stutter.

Instead of a punch, which I could endure, I felt the lightest of touches on my scars. I opened my eyes.

He was staring at my scars. Without revulsion, without the murky brown of disgust tinting his rapidly shifting eye color. Anger, possessiveness, and disgust—there was none of that. Instead, there was worry, a hint of fear, and many colors I couldn't clearly decipher. And buried deep in the colors of his eyes, something I wasn't sure I wanted to recognize.

"Are you all right?" Stone moved to cup his hand around my face.

I turned away from his gentleness. A punch I could handle. This, I had no idea what to do. I couldn't answer him, so I just nodded my head. He looked slightly hurt. His eyebrows pinched and his lips drew into a tight line. He sat and tugged delicately on my hand to encourage me to join him on the seat. Still breathing out the last traces of fear, my heart resumed a more normal beat.

After a few more moments of silence, Marcus cleared his throat.

"Lassie, there are some things we need tae be discussin'," the unusual yellow in his eyes scared me, chasing my eyes into a downward glance.

Marcus sat close to Nixie. His arm touched hers, and she didn't flinch. She didn't even look bothered. In fact, she looked like she enjoyed it. She turned to Marcus and smiled faintly before grabbing his hand and squeezing. I glanced again at Marcus, his whole body looked out of sorts, like there was something underneath his skin waiting to break free. The air around him shimmered like a disguise woven from light. It hit a familiar cord in me. A long forgotten memory. Ever since Elijah had removed that thing from my mind, the memories had been closer to the surface. Now they were easier to access than I wanted.

"There are things we need tae tell ye, Audrey."

I looked back to Stone. Everything about him was completely different. Moments before, he had been sitting tall, like a mountain. Unmovable. Impenetrable. Now, he slumped, his shoulders sagged, his hair was mussed as if he had just run his hand through it.

He seemed as twitchy as I felt.

Chapter 18

STONE

How could I explain to her that supernatural creatures were real, that she might be one herself? We weren't even sure how much of her memory was intact. And the way she looked at me … I felt like scum. My skin crawled under her gaze.

Audrey's eyes tightened around the edges, her lips pressed tight. She had turned her head to the side and tilted it down. Anger rushed through me, hot and dangerous. Breathing heavily through my nose, I tried to calm myself with little success. Everything in her posture told me that she thought I was going to attack. To hurt her.

I could never do that. I felt the softness of her cheek before I could think. My fingers brushed the side of her face. I had to reassure myself that the woman in front of me was really okay. My eyes fixated on her scars. Those unimaginable scars and the pain that had caused them. Gods, I had wanted to kiss them so badly.

"There are things we need tae tell ye, Audrey," Marcus announced. He was watching me with that pointed look. I ground my teeth and pulled back my hand, tightening it into a fist.

My heart took on an erratic rhythm as she looked up at me, wide-eyed. Through the milky one she could somehow see my emotions. Even the ones I wanted to hide. That was something no sorcerer or witch I had heard of could do. There was no supernatural being out there that could do that, as far as I knew. When Jacobs had told me about her power, I doubted him. But, reflecting on the sensitivity of her responses and reactions, it must be true. But both eyes were a sight to behold. One, filmed with the cruel damage of a past life, the other shining bright and blue. The stare unnerved me. What could I tell her? How could I tell her?

"There is more to this world than the human," I started off lightly. I watched her face, waiting for the confusion. Waiting for her sense of reality and normalcy to break. How much could she take?

"Normal isn't really all that normal. There are creatures that you probably only thought existed in your dreams." I paused, running my hand through my hair. "Let me start over. I've never had to explain this before. You could say that we're similar to the humans. Vampires, werewolves, fey —not all of us are good, and not all of us are bad. Most of us are complicated and just trying to live our lives."

Audrey's brow was furrowed as if she was recalling something. My mind raced with all the different ways I could have brought this up. I was too direct. I had never doubted myself as much as I did with her. And it didn't look like Nixie was impressed by my efforts either.

And if looks could kill, Nixie would have murdered me by now. Shit, as if I wasn't ready to do that myself. Not only had I made a complete ass out of myself, but what terrible memories had I stirred up for Audrey? She had been prisoner to the Vedenin Clan, and it was doubtful they hid their true forms from her.

"I know," she whispered, so quietly that I wasn't sure she had said it. Audrey looked up, her eyes were filled with fear, her lips parted a little as she breathed more heavily. The fear pulsating from her sickened me, it clouded my mind with a desire to somehow, someway—*to set her free*. I wanted to pull her into my arms and never let go. She shouldn't be at the center of all this.

"What?" Nixie asked leaning toward Audrey. Audrey was still hunched over her seat, but I saw how her eyes darted to Nixie. The lines that had been drawn tight on Audrey's face started to relax. A new a calm came over her. I raised my eyebrows when I saw her reaction to Nixie's concern and care. I have to admit, I was impressed at her ability to calm Audrey.

Nixie was a skilled siren, but Audrey wasn't the easiest to keep in hand. Even so, she had an obvious positive effect on Audrey, who remained still a moment longer. Then her shoulders dropped an inch, but when she raised her eyes to us, I caught a glimmer of something new. Courage. There was no reason for me to feel it, but still I puffed out my chest in pride.

"I believe you. Go on," she said, pausing for me to continue. I relaxed as Audrey's eyes swept over me, this time with curiosity. Gods, I loved it when she looked at me like that. Right now, in this moment, she wasn't afraid of me. She was calm, stable, safe. But when she looked into my eyes, I saw her retreat from me just a bit. Shit. I blinked, trying to think of something else to say. But she could see how I felt in those eyes of hers, couldn't she? My eyes gave me away. I was saying a lot already without saying anything at all.

"All right, lassie. Weel, I'm what ye would call a fey. I don't hae wings, so don't ask. I can shed mah glamour if ye want."

Without waiting for her answer, Marcus's glamour melted away. It unsettled me. His short hair grew in length until it reached a little beyond his shoulders. He grew in height and his features sharpened. All fey had an unearthly look to them, and Marcus was no exception. Watching him I knew why humans so often fell for a fey's allure. His eyes before had been an odd shade of yellow, but now they were deeper, resembling the color of summer flowers. Audrey's eyes widened for a second before her brow furled and her lips tightened.

"I miss your human form already," Nixie whispered, sighing loudly. Sirens and fey usually got along pretty well, but once fey started to take the spotlight, sirens got a tad jealous.

Audrey said nothing, so Marcus continued in his explanation of the fey. They had their own realm, called the Shade. Many had escaped back to that place centuries before the Council fell, which was when the clans began their rule. But fey were a secretive sort, and Marcus was very private about his reasons for staying in the human realm. I didn't trust rumors I had heard one bit. Something about him searching for the paranormal who murdered his mate, though in all the time I had known him, I had never seen anything to substantiate this.

Marcus continued, telling her that though fey seemed chaotic to many, they were bound by an intricate system of rules. They technically couldn't lie, but they could easily confound normal people, avoiding the whole truth in a way that blinded them to the questions they sought in the first place.

Then Nixie joined in and told Audrey more about sirens and the differences between them and mermaids. She explained that mermaids couldn't leave water, and also had a special form they could use while in water. It was news to me. I wasn't very knowledgeable about mermaids, as I had never lived close to the sea. She told Audrey about the siren's song. How it could persuade humans into doing things. Anything really, but some sirens, those who were gifted, could persuade paranormals as well. She grinned proudly when she told Audrey that she was one of the few who had this gift.

"Beyond that," Nixie went on, "sirens have a tendency to form a sort of magic bond. It's an instinctual thing, and that's the reason why our communities are so close-knit. Breaking these bonds can be very painful for a siren. They can be created through personal relationships and are an asset for us when far away from large bodies of water. Too long away from water can be dangerous for us, and having these bonds to land dwellers makes being away from the water more bearable. We rarely choose who we form bonds with. Generally, it just happens if there is a strong personal connection."

I watched Audrey the whole time. She remained quiet and kept pulling her arms closer to her sides. Then her back began to curl. It was like she was trying to disappear, to compact herself until there was nothing left. Her eyes darted quickly around our group, the information overwhelming her.

Nixie finished explaining about siren pair-bonds while I remained silent. Marcus watched Audrey, his eyes flashing with recognition at something before returning to a guarded neutral. His gaze unnerved me and my hand tightened into a fist under the table. He was very old, but that was natural. Fey were very long lived. What if he knew something? In the corner of my vision, Audrey squirmed in her seat. She was watching me now. Hesitation and curiosity swam in her eyes. She swallowed, as though to gather courage.

"And what are you?"

I couldn't help but wonder what she saw.

"I'm a shape-shifter," I said. I was facing forward, staring at nothing, really. Her reactions to the rest of what was said didn't feel like it mattered. Not like it did now. Like it did with me. Would she see me as a fraud? My own skin as a façade? Anxiety tinged with desperation fluttered through me. What did she think of the man before her? I breathed out in relief. But she had taken it all in stride, which was impressive considering the situation. Considering what Marcus and Nixie were. Though when it came to Audrey's opinion of them, I felt disconnected. Not that it was personal. I didn't really know what it was or why I felt the way I did.

Fingertips brushed against my arm underneath the table. My back tensed and my nostrils flared. Seldom did someone surprise me like she did. She was looking at me with open curiosity, her lips parted in an unspoken question.

"I can change my form into either human or animal."

With Audrey's attention on me, I started to shift for her. My cells shook, preparing to reform. It didn't hurt. It was second nature to me. My skin rippled, the muscle underneath reshaping and changing to a leaner, corded shape. My once tan skin faded to a silkier, paler tone. My shorter dark hair tingled across my scalp as it grew until it fell beyond my shoulders, red as fire. I shook it out so it laid more naturally. Now, I was sitting taller. I wasn't especially fond of my new height. I didn't care to take fey form. Most of the time it made my skin feel tight, and when all was said and done, it took more energy to imitate their kind than I cared to expend.

Audrey sat back in her seat, scooting to the farthest edge as she took in both Marcus and myself. We had, for all intents purposes, turned into twins. I was a complete copy of him, down to the very cell. It had more of an effect on her than I had hoped, and I could see her chest heaving with shaky breaths. And while she regarded him more closely, I slipped back into the skin I had always worn around her. My chosen skin.

Nerves had me talking immediately again, without giving her much time to take it in. Part of me worried what she might say.

"There are three different types of shifters. First are shape-shifters like me. We are rarer, and, like I mentioned, we can change both our human form or into any animal we desire. There are human-shifters that can only change into human forms. And lastly, animal-shifters, who have one human form and can change from that into any animal. Unlike *were*-creatures, we don't co-exist in our bodies with an animal spirit, so we aren't driven by animal instincts."

Audrey relaxed in her seat.

"Why do your eyes change color?"

It was probably the first time I had heard her ask a question without any trace of fear. Her voice didn't shake, and she didn't clam up like when she had listened to Nixie and Marcus. She was more open, her arms were loosely folded across her stomach, and her legs turned toward me. I was pleased. I sat a little taller.

"Shape-shifters, like me, or human-shifters can change our eye color, but that takes concentration. Mostly our eye color changes unconsciously to reflect our emotions. If I was in a human populated place, I would choose a single eye color, but here it's safe to be myself."

I looked at her pointedly now.

"*Were*-creatures are different from shape-shifters though. *Weres* are people who have an animal spirit in them as well. Dallas and Jacobs are both werewolves. They can only change into wolves, but it's not only that. Part of who they are is tied to their wolf nature. Their animal spirit naturally extends into all aspects of their being, including their instincts."

She didn't look at me as I said this. Instead, she wrung her hands together in tiny, barely perceptible motions. I found myself wishing I knew what was going through her head.

Chapter 19

AUDREY

Our small group stayed in the cafeteria for a while longer. I was still digesting the information they had given me. I had such a limited view on everything. It was all strange and new. People started to filter into the cafeteria and my leg started to twitch under the table. My hands became restless. Stone noticed and told me that he would be right back.

Nixie gave me a bright smile and told me more about her race. She explained the finer points, mostly about the difference between mermaids and sirens. She was in the middle of sticking out her tongue to show me that sirens generally had darker colored tongues while mermaids had lighter colors when Stone returned. He held white boxes in his hands. He silently sat and started to place my uneaten food into them.

"How about we take you to Nixie's room?"

He wasn't really asking, but he looked at her as her tongue peeked out of her mouth, communicating something silently.

"Oh, yes! Guppy, you can bunk with me! I would love that, love it! It's such a guy's club most of the time. I definitely would love some girl time."

She instantly blossomed into a full smile at the prospect of us rooming together. She was practically bouncing in her seat. And her excitement was infectious, in a way. I felt a tingle of excitement jolt through me. It was an odd sensation, even if it didn't last long. But I couldn't help recalling their unspoken communication. The look they had shared.

It jarred me, the realization that these people weren't technically my friends. I deflated, my shoulders drooping, my heart heavy. They were probably just trying to keep tabs on me rather than make me comfortable. Rather than trying to be my friends. But …

Stone grabbed the boxes for me and waited for me to get to my feet. Marcus stood in one fluid movement that was unnaturally graceful. Nixie slid out of the booth and jumped up. As soon as I followed, she twined her arm around my own. She was a little taller than me, and in an affectionate gesture, rested her head on top of mine for a second. My muscles tensed, but the longer she kept her head pressed against mine, the looser my muscles became. I wanted to savor the touch, the affection. I wanted to believe it was real.

"I'm so, so, so happy that you agreed to stay with me."

Nixie held on to my arm and lifted her head as we headed to her room. She was explaining to me that she could sense when she was forming a connection with another person. The bonds of a siren were like lifelines. When she told me that she could feel one forming between us, I was curious. I asked her to explain it more. It was an exchange of energy that would intensify with the strengthening of our friendship. Nixie said the bond formed between suitable pairs. It was impossible to bond with someone unless you were compatible. The idea sunk deep roots of fear in me. Fear at what the connection might reveal to her, and of what she might do with it.

I believed her. I believe what they all said. Because, aside from the apparent truth in their words, I could clearly read it in their eyes. I already knew the paranormal world. Somewhat. Not as much of it as they had told me, but I had known my father wasn't entirely human. He had shown me that. Had even punished me for not being more like him. He had demanded many times when I was growing up to *change*. But, even then, I had been broken. But how had I been broken?

The memories were foggy. Perhaps a better way of thinking about it was that there was something lost deep inside of me. I had felt that loss, even before he started pushing me to *change*. I was too scared to think

120

about it too much. If I had remembered what it was, if I remembered now, would Nixie and Stone treat me the same? Would they try force me the same way my father had? Would they be as unyielding? Would they punish me as well for not being able to do as they asked?

The waters of fear in my stomach bubbled unpleasantness within me. What might they do? I thought all this as we walked. When we passed a man that looked a lot like Elijah, I remembered what they had called him. A wraith. They made him seem like a fearful creature. Like a being I should fear naturally. And yet he was the one I had felt the safest with since I had arrived. Somehow, he understood me without me having to say anything. Even with the sense of comfort I felt around Nixie and Stone, I hadn't yet thought of them as safe.

"What is Elijah?"

My voice was a little louder. I wouldn't normally have said anything, but something about being around these kind people. They gave me courage to speak, though I was still nervous. My hands sweated, and I got a sharp glance from Stone in response to my question. Nixie's hand tightened around my wrist, as well. Stone's eyes turned an ugly shade of red, and his nostrils flared. Should I not have asked? Marcus gave a chiding look to both Stone and Nixie before explaining.

"Elijah is a wraith."

Marcus's carefree expression melted into something hard and stony. The lines around his mouth deepened and his movements stiffened.

"Wraiths are creatures from th' underworld. They aren't pure demons, but nobody really knows what they are. What we dae know, is that they donae hae a form of their own in this warld. They tak' over a human or paranormal host, and if they remain in one body too lang, then th' host body's sool dies."

Marcus got quiet. Stone's neck was flushed and his nostrils flared. I felt bad that my question had upset him so much.

When we arrived at Nixie's doorway, the two men looked tense. The lines around Marcus's lips weren't as creased as before when he had told me about Elijah, but his shoulders were still tight. Stone's face hadn't changed from its grim look. He looked utterly unpleasant in that moment, but the usual stab of fear that would come upon me in these times was absent.

"We'll continue this conversation tomorrow," Stone said with a grim tone.

My lips twitched upwards and back down again. I didn't think that I was ready to keep learning more. It was already overwhelming. True, I knew about of some creatures, but the small world I had been kept in for so long was exploding in every direction. All I could do, though, was follow Nixie into her apartment.

Nixie offered to share her bed with me so I wouldn't have to sleep on the couch. It was certainly big enough, but the thought scared me. I was afraid of strengthening the bond she had spoken of earlier. I couldn't bear the thought of her suffering through my nightmares. So I declined, and we made a small bed for me on the couch. I cast a longing look at the floor. It might seem strange, but in the face of all these changes, something familiar, even the thought of sleeping on the floor, was a comfort. But it was only moments before the couch engulfed me and pulled me into a deep sleep.

That night I dreamt of the last time I saw my father. In the dream, I was in bed. That's when it happened. But in that disoriented, displaced sort of way, I knew I was also in the kitchen. Why was I here? I would feel safer in my small room. I could hear the noises muffled through the door. They amplified as I approached the door, standing there in the middle of that dark and shadowed place, only sixteen years of age when they came. I was no child, but even then, even before they took me, I felt small and brittle.

The crashing became louder, stomping feet came to my room. The door was thrown open. My father's eyes, now slit-shaped, watched me. I knew what he was. What I was meant to be.

"Get up!" he had roared. His voice was always deeper when he was angry. I threw off my covers. He grabbed my arm and started to pull me from the room. I tried to reach out for my only companion—Aiden, my stuffed dragon. Missing an eye and threadbare, he was my only possession. He was my only friend. I needed him. As I tried to tug my arm from my father's grip, he pulled me harder.

"Let's go!"

Helplessness gripped me tight, my throat closed up. I had only one thing in my life that I truly cared for and I was losing it. I needed my dragon. I needed Aiden. I loved him. I couldn't leave without him. He was my only source of comfort. But I should have known better. Pulling away from my father was a mistake.

My father often didn't know his own strength. And though he was holding tightly, he misjudged my desire to retrieve Aiden. I wrenched away just as he tried to pull me to safety. My shoulder *popped* loose from its socket. Even then, I had learned to not scream. He had no idea the pain I was in. And though I hadn't noticed it then, there had been a desperation in his blind urge to escape.

He dragged me along. I was in a world of agony. I couldn't move. Couldn't focus. Couldn't breathe. He tried to lift me, I think. Finally, the pain caused me to scream. I would scream until my throat was raw. And then things faded. Grew hazy. I slipped from one moment to the next. My faint memories bridged detached moments in time seamlessly.

A distant part of myself thought of the white room, how I preferred the dreams of that place. Not this room. Not where the entrance to hell opened up. Any room but this one. *No. No. No.* Not here. Not the room carved from stone. Where it hurt to sit. Where it hurt to lie down. Where everything was meant to hurt, hurt, hurt.

I had been kept there a year. Each day I was visited by creatures from my nightmares. Men with soulless eyes. Not like Elijah's. No, these men had no goal aside from their desire to inflict pain.

Pain. Pain. Pain. So much pain.

Each day it became harder to hang on. Each day existence became more of a struggle. Each day, I became less. At least with my father, I had his love, as twisted as it was. He just didn't understand the pain he caused. He was too strong, and I too fragile. But I could see it in his eyes, as I could with everyone. Two sides. One that loved, and one that possessed. But he couldn't help being a slave to his nature. He couldn't help being possessive.

Those men in the stone room beat me until my skin was different shades of black and blue. They touched my body roughly. Without decency or restraint. They screamed at me. Destroyed me and put me back together again.

Over and over.

I lost track of time. Days blended one into the next, stretching out into a path through time leading inevitably to the white room. I was finally moved because I wouldn't break. Or, more accurately, because I couldn't tell them where my father was. Not that they believed me when I said it. I couldn't be what my father demanded any more than I could be what they demanded. I couldn't *change*. But that was a secret I would keep from them no matter what.

And then, a voice in the darkness. The voice of one of the guards. When I heard him say the year, I was shocked. Had I lived in this hell for a whole year? That guard, the talkative one, he was my favorite. Something in him was hesitant. He hit a little less hard. He screamed a little less loudly than the rest. His touch, though unwelcome, was more a caress. The side without the scars. *What a shame it was*, he had told me. Who was this man? Was he only a dream in the dark night of my captivity, or had he been real? He might have been a manifestation of my hope. My hope for something, or someone, that was different from my constant torture. In the midst of a world of nightmares, my imagination had worked to save me. I had gotten free ... almost.

The dream touch still lingered. This time on the wrong side of my face. The memory of his gentleness was as though it were with me now. I moved my face so that the feeling wouldn't stop. I wanted more of it. I breathed in.

The air smelled different. It was a mixture of sandalwood and a hint of pine. My eyes opened to soft, violet-colored eyes. The violet changed rapidly to ocean blue. And then my hand was moving, moving with a mind of its own, pushing Stone's hair from his eyes. He watched me, reining in his shock, as if terrified to scare me away.

Why would he be scared?

"How did you sleep?" he asked, as I jerked my hand away. Why had I reached out as I had? My jumbled thoughts refused to resolve into something more sensible.

"I slept?"

The way the nightmares and memories mixed together left me unsure what was real and what was not. He smiled at my confusion, and I saw a light yellow glow in his eyes.

He was laughing, honestly, and not out of cruelty either.

"Come on, you have a lot to learn today."

His voice trailed off, as though he had more to say, but had decided against it. And then Stone left me alone so that I could change. I hadn't had so many different choices for clothing in so long. The thought of pajamas hadn't even occurred to me. I had slept in what I had worn the day before. But once upon a time, I had slipped my father's old shirts over my head and worn them as nighties. They hung past my knees and brushed my toes.

When I came out of the room, I was wearing a dress with a sweater. The knit fabric of her sweater reached well below my knees. It was more comfortable than what Nixie had recommended to me. I looked up when I heard Stone's breath. It was sharp, like a gasp. I flinched and my eyes widened with fear. I frantically looked to see what had caused his reaction.

Stone stood motionless while my eyes flickered around the room. His eyes raked their way up and down the length of my body. His glance slid up the length of my legs, causing me to shift my weight under his stare. Stone shook his head and took a step back. I crossed my arms and looked down. Heat coursed up my neck, starting high on my cheeks until it reddened my whole face. While other stares made me shrink in fear, his made me squirm. Years of abuse had made me believe the attention of another a dangerous thing, but my heart fluttered with excitement with him.

"I can change if these clothes aren't good enough."

I was already withdrawing into the room with the intention of changing. Stone grabbed me before I could get too far.

"No. Gods, no. You look … amazing." His voice was breathless with an emotion I knew but didn't understand.

He stood so close. Too close. Yet he was somehow farther than I wanted him at the same time. I didn't dare look past his chest, which was eye level. His hands, gods, they had been the softest things I had ever felt on my skin. Though they were still rough with callouses, his gentle, tender touches somehow felt like silk. It was completely foreign. Hands tightened into fists and brutal slaps, these were what I knew best. His touch was different. I closed my eyes as I leaned into it. He lifted my chin and my entire body followed the motion, not wanting him to let go. For once, the touch of another, besides my stuffed dragon, my Aiden, made me feel safe. I didn't know why.

"You should stand tall. No more hiding."

His warm breath ghosted over the sensitive skin of my closed eyelids, making them flutter. The warmth. The safety.

"Audrey."

His voice was so, so, *so* close. I felt his hands slip through the tangles of my thick hair, strands wrapping around his fingers, knotting, trapping him, refusing to let him go.

"Audrey! Are you—?! Well, isn't this the most awkward time to walk in," Nixie said with a sly tone as Stone and I jumped away from each other. If my heart raced any more, I would surely collapse.

Overwhelmed with embarrassment, I looked away from Stone, flushing red once again. I kept my eyes downcast and my hands curled. My nails dug into my fragile skin. Out of the corner of my eye, Stone's lips were firm, the muscle in his jaw ticking incessantly. Dragging my bottom lip between my teeth, I wondered if he was angry with me or if it was something else.

"Yes, Nixie, a horrible time to come in. But now that you're here, I suppose we might as well head down for breakfast."

And with that, Stone stomped out of the room.

"What fish swam up his ass this morning?"

Nixie looked at me with a bright smile, apparently pleased with herself.

"Look at you! You're practically glowing! You're looking very alive this morning," she said with a huge wink.

I tilted my head so my hair would fall in front of my face. I felt more at ease when it was in front of my scars. Beyond that, my face was still red from when he had touched me so tenderly. The scars he had traced so delicately with his fingertips felt almost branded by the heat he left behind. The air in my lungs felt thin. My head swam with confusion.

"Well, come on. You can tell me all about that steamy moment I interrupted while we head down to the cafeteria."

Nixie grabbed my hand, the contact with her oddly normal. Maybe the familiarity I felt was a result of our bond? On our way down, Nixie started to tell me more about the siren song. The elevator jerked into motion, causing me to start. My hand flew out to the wall to hold myself steady. It would be a long while before I got use to these things.

"Sirens usually can only use it on humans. I'm the only one that I know of who can use it effectively on paranormals. But don't tell anyone. Let's let that be our little secret," she winked again as she said this, a large smile spreading across her features.

"Well, not on *all* paranormals. Wraiths seem to be immune, and so do a few others. Like spirit element paranormals. You know, wraiths, djinns—creatures of that nature. For some reason they're resistant. And, well, I imagine the legendary dragon shifters as well, but I think that's because of their iron will. Or at least that's what they say in fairy tales! The last time anyone even thought they saw a dragon was over three hundred years ago. Maybe longer."

"The gods, there were five right?" Some of this sounded so familiar to me. But my memories were still elusive and kept slipping from my grasp.

"Yup! Each for every element, or at least that is how the legend goes. Air, fire, earth, water, and spirit."

But now Nixie sounded distracted, as if she was still caught on a different thought. I absorbed the information easily. It felt so natural, anyway, like remembering a forgotten fact that I knew to be true.

"It's such a shame so many of the Elder Races have died off or disappeared. If the stories are true about the dragons, they were dangerous, beautiful folk. Of course it is not like I met one before, the stories could be all made up, but if they're true! Man! They had to be the most possessive creatures out there. I heard the males were like a pack of alpha werewolves mixed with Leprechauns. And let me tell you, Leprechauns are *insanely* possessive."

Nixie rolled her eyes while shaking her head.

"Oh and if you think leprechauns are bad, you should have met this gargoyle I went out with once. Hot, especially with that tail! Gods, the things that man could do with his tail … of course they are only playful with their tails when they *really* like you."

Nixie drifted off with a mischievous glint in her eye as we entered the cafeteria. Stone was already sitting at the table in the back corner. I felt a pang of something deep in my heart. He was being considerate. The thought almost put tears in my eyes.

"I'll grab your food. Is there anything you want in particular?" Nixie asked.

I started to shake my head, but I found that, surprisingly, I did have a request.

"Grapes, please."

My voice was still barely a whisper, but I noticed how it was getting stronger with more use. Less hoarse and more musical. Nixie's face broke into a shining smile, her matching coral lips spreading wide, thin lipped with joy. She squeaked and wrapped her arms around me in a quick hug before she disappeared. Stone saw and made a move to get up. He didn't stand quickly, but watched me as I headed in his direction.

Chapter 20

STONE

Gods, seeing her in that dress. Those long narrow legs. Granted, they were skinnier than I liked, but it was the most skin I had seen her show since meeting her. And I wanted to touch every exposed part of her. I shook my head, dislodging the thought as a hot flush crawled up my neck. It was wrong for me to think that way of her, and not just because she was our pseudo prisoner, but also because of what she had been through. She crossed her arms defensively, as if a look alone could harm her.

Standing so close to her, I could smell jasmine and lavender. I moved closer; I couldn't seem to stop myself. For once, she didn't move back or flinch, but she did avert her eyes. How could she not see how beautiful she was? I wanted her to stand tall, to be proud of who she was.

I touched her scars again. I knew how they would feel from experience. Raised, leathery, and tight. When a person grew into scars, the skin around them didn't grow quite right.

Gently I pressed my fingers under her chin, pushing her head up. Her eyes locked with mine. It was electric. I was seconds from pressing my lips against hers before Nixie came and stole her away. Her timing couldn't have been worse.

It was such a near thing, I could practically taste the kiss we had almost shared. It hung before me in the air, a beautiful illusion that shattered to pieces when Nixie's delighted squeal pierced the air. And then Audrey was in her clutches. I rose, transfixed by the black sweater she wore over her dark green dress. The red-maroon of her hair stood out against the black and green, making it all the more prominent. I thought back to when my fingers had tangled in those locks.

"What were you two discussing?" I asked when Audrey arrived back at my side. She sat next to me, at least a foot away. Too far for my liking, but I knew she needed to come to me, not the other way around. I didn't want to push her.

"Mermaids versus sirens. It was … enlightening. Is there more you could tell me about?"

She looked up at me with those eyes, almost as if she could trust me. I felt my insides tighten. I ran my hand through my hair.

"Is there anything specific you want to know?" I asked. My mind raced to think of all the information she needed to know, and other information she wasn't yet ready for. She didn't need to know every sad truth about paranormal history. And I couldn't shake this desire to protect her. To keep her safe.

"Everything."

Her eyes lit up for a moment, it was like catching a glimpse of who she must've been before she was … and then, something else? A thought flashed across her face, and she slouched back down in her seat.

"That's a lot of information."

My tone was smooth. My words charming. All in an effort to perk her up again. To return her to the state she was in when she sat down. I wanted to see her excited again. She responded, but not with her initial verve.

"Last night we started telling you about the different races," as I started, Audrey's mouth opened a little as if she had something to add. I waited for her to speak.

"Nixie told, uh, she more reminded me, I guess, about the gods. The five different gods."

"Well, each race is descended from one of the five. It can cause a lot of friction between different races, since some are natural enemies. Witches and Wraiths, in particular, are known for their lack of love. Centuries ago, the Council that ruled the paranormal world was ready to reveal itself to the humans. It started quietly, but from the stories we have of that time, humans learned about the rivalries between races, and they used those against us. Paranormals were pitted against one another. So we fashioned stories intentionally inaccurate so our secrets would be kept safe from the humans. Some paranormals, though, became endangered, extremely rare, or in some cases, extinct."

"Like dragon shifters?" Audrey gave me a strange look. I was baffled that she knew about dragon shifters. It must have shown.

"Nixie just finished telling me a little about them."

"Uh, yeah. Like the dragon shifters. They were a proud, powerful race. Many paranormals feared their power. You see, the dragons were on the Council of ruling paranormals. They were the muscle, being the top of the food chain and all that. According to legend, they were deadly creatures.

"The Council was disbanded after what had happened with the humans. We are now ruled by families, or clans. The family you belong to says a lot about you. Each family bears the characteristics of its leading members. The heads of families can be great, noble paranormals, but some are brutal. Like the Vedenins, who held you captive. They're one of the worst. Slavers and butchers, all in the name of their clan."

She flinched away, but there was nothing I could do about that. She needed to know the truth about our world. We weren't safe. No one was. And happiness? Friction between the clans left most of us victims of senseless tragedy. Paranormals, much like humans, were greedy for power and willing to do almost anything to get what they wanted.

Nixie set a tray down in front of Audrey, who looked at it for the first time with enthusiasm. Her eyes betrayed her, and suddenly I knew what she was excited about.

The grapes. It was a simple and unimportant realization, but something changed in me at that moment. This simple fruit made her seem more alive than anything else had up to this point. When I looked at Audrey, I saw more of the mystery we had to solve. That *I* had to solve. I was the one who found her; I was responsible for her, wasn't I?

Nixie was telling Audrey stories about the time she lived in the sea. Audrey seemed fascinated, but at the same time, she guarded her emotions. She didn't ask as many questions as I knew she wanted, though

131

I saw those questions dance in her eyes. At times she would start to sit up a little taller, as though she were gathering courage, but she would only to slouched back down again. I wondered if she would always hold back.

"Audrey."

Elijah's detached voice came from behind us.

She turned to look at him. She was the only person I knew that could look a wraith in the eye without being effected. She released a slow breath. The lines marring her face with worry, smoothed. What about him was it that made her feel relaxed?

"Jacobs would like to have a word."

Elijah headed out of the cafeteria without looking back and headed toward Jacobs' office. We all knew he probably wanted this to be a one-on-one meeting. That wouldn't stop me though. Things had changed. She … needed me there? No. That wasn't it. I *wanted* her to need me there.

When Audrey didn't automatically go after Elijah, my heart swelled. I stood and motioned her to follow, barely containing my smile. I wanted to hold out my hand, take her waist in my arm and lead her, but I knew even offering her a hand would be too much. She took one last glance at the grapes and stood. It was as if she were expecting this to happen. Nixie worried her bottom lip and her eyes filled with longing as Audrey started to pull away.

"Come back and finish eating when you're done, okay, Audrey?"

She looked up at me with those big frightened eyes and I didn't know what to say. I didn't know if that look was rooted in fear of punishment or fear of hope. But both inspired my need to protect her more. Just what exactly had those cruel bastards done to make her this way? Elijah waited at the elevators for us, his blank gaze coming to rest on me.

"You can stay. Jacobs needs to speak with her alone."

As soon as the doors opened, Elijah turned on his heel, marched in, and waited for Audrey to follow. She looked back at me, tucked her head down, and wrapped her arms around her torso as she followed.

Shit. I wanted to follow her. I wanted to hold her in my arms and tell her that she was fine, that she was safe here. But I didn't know that for sure, did I? There had to be a reason Jacobs wanted to see her. He knew more than he had said. But then the doors shut, trapping Audrey with Elijah. I waited like the good little solider that I was.

Chapter 21

AUDREY

The doors shut. I remembered how my father had hated elevators. I hated them too. They were small, far too small. My lungs constricted painfully. The air tasted bland, much like the recycled air I had tasted every day of my imprisonment.

My pulse began to race. This was all too similar for me to simply ignore. Memories stirred uneasily. With each rhythmic passing of each floor, those memories whispered hateful words. *This is the same. The same. The same. The same.*

The walls began to draw close. They loomed large and imposing. The space was suffocating.

Elijah stood still, a stone statue, safe in the center of his unshakable indifference and dispassion. I was the opposite. I was fragile. My skin, I well knew, would part easily under blade or knife. My breakable bones would snap easily in angry hands. Pieces of me could be ripped away.

Breakable. I was so very … breakable.

The doors opened, though we weren't on the right floor. My eyes had been trained on the glowing number that was our destination. Elijah grabbed my upper arm and pulled me free of the small prison. His thin lips were pressed so tightly together, the skin around them white.

"From here, we take the stairs."

He moved to the door next to the elevators, leading me on our upward climb.

For a moment I felt grateful for Elijah's actions. But gratitude was something I was no longer practiced in expressing. I could only remain silent and keep my head down.

"Your fear was stifling. I can taste such things. Are you claustrophobic?"

My head shot up before I could stop myself. He had sounded different when he asked me that, almost perplexed. I had to see if it was true, if he really was puzzled. I looked closely, but his eyes remained the same impenetrable black.

"To be claustrophobic means to have a phobia, or fear, of enclosed spaces."

Back to the logical, unexpressive voice.

"I suppose. I-I don't know."

It was true. I didn't know. Most of the time I felt safe in small spaces. I felt a comfort there, but in that metal box, I had felt like I couldn't breathe.

"This way."

He opened the door, and I stepped out into a familiar looking hallway. The floor was decorated in a soft green. It was a comforting color that I couldn't get enough of. I stopped and took it in for a moment. Hidden deep in the secret part of its pigment, I saw lust, hate, and every other emotion powerful enough to leave an impression in the depths of its dye.

The color remembered it all. Held the emotion. This wasn't the first time I felt memories through colors. But it had to be examined carefully, lest it be missed. It was so subtle. I hadn't looked carefully enough till now, but I could feel the memories locked there, like the shadows of animals caught in a cage. A shiver would run through the fabric of it. A deep motion, like a creature of the deep sea churning the upper waters from far below. In my white room I was safe from anything like this.

We arrived in Jacobs' office. I kept my head down and caught a glimpse of polished wood, a desk cleared of clutter, and demanding, unyielding eyes. Submission to males like Jacobs' was always the safest course of action. Men like him could smell your fear, but at least I could hide it in my eyes. Elijah left me in front of Jacobs' desk, and I soon heard the door click shut. My body trembled and my stomach plummeted to my feet. My muscles itched, the room felt smaller and smaller. The beatings would start, soon. My punishments. I had grown accustomed to unbruised and unbeaten skin in my short time here. That would end here. Jacobs cleared his throat and began.

"No more games, Audrey. Elijah informed me that your memories were unlocked when the wraith was extracted. I demand to know everything."

Jacobs' voice was biting, and a flinch jumped through me. It was the way his words nipped at the air, the way the subtle flecks in his eyes changed. The colors changed, darkening to reveal his vicious anger.

I didn't want to remember those memories. I didn't want to talk about them. I knew what the Vedenins had wanted. I remembered the moment I woke up. But I had pushed them away. I pushed them all away. Jacobs wanted the same thing. He wanted to know about my father. Like they had. Keeping my eyes lowered and my stance vulnerable, I waited. It was all I could do.

It didn't take long. Jacobs' fist came down on the desk with a loud crash.

"Gods dammit! Speak! Do you know how much I risked coming for you?" Jacobs' anger tore through the air in a yell. His face was bright red and spittle flew from his mouth. I shrunk into myself, waiting for the blow.

"Jacobs," Elijah spoke up. His voice only slightly more raised than normal. Jacobs ignored him.

"I'm done tip-toeing around. I told you, Elijah, to look into her mind while you were in there. I need that information. Cain wants it. Now. And I know she is hiding something. You do too. So either you tell me what I want to know or I'll make her tell me. The Vedenins aren't stupid. They know who took her and are attacking our smaller facilities already. And somehow, gods damn all you fools, the York Clan has also found out about her. Cain is *displeased*. The York Clan breathing down our necks was the last thing he wanted. I won't put our clan in danger because of this girl. And neither should you, wraith."

Jacobs was slowly rounding the corner of his desk, crossing in front of it, eyes locked onto mine as he spoke. He sucked in a sharp breath, crossing one leg over the other so his polished, black shoes touched my open-toed sandals. He grabbed my chin roughly. Forced me to look into his eyes. I saw pure determination there, mingled with the need to protect. The emotions practically radiated from the twin suns that were his yellow eyes. The force of his emotions was too much. His grip too tight. I tried to pull away but he held like a vice, roughly keeping me in his grasp.

I let out a whimper.

"Jacobs, I will only tell you this once. Release her."

Elijah's tone was more demanding than I could ever remember having heard from him.

"You don't give me orders, Elijah. You may be a wraith, but I am still your superior and this girl is going to tell me what I need to know. By any means."

Jacobs' eyes had flickered from me to Elijah. His hold on my jaw tightened, extracting another cry from me.

My stomach hollowed out and tears formed before I could hold them back. One hell to another. Wasn't this supposed to be a safe place? This was worse. Much worse. They had lied. All those touches. The false kindnesses. Those deceitful words.

Fake. Fake. Fake.

"Release her."

I felt the air around me suddenly drop in temperature. Elijah's pale hand gripped Jacob's wrist. There was a fleshy, cracking sound of bone breaking. Jacobs' widened his eyes a little, but soon relinquished his hold on my jaw. I didn't think it was voluntarily. Tears stung my eyes as I staggered backwards, a feeling of doom brewing inside of me.

There was the sound of tendons straining and a reluctant grunt. My hands shook as I blinked back the building tears and looked ahead of me. Jacob was on his knees, and Elijah held his wrist effortlessly in a painful grasp.

"I do not repeat myself, Jacobs. Not to you. Not to Cain. Not to anybody. Do not touch her again. I decide what I do. Not you." Elijah's voice had changed. It had deepened, darkening to the point it was

137

distorted. Hardly recognizable. My breathing came in erratic gasps. I couldn't get my eyes to focus. My heart was throbbing a chaotic, galloping rhythm. Pound, pound, pounding away. My legs felt far off, my body disconnected. I felt myself drifting. Light. Effortless. Down, down, down to meet the floor. But I didn't. Not this time.

Elijah was there to catch me.

"Come."

He picked me up with ease, and I made no movement of protest. I couldn't focus enough to react to his hold. My mind played the same broken record.

Fake. Fake. Fake.

Still I craved the contact of another being. *Pathetic.*

Fake. Fake. Fake.

I craved friendship.

Fake. Fake. Fake.

The comfort they offered.

Fake, fake, FAKE!

Fake.

Fake …

Fake. At least at long last, I knew.

Elijah placed me onto a bed. I saw the room in shades of black. While white was the absence of color, black was all colors. It was overwhelming, but only at first. Only until I closed my eyes.

Then the darkness was truly colorless.

Chapter 22

STONE

"Find her," Jacobs said, dismissing the guards.

I waited for them to leave. I wanted to know who he was talking about, even though the sinking feeling in my gut told me all I needed to know.

"Are you coming in, Stone?"

I rounded the corner into his office. Jacobs's eyes were a deep yellow, the sure sign of an excited *were*. His voice gruff. He was not happy.

"Maybe it would be a good time for you to go for a run, Jacobs."

I was only somewhat sarcastic.

"Where the hell is she?" his alpha voice rang out in those words. Alpha orders were law. *Weres* could not deny the command of their alpha. Us shape-shifters, on the other hand, weren't compelled by the commanding presence of an Alpha *were*. And we were certainly not inspired by a werewolf Alpha without a pack.

"You're overstepping your bounds, Jacobs. You've been keeping us in the dark, and we're pretty damn sick of it."

I stood a couple inches taller than Jacobs. Looking down at the werewolf, I took in the wrinkles that lined his skin. He was getting too old for this job, but I could respect the fierceness in his eyes. No matter. Something else inside me was in control. A driving force that made me throw consequence out the window.

"Stop acting like an overgrown pup. You haven't been able to control yourself since we found the damn girl. You can't even trust yourself around her, why should I?"

That pissed me off. Jacobs had pushed me a little too far. I didn't care anymore. I needed to find out exactly what the hell was going on. I took a step forward. He didn't step back, but his frown deepened.

"Look, mutt, I respected your decisions because I thought you had the best interest of the clan in mind, but Audrey needs to be protected. So, believe me when I say I will not listen to you unless it is in her best interests."

I had him by the front of his shirt, which had ripped under the strain of my grip. His thick nails found my skin and dug in, but I didn't flinch, didn't turn my eyes away. The first to look away submitted.

I would not be submitting this time.

"Dad!" Dallas stepped forward from his place against the wall, he shoved me away. Dallas stood in front of his father, hackles raised, crouched, ready to attack at a moment's notice. Behind him, Jacobs started to adjust his shirt, composing himself. Jacobs laid a heavy hand on his son's shoulder.

"Back down, Dallas. Stone is letting his *emotions* get the best of him."

I didn't like how he stressed that word, the bastard.

"Dallas, let the guards know that Audrey is unstable. She needs to be brought directly back to me. For her own good."

Jacobs didn't take his yellow eyes off of me. He gave me a smirk, as if to gloat. He thought he had won this round.

Little did he know, I would be the one to protect Audrey. Even if that meant protecting her against Jacobs. I gritted my teeth. I would find her. I headed out of the room, but Jacobs called, stopping me where I stood in the door.

"Dallas, go with Stone."

"I don't need a babysitter. I know where my loyalties lie," I ground out between clenched teeth. Dallas growled.

I ignored him and continued my way out of the room. I heard Dallas mutter something to his father, then he followed me out of the door. I needed him away from me while I looked for Audrey. She would never

140

believe that I was trying to keep her safe from Jacobs if I had Dallas in tow.

"Dallas, maybe you should sniff out Nixie. She may be with Audrey already."

"Whatever the fuck is going on with you, Stone, figure it out. And deal with it."

"Nothing is going on with me. But something is obviously going on with you and your father. You've been keeping too many secrets from the rest of us. Care to fess up?"

Dallas's lips curled back in his disgust, a hint of yellow starting to bleed into his irises.

"We don't keep secrets from our troops, shifter. Maybe you should just do your fucking job. I'm going to do mine and find Nixie."

I had no idea where to look, but I was going to find her. I had to.

Chapter 23

AUDREY

"Audrey."

I rolled into the cool folds of the sheets, away from the voice. I preferred to stare at the wall than the open space around me. More than ever, I missed my white walls. I missed their blankness. White was the only color free from the attachment of feelings. Though few knew it, color had the unique quality of absorbing various emotions and energies in its tints and hues. All colors, save white.

Finally, I looked up at Elijah. He remained unwavering in his dispassionate state.

"Why are you helping me?"

I didn't turn away from his black eyes.

"I do not know. For once, fear did not taste that sweet."

Elijah's head cocked toward the door as if he heard something that I couldn't.

"Stone is at the door. Would you prefer to be kept a secret or would you like him to be aware of your presence?"

Stone's name made my heart beat a little faster. Whether out of fear or something else, I was not certain. Why was he here? Would he tell me I needed to go back to Jacobs' office? To face his torture?

I felt helpless and, for some reason, the idea of losing this place, a place that had finally started to feel like home, felt like too much. Who did

I belong with? I had no one to run to. No clan. My safe haven had turned into the thing I feared the most. Another prison.

"I suppose … let him in?"

A knock came from the door as soon as I answered. Elijah disappeared and I heard grunts, the sickening sound of flesh striking flesh, a sound that had filled my nightmares for years and years. Finally, there came the sound of heavy footfalls, quick and hurried.

"Audrey."

Stone's black hair was disheveled.

"I've been looking for you all night. Jacobs is demanding answers. We need to get you out of here."

Stone looked at the entranceway where Elijah stood watching us.

"Elijah, you won't stop me." Stone's nostrils flared once with his threat.

"What is your decision, Audrey?"

Elijah's eyes met mine.

Stone had gone quiet. The man who had sought me out moments ago had vanished. In his place, Stone stood quiet, regal, his lips pressed together, his brow stern over his eyes. Otherwise gave away nothing. But he offered me something I'd been hoping for this entire time: escape. Jacobs only offered imprisonment, or worse. Intimidation, at minimum. A return to torture, possibly. I couldn't go back to that. I wouldn't survive.

"I … I want to be free!"

"Then I shall help you."

Elijah glided past Stone whose brows had furrowed at the wraith's words. The skin under his eye twitched.

"Excuse me? You're going to help us?"

Stone moved a little closer to me, taking my hand in a reflex I wasn't sure he was aware of. Though it was tight, something about it was also … reassuring?

"Not you. I will help her. There are things you do not know about her. Things that I will not share with you. She needs more protection than just you."

While Elijah spoke, Stone's grip got tighter. My hand began to ache. A small murmur slipped from my lips to bring his attention to my hand.

Stone looked down, his grip loosening instantly, his face clouded with worry at any harm he might have caused. Then he let go, and I immediately regretted drawing his attention to it. My fingertips brushed his wrist in an attempt to reassure him everything was okay. He wasn't trying to hurt me, he was trying to protect me.

"Is that why Jacobs wanted to see her?" Stone growled.

"Calm yourself, shapeshifter. Yes, but it is too dangerous to allow anyone to know her secrets. At least not before she is ready to decide what she will do with them herself."

Elijah moved around his room picking up random objects and placing them in a duffle bag.

"I would recommend you get your overnight bag. We may be gone for a while. Her memories will return at their own pace. Pushing her will only do harm. I will not allow it. Meet me in the garage. I will be waiting."

Elijah's words were monotone and without inflection, but his eyes watched Stone carefully. I was too scared to look into Stone's eyes and read what he might be feeling.

"She is mine to protect."

I peeked up at him. His jaw was tight, his eyes were locked with Elijah's. He nodded once and started to pull me from the room.

When we left Elijah's room, Stone continued to drag me through the building. He would stop every so often to listen intently or peer around a wall. I remained quiet and tried to be as small as possible. When we arrived at his room, he pulled me in, but as soon as he shut the door, he pushed me against it. He wasn't rough about it, but it startled me. He moved so close that our bodies were touching, although only barely. His muscles tensed against my soft skin. He pressed his forehead to mine. His eyes were shut tight.

Stone was an unstoppable force that had entered my life less than a week ago, and yet he made my heart pulse in a way I hadn't know it could. He brought me the hope of peace. I had begun to rely on him even though I didn't truly *know* him.

"I thought ..."

His hand parted the tangles in my hair. I don't know why, but I couldn't stop myself from bringing my hand up and smoothing the tight lines around his eyes. The desire to calm him was too great to ignore.

He relaxed under my touch and opened his eyes. They were a stormy grey color that I had never seen before. His hand pulled free of my hair and touched my face. He ran his thumb across my lips.

"I …"

He straightened suddenly.

"I need to get some stuff then we will head to Nixie's."

He pushed off from the door. I swallowed hard, remaining where I was, trembling. He headed for his bedroom.

Stone grabbed a bag from inside his room while I sat tensely on the couch. I could still feel the rapid beat of my heart when he came out, his eyes a calmer shade of grey now. Not like earlier. What had that color been? Stone stopped in front of me. He held his hand, palm outstretched for me to take. If I did, everything would change. He offered me freedom. The prospect excited me. My heart suddenly beat with a new tempo. Faster and more unsteady than before.

Stone and I carefully made our way through the hallways, making it to Nixie's room without incident. When we arrived, though, we both could clearly hear shouting from inside.

Stone stopped me and listened for a moment.

"It's Dallas."

He grabbed my arm and pulled me around the next corner. Within a few seconds the door opened and Nixie's voice screamed.

"You're an asshole, Dallas! Fuck you!"

Then the door slammed shut. We heard Dallas rumble a few things under his breath. He stopped for moment, his nose tilted upward. He turned his head in our direction and my heart stopped. Dallas pulled in another breath only to sneeze and head off in the other direction. Stone looked down at me with a smile.

"We're lucky Nixie got him all riled up. Otherwise he would have scented us. Come on."

Stone grabbed my hand. I was mystified at how quickly I had become okay with his touch. He somehow made it bearable. For the first time, it felt safe.

Without knocking, Stone rushed through the doorway, shutting it immediately behind us. He started barking orders before Nixie could get a word in, but the living room was empty. I took a step away from Stone and looked into the kitchen. Nixie wasn't anywhere to be found, but we knew she was here.

"Give me a minute, just wait for me there, okay?"

Stone slipped ahead of me. He was watching the room as closely as I had been. His muscles were tense. He was ready for anything. I didn't think that either of us was expecting what happened next though.

Nixie flounced out of her room with every ounce of grace she had in her. Dangling from both of her hands were seafoam green luggage bags.

"Took you long enough."

Nixie blinked at Stone who took a step back appraising her. I think he was looking for some kind of sign that she might be trying to stall us.

"Well? Are you going to take the bags or not?" she asked.

"I don't need that much stuff," I said quietly, mostly to myself. I didn't want to take so many of her things. I had felt like I had found a friend in Nixie and leaving her was going to be hard enough. But to take her clothes as a constant reminder hurt too much, like a phantom pain in my chest. I rubbed absently at my heart.

Nixie let out a snort.

"Oh, guppy. These are my bags. I still have to go grab yours. Here you go, Stoney boy." She pushed the bags at Stone. He didn't even flinch as they fell to the ground in front of him.

"You don't know what you are getting yourself into, Nixie."

"The walls have ears here, hun. I know exactly what is happening. You aren't the only one who cares about her. I have nothing keeping me here anymore."

Nixie's coral eyes had taken a shaded hue, her deep seated sadness shining through. She gripped her own wrist and rubbed her thumb in small circles there. Her brows had pinched. I could actually feel the pain she was holding in. Was this an effect of the bond she had told me of?

"You made your decision. And now I am making mine."

Nixie was stern. It was the first time I heard her voice take on a steely edge. She brought her gaze back to us, pulling herself out of her own thoughts. The look lasted only until Stone nodded. Then she rushed over to me and gave me a quick hug, but paused last minute and backed away. She was catching on. Though I was becoming more comfortable with her every passing day, I still wasn't ready to be touched casually. I think she was beginning to understand that her attempts at comforting me might hurt me more in the end if she didn't respect my boundaries.

"Audrey, you need to tell us exactly what Jacobs said."

Stone turned to me. I told them everything. And Stone—well I trusted him completely. I already knew his intentions. The look in his eyes told me all I needed to know, though it was a little hard to believe. How could he be willing to do anything for me? To go to any lengths?

"Nixie, did Dallas give you any information?"

"No, the blowhole just came in here acting like he owned the place. Demanding this, demanding that. Blah, blah, blah. Said something about Audrey being unstable. Then I, of course replied, 'Well, aren't we all a bit crazy?' Then he went all wolfy on me and started to growl and throw a fit. I threatened him with a newspaper to the nose." Nixie was getting geared up to talk some more before Stone interrupted her by clearing his throat.

"All right. Well, being that I am pretty sure I know exactly what Jacobs will do if he gets his hands on her, we need to move."

"Let me grab one more bag."

Nixie disappeared back into her bedroom. Stone moved into her small kitchen, rummaging through the fridge and cabinets. He grabbed bags of food and a couple bottles of water.

"I want you to know that I had no idea and don't agree with what Jacobs wants to do."

He was watching me. I could see guilt, small though it was, in his eyes. It was murky green, swamp-like in color, with a tinge of red from shame. He was ashamed he hadn't known sooner.

"Have you tortured others to get answers before?" I knew what a man like Jacobs was willing to do. Whatever it took.

"When I was instructed to, yes."

His eyes were now a cold distant silver.

"Not everyone is innocent," I answered, shame heated my cheeks. My desire to both comfort him and assure myself overwhelmed me.

"No, I suppose not. But there are better people out there than me. You are one of those people, Audrey."

"No, I really am not," I whispered. I stared at my hands while I waited for Stone.

I slowly looked up. Stone had stepped forward so that he stood in front of me. I had been so locked in the memories I wanted to forget, that I didn't hear him. His eyes were a beautiful shade of violet, showing his deep compassion.

"You shouldn't think so little of yourself. Your crimes may not be as horrible as you assume."

His eyes drifted down to my lips. I felt the need to both move forward and away. I did neither, we only stared at each other a while longer. He took my hand.

"You'll be safe."

I looked at Stone, his eyes a light grey, almost blue color now. I could tell that he was calming down, even if his grip on my hand hadn't changed. It remained as tight as before, but not tight enough to hurt.

"Why would you do this for me?"

"You never deserved what happened to you. You've been innocent in all this."

"And who is to say that I am any more innocent than the people you tortured?"

It was the first time I felt fearless talking to him. To anyone. I wanted to understand why he believed what he did. His eyes turned a murky brown, a mixture of brown and rusty red. His fists tightened at his side.

"I can't change my past. But I won't make the same mistakes I made then. You are innocent. I've known since the moment I met you, though I don't know why, that you are not evil. You didn't deserve of any of the torture you received. You have done nothing wrong. Nothing to deserve it."

He moved closer to me. My eyes stung with the threat of tears, so I shut them, hoping that would dam up the emotions. His breath fanned my cheeks.

"Audrey ..."

"I got the last bag!" Nixie announced, pulling me out of the moment. My eyes opened to see her coming into the room with her luggage. Stone's face went blank as he took a step back.

Nixie fists turned white at the weight of the sleek, black duffle bag. She pushed back her shoulders and tipped her jaw up.

"Are you two ready?" This Nixie was so different from the bubbly woman I knew. She had pulled her hair back in a tight ponytail. Her expression looked grim, but when her gaze met mine, the tight lines around her mouth softened.

* * *

We only had a few incidents after that. The hallways were crawling with guards, but both Stone and Nixie knew the building. It was an achingly petrifying time getting through the building. If a guard had come too close, Nixie would start to sing a quiet song. I could barely hear it, but each time a guard would straighten his back and turn in the opposite direction, away from us. Stone had shifted his body so he wore a new face, and he was already dressed like the other guards. It had been chilling to watch his features melt away into someone else.

Stone stood tall, easing into his new body. Nixie held onto my arm and steered me closer to the wall. We had made it to the stairs, but had to make a quick escape onto one of the floors when a thunder of feet came from above us. Where we were headed now, I wasn't sure. My stomach was in knots, and I kept twisting my head looking around us.

Nixie tugged a large sweatshirt from her pack. She gripped it tight in her hands. For a second there was a longing in her eyes. She blinked once, twice, and the look was gone. Quietly she motioned for me to lift my arms. I did so, and the sweater came down heavily on my shoulders. The scent was masculine, not a bad smell, but I wrinkled my nose all the same.

149

Nixie took a step back assessing her work. I continued to stay in my crouched position for a moment longer. Straightening my knees, the sweatshirt unrolled and it went well past my hips to reach my knees. The arms went past my fingers; the entire sweatshirt was huge on me. Stone stepped forward and pulled the hood over my head. He nodded.

"We'll make our way back to the stairs and get to the garage that way."

Stone lead the way, and I curled into the sweatshirt. Nixie walked boldly next to Stone. She looked much like a warrior—jaw tipped up, eyes hard and forward. She had a confidence I couldn't dream of having. We had to go through a variety of hallways, taking the long way around to the stairs.

My heart pounded loudly in my chest as I would continually peek from the lip of the hood and take in our surroundings. We still hid from passing guards, and there were fewer patrolling the stairs.

I was nervous at the exit. Even thinking of going outside made my heart quicken. I hadn't been outside in years. But instead of daylight, we found ourselves in another dark, cement building.

In the parking garage, Elijah waited in a nondescript car. It was a black number with slightly tinted windows. Elijah said nothing as Nixie and I slipped in the back. I jumped when the trunk slammed. I twisted, looking around, feeling oddly exposed and trapped at the same time. Nixie tried to hum a tone near my ear to calm me. I shifted in my seat, my leg twitching, adrenaline rushing through my blood.

Every stitch of the seats pressed upon my skin. I closed my eyes. I touched the stitching intentionally, counting. *One. Two. Three.* I took a deep breath.

The car rumbled and we moved, my hand remaining steady as I counted. At twenty, light exploded before my tightly shut eyes. I closed my eyelids tighter. I pulled my limbs inward, tucking them to my chest, except for my one hand that continued tracing each thread. *Thirty-nine.* The breeze. I could taste it. I could smell it, feel it—I could taste its unrestrained freedom. My freedom. *Forty-three.* I was safe. I was free. No more concrete cages. *Fifty-seven.*

"Audrey …"

Nixie's humming was interrupted by a masculine voice. Not his. Never again. *Eight-two.*

"Audrey ..."

Eighty-seven.

"Don't you want to look outside?"

Ninety-six.

A trick. It had to be. The breeze—the smell of it, the feel of it, the taste. They had used a flashlight once on my blindfold. How my heart had broken, but now I knew all their tricks. *One hundred twenty-one.* I knew them all. But the heat touching my eyelids, the unwavering truth in his voice.

One hundred twenty-four.

How could I not believe him? I opened my eyes and forgot to count.

Chapter 24

STONE

It was like watching a newborn open its eyes for the very first time. Fresh and eager. Even her dead eye shone brighter. Her wild maroon hair flew around her head, propelled by the gust billowing in from the window. Finally, her lips twitched in response to the sight. Before I knew it, her entire face lit up with a full smile. I had never seen anything as heartbreakingly beautiful. Unconsciously, she began unfolding her limbs, straightening her back, and stretching her lithe body.

"Beautiful."

The word slipped out before I knew I said it. Nixie heard me, giggled, and punched the back of my seat. My attention was on Audrey, though, who remained next to the window. When her eyes weren't drinking in the sights, she would close them and let the breeze rush against her face.

In those moments she looked truly free.

A few times during the drive, she questioned what was happening. She flickered back and forth between the scared, damaged woman we rescued and the freed woman she was starting to become. But then she would touch the stitching on the seats and her lips would move. Watching her during those moments was like watching a beautiful snowflake melt away. I wasn't sure what she was doing in those moments, but I watched. I learned.

I wanted her to be able to hold onto this free, majestically enchanting woman that was finally shining through. It was the brokenness that I couldn't stand. Seeing her that way made my heart twist.

Thinking of her that way reminded me of my own sins. How many times had I killed in the name of Braden, my clan? How many times had I tortured men and women alike for a simple answer?

"She is no saint. And if you keep painting her in that light, she will not thank you."

Elijah's head tilted toward me slightly, but the night-black pits of his eyes offered no clue as to where he was really looking.

"No one is a saint. But some of people are better than others," I answered, watching as we passed another state line. We had been driving for hours. When we had left it was bright and sunny, now night was upon us.

We were headed north up the coast. I wasn't sure where Elijah would take us, but I hoped it wasn't near York land. The York's were one of the biggest, strongest families in the world, with land on every continent. They weren't too fond of the Braden Clan, and worst of all for us, they had occasionally worked with the Vedenins.

Hours later, after Nixie and Audrey had fallen asleep, after two stops for food and gas, we finally arrived. I found myself starting to drift off, even though moments before I had been wide awake. The sleep that overcame me felt unnatural, but I couldn't stop it either.

I woke before either woman in the back seat and twisted to look at them both. Audrey was curled up, head pressed against the window. That's when I realized what had happened. Annoyance slithered through me, tightening my muscles. I turned my irritated gaze to Elijah. He shouldn't have pulled me under. Shouldn't have force me to sleep. It could have endangered us.

"Why did you do that?"

"I am the only one here that cannot be compromised in any way. It is … *safer* for her this way," Elijah said, the word *safe* sounding unnatural coming for him. I didn't think he fully understood why he was doing this. I sure as hell didn't, but if the wraith was helping her, I wasn't going to reject his aid.

As much as I hated his reasoning, I also respected it. There were many different resources Jacobs had at his disposal. Nixie, Audrey, and I could potentially be a danger to ourselves without intending to be. He could use the talents of a warlock or witch to scry for us. Judging by the time on the clock, Elijah had put me under for about three hours.

We'd all ditched our phones. Nixie had even reluctantly parted with her iPod. Jacobs had tracking devices in all our electronics, for our "protection" in the event one in our clan was kidnapped. But this car was a different story. I'd never seen it before, so I was guessing Elijah had obtained it, somehow. I wasn't going to ask. I was pretty sure he wasn't going to tell.

"This is my cabin. Only one other person knew about it. And that person is dead now."

Elijah rarely ever smiled and I was glad for it. But now, he bared his sharp, dagger-like teeth in an unsettlingly empty grin.

"There are two bedrooms, a kitchen, and a living room with a couch. You can all take the rooms."

He didn't even look at us.

The forest spreading around us felt like heaven. There was plenty of space to run, to stretch my tight muscles. I looked over at Audrey. Her lips were parted, almost tipped upwards into a smile, but also frozen as she took in all there was to see. Standing within the trees, she looked at peace. She looked at home in nature.

Nixie joined Audrey and touched her shoulder. Audrey flinched at the contact, but relaxed when she saw it was only Nixie. While they headed in, I retrieved the bags from the trunk.

"How safe are we here?" I asked, hoping he'd give me a good answer.

"I made our scent untraceable, but the magic will fade. This remote, I estimate at least a month before they have a chance at detecting us."

I nodded. Better than I thought originally.

"Could you get me a few extra things?"

This time Elijah looked at me with his head quirked quizzically to one side. I knew wraiths weren't easily surprised, but he looked at me with their closest equivalent. I handed him a list, and after looking it over, he nodded.

"I will be a couple of hours. But I will return."

I turned back to the wraith's secret cabin.

Chapter 25

AUDREY

Waking up, my memory of the outside lingered. I had touched the ground with my toes. I had felt the freedom of fresh air all around me. Being in the car was different. The outside zipped past as if eager to pass by. The air here was different, too. It was stiller, more patient.

Nixie had urged me into the house too soon. She was asleep next to me on the same bed, being respectful enough to keep as much distance between us as she could. I feared sharing a bed with her. More times than not I had violent dreams. Violent memories. She wasn't the reason I couldn't sleep, though. I was just too eager to go back outside. I had been starved of this for four years.

I needed this.

And so, I closed my eyes and reached out with my senses. I could hear everything. A cricket northwest, a frog southeast, and a deer to the west. Leaves rustled. I had long dreamt of these sounds, longed for them. Being able to hear them again—nothing compared.

The temptation was too much. As silently as I could, I slipped my legs off the bed and lifted my weight carefully and evenly. I slowly made my way through the house. I feared waking anyone. Feared they would take this away. But their exhaustion must have driven them to a deep sleep. At last, my bare feet touched the damp, gritty ground. I didn't care. I soaked up the moisture like a plant. The further I walked, the more vibrant the colors became. This place was so full of life. Color exploded, one transformed into the next, new colors forming before my eyes. I should have felt overwhelmed, but I felt strangely at ease. I ran over to a tree eager to peer at its every contour and variation. At its shades of brown and green. I was utterly entranced.

"Audrey!"

Nixie's musical voice came out strained and broken from the direction of the cabin.

I looked up at the sky, to see the top of the trees reaching up high into the blue. White fluffy clouds leisurely made their way across the sky. When I emerged from the cabin, the sky had been full of stars and their gentle light, but now they were gone. The cool, icy blue of early morning had crept up from the horizon. Had I been out here long?

I turned to head back to Nixie when I saw a black panther step out from behind a tree. It was huge, its sleek body rippling with muscle as it settled on its haunches in front of me. Its tail flicked irritably. My heart stopped, my breath stuck in my lungs. Its murky brown eyes changed to a bright yellow.

Stone.

I let out a slow breath and swallowed my fear. He walked over to me and placed his large feline head under my hand.

Nuzzling inward, he nipped the edge of my shirt with his teeth and pulled me back toward the cabin. A small smile tugged at the corners of my mouth, but he just flicked his tail at me and walked ahead.

A couple of times, when I stopped to smell a flower or inspect something more closely, he would turn and nudge me onwards. I suppressed another smile at this worrying. But I couldn't help myself. It was a strange sensation being outside after being trapped for so long in my white room. I felt untouchable and utterly exposed at the same time. My joy left little room for any other feelings I had at the time.

A low growl rumbled from panther-Stone.

At this point, I had my back to him and could hide the smile that crossed my lips. I bit down on my bottom lip. Trailing my hand against the rough bark of the tree that had demanded my attention as I came back around to face Stone. His head was low, but his ears were perked up. It felt surprisingly easier to be around panther-Stone than human-Stone.

"Sorry," I whispered to the ground. Deep down, I knew that I should be scared that Jacobs would find us. But I couldn't bring myself to worry about that. Not yet. Not when I felt, for once, content. Almost happy.

Almost.

As soon as we emerged into the clearing that surrounded the cabin, Stone bounded off somewhere inside. Nixie rushed from the porch of the cabin and bent down a little so that we were eye to eye.

"Are you all right?" Nixie's coral eyes flashed her worry.

"I ... I'm the happiest I've been in years."

I hadn't been this happy since I lost my dragon companion, Aiden. But even now, the pain in my heart ached dully. At least now it was less noticeable.

"You had tears in your eyes. I was worried about you, is all." Nixie smoothed my hair back as she spoke. "I'm sorry I got scared. When I woke up, you were gone."

Nixie pulled me into a hug. She took in a long, shaky breath. I couldn't find it in myself to pull away from her touch. It felt soothing. Like ... family?

"I can't believe a wraith would offer up his totally top secret cabin for us. Are you working your womanly charms on him?"

Nixie moved to my side, bumping me with her hip lightly, laughing.

"My womanly charms?" I asked, but my mind was still caught up on the fact Elijah had given up this place for ... for me? The cabin right before my eyes reminded me of all that he had given to help me.

"Yes, guppy. Womanly charms."

She leaned forward, bringing her arms together to exaggerate her already well-endowed chest. Her voice took a husky, seductive tone.

"Elijah may be a wraith, but he is still male. A male with creepy ass eyes, but eyes for you, nonetheless."

She ran her green tongue over her teeth as Stone emerged from the cabin. His chest was bare, a shirt in his hands and his pants low hung on his trim waist.

"But if you want to see *real* creepy eyes, you should meet a weresnake. Creepy. Especially when their second eyelid blinks. See, snakes don't have eyelids, so when a weresnake is in its human form, their eyes don't quite adjust right. They have eyelids like normal humans, but they rarely use them. It takes more conscious thought for them to remember to do that," Stone commented as he pulled on his shirt.

"I haven't met a weresnake before! I wonder how creepy they really are ..." Nixie stopped and looked at us both with a sly smile, her eyes twinkling with mischief at her own thoughts. "Never mind. Anyways, what is the plan, cuttlefish?"

"I know you've been enjoying the outdoors, Audrey, but you need to be more careful. Also, we need to start teaching you. If we hadn't been on high alert in the car, we'd have given you a crash course then. It's too dangerous for you to be unaware of our world and how it works."

"Elijah should be back soon. Hopefully he will be able to give us more insight into exactly what it is Jacobs is after. Come inside, I'll start making lunch."

Nixie and I headed up the stairs leading to the porch, and Stone was already back in the cabin. My heart beat in my throat, pulsating steadily with fear. Would they demand to know my secrets? Stone was in the kitchen already preparing food. Nixie and I took seats at the table.

The cabin wasn't huge by any means, but to me, after living so long in that room, it felt like the perfect space. The first room was the living room, which was followed by the kitchen and, after that, a dining room.

The kitchen was small and looked barely equipped with the essentials. The living room had a stiff couch that sat next to a fireplace. The table, where Nixie and I were, seated only four. Three doorways led out of the living room. Two toward bedrooms, each bedroom decorated the same. One bed, one dresser, muted colors. Ah, the decorating sense of a wraith.

The last door lead to a small bathroom with a stall shower, toilet, and sink. It felt like a skeleton of a home. We had filled it with a human kind of warmth, but the décor held an aloof, chill feel to it. Much like Elijah.

"What do you want to know more about? Let's start there," Nixie asked, resting her chin on her folded hands.

"What do I need to know?"

"There is a lot you need to know," Stone added from the kitchen. He looked like he wanted to say more, but instead he remained quiet.

"We never finished telling you about all the different kinds of *weres*!" Nixie waved Stone off.

"So there are *weres* for almost every kind of animal out there. Were-creatures have the spirit of their animal living inside of them. But their human and animal sides aren't separate—they're one in the same. At least that is how it was always explained to me. Like for an example a weresloth." Nixie paused for a second, giving me a knowing smile.

"Yeah, I met a weresloth. Don't pretend you're not jealous! Anyways, so he was really slow, and when he talked, it took him forever to get out a sentence. Oh, and I met a wereraccoon once. Gross! Don't hang around them too often. They smell horrible and they are super possessive of their food. The one I met hissed at me once. That's pretty much the gist of *weres*. They are pretty simple creatures to understand."

Stone set the food he had been preparing on the table. The noodles were tangled in a broth that smelled strongly of beef.

"Ramen noodles. It was all he had that was still okay to eat. I think he should be back soon. And he'll be bringing better food," Stone explained as he handed another bowl to Nixie, who immediately wrinkled her nose. Stone had told me before that Elijah had gone to shop far from the cabin, just in case some type of tracking paranormal was trying to catch our scent.

"I am guessing he won't be bringing me my seaweed salad. He is bringing fish, right?"

She looked up at Stone who moved to the other side of the table.

"Yeah, I told him."

"Whew, for a second there I was really worried. Thanks, Stone. You are a true guppy!"

Nixie smiled, looking back down at her food.

"I know it says shrimp flavored, but this does not smell like shrimp." She sighed, and started to eat it despite her reluctance.

160

"What are some other paranormal creatures?" I asked quietly.

"Well, there are nature based ones, like the dryads, elves, fey, fairies and pixies," Nixie replied. "Those are usually the most common. Elves are not small little things, like you might imagine. Actually, those are gnomes. And where gnomes are concerned, my advice is to stay far away from them. The bastards drive people insane. There are a lot of different paranormals, but more importantly, we need to start educating you about the families that form the government of our world, in a manner of speaking.

"There are ten ruling families, plus a few smaller ones, but they connect, in some way, back to the original ten. The Bradens, our family, will not be the only ones looking for us."

They exchanged a glance when Nixie finished. Both got really quiet. I watched them, waiting for one of them to explain.

"Elijah mentioned we were near the York family's land."

"The Yorks?" Nixie's usually pale green skin looked even paler.

"Sorry, Nixie. I should've said something sooner," Stone sounded sincere.

Crash.

I jumped in my seat, eyes wide as I searched for the source of the sound. I had been so focused on Stone that Nixie's abrupt movements caught me off guard. She was standing, her chair had fallen backwards. Her hands shook as she brushed them over her shirt.

"I think I smelled a lake nearby. I'm going to take a walk."

Her words were stiff and lacked their normal musical lilt. The door slammed shut following her exit. I stirred my food. Stone touched my hand bringing my eyes to his.

"There is history there. Something she'll have to tell you, but for now, how about you and I take a walk in the woods? I know you weren't done this morning. I just wanted you to eat something. You still look a little on the thin side."

Stone's voice was low and smooth. His quiet tone brought my unsteady heartbeat back to a normal pace. We stood together and went outside.

"Would you be willing to tell me about your past? Anything that you remember?"

I stiffened at his words. It was instinct. I didn't know how long it would take before the suspicion that this was just another elaborate trick faded. If this didn't work out for a day, then would they send me back to Jacobs? Was this part of Jacobs' plan? I didn't want to be sent back to that man. Stone touched my elbow, his hand trailing down my arm. My eyes closed at the touch. My breath quickened. His fingers left a trail of sweet fire behind. He cupped his hand around mine, his fingers twitched as though they were trying to get even closer.

"I'm not asking for them. I want to know about you."

I looked up at Stone.

"I don't know what you want me to tell you …" I whispered, looking away from his forest green eyes.

Chapter 26

STONE

"Tell me anything," I said watching her. My desire to know more about her was all consuming at this point. Part of me believed the more she told me the better I could protect her, but the selfish part of me simply wanted to know her better. To be the one she really opened up to. It was a need I couldn't quite understand. Usually I was happy enough staying uninvolved—it was easier that way. But looking at her now, I wanted to know everything about her. I waited patiently as we walked.

Audrey looked down at the ground as though ashamed to even think about her past. I had to wait for her to come to me if there was to be any trust between us at all.

"I had a stuffed animal—Aiden. He was my only friend for so long that when I lost him, I felt like I lost the only good thing in this world. It was just a small, little thing I remember my father gave to me."

Her lips twitched for a moment. The lines around her eyes dropped; the eye that was scarred, shut a little farther than the other. The scar near her lip looked tight.

"How did you lose him?" I asked before I realized that it was the wrong thing to say. "Wait, you don't have to ..."

"I was in my room that morning, holding Aiden. I had been holding him tight because I'd been crying. My dad knocked on the door. It startled me, and I let go of Aiden. I let go of him. When I opened the door, my father looked worried and pulled me from the room. I told him I had to go back for Aiden. All I remember was turning back to grab him. It was the last time I ever saw him."

She gripped my hand even tighter, like some sort of life-line. I wasn't sure if she was speaking about what had obviously been her only friend in her short life, or if she was speaking of her father.

"Audrey." My free hand grasped at the air emptily, as if I could physically grasp what I needed to say to help her. Words never felt like enough. What could I say? I understood the pain of loss. Which, naturally, made me think of my mother. Suddenly, my insides were teeming with old pain and guilt.

Audrey's arm brushed against mine, bringing me back to the present. I would do anything to make sure she wouldn't have to suffer anymore. Hadn't she suffered enough? I stopped walking and turned toward her. All I wanted to do was wrap her in my arms and never let go.

My hands moved to her hips without a thought, and I guided her gently to a tree. I looked down at her eyes. There was a hint of fear there. Uncertainty, too, and something I couldn't quite place. Could it be that she felt it too? Did she feel the same desire I did?

I doubted she fully understood her own feelings. Acting on instinct, she leaned forward, nuzzling against me. Her soft body pressed against mine. I closed my eyes to better savor the feeling, but only for a moment before they hungrily opened again.

Logic flew out the window. The desire to protect her from fear or sadness was overpowering. Her irresistible lips had become a seductive focal point in my mind. I leaned down and she leaned back. I sensed a hint of fear, but with her back against the tree, she couldn't escape.

I hovered close to her, the palm of my hand pressing into the bark of the tree. It dug into my skin, keeping me grounded. The desire to claim her lips was strong in me, but I had to remind myself that this wasn't the time to let instincts overrule logic. If I moved too quickly, if I forced this on her, she would run.

I anchored myself by holding the delicate, flared part of her hip. I released my hold on the tree, allowing the fingers of my other hand to swim through her locks, tracing the graceful line of her scalp to the back of her head. The silkiness thrilled me. I had been anxious to run my hands through her hair again and again. It twisted around my hand like something alive. I savored the luxurious feel of each and every strand.

Audrey's lashes touched her cheeks, her lush lips parted as she let out a breath. She lifted those lashes to look up at me. Desire darkened her eyes a shade and her hip moved in my hand. She leaned a little closer. And that's when my brain switched off and my body took over. Basic instincts and pure desire drove me forward.

I needed to feel her entire body against mine. My body moved without permission, desperate to draw as close to her as possible. My lips, quite suddenly, were against hers. They were as soft as I'd imagined. She tasted like she smelled: wild, untamed, and sweet.

She stiffened in surprise for a moment, but before long she followed my lead. My tongue traced the bottom of her lip, releasing a gasp from her sweet mouth. I pressed my advantage. She froze, again, but only for a moment. Then her tongue melded with mine. Dancing a passionate dance. I was lighter. A burden I hadn't known I carried suddenly lifted from inside me.

I was free.

It was an odd sensation. I was lightheaded. And though every part of me ached for her, the need for air already burned in my lungs. I didn't want to pull away, but soon did.

My forehead pressed against hers. She breathed heavily, eyes downcast.

Shame flooded through me. I hadn't meant to initiate the kiss. She should have been the one in control of the situation, but lust had taken control. After all she had suffered, I never wanted her to feel out of control in a situation. The fog that had clouded my judgements while watching her before had dissipated, leaving me feeling like scum.

Gods, I needed to know what she was feeling. *What have I done?* I needed to know if I had destroyed what little trust we had between us.

"Audrey."

I needed her to look at me. Only then would I know the truth. Only then would I know if my thoughtless desire had hurt her. When she did, the tear-tracks caused my heart to lurch. It was a terrifying, weightless feeling followed by a stab of bitter pain. Those tears in her eyes.

Shit.

"Did I hurt you?"

"No … it was … nice."

She looked down, her cheeks reddening to a beautiful rosy color. Her skin, though, was still unnaturally pale from the lack of sunlight she had suffered in her captivity. She all but glowed with the pink blush that infused her cheeks. And her lips! Audrey's lips were pulled wide into a bright smile. Her eyes were lit up.

"I've never been kissed before."

Looking down at her, my heart started to pound. Something inside of me was devilishly pleased that I had stolen that sweet first kiss from those innocent lips. This made her more surely mine than anything else. I felt an intense moment of pure pride. I was the one who had put that look on her face.

Reality brought me back to earth, though. Moments before I had been terrified that I had scared her. And while she looked pleased with the kiss, I couldn't shake the feeling that I moved too far with her too soon. She needed to be the one who set the pace. I didn't want to lose her because I couldn't control myself.

I stepped back, allowing her room to decide what she wanted to do. She slipped through the space separating her and me, picking up her meandering path where we had stopped. We were quiet for a while.

"Audrey."

"It's okay. I'm okay."

Her voice seemed to hold a note of disbelief.

"Did you want to keep walking or head back to the cabin?"

"I want to keep going."

She lifted her chin a little in determination. I suppressed the smile.

"The first girl who kissed me punched me afterwards and told me that I was a terrible kisser. I was the laughing stock of the playground."

I ducked down to whisper this to her like a well-kept secret. A little giggle slipped past her lips before she reined it in. It was almost like she couldn't quite believe what had just happened.

166

"What was school like for you?" I asked, curious about the mysterious woman next to me. Hopefully this topic would keep things light.

"I went to school for a bit, but my father … he was trying to protect me."

She stopped. I watched as her eyes darkened. My own instincts were already kicking in. She needed to be protected. From what, I had no idea. But the hurt expression now crawling across her features was enough to make me want to kill somebody.

"There was a boy there. He was nice to me. He told me I could be his friend. I never got along well with the other kids because …"

Again she paused, as if debating what she could say. What she should say.

"I was different. But he was brave. And then we spent the whole day together. I think it was one of the happiest days of my life. When I came home that day, I was smiling ear to ear. But …"

She stopped and swallowed hard. I watched the tears bead first in the corners of her eyes. Tragic jewels. Her hand touched the scar on her face. Fingers pressed against old wounds. I touched my forearm rubbing a scar hidden by the form I wore. Watching her relive her pain reminded me of my own dark memories. The scars hidden beneath my skin, untouchable, but I knew them by heart. I knew every jagged end and puckered piece.

"After school, my father had asked me why I was so happy. I told him I had a friend. I'd never seen him so out of control. He had punished me before, when I had been bad. But I deserved this one. We were in hiding, my father and I. I knew I wasn't supposed to make friends. I had promised him."

She was muttering, and as she did, her words began to lose their focus. Her eyes became distant. Audrey dug her blunt nails into the scars on her face. She raked them down the trail of scars.

Slowly, and with a gentle touch, I wrapped my fingers around her wrist. I tugged lightly, pulling her hand away from her face. She blinked a couple of times, allowing me to do it. Unsure of what else I could do, I pulled her close and whispered to her that she was safe.

It wasn't unheard of for rouge paranormals to live without a clan. And from what she had just said, it seemed to me that her father feared being discovered. Who knew how old she had been at the time? But it was wrong for him to punish her for making a friend. I felt hatred for this man burn inside me. It was strange, feeling so strongly about someone I had never met.

She latched onto my shirt, clinging to me in a way that made me swell with pride for a fleeting moment. Then she pulled away, breathing hard. Was it fear that made her pull away? Fear of me? But I saw her eyes were focused again. She had pulled herself from the panic of her memories and continued on. I immediately admired her courage.

"After that I stopped going to school. My father took care of me, though. That's when he gave me Aiden. My friend, the stuffed dragon. I named him secretly because if my father had known I named him after my first *real* friend, the one I had made at school, I was scared he would take him away as well. Aiden was the boy who promised me he would hold my hand anytime I was scared. But I never went back. I wasn't there for him. We were only six."

Audrey looked away from me. The tortured look in her eyes compelled me to take a step forward. The muscles in arms ached to hold her close again. The desire to pull her close and hide her away was almost too much. I took a step forward, but then mastered myself and stayed right where I was. It hurt to be away from her, but I'd be damned if I made the same mistake twice.

However, I couldn't allow her to believe that it was her fault. It had all been out of her control. Her childhood friend would have understood. Her father too. Any father would—she had to know that.

"Audrey, I'm sure that neither Aiden nor your father feel like you betrayed him."

She wouldn't look at me, so I took her hand in mine. I brought it to my lips and her gaze met mine. I wrapped her hand in my fist and placed it over my heart.

"I promise to hold your hand whenever you are scared, as long as you promise to do the same for me."

I searched her eyes, and that guarded look that had been there from the moment we met softened. Her chronically tense shoulders slackened. She looked at me like she completely believed I would never hurt her. I felt like I was asking her for more than I was willing to offer.

With her hand in mine, we continued our walk. Our conversation turned from her past to lighter things. I told her some more about the world we lived in, or the world as it had come to be since the paranormals had made their presence known. And, in the quiet moments between the lazy topics of conversation we both seemed to enjoy, I tried to guess at the secrets locked inside her. What might her paranormal affinity be? Was she a creature of fire, air, water, or earth? Or was she a rarity and a mixture of the two? She trusted me to protect her—that much was clear. But it would be a while before she was ready to tell me the whole story.

Audrey reached out her free arm at intervals, caressing the trees and the plants we passed with her fingers on our return to the cabin. It was an enchanting sight, seeing her rediscover nature. Her eyes would brighten as her lips twitched upwards. At times she would release a subtle gasp of delight. But the closer we got to the cabin, the more subdued she became. She kept her focus straight ahead. We came into the small clearing in front of the cabin, and walked up the stairs together. She released her hold on my hand and walked through the door ahead of me.

Without a word, she took up residence on the couch beside Nixie while I headed back outside to go for a run. There was a lot on my mind, and the cabin was starting to feel cramped, anyway.

Elijah returned around midday, driving an old deep blue colored Impala LT with tinted windows. It smelled clean and new. Either he bought it off the lot or stole it. I didn't care to ask. From the look of the paper bags occupying the passenger seat beside him, he'd purchased some real food. There was seafood, especially for Nixie, and an assortment of mouthwatering red meats.

The next few days followed this pattern. Nixie usually accompanied us on our walks, no matter that she wasn't wanted, or at least not wanted by me. That being the case, I didn't get a chance to spend much time alone with Audrey. I longed to kiss her lips again. To feel her skin so close.

I dreamt of it, yearned for it, but deep down I knew it was better this way. It had to be this way for now. Yet …

In the dark of the night, my dreams of her kisses turned to more. I shifted forms daily, hoping one of them would help me shake the feeling in my bones that I needed more of her. But it wasn't only her body that I craved, it was her trust and affection. I realized that I had dreamt of being a hero of sorts for her. I wasn't though. When she and I left on her walks, I did so with a basic need to protect in my heart, but the feeling was growing. It was changing, and I didn't know into what.

On our fifth night we were setting up for dinner when Elijah walked in. He never joined in on our meals. I wasn't sure that wraiths even ate real food.

"Tomorrow I will have to go get more supplies. If anyone needs something, add it to the list."

Always to the point and completely unemotional. Even after spending so much time with him, I still felt uncomfortable in his presence.

Chapter 27

AUDREY

Elijah had left the room, disappearing to where ever it is that he went. Nixie and Stone always got noticeably less tense once he left. Nixie had been poking around the drawers and cabinets in the cabin. The place's sparse furniture had only the bare necessities. During Nixie's searching she had come across a deck of cards. Each night she and Stone taught me a new game to play. Nixie had pulled them out again tonight and started to explain the newest game to me.

I couldn't keep myself from peeking up at Stone. A couple of days had passed since he kissed me in the woods. I had never felt anything quite like it. I remembered how sweet it had been to lose all sense, as I had when his tongue glided along my bottom lip.

Looking at him and thinking of that kiss, I yearned for the closeness we had shared. Even if it was for such a small bit of time.

A hand with a card crossed my line of vision, jolting me from my daydreaming. My eyes met Nixie's who gave me a wink. My cheeks reddened and I looked down, feeling bashful. I hadn't told her what happened between Stone and me because I felt that it was our moment and ours alone. It was a foreign feeling. Having something that belonged entirely to me, even if it was only a moment. Even if it was just a memory. It was *mine.*

Stone came over to the table and started to argue with Nixie about what game we would play tonight. Movement outside the window caught my attention. My heart had started to pound, but when Elijah's dark hair caught the moonlight, my fear calmed.

"I'll be right back."

I kept my voice quiet. Stone watched me as I stood up and headed toward the door, his eye color changing rapidly, shifting with the changes in his emotions. Open curiosity was written all over Nixie's face. But Elijah stared at me through the window, with his head slightly tilted, a silent inquiry expressed in body language alone, as if he knew my intentions.

I had reached the door already when I heard a chair scrape against the hardwood floor. Stone was standing, gripping the edge of the table. Nixie's glance flickered between us, her lips pressed together. Staring right into his eyes, I mouthed that I was okay and tried to give him my best reassuring look. He sat down stiffly, but his hands didn't loosen on the table.

"What is it that you wanted?" Elijah asked.

I swallowed hard. Elijah scared Stone and Nixie for entirely different reasons than me. They feared the creature that he was. I feared that he would see through me. That he would tell them everything.

Elijah stood next to the railing of the porch and I moved so that I was standing nearby him. He stood so tall and straight. There wasn't a muscle in his body that wasted any movement. He was in control, as ever.

"Why would you do this for us?" I asked quietly, not able to look at him. Instead I looked out to the moonlit ground. What I had really wanted to ask him is why he would do this for *me*. I had no doubts that Elijah didn't care what happened to Nixie and Stone. I wasn't even sure he cared what happened to me.

I hadn't been able to let the thought go. The whole week we had been here, it had been on my mind. Elijah was distant and unfeeling most of the time, but there were moments like now when he would join us and I could feel him watching me. But I didn't know what that meant.

"You intrigue me."

Something in his tone made him almost sound like he was surprised at his own answer. We were standing on the deck, Elijah a few steps away from the railing. I was pressed against it, silently counting the poles. A heavy sigh slipped from my lungs, relaxing me.

"Do …"

My words trailed off as my courage failed. But slowly I was becoming aware that … these people could be trusted. What did I have to lose?

"Do you remember anything from," a shiver of fear worked down my spine, "when you extracted the wraith from me?"

"Yes. I remember everything. Do not mistake my intrigue for compassion, Audrey. I am more likely to steal your soul and devour every last piece of it before comforting you. Your soul has been darkened by your experiences. Fear and pain have become a permanent part of you. Yet I have not even tried to take any of your fear as food. Intriguing, isn't it?"

I nodded. I could only accept his blunt answer. I didn't expect him to give me a heartfelt answer as to why he would help us. Elijah had made it blatantly obvious that he didn't feel emotions like the rest of us. His lack or complete control of his emotions made him easier for me to deal with. He didn't play games or hide anything.

"Is there anything …"

"I will not tell you about your past. As I told Jacobs, when it is time for you to know your past and the secrets locked away there, you will know."

With that Elijah walked back into the cabin.

My fingers twitched over the railing. *Thirty-eight, thirty-nine.* The veins of the wood kept me grounded. I was becoming too comfortable with the idea of hope. Frustration and anger built inside of me. I was living on the edge of knowing.

"What were you two talking about?"

When Nixie appeared, she took the position that Elijah had vacated. I heard the floor creak and was expecting to see Stone, not her. My fingers still fluttered over the veins in the wood I was counting.

"I was just asking him about the wraith, if he would tell me anything."

"It will come back to you," Nixie leaned her elbows onto the flat railing. We were quiet for a few moments. Nixie's lips made a rare downturn, turning her usual smile into a small scowl. Her brows pinched.

"Sorry. I didn't mean to intrude, but Stone was getting anxious. I offered to come out, otherwise he would've been all overbearing-man on you. Stone really has taken a shine to you, guppy. I think he's overreacting, but like I said, it was better than the alternative."

I didn't say anything. I continued to stare out into the blankness of the night. Frustration built a tight knot in my stomach. A hint of anger bit at me. I was so used to suppressing my anger in fear of retaliation that it felt unnerving to feel it against Elijah.

"Sometimes we have to forget the past."

Nixie's coral eyes were downcast and moisture glistened on their surface. I reached over and touched her arm trying to offer her some comfort. She obviously wanted to forget her past, but not knowing— being in a void—that was even worse. I felt adrift, like my grasp on reality had slipped, and weightless, I hung for a moment.

"Maybe it's better to know."

"I'm sorry." Nixie wrapped her arm around my shoulder and pulled me close for a second. "I shouldn't have said that."

"We all have our own demons," I whispered, feeling the chill of the night starting to seep into my skin. Nixie slipped on her smile and bright eyes like a mask.

"Come on, sweetie. Let's go play a card game!" Nixie skipped back into the cabin dragging me along.

The hours crawled into the early morning as Elijah and I learned how to play the new card game. He turned out to be very good at it, and I didn't do too bad myself, either. We finally started to wrap up the game at about two o'clock in the morning. Nixie and Stone had managed to keep me smiling for most of the night. To all our surprise, I almost laughed at one point. How long had it been since I'd done that? My heart filled with a sort of lightness as the laughter shook its playful way through my body, relaxing my muscles, loosening them in a way that hadn't happened in a long time.

Nixie had left the table after we finished cleaning up the card game, saying she was going to take a shower. Elijah left claiming that he was going to check the perimeter of the cabin. I got up from the table and headed to the bedroom that Nixie and I had been using.

"Audrey," Stone called, sounding closer than I thought he would be. I turned to see him only a few feet away. His hands were open at his side, and he uncharacteristically shifted his weight back and forth for a second. He looked lost.

"Mind talking for a second?"

He jerked his head toward the door and I realized he probably wanted to talk about the private conversation I'd had with Elijah. Stone had taken his promise seriously. All this time he had stayed with me whenever he could. He had calmed me when I was unmanageable. He was a constant. He made things easier. Bearable.

When we stepped outside, Stone pulled me around to the side of the building. Without warning and without any hesitation, he claimed my lips. I responded without hesitation this time, understanding the movements, understanding how he would make me *feel*. The moment stretched on forever, but before long he parted his lips from mine.

My heart constricted, other parts of my body reacted so violently to his touch. I was drawn to him like a magnet. When he pulled away, my body followed, determined to keep the closeness between us. My body shook with a desperation, a need that I didn't understand. His hands moved up and down my back. His very touch left lingering trails of warmth on my skin. He pressed his forehead against mine again. I squirmed. My brain was the source of so many dark memories. I wasn't ready for him to touch me intimately, but I couldn't move away from him. I wouldn't. The sensations still scared me, caused my heart to flutter, caused my breath to thicken in my throat. Still, I couldn't stop.

"Stone ..."

"Gods, I don't even want you to call me that."

His eyes were shut tight, and his smooth hands that had explored the edge of my shirt, touched the skin beneath it, his thumbs rubbing circles. The wind brushed through the tree tops, the leaves brushed one against the other. An owl called out in the night, but all this noise, all this wilderness was drowned by the hot rush of blood in my ears.

My body quaked. I swallowed, watching his chest rise and fall. His legs brushed against mine, one tucked between mine. His intoxicating scent started to overwhelm me. I bit my lip as I met the soft red hues of his eyes.

"Audrey ... my real name is Gabriel."

"Gabriel?"

When I said his name, his lips tilted upwards, the crease between his brows smoothed. There was a new color, a light peach abloom in his irises that quickly shifted before it was even fully formed. Instead his eyes turned a deep purple color, the color of deep affection. I wondered what he was thinking. What had forced his eyes to shift to this new color?

Reaching up I traced his jawline with my fingertips. Faint bristles of hair scraped against my skin. I didn't hate the sensation, but it was new, strange, and caused a steady warmth to build inside me.

"It's been years since I've heard someone call me by my real name. Hearing you say it though ..." He opened his eyes again and kissed me. This time it was as short as it was sweet. It was a tender press.

"Why do people call you Stone?"

"I haven't ever been known for my sensitivity. I trained from a young age to be the man, the killer that you see in front of you today," he replied. His hand moved to my face, touching my cheek, my lips, anything he could.

"How can you just stand there and let me kiss you? Let me touch you when I am no better than the men who attacked you? Who tortured you?"

And yet he didn't stop. Still he touched me. His hand moved to trace the lines of my hair. His soft touch left a trail of tingles on my skin. I wanted to close my eyes, but I wanted to watch him as well. The chilly air swept across us, his hair blowing in the wind, mine mimicking his.

"Why do you insist on having people call you Stone?" I asked, curious as to why he would hide his name.

"I couldn't bear to hear strangers say the name my mother gave me. I didn't trust anyone enough to tell them that."

Gabriel stepped back a little, but his hands never left me. His right hand, which played with my hair absently, slid downward to rest on my hip.

"But you trust me enough to tell me your name?"

Instead of answering me, he tilted my head back to kiss me again. He meant it to be quick, but I followed as he pulled away. My heart raced. My body knew what it wanted, and slowly, I was figuring out what I wanted as well.

"Gods help me, but I trust you."

After that we headed back into the cabin. He brought me to my door and kissed me one more time. His lips were tense against mine. He held back, but knowing he did made it taste sweeter. His lips capturing mine, holding them without moving. He pulled away, walking backwards toward his room. Only when he entered did I find the courage to lick my lips. His lingering taste still there. So many touches in one night. My fingers drifted to my lips in wonder.

I hoped that my dreams would be as kind.

***

As the days passed, old memories bubbled up from some deep, dark well inside of me. Some of them I relished, but those were the good ones, and few and far between. Most were tainted with bitterness and cruelty. I had spent a year as a prisoner before they had taken me to the room with white walls. A year had passed between the last time I saw my father and my isolation. Loneliness was more favorable than the memories.

Drip, drip. Drip, drip. Drip, drip. My body shook with pain and fear. It radiated through me, pulsating with every drip. My eyes were swollen with tears, with pain, I wasn't even sure. My vision was limited by the darkness. Stone walls. Grey. Grey. Grey.

The more conscious I became, the more the pain grew. I pressed my swollen cheek against to the uneven ground, hoping for relief from the burning pain. Drip, drip. All silence but those drips and my labored breathing. My tears had dried up, my throat and mouth painfully dry. Drip, drip.

My legs involuntarily pressed closer together. A shudder racked my body.

I lied. My tears hadn't yet dried up.

Drip, drip, drip.

I must have lost consciousness. I wasn't shocked. My whole body was exhausted with pain. They—the guards, the ones who looked human but were really monsters—had done this to me. Had broken me to pieces. Only monsters could break three bones without remorse. It was a blessing honestly. Only three. Drip, drip. Three. Cracks. Snaps. Drip, drip. Agonizing screams. No relief.

Drip.

I shuddered at the memory. The broken bones throbbed together in a chorus of pain, as if groaning under the pain they had endured. I pressed my face into the pillow, my tears smeared across my cheeks, absorbing into the fabric.

Stone. Gabriel. Think about him. Think about that kiss. Think about *anything else.*

It helped. The memories faded some, to the point that I could breathe. I don't know how long of a reprieve I would have from my memories. They occurred at unexpected times and were triggered by unexpected things. And they felt so *real.* They assembled like a cruel puzzle, taking shape only as the moments were remembered.

The dark memories started to melt away into a new scene.

I was five.

He lifted me up and placed me on his shoulders. I always liked this view; he was so tall! I felt like I could touch the clouds. I giggled, a sound foreign to me now, but natural to hear from my past self. My dad touched my exposed toes pretending to bite them. I giggled more.

"My little survivor."

His voice was much gentler this time. He sounded care-free. Maybe even happy. I smiled, my hands grasping tufts of his hair. He was taking me out to our spot, as he called it. Our little safe haven. It was just past the woods behind our house. There was an open meadow where long grass grew.

I would run around with my father and we would play games. He would search and I would hide, though it was never quite hide and seek. He never let me out of his sight for too long, and whenever he did catch me, he would carry me back to an area where the grass was flattened from our excursions. I jostled in his arms as he ran. He always seemed just as excited as me when we came out here. I was about to ask him if he was going to change when a growl rumbled through his chest.

My father pulled me down from my perch around his neck and placed me on the ground. His blue eyes stared back at me with urgency.

"If I say run, you run back to the house as fast as you can. Don't look back and don't stop no matter what."

Fear shot through my blood, icing it cold, cutting off any reply I might have made. I whimpered, trying to pull away from his urgent stare and his tightening hold.

"Promise me, Audrey."

"Okay, daddy."

He nodded once and adjusted his grip as he straightened. We walked slowly, returning to our circle where a man as tall as my father was waiting. Massive grey wings the color of stone sprouted from his back. I couldn't stop looking at them. They were majestic, moving about in graceful arcs. When I sensed his gaze on me, I looked up into his eyes. They were black. I hid behind my father's leg as he pressed his hand on my head.

"What do you want?"

"You know what I want. You've always known."

"This isn't a good time. It hasn't been long since she passed. Not for me."

My father's voice darkened, taking on a tone I knew to hide from. The other man didn't even flinch, but his stare lingered on me for a moment. He smiled sweetly, but the expression disappeared as his eyes returned to my father.

"And I told you years ago …"

The memory faded as new voices filtered in from outside my door.

***

We were out on a picnic. Stone had taken me. We walked until we hit the edge of the lake. Nixie had left on her own when we first arrived. A clearing stood at the edge of the lake. Surrounding it were trees so thick the leaves cast shadows tinted green.

The lake stretched out so far that I couldn't see where it ended. It formed an aqueous horizon that shifted and changed serenely. This was the largest body of water I had ever seen. Its water was murky, but in a beautiful way that mixed greens and dark browns comfortingly. The water, itself, moved in quiet waves.

We had been at the cabin for two weeks. Nixie seemed content enough. When not spending time with me, she would go to the lake. Stone would only take off once in a while on a run, usually in the form of a wolf. Elijah would disappear often, but I never knew where he went. I never asked. I didn't have the courage to.

Night started to settle in around us. The sun had been high in the sky when we arrived, and it had slowly made its journey, finally sinking toward the horizon where it had set moments before. I moved closer to Stone. Over the past two weeks I had grown comfortable around him. As we sat there, we didn't speak, we just enjoyed the calming sound of the lapping water. There were hoots and calls from different birds. Crickets chirped, and the leaves rustled with the wind. Stone traced his fingertips up my arm absently, moving from there to my shoulder. My eyes fluttered shut under his tactile exploration.

That's when it came. Unbidden. A dark memory that summoned words to my lips. I needed to be heard. I needed *him* to hear.

"When they first took me, I just remember hands. Everywhere. Pulling and tugging. My clothes, skin, and hair."

Stone stiffened and his movements became wooden.

"I don't know where they took me. The blindfold they used made sure of that. I couldn't even scream because they gagged me. The room I eventually found myself in was made of stone. Anywhere I lay, anywhere I stepped, the jagged floor pricked like a knife. It was cold. Damp. Unforgiving. I was trapped in that cave. And they left me there blindfolded and gagged for the first couple of days. My arm had been dislocated, and my hands were tied together. No one came. I wasn't given food or water. My throat was raw from trying to scream through the gag. It wasn't long before I gave up and collapsed. Then they came. It felt like every day they would torture me. I fought back for a while. But they tied my hands back together after I clawed them the one time. I …"

I moved my weight, feeling uncomfortable with the memory.

"I wrapped the loose rope around one of the guard's necks. The others tried to pull me off, but I managed to …"

My teeth clenched together. My fist opened and closed; the memory of the weight and rough strands of the rope burned in the skin of my hands. The fear and desperation I had felt that night echoed through me. I had never been so scared or out of control in my entire life. I had acted, but I hadn't thought. Stone was watching me. He saw me as this innocent creature that he should protect. Now though he would see the truth.

I was a monster.

"You killed him, which is more than he deserved," Stone whispered in my ear. He was sitting right next to me now. I hadn't notice him draw so close. His eyes were now a murky red color that screamed his murderous intentions and rage.

I nodded meekly. He wrapped his arms around me trying to offer me comfort.

"I killed."

"In your place, I would have tortured him. I would have made sure that he suffered longer and more completely than you had. And then, I would've taken his life."

Stone held me tighter.

Save for that sole conversation, the rest of our time by the lake was spent in silence. My head and heart were thick with memories. They had surged forward, had trapped me in times and places distant from now. But he was patient. He was cautious.

I was touched at how careful he was. How he protected me even from my own memories.

***

We took many walks in the forest over the next few days. I was eager to get out and taste the air. Sometimes only Gabriel and I would go exploring, sometimes Nixie would come as well. Gabriel told me to call him Stone only when other people were around. I could respect that. And, as much as my friendship with Nixie had grown, I still felt hesitant with her.

The trust I felt in Gabriel was a mystery to me. It felt too easy, too simple. At times reflex would make me shy away from him without realizing it. He was constantly patient. He was careful and understanding. At times I could see the frustration set in. His jaw would tighten. His eyes would flicker to a different color. He explained that he was never upset with me. He knew, at least in some way, how I felt about him.

On our third week in the cabin, Elijah announced he would be going into town to gather some essentials and doing a check in the town. He explained that he wanted to make sure there were only the local paranormals, and he wanted to check the progress of those still hunting us.

"Audrey, do you want to go?" Stone asked standing near the door. Nixie was keeping busy playing a card game by herself.

"Nixie said she is okay with staying here holding down the fort."

Nixie perked up at her name. But then she realized what had been said, twisted her lips, and went back to laying cards down on the table.

"Yeah, it's all good, guppy. Go with them."

Stone pulled me outside.

Elijah was already waiting inside the car, face forward. He rarely acknowledged our company. Stone held the door open for me, allowing me to slip in. He walked to the other side before climbing in next to me. I hadn't been in a car since we had arrived to the cabin. Immediately I grabbed onto the door's armrest and twisted in my seat so I could watch the forest pass by. Nerves got the better of me, and soon my blood was rushing fast, my heartbeat pounding in my ears.

Part of it, I knew, was the fear that this would be the first time in *years* I'd be in a town. Near humans. Stone had mentioned that we had to shop as far from the cabin as possible. Many paranormals were expert trackers, and they might catch our scent if we weren't careful. I swallowed the lump in my throat. My other hand reached to touch the stitching. *One. Two. Three.* My eyes closed. The jitters started to calm.

Fingers brushed against my counting hand. My eyes popped open and I looked to Stone. He watched me as he wrapped his hand around mine. Slowly he brought my hand to his lips and pressed a small kiss before releasing it.

Stone was trying to help me relax, but his tender actions had my heart pounding for a different reason. I couldn't bring myself to make it stop. I never had anything like this before.

On the drive into town, I stared out the window. I couldn't get enough of the outside world. I wanted to feel the air. I wanted it flying through my hair so fast that it felt like I was flying. I dreamed of that sometimes. Those were the good dreams. Dreams of flying high above the world, looking down at it and seeing how small it was. Being so high up made me want to be more than I was. But even more importantly, in the skies of my dreams I was safe. I was free.

The transition from backroads to the expressway jarred me from my thoughts. The cars became more abundant. I watched other people in their vehicles, and when I tired of that, I went back to watching the scenery. Elijah drove for another two hours before stopping. On the way, we passed through a small town. It was charming, with its glistening storefronts and buildings. We were moving too quickly for me to read all the names. And along the sidewalks and in front of the displays of the stores, people went this way and that. Some walked hand in hand, others rushed past toward things I couldn't guess at.

Elijah stopped the car.

"I will pick you up in four hours."

Stone told me to wait a sec as he climbed out of his seat. He appeared at my door a few moments later. He opened it and took my hand. I was in awe of the buildings. As I slipped from the car, I was unable to tear my gaze away from the city surrounding us.

"I have a surprise for you."

Stone seemed eager about his surprise. A tremor of fear slipped down my spine. Most experiences I had with surprises weren't good. I licked my lips and reminded myself that Stone had never given me a reason to fear his intentions.

"What- what is it?"

Stone held my hand as he towed me down the street. A cold fist wrapped its way around my heart. Old doubts were still difficult to shake and soon started to take over. But Stone wouldn't hurt me. He wouldn't lie to me. He wanted to protect me. But was he? Hadn't I been tricked before? Was he lying to me?

I shook my head violently.

No, no, no ... Liar. Liar! But who? Me or him?

"Easy. Hey, easy, Audrey. Look at me."

I heard his voice over the cold, insistent fear in my head. Had I been speaking out loud? Stone's eyes were clouded grey with his worry.

"I would never hurt you. I was just going to take you to a movie. I promise. Everything will be okay. I'll always make sure you are safe."

Stone grabbed my hand and brushed his thumb over my knuckles.

"Okay?"

I nodded. When he asked again, I could tell he wanted to hear me say it. And so I did.

"Okay."

It came out quick and shaky. He accepted it, though. I had been so caught up in my own head I hadn't realized that he had pulled us into an alleyway. Stone waited with bated breath for a moment before nodding in response. Moments later, we were back to strolling along the sidewalk. We didn't walk far before we arrived at a stunning building. It had a tall, old marquee sign. Running top to bottom, spelled out in fat yellow bulbs was the word "Theater."

There were movie titles, too, but we were under the awning before I could get a good look. I didn't think they would have told me much anyway. I hadn't actually ever been to a movie theater before. My father and I lived far away from others, and it had been rare for us to even go into town.

Inside, a salty, buttery aroma filled my senses. My stomach rumbled quietly as a sudden hunger took over me. The carpet was an old, faded red. Ahead of us was a concession stand. The glass display had candy

184

inside, and popcorn. I bit my lip suppressing a smile that all but consumed me. The walls were decorated with glass frames, each lit up around the edges, with posters on the inside. The posters had different features. Some had couples, others a single hero. The posters kept my attention until Stone spoke up.

"What would you like to see? Romance? Action? Comedy? … Horror?" Stone looked down at me, his eyes for once a constant shade of blue. Still, his merriment made them dance. His excitement was infectious.

"I think … a comedy would be nice," I replied timidly. The anticipation I was feeling made the words lighter.

He purchased the tickets and a few other treats, then asked if I was ready. I nodded and went with him into the theatre. When we sat, he handed me a tub of popcorn and a drink.

Chapter 28

STONE

When I saw her lips part in a smile, I knew it had been a good idea. I could see positive changes in her already. Her usually drawn cheeks filled with a smile. Looking at her now, her emaciated body was regaining healthy curves. She stood a little taller each day, and her eyes would even shine at times, now and then. Sometimes, like when we had arrived at the cabin, she would revert to the scared and timid girl we had rescued from that cell. Hiding in herself. Fearing everything around her. Whenever I saw her struggling, I wanted to step in and remind her she was safe.

"Ready?" I asked.

She nodded. I was trying to get her to become more vocal. Since she started to speak more often, I realized how beautiful her voice really was. It wasn't light and musical like Nixie's, and it wasn't hesitant and quiet like when I first met her. It was deep, sultry, and damn sexy.

We headed into our theatre and I felt her hold tighten around my hand. I knew that she felt more comfortable in dark places. She was always a little more at ease in the dark. She had told me some things, pieces of her history, but the way she stirred and winced in fear when she told me broke my heart. Understandably, she avoided her past. It wasn't as though I had told her about my past. And still, she told me about the white room, about her experiences. Everything she told me made me care more. She was stronger than she realized, and watching her grow in such a short time since we left Jacobs, I knew I had chosen right.

I let her take the lead as we walked to our amphitheater. She picked a spot close to the exit at the edge of a row. Audrey's head twisted to view the large cushioned chairs around us, the scattered popcorn on the floor, the other people filtering in.

Her thick hair covered the scarred side of her face. I couldn't help wanting to push it away. To soothe her scars. To touch the jagged part of her lips tenderly. I always kissed it lightly. It was my way of reminding her how gorgeous she was. She would blush, never saying anything about her disfigurement. People stared, but she didn't seem to notice. She continued taking in this new world wide-eyed. A world she was just discovering.

It was an innocence I hadn't thought existed in this world.

She settled into her seat and I held out the popcorn to her. She reached out hesitantly before curling her fingers back. She had been cautious about food since she arrived, so I popped some into my mouth to show it was okay. Well, that and I was kind of hoping she'd watch me and be reminded of my mouth, just as I constantly was of hers. She let me kiss her, but I hungered for a time she would be comfortable enough to come to me.

As the movie started, I saw Audrey move her hair from her eyes. It was the first time I saw her do this on her own, instead of hiding behind it. During our time together she had confirmed what Jacobs said about her damaged eye. Somehow she could see through it in a way that was unique only to her.

Thinking about her supposedly blind eye, I couldn't help but wonder how that was possible. Around others she wanted to hide her scars. After all, humans didn't usually have scars like we did. Other paranormals would know from a look. Our kind understood that the world was ugly and the scars it left constant. They weren't usually as bad as Audrey's, but that's what made her all the more lovely, in my opinion. That she had pulled through all that and somehow retained a gentle spirit. What no one else realized, I was sure, was the extent of her scars.

Humans saw it as hideous. They would assume it was the result of some accident. Something to be pitied. They would shy away. I, on the other hand, was glad that for once I could see her entire face. I had to resist the urge to trace a scar I had yet to touch. It was the smallest, but its jagged appearance filled me with a yearning to offer comfort.

I shook my head, trying to regain control of my thoughts. I couldn't focus on the movie. I kept finding myself in times and places I had inflicted similar pain on others. I had left scars that would never fully heal. One of my first missions, one that I wished that I could forget, would forever haunt me.

There was no denying it. Even with Audrey beside me, I couldn't ignore that horror. The events unfolded smoothly before my eyes.

Children cried out for their mothers, and mothers' cried out for their children. Not that it mattered. Only one thing mattered now, and that was finding the paranormal Jacobs wanted. I was determined. I would be the one who caught her. I still felt the need to prove myself, even though I already had. I wouldn't be on the team if I hadn't. But that didn't matter to me. I had to be the best. I always had to prove myself.

Jacobs had described her to us. Young. Female. Fiery red hair. She wasn't a normal human, otherwise she wouldn't have merited her own mission. From what Jacobs hinted at, there was something ... wrong with her. Jacobs had said something about a werebird. I was young and inexperienced. I was letting the adrenaline get the best of me. That's why I wasn't paying as close of attention as I should have. Even if, like he said, she was mentally disturbed, walking around like some half-shifted fool, I would retrieve her.

I would be the best.

I saw her herding children into a house that we had already searched. I ran in after her, but she was gone. Three young children and a mother, maybe even their mother, hunched in a corner, eyeing me with fear I had earned. She was trying to protect them. I called out a warning. I took them, those children. And the mother, too. I had no connection to them after they were in Jacobs' hands, but he had been convinced they wouldn't voluntarily tell us anything, I knew what that meant.

Torture. And I had made it possible.

In the end, we never caught the red-headed paranormal. But in the pursuit of her, we had destroyed innocent people's lives. Hurt little children.

The revving of an engine snapped me from my memories. I shook my head, taking in a long breath through my nose. A cherry red Ferrari flew through the air on the screen. Audrey was sitting close to the edge of her seat, the popcorn completely forgotten. A playful smile crept across her lips, crinkling the scars. The theatre was showing old classics, and this was probably the best choice. She seemed to be really enjoying it.

My attention was mostly on Audrey, though I spared some glances for the action on the screen. I would watch her reaction at certain parts of the movie I knew would get a reaction out of her. Audrey's smile would dim at certain times, a look of wonderment replacing it. I felt a moment of peace when she looked like that. I settled back in my seat and reached out to touch the edge of her long hair. She didn't even notice my actions. She was too busy furrowing her brows together in response to the events unfolding on the screen. One of my favorite parts was about to happen, and I covertly watched her out of the corner of my eye, eager to see her react.

Anticipation rushed through my blood, making my heart beat twice as fast. Excitement uncoiled in my stomach. Nothing could sound as beautiful as her voice, save one thing: her laugh. All the tension that had built up in me slipped away like a wave crashing over me. Her laugh undid me.

The laugh was boisterous and all-consuming. Her shoulders shook with delight. My lips pulled tight into an unbreakable smile. I hadn't felt this kind of happiness in years. Every muscle felt light, and everything we were running from disappeared from my mind in that moment. Her eyes lit up, and the air caught in my lungs.

Her laughter started to die down, breaking up into smaller fits of giggles. Suddenly, she bit her lip and looked down, as if shocked by her reaction. I hadn't realized that I had moved in my seat so that my knee now brushed against hers. Her laugh was a siren's song that I couldn't resist. She brought her hand to her mouth and nipped down on her thumb, the sweet sound of a single laugh echoing through her. She looked bashful as she peeked over at me. I did my best to compose myself, I knew I was watching her mouth slightly agape, my lips upturned.

Audrey took hold of my hand, leaned over, and kissed my cheek.

"Thank you, Gabriel," she whispered before resuming her previous position.

The rest of the movie didn't even register for me. Bliss took over all my other senses. I still tingled with the touch where her lips had pressed. Disbelief mingled with my delight had me touching the spot on my cheek. My body tensed. I had to be careful. For her sake. This wasn't something I could rush, no matter the impatience I felt.

This wasn't just a one-night romance. This was different.

A new feeling had been building in me since we met. Silent. Stealthy. Without being aware of its coming, fear crashed into my body like a splash of cold water. Could I love this girl? Would that be fair to her?

No. I couldn't. I *wouldn't* do that to her. But on the heels of that thought—the remembrance of how it felt for her to say my name. It was right. Every way she said it would fill my heart with joy. Again lost in my fantasies, it took a while before I realized the credits were rolling. Audrey was still smiling. The few scattered people that had come to watch started to steadily stream out.

"That was … it was amazing. Thank you, Gabriel. Thank you!"

She threw her arms around my neck and hugged me tight. Our bodies pressed together, flushing me with warmth. She pulled back slightly and watched my eyes. She was probably waiting to see if they would flash a different color, but around humans I put extra effort into keeping them one color at all times. I knew she would still see subtle changes with her special sight, but that was something no human would ever see.

She had explained it to me a little better on one of our walks together. She could actually see different flecks of color in people's eyes with every change in their moods. Audrey said that she had been able to do this for as long as she could remember. At this point in our relationship, I could tell when she was holding something back, and she definitely had been when she told me about this. Was it something that she remembered? Or something she was still scared to share? But then her eyes slid to my lips and the thought vanished.

I waited. In my impatience, I had pushed her limits before, but it was time she started to make her own decisions. She was brave and courageous. She knew what she wanted, and I wanted to help her learn how to express that. My muscles burned with the urge to pull her close and give her what her eager eyes were asking. But I wanted this to be *her* choice.

She moved tentatively, her eyes flickered to my lips again as she gathered her courage. She was centimeters away from me, and took all my self-control not to take her lips the way I wanted. Like one who is starved. She made me feel that way, though. I couldn't get enough of her. Her quiet strength, her broken spirit slowly mending into something beautiful. She was damaged, but she wasn't shattered. There was time yet for her to heal.

Finally, she moved in. Still hesitant, she barely touched my lips with her own. I watched her closely as she pulled back barely an inch. Her eyelids dropped heavily, a subtle shiver went through her body, and she moved forward. Audrey's touch alone electrified my blood in a way I had never experienced before. She grew bolder, leaning forward and directing the tempo of the kiss. I could taste her hunger.

My hands clutched tightly at the cushioned arm rest, the veins in my forearms pulsing with my desire. A need to pull her close and kiss her deeply filled me. But this was a step she needed to take. A moment she needed to own. She scooted a little closer. This was the part that would be most difficult for her. I knew. It had to be. Especially if she felt even a part of the agony I did as I waited for her lips. I wet them, parting them just enough to let her know she wouldn't be denied if this was what she wanted.

It didn't take her long. She naturally fell into a rhythm we both shared. We kissed in the way I had wanted to kiss her all along. I kept my arms from wrapping around her. I didn't want to startle her or make her feel confined. I wanted her to have the option to move away if she chose to. I didn't want her to feel trapped, not right now, not when she was in control.

Mostly, I didn't want to see fear in her eyes again. Not if I could help it, and never on my account. The armrest creaked under the strain of my forearm. My grip on the armrest had tightened to the point of being painful. The hard edges bit into my skin and put pressure on my joints. But it was worth it. It was well worth it.

When she pulled away, she was blushing and her lips, just barely swollen now, made me want to pull her closer. My tongue darted out to catch what lingered of her taste. She watched the movement, her own desire clouding her eyes. My gut tightened with the hunger of lust. Bravely, she looked back up to me without showing any hint of fear.

"Thank you, Audrey."

I took her hand, my lips brushed the valleys of her knuckles gently, she released a heavy sigh, her eyelids heavy. She smiled, not in the way I had hoped, but at the same time, it was more than I had thought she'd be capable of at this point.

This was all new to her. I had to remember that. I had to remember that she wasn't like other women.

"You ready?"

She nodded. I was about to let go of her hand, but she tightened her hold on me. As we walked out, she told her favorite parts of the movie. It had been her first experience at a movie theater. She allowed me some more insight into her past, telling me about the small TV in her childhood home. She had rarely watched it. She got a bit quiet after that.

"I like hearing about your past with your father."

She looked up at me. I could see the fear pulsing through her, causing a tremor to pass through her extremities. Immediately I regretted my words and wished I could take them back.

I thought that she might deny that she remembered anything. To forget. The way she had been for the past week. We left the theater with an hour to spare before Elijah showed up. Placing my hand on the small of Audrey's back, I felt her breathing catch. Her body shivered. Was it fear? Was it something I had done? I hoped that it wasn't.

"Audrey, I promise you're safe. I don't think I could ever hate you, not because of your past, not for anything at all."

192

I pulled her closer as I said this. Her hair cascaded down her face, on the side closest to me, and as much as I wanted to push away those strands, I knew she preferred them there. Let her hide for now. She could hide from the world as long as she didn't hide from me. She thought herself a monster. I knew that much. But looking down at her, I couldn't see it.

I kissed the top of her head, surprising her. Surprising myself. My nose filled with her scent. Sweet. A tantalizing fragrance. She looked up at me, I blanked my features to their default state. My jaw loose, lips resting—I waited for her.

"I would hide in my room most of the time. My father wasn't a bad man. He would spend time with me when he wasn't busy. I loved him. I know he loved me, too."

She tripped over the word loved. She still loved him, though there was something more there. She was so vague about her past it was maddening, but there had to be something special about her. Three clans wouldn't be interested in her otherwise. And maybe not her alone, but her father as well.

What had driven them to hiding from the clans? In my eyes, it seemed like she had done all this to protect him. But the way she spoke of him, that hint of fear that shone through her eyes, and the way she reassured me that he was a good man hinted at more. That she still cared for him—all this was pretty decent evidence that there was more to their story. He was her father, and even with a past as horrible as hers, she still loved him. Still, I had a hard time holding any respect for a man who left his child in the hands of a cruel clan.

"He didn't mean to hurt me so much. It was the only way he knew how to punish. He was driven to do it. He had lost so much. My mother. His family. He was scared too. Most times I deserved it. I understood the rules and yet ... and I broke them."

She paused, biting the inside of her lip. It was a new bad-habit she picked up from Nixie, who did the same when nervous.

"You needed something more. *Wanted* something more."

I understood. She nodded sheepishly, avoiding eye contact, and this time I realized it wasn't out of fear. She was ashamed. She was ashamed that she wanted to have friends. A life outside of her home. For me, it was impossible to believe that she still held such affection for her father. He had abandoned her. And yet, he still meant something to her.

"You said he lost your mother, but you did, too."

"Yes, but I was the one who killed her."

Audrey looked me straight in the eye as she said this. There was only acceptance in her face. It was a fact to her. That was all. A serious line creased her brow.

"My dad reminded me every birthday. She didn't survive, but I did. He loved her very much. He called me his little survivor."

Audrey hadn't yet talked about her family so freely. I didn't know why, but this apparently was a safe topic for her. I didn't know what to say. I wanted to tell her that her father was wrong. That father was abusive to her in a way she couldn't plainly see. I couldn't, though. I couldn't tell her. Not even if these obvious facts had my blood boiling and my vision turning red.

"What about your father?"

She reached out and touched my arm, her brows arching over her eyes. I closed my eyes and focused on my irises from the red of anger back to the blue they had been all day. When I opened them again she was still waiting for my answer, without judging me for losing my cool. She didn't even question it.

"I had one."

My bitter mood lingered.

Audrey's face fell with disappointment. My heart clenched. I hated that I had caused her to look at me like that. Then her lips twisted, and her eyes sparkled with mischief. Whatever damage I might have caused with my careless response slipped away.

"That was a joke, right?"

Her eyes climbed their way to mine haltingly, full of a hopefulness that broke my heart. My reluctance to tell her stemmed from her playful mood. I didn't want my sad story to cause her to lose the joy she had just started to discover. I knew how hard it was for her to share her past. And I didn't want to hurt her by pushing too much of my baggage on her too soon. My own past wasn't happy. But she had given a piece of her past. I couldn't deny her.

"Yes."

I leaned down and kissed her head once again.

"My father was also a shape-shifter. He was a strict man. He demanded the best from me whenever he was around. He was of the opinion that paranormal creatures should stick to their own kind, but he didn't really like the idea of clans either. Not that he had a choice. There's no real way around how our world is set up. He tried to keep me around our own kind as much as he could. At least it was easier then. The clans had yet to come into their full power."

"How old are you?" Audrey blurted. Her cheeks immediately tinting tomato-red. I wanted to laugh at her expression, but feared she might take it the wrong way.

"Shape-shifters, like many paranormals, have longer life spans. Ours, much like some were-creatures, range up to seven hundred years. In human terms, I'm about twenty-six, but actually … 95."

Her jaw dropped. I lifted my finger under her chin and closed it gently.

"I'm considered to be quite young. Especially for the position that I hold, but with a father who demanded only the best, it was hard not accomplishing what he wanted. He wanted a son who would be a killer. That's exactly what I am."

"I don't think you're a killer."

Audrey bravely moved, snaking her arm around my waist, pulling me into a timid sideways hug. Gods, it felt wrong to have her hold me. I didn't deserve her, but I wouldn't give her up for anything. Not now.

"That's because you don't know the real me, yet. This person now, I don't know who he is, but I'm starting to like him. You've made me a better person, Audrey."

I didn't look at her. Instead, I pulled her to my chest and held her close. Audrey and I continued to walk, and she held onto me as we did. People slipped past us, some turned to take a second glance at Audrey, but she didn't even notice. She bit her lip every so often, and she would occasionally tighten her grip around my arm. She was so caught up in her thoughts that she jumped when a car roared up beside us. I had been watching it since it turned the corner. Even with the window tinted, I recognized the car that Elijah had brought us in.

"Fools! How could you not notice the *were* that has been on your trail the past half hour?"

The wraith sounded mad. He remained in the car and rolled up the window he had just yelled through. I opened the door for Audrey. Looking around, I couldn't see anyone who struck me as paranormal. They were easy to spot when you were one yourself, or if you knew what to look for.

My hand was pressed against Audrey's back. She was quaking, but her lips were set in a tight line. She kept her back straight. Once she was in the car, her hand went to the stitching in the seat. I moved to sit in the front with Elijah, scanning the surrounding area. I cracked the window shifting my senses to animal sharpness, hoping to catch a scent or sound that could be helpful.

Chapter 29

AUDREY

I had counted the stitching in my seat three times before we arrived back at the cabin. Stone didn't try to comfort me at all during that time. I was disappointed, but he was on high alert, the tendons in his neck cording out. His eyes watched the distance warily. He would open his window periodically and take deep breaths. Then Elijah would shoot him a look and the window would go back up. It was as if they were having a silent conversation. What about, I couldn't guess. I wanted so badly to ask, but Elijah's face was set in a fierce, dangerous scowl. I was scared to look into his eyes. I was scared I would finally see something there. I was scared that I would see anger in that blackness.

I climbed out of the car. Nixie was already waiting by the cabin door. She wrung her hands together, but at seeing us, let out a long breath.

"Gods, I was so worried about you guys!"

She rushed over and hugged me.

"Elijah called and said he sensed other paranormals. That I should stick close to the cabin. I was frantic wondering what was happening to you two!"

"Elijah …" Stone started, but when Elijah got out of the car, his eyes darted to the woods.

"We don't have time."

He looked back at us. His voice never changed from its expressionless tone, but this time his words sent shivers down my spine.

"Can we at least …" Nixie began, but when Elijah's black eyes came to a rest on her, she stopped talking.

"No. At best we have an hour before York's clan invades."

Nixie tightened her arms around me. I could feel her body shaking along with mine.

"There is a lake nearby. I'm sure that I could hide us. At least sing them away," she offered, sounding smaller and quieter than the usual alive and bubbly Nixie I knew.

"There are too many," Elijah stated. Then he turned his gaze on Stone. They stared at each other for several moments. Stone's jaw tightened, his eyes narrowed. Whatever passed between them ended when Stone looked away, his fists tightening.

"So what? You want us to stand around for an hour and wait for them to attack? Wait for our deaths? No thank you!"

Nixie let go of me and started to pace.

I felt hopeless. I didn't know what transpired between the York Clan and Nixie, or Stone for that matter. They both looked nervous. Stone hadn't moved. His jaw ticked as he looked out at the woods. Elijah eyes were on me now. I didn't know what to do. The world began to feel too open, too free, full of too much space.

Too much space. *Too much space.* My breathing caught in my chest, becoming irregular. Stone moved quickly to my side. He caught me in his arms before my legs gave away. I wanted to be somewhere safe. I needed to be somewhere protected. It was safer where it was smaller. It was manageable.

"Audrey …" Stone holding me up. My eyes were losing focus.

"Pay attention. You will be safe. I won't let anything hurt you ever again. I promise."

He stopped, looked up at Elijah, then back at me.

"I need you to trust me," he whispered as he kissed my head. Then his arms were gone.

Elijah walked over to him and nodded. My back was supported by the car but my knees had buckled. I slid down to the ground. My head was light, and I couldn't feel my legs. It was as if they had floated away. Before long, the Stone I knew melted away. He transformed into a small squirrel and ran up to a tree.

Elijah took Stone's place and grabbed my arm to pull me up. He held most of my weight. The pins and needles stabbing my legs made it unbearable to stand. But I could only focus on Stone leaving us. Leaving me. In the face of everything I had hoped to believe, he was slipping away while the rest of us would have to wait out our fates. My heart felt like the fragile pieces he had restored in our time together were cracking apart all over again.

It hurt.

"Stand strong, Audrey."

Nixie watched Stone's betrayal with the same acceptance that Elijah had. She remained calm and came to stand closer to us.

"I'm so sorry, Audrey," Nixie whispered.

Something rustled in the nearby trees. I felt a prick in my neck. I fell limply, with my head pressed into the grass. The last thing I saw was Nixie lying next to me with her eyes shut. Seconds later, darkness rushed over me.

Chapter 30

STONE

The moment Elijah met my eyes he started speaking to me—in my mind. It was painful. His voice took up too much space, but I kept a straight face. I had to. He told me what I already knew I should do. I didn't want to leave Audrey, though. While our connection to Braden Clan would protect us, Audrey had no such protection. The York Clan might try to force an alliance on her. She'd survived the Vedenin Clan's attempt, but a second round … it might break her. I couldn't leave her. I wouldn't. But Elijah interrupted those thoughts.

You must abandon her for now. Change forms. Wait. Take out a guard and assume his shape. I can hide your scent.

Sure, his logic was sound, and I knew his plan was the only way that could save us, but I wasn't sure I could do it. I needed to protect her, I needed to be here. Looking down at her and seeing how fragile she was in this state of fear. How could I walk away?

And yet I did.

Somehow I changed my form and fled just before the Yorks moved in, knocking out Nixie and Audrey with darts. Elijah wouldn't be affected by the sleeping poison, but the host form he now inhabited couldn't fight off a full-blooded witch. Any witch worth her salt could wield lightning, and from past experiences, I knew that Elijah was vulnerable to that kind of attack.

Two goblins and a weresnake moved in. Elijah moved fast, taking out the goblins with a twist of his wrist and a snap of their neck. He moved quickly, almost seeming to appear in a flash beside his enemies. The weresnake somehow managed to match his pace. She mirrored him dangerously, almost seeming to have the upper hand at one point. In the end, Elijah slipped out of its path just in time and slammed the weresnake's head into a tree.

But these, as I well knew, were only grunts. Shock troops. Expendables. More would arrive.

I would have to wait until the main players showed their faces. I could change into the witch, but if she were asked to perform a spell of any sort, I'd be found out. I can take different forms, but paranormals like witches had magic. I did not. No, it would be safest for me to wait for a *were* or another animal paranormal.

I was surprised when a male zana came out. Zana's, normally peaceful creatures, lived in the forests of Romania. His skin was tree-bark brown and his eyes leafy green. It was odd, though. Males of this species were rare, and his stature was incredible for his species. One over five-foot-five-inches was unheard of. This one though was at least five-foot-nine, though his build was a little on the trim side. He strode toward Audrey, his long legs taking him to her unconscious body.

Then I saw the witch. A short, little thing with long black hair. Her entire body seemed to be marked by tattoos of some sort. Some were runes, which indicated her as a lower acolyte, but there were also glyphs of power. Elijah went down at last after a jagged arc of light leapt at him from her fingertips.

Two werecheetahs loped from the vans now parked in the driveway toward Nixie. They looked like brothers, which meant I wouldn't be able to assume one of their forms. They'd know each other too well. No. I needed a loner paranormal. Someone the others were less likely to talk to.

I was beginning to worry when a dwarf clomped into view. The dwarf strode over to Elijah. In my squirrel body, I trailed him from atop the branches, remaining as silent as I could. The witch walked ahead of him at all times, seeming both eager to get where she was going and to put distance between herself and the dwarf. I scaled down the tree and waited for the two paranormals to gain more distance from each other.

I studied the dwarf carefully until I memorized his every feature. His height was barely over five-feet, he had a stout figure, thick with muscles. His hair was a dark dirty blond shade and was tangled in mats. His beard was coarse and thick. Heavy lips and eyebrows adjourned his face. A single mole set on the right side of his cheek occupied the space close to his jaw line, but not quite hidden by his beard.

My cells started to reform and stretch. It felt liberating for a moment. It always did when shifting from a small compact form. Now my body reshaped to a wider, stouter stature. My next few steps I grew in height and began mimicking his actions. It took moments before I was fully changed into his form and felt comfortable in his skin. I could mimic his gait and stride, so I moved into position behind some underbrush beneath the dense trees.

The dwarf kneeled down and picked up Elijah's unconscious body. He hastily threw him over his shoulder with a grunt and turned on his heel. He started his march back to the direction he had come from—back toward me.

I waited, my heart beating steadily, my breathing calm, every part of my being focused to a pinpoint, focused on the task at hand. I had to be quick. After the shift, I was left completely naked. The transformation to the squirrel had left me without clothes. I would have to steal the dwarf's, and I'd have to do it without alerting anyone.

The dwarf passed and I slipped silently out from behind the trees. My fingers instinctively sought out the pressure points on his neck. Even though my now beefy hands wouldn't be able to wrap around his neck, I hit the points I needed, rendering him unconscious. I gripped his neck. He grunted and tried to pull away, but his legs buckled beneath him uselessly, and then he was on his knees.

I held onto his shoulder keeping him upright, but the arm he had wrapped around Elijah released and he went rolling off the dwarf's shoulder. He landed with a thump and my head shot up to look around. I kept my grip tight on the dwarf. Finally, the breath left his lungs and I slowly rolled him quietly to the ground.

202

Efficiently, in the way that only my kind could, I stripped him of his clothes. With unnatural swiftness, I tucked the dwarf into a shadowed cleft in the roots of a tree. I now stood in his stead. I lifted Elijah onto my shoulder. I picked up my pace to catch up with the witch.

It would have been easy to dispatch the witch, but for the moment I didn't know where Audrey and Nixie were. If the others in the York Clan had caught them, they'd certainly use them as leverage or maybe even just take off.

The walk to their vehicles wasn't long. Three separate vehicles awaited us. One was so normal it looked out of place—a simple family van, but I knew that was only camouflage. The back would be gutted. I was familiar with how the clans transported prisoners. The two black SUVs, tinted windows darkly gleaming, were far less innocent looking.

I caught sight of the zana and Audrey, who he held in his arms bridal style. He was taking her to the last SUV. At the sight, a growl almost escaped my lips. It was hard to deny the impulse to tell him to get his hands off of her, but I knew that would only hurt our chances.

"I have a special spot for that one," the witch said as she eyed Elijah on my shoulder. Her lips were pressed together as if she were suspicious her spell had worked so well. From what I knew about dwarves, they rarely spoke. So I said nothing and hiked him a little farther up on my shoulder. Elijah's body flopped around like a ragdoll, which seemed to satisfy the witch in some way. She turned away and led me to the cargo van. Elijah's muscles tensed under my grip, silently letting me know he was conscious.

I followed the witch, stomping my feet a bit louder. Things were moving faster than I anticipated. I normally watched a creature for at least a few hours before imitating them. It was the only way to figure out their mannerisms, habits, speech ... this had been spontaneous. All I had to go off of was what I already knew about dwarves. And, besides being uncommunicative, they also tended to walk heavy.

It had been a long time since I had to imitate a dwarf, and the movements still felt unnatural. The witch opened the double back doors of the van. The inside was gutted, the metal bottom gleaming in the light from the setting sun. Into the walls were bolted short, heavy chains. At the end of the chains were manacles. The witched stepped back, allowing me to move forward. Elijah's muscles loosened in my hold as I flopped him roughly onto the floor of the van.

The witch took a step forward, her nose scrunched up as she looked at Elijah's unconscious body. He was sprawled out, and she climbed in to inspect him more closely, stepping over his body warily. She kept eyeing him like he would suddenly come to and attack her.

"Help me out." She started to tug at his arm. I stepped up into the van and it rocked under my weight. I helped her hoist him up and lock his first wrist into the tight, metal manacle. We repeated the process with the next one until his arms were tightly secured behind him. His head flopped forward. I briefly considered moving him so that his muscles wouldn't get sore. I was torn between the need I would have for him in the near future and putting on a convincing act. He had to be at the top of his game, but there was nothing I could do. He would have to suffer.

I took a step back, getting out of the back of the van. The witch remained there and started another spell. I had heard those words before. Previous experience told me she was trying to bind Elijah to his current body.

I stood to the side and watched as the zana carefully settled Audrey into place on the seat. When his hand touched the bare skin of her waist in an innocent slip as he fastened her seatbelt, a snarl involuntarily passed my lips.

I stiffened, then immediately relaxed into a more normal posture. Had anybody heard that? No one turned in my direction. I sure hoped to hell they hadn't.

Nixie was set in the middle of a bench seat between the two werecheetahs, each of whom wore earplugs. Clever, though even the earplugs wouldn't save them. On a mission a couple of years back, she had used her skills to get us out of a similar sticky situation. The other paranormals had been prepared with earplugs, but she had still managed to use her siren song and send them away. She looked safe for the most part. The zana had handcuffed Nixie before arranging her upright between the cheetahs. But why hadn't he handcuffed Audrey? True, she probably wouldn't cause them trouble. But *they* didn't know that.

The witch and I stood at the back of the second van watching the others work. She peered in to get a better look at something. I slid my eyes to whatever she was fixated on.

Elijah's leg. It was lying in a different position. Shit.

"Zeke!" she called out to the zana who was closing Audrey's door. "I think that the wraith might be waking up!"

She sounded worried. Zeke, the zana, moved over to the van, checking the inside.

"Imogen, trust your magic. Ride with her, will ya?" he said, nodding his head toward me.

The group moved out. Imogen, the tattooed witch, drove the van and I sat beside her. Throughout our drive I kept silent, and Imogen kept nervously peeping over her shoulder at the form chained in the back. At times, she would tap her fingers against the steering-wheel in a strange rhythm. She made it two hours before she finally said something.

"Can you check on him?"

Imogen bit her lip, her eyes flickering between the rearview mirror and the road. She must not have trusted what she was seeing. Each time she looked over her shoulder, it was only for a second. But Elijah's posture was a little too stiff for someone unconscious. Not that I was going to tell her that. I doubt anyone but a shifter would have noticed. I responded to her question with a nod, and then pivoted in my seat.

She released a relieved sigh. Her shoulders dropped, and for the following three hours she but rarely looked over her shoulder. She even pushed a CD into the player. We drove east and north the entire time. I kept my eyes on the mile markers, looking for any and all indications of where we might be headed.

Imogen followed the SUV in front of us as it exited the highway to a road that looked like it lead nowhere. There weren't even signs pointing the way to any gas stations, restaurants, not even a supermarket. We drove for another hour, this time headed west. The caravan proceeded down more backroads, following twists and turns until we were bouncing around in our seats from the unevenness of the ground. The roads were a mixture of dirt, but there were signs the route had been manmade. The final road took us through thick forestry. The first van paused before driving on.

Their facility was less imposing than I expected. We pulled up to a single story building with a domed glass ceiling at one end. But the York Clan was a large family. I didn't see how this facility could house them all, unless there were more levels underground? Imogen pulled into a large garage attached to the side of the compound. The rest of the vehicles followed. The doors to the SUV holding Nixie opened as we parked.

The cheetahs flanked Nixie, who was awake and standing without assistance. They had gotten rid of the earplugs after they had gagged her. Nixie chewed vigorously, though ineffectively, on the cloth they used.

My relief, however, was short lived. I felt better seeing Nixie conscious and was pleased they were allowing her move about a little bit on her own. But my gut was still tight with worry over Audrey. The drive here had been torture for me. My anxiety and anger, trapped inside of me with nowhere to go, were giving me a headache. I needed to know what was happening to her. Why she hadn't arrived yet?

Imogen paced at the back of the van, her hands moving swiftly, sparks of her magic crackling between her fingers. I leaned against the side of the van waiting for the last of the SUVs to arrive. The others would wait to move Elijah until the last SUV arrived. They would want to move the prisoners together. Less chance of someone sneaking off or overpowering a single guard on his own.

The last SUV pulled to a stop. The door opened, and Zeke lifted Audrey out and set her down next to the SUV. The pull was magnetic. I lifted my foot to move toward her, but Nixie's eyes immediately found mine. Her eyes narrowed. It hadn't taken her long to figure out whose form I had taken. But she must have, because she imperceptibly gave me a shake of her head. I put my foot back down on the ground. No one else had noticed.

Audrey started to stir. She had a cloth-bag over her head, and she blindly reached out with her hands to feel around. Her arms were still free of restraints, same as her legs. She was looking for a comforting touch. My body shook with anger. She was searching for *me*. Gods, I hoped it was for me.

Zeke helped her up. When she flinched away from him, my fist tightened. If I couldn't control myself, I was going to get myself captured as well, if not killed. I would control myself. For her.

"Fuck. He's awake."

Imogen opened the back doors of the van. Her nerves were obviously getting the better of her. She paced an impatient circuit back and forth where she stood. But that was to be expected. Any paranormal that wasn't afraid of wraiths was stupid. They were powerful creatures, not being careful around one would be the same as suicide. Turning on my heel, I stomped toward the back of the van. Elijah had, until then, been silent. He had broken his act when we parked. Now that the doors were open he didn't take his eyes off the witch. In a show of uncharacteristic emotion, Elijah's lips pulled back in a snarl. He was the one who had thought up this insane plan. Now he was losing his temper at the indignity of it.

I had hoped Elijah's mental communication would be a one-time thing. But again, I found him speaking inside my head. The sensation could only be described as unpleasant. His voice carried a chill in it, and the way it pushed through my thoughts made my head feel overfull. His plan had called for us allowing the York Clan to take us. I hadn't liked it. Still didn't, truth be told. But we were committed to it now. I would follow it until we could escape safely.

As I approached the rear of the car, the witch Imogen glided out of my path as I stomped along. The van again rocked under my weight as I climbed in. The chains around Elijah's limbs rattled as the vehicle shifted. I pulled out the key that Imogen had given me from my pocket. I started to unlocked the first chain around his wrist. Imogen took a step forward.

"Here," she kept her focus on Elijah, stretching as far as she could to hand me thick and heavy handcuffs.

Elijah didn't spare me a glance. His eyes were fixed on the witch. His lips were pulled back in a sneer, showing off his jagged teeth, and his pitch black eyes narrowed maliciously. It was terrifying to witness. She took rapid steps backwards, her lips now pressed together in barely restrained fear. The magic that had crackled along her hands was now sparking off and leaving burnt spots wherever the energy landed.

"Damn witch! I will kill you!" Elijah rasped. His voice was hoarse. It was different from the monotone he normally spoke in. I stumbled backwards as he pushed by me, eager to get at the witch. The chains I had yet to remove pulled tight, holding him back. Both his arms strained at his remaining shackles, the metal groaning under his power. But the chains held. They had been spelled with runes expressly for this purpose.

Elijah's unnaturally emotional reaction made my gut twist. I stepped forward, the witch watching my every move. I had to remind myself that I was not his friend, or even his teammate in this moment. To the witch who now stood watching and waiting. I was part of her team. She was my ally. With my meaty hand, I slammed Elijah back against the side of the van. He didn't take his gaze off the witch, though.

"Nixie …" A desperate strangling sounded from outside the van. I kept my hand loose around Elijah's neck, but my back tensed at hearing her and my ears perked. Audrey was awake and I felt the dread of what was to follow. Elijah heard her voice as well, some of the madness that had overtaken him slipped away. He stopped struggling against me. I took a step back, Elijah's face melted back to his indifferent calm façade.

A deep and selfish disappointment filled me as I listened to Audrey call out for Nixie. I stood by my decision to abandon them when I did. It had been our only chance. Audrey would believe me once this was all over and I could explain. I turned back to Elijah, clapping new manacles onto his wrists and unlocking him from the chains bolted into the van. Imogen watched us, but took several steps backwards as we edged our way out of the van. Elijah's muscles were tight under my hold, but he made no other move to make me think he would act irrationally. I didn't know much about the dynamics between wraiths and witches, but I did know Imogen's magic could affect Elijah.

Elijah stepped down from the van first, I followed. In the dwarf form I was much shorter than him, but I had twice as much bulk. My thick hand closed around his arm keeping him close, even though I knew he wouldn't do anything to jeopardize our escape. At least I hoped so.

"Take the sirenă and the fantomă to the prison cells. We will question them later," the zana commanded.

"Get your filthy paws off me, you mother-fishing were," Nixie's voice slurred.

I moved to pull Elijah out of the van, but he stepped out on his own. The cheetahs stood with Nixie between them. She watched Zeke who held Audrey's upper arm like a vice.

"Come along, Balaur," Zeke said, pulling Audrey away from us.

Imogen led us in the opposite direction from Zeke and Audrey. Nixie was already at work, whispering things to the werecheetahs. I knew she would soon have them under her spell. One of them had already slackened his grasp. The other still resisted, but that wouldn't last for long. He kept shaking his head as if to rid himself of something at the edge of his awareness. Something insistent. Eventually his eyes glazed over until he was much like the first *were*.

Imogen walked in silence. She kept an eye on Elijah, who remained in control of himself for now. The relative calmness of the moment gave me time to think. Time to plan. Nixie was now in control of the cheetahs. She had done it quietly. But that was her special talent—she was the only siren I knew who could sing paranormals under her thrall. I would be able to take down Imogen, but while we might subdue our captors, we couldn't be sure where Audrey had been taken. If I revealed myself too soon, they would probably catch us all and lock me away, too. That wouldn't do anyone any good.

We would have to bide our time. That meant both Elijah and Nixie would have to be locked prison cells, but with cheetahs under Nixie's control, the doors of those cells would be no obstacle. I would come back for the two of them after I found Audrey. The problem would be finding her. I was fearful that they might take her right away to exchange with the Vedenins. The Yorks had been working closely with the Vedenins for a while, and if their partnership was still intact, I had to move fast. The Vedenins would expect the Bradens to come after her again. We knew she existed, even if we weren't exactly sure what she might be. Not that that mattered to me anymore. All that mattered was saving her.

We moved farther into the building and stopped at a pair of industrial elevators. The buttons showed two subfloors. Along the way we passed other paranormals, but they barely took a second glance at our strange group.

At the elevators, Imogen had to place her hand on a scanner and punch in a code. I watched her closely from the corner of my eye. There were no other guards with us, Imogen and I were Elijah's guard detail while the cheetahs "watched" Nixie. It all felt too easy. Their security seemed lacking. It put me on edge.

The elevator lurched and started its descent. The freight elevator was large, but with so many bodies crowding it, it felt tight. If we had to start a fight in here, it would get messy. But it wasn't long before I felt us slow and the elevator stuttered to a stop.

The doors to the elevator opened to a Valkyrie and a stone giant. Valkyries were born warriors. They had an innate knack for combat and mature ones could learn new martial techniques in a glance. And the stone giant—I was still in shock. I hadn't thought they existed anymore. They were large, dangerous creatures, with bodies made of stone, like their species' name implied.

This was going to be a lot harder than I had originally thought.

Chapter 31

AUDREY

My eyes were open. Still it was dark. Fear crowded out all other thought. I couldn't breathe properly. The space was suffocating. It was limited by darkness. My breath caught in my lungs in broken, gasping intervals. And every time I tried to breathe in, something would brush against my lips. I remembered this feeling—the last night I'd seen my father. I struggled to recall it, but couldn't.

I was desperate for the comfort of a friendly hand in my own. I hadn't realized how dependent I had become to Gabriel's small touches. There were times I wasn't sure he was aware of how his hand would absently skim the edges of my arms, or how his hands would play with my hair.

I missed Nixie and Gabriel, and even Elijah. I needed them. I needed the strength they offered me. But they were gone. I had tried to blindly reach out to Nixie earlier, but no one existed in my new world of darkness.

"Stop moving your head, Balaur," an accented voice demanded. His voice was so close it sent shivers of fear down my spine. A hand touched my upper arm.

"We are standing now. Walk."

His words were clipped. We paused after a few steps.

"Take the sirena and the fantoma to the prison cells. We will question them later." His hand gripped my arm a little tighter. The hand tugged my arm, effectively towing me with them. I kept searching for the sound of my friends' scuffling feet. I strained my ears to hear Nixie, to hear *any* familiar voice.

"Nixie?" I called out quietly.

"Get your filthy paws off me, you mother-fishing *were*!" Nixie's voice rang out and I tried to move toward it. I could tell she was being pulled away from me, in the opposite direction.

Then we walked—blindly—down a labyrinth of twists and turns for moments that stretched off in a dark eternity. We stopped and some words were muttered. Then we were inside, though inside where, I did not know. The comforting brush of the wind was gone. The sound of my friends' footfalls was gone. Instead, it was only me and my captor.

"Well, Balaur, it's time for a family reunion, I think."

The accented man tugged the cloth from my head. The fabric rasped across my skin. It wasn't rough, but my hair caught in it, causing it to scrape against my face.

I blinked. The room was bright and big. The high ceilings were bright and open. Light reflected off glass casting a rainbow of shining colors. The thick stone walls surrounding the room. There were so many details that it was overwhelming. But those all drifted away into the peripheral.

My heart pounded against my ribs, painfully. Denial pulsed a monosyllable of refusal in my brain. *No. No!* It couldn't be …

I couldn't take my eyes off the creature in the middle of the room.

Its eyes were shut, body curled around itself. Its steady even breathing told me he slept. The scales were iridescent in their lurid redness. Smooth, too. Ruby red and ruby smooth.

That coloring. So familiar. I felt my vision swim. It couldn't be, but it couldn't be anyone else. My breath was hollow. The ridges of his spikes looked more deadly than ever, each point sharp enough to draw blood from a touch. He was so beautiful in this form. He had taken it so rarely when I was a child.

There was a change in his breathing. He had scented me. Fear stole my air, chilled the sweat upon my forehead, made my hands shake. His

212

eyes opened to slits and stared at me. Uncurling his front legs, he pushed with his hind legs and stood. Sharp, long talons *clicked* against the ground. I remembered those claws well. In his half human form, they were smaller, more needle like. Now they were thick and heavy.

Ice filled my veins, rushing in little floes of terror back to my heart. Every beat ached with cold dread. He opened his mouth to reveal shining white fangs and threw back his head. The room shook with his roar. It vibrated its way through my entire body.

Zeke's hand gripped me a little tighter. My feet took halting steps backwards. His roar. It reminded me of past failures. My fear of his punishment still ran deep. What would happen this time? Even after so long. I touched the scar on my face. That scar had been the price of friendship.

How would he punish me for being absent these five years? For disobeying him and getting myself captured? I had only wanted to go back for Aiden.

The dragon that stood before me began to shift. It was fluid movement, bones collapsed inwards, scales sliding together, scales blending into ruddy colored skin which then mellowed to a more human tone. I gaped up at his six-foot-seven-inch height. His body was thickly built and sturdy. It was the body of a real dragon shifter. He had always told me that I was too small, even for a girl. That I wasn't a real dragon. It was true. I wasn't. After all, I had never shifted, even before I was taken away from him. No matter how hard he tried, I never could.

I remembered the half attempts, I remembered how frustrated he had been. His exasperation. How it inevitably led to more punishments. The memories came quick, one upon another. All the nights I spent whispering to my precious toy, my friend, my Aiden, about how I wished I could be a dragon like him. As he sauntered toward me the memories came quick. They were a flash, a glimmer, a streak of light reflecting from my cold, hard past. Like metal, dazzling reflections of memory were cast into the farthest corners of my mind. His voice came unbidden from out of those memories. *You're the reason why I fight so hard to master my demons*. Even after I took my mother.

"Audrey ..."

His voice was deeper than I remembered. A strangled whimper sounded in the back of my throat.

I flinched as he moved toward us. The primal connection shifters had to their paranormal side put our kind more at ease with nudity, and his freshly shifted bare skin didn't stop him from advancing toward us.

His deep red hair was longer now, its ends brushing his shoulders. He'd once told me I was fortunate to inherit his hair. I had mostly inherited my mother's softer looks. And her height. But looking now at his strong, square jaw, it dawned on me just how different we looked. I found myself thinking about the blue eyes we shared and the same lopsided smile. At least that was what the few people we interacted with had said. I doubt anyone would say that now. I rarely smiled. When I did, it felt wrong. A little too tight, a little too scarred. I stared at my father's chest, afraid to look him in the eyes.

Afraid to see the anger there.

"Audrey."

His voice was rough and much closer than before. He was getting annoyed, but I was too afraid to move. He gently nudged my head up with his fingertips.

My father had lived his entire life with paranormal creatures, he never had to control his strength to the point of dealing with a human. He refused to really learn to control his strength until one time, when I was a child, he had grabbed my arm too roughly. I had cried out, wailed from the pain of it. The memory blinked out of remembrance before I could recall anything more. He told me I was the reason why we couldn't live with other paranormals. Weakness in a dragon-shifter was the same as embarrassment. I was too weak to be with our kind. Too weak to be a part of the paranormal world at all.

"What do I always say?" he demanded.

"Head stays up," I answered, meeting his eyes.

He nodded his approval and pulled me into a hug.

"My little babe is all grown now."

He took a step back and inspected his scar. I could see a glimmer of approval in his eye. Dragons were the most possessive kind of creature. My father had never told me much about his past, but I knew his dragon ruled him at times. There wasn't a clear barrier between man and dragon, like there should have been. In all reality, my father was more dragon than he was man. And the dragon in him couldn't understand the human side of things. All it knew was to possess and protect.

I looked away as fear slipped down my spine. The scar was a lie. I no longer belonged to him. I belonged to another.

"Zeke, grab me some clothes."

Zeke nodded and went to get my father his clothes.

"I've missed you."

He cupped my cheek gently, his blue eyes showing the depth of his sadness. He was too controlling, but we were happy at times, too. It was hard to dismiss the man who had taken care of me for so much of my life. Zeke returned with clothes for my father, who pulled them on easily.

With his attention momentarily elsewhere, I finally had a chance to really take in the room. The ceiling was jeweled with glass panels that formed a dome and made the sky glitter. It was quite beautiful, and the brilliant sun shined onto the white marble of the floor, highlighting black, lustrous veins that ran through it. A concrete ceiling overhung the edges of the room, shrouding the perimeter in shadows. Across the room I could see a bed and some furniture.

Black. His favorite color. He said others were weak. Black was the color of strength, and our kind were strong. My father returned his attention to me.

He stood in front of me again. He took me in, a look of awe entered his eyes.

"My little daughter ..."

He pulled me tight against him in another hug. He took a step back, his hands still gripping my upper arms. He continued to watch me, his grip never loosening. I swallowed hard, taking him in. There was so little, but also so much, that had changed in him. Rarely in my youth did I remember him not being tense. Ready to move at a moment's notice. Now he stood in front of me leisurely. It didn't last as a thought crossed his mind, marring his excitement with a pensive look. He switched his grip and steered me with a single arm. There was a sense of urgency to his movements now as he led us to a door on the other side of the room down a hallway.

I was soon lost in the many twists and turns. The compound was more like a maze than any building I had been in before. Finally, we arrived at a dark wood door inscribed with small, intricate designs. I didn't have long to look at them before my father took his place in front of me. It was common for our kind, or so he had told me once. It was a way of protecting the young, and it kept me hidden until he was ready to let someone see me. He knocked on the door. A gruff, distorted voice answered.

"What do you want, Drake?"

My father opened the door. As he did, I glimpsed the man on the other side. But it was all jumbled together, the form behind a desk blending with the dark mahogany, warm incandescent lights shedding yellow light that cast long shadows upon a strong figure sitting behind a meticulously clean desk.

Father didn't have to remind me my place. I already knew. I would stand behind him until he said otherwise.

"Look, Drake, I don't want to fight with you."

"Xavier, I would like to introduce you to my daughter, Audrey."

My father moved a single step out of the way. He pulled me close, protectively tucking me under his arm.

Even in full view, I had difficulty believing my eyes. His skin was a deep grey color. Not as though he was sick. It looked more like grey concrete than actual skin. His eyes were a deep purple color, and in them I saw shock, even if his face remained passive and blank. A small smile curled the end of his very dark lips.

"You found her."

It was almost a question. But he moved on before anyone could answer.

"I am so sorry, where are my manners? I am Xavier York. Head of the York Clan."

He offered me his hand, and I wondered at his sharp clawed nails. There was the swish of a tail behind him and, pressed to his back but still visible, were huge bat-like wings.

216

I didn't take his hand. I only stared.

"Are you going to kill my ... my friends?" the words staggered out from me. I wished my voice were stronger as I said them. But in these circumstances, I was amazed I spoke at all.

My father's hold tightened until it made me wince. The bat-thing, Xavier, gave my father a look of annoyance bordering on anger. My father released his grip on me, but his arm remained around my shoulders. I had never seen my father listen to anyone's advice where I was concerned.

"No, my dear. We would never do that."

Xavier flashed a sharp-toothed grin at me. His incisors were longer than a normal human's were, but besids them were normal sized teeth.

"There is much—"

But before he could finish, the door behind us buckled inward in a shower of splinters. All hell broke loose after that.

Chapter 32

STONE

Our small group stepped off the elevator. The Valkyrie and the stone giant who stood guard in front of the double doors straight ahead of us didn't budge an inch. The giant looked down at us, but otherwise they remained at attention, on alert for other threats. The stark white room between the elevator and the double doors that lead to the prison block provided a buffer of security. Close to both the Valkyrie and the giant were hand scanners, and next to the Valkyrie was a keypad.

The ride down had been quiet and tense. Nixie's mouth twitched into a smile every now and then. She must be damn proud of herself. I know I was. She had those cheetahs in her thrall without anyone realizing, which was no small feat. Elijah remained still. His attitudes and reactions were becoming more predictable. His outburst earlier was unlike him. But apparently he had himself under control now.

We stepped farther into the room. The cheetahs had a loose grip on Nixie, whereas Imogen and I kept Elijah tightly in hand. The giant moved first, it's body rumbling, clicking together as it turned to press its hand against the scanner behind it. The Valkyrie waited until the giant finished.

I realized freeing Elijah and Nixie later might be harder than I thought. Counting the stone giant, I had seen two endangered paranormals in the ranks of the York Clan. I had been under the impression that the York Clan was primarily made up of Middle Eastern American paranormals. Regional types tended to stick together. I eyed the Valkyrie sidelong, wondering how old she really was. Age was an important factor to consider when dealing with her kind. The older they were, the more difficult they'd be to beat, not that it would be an easy fight in any case. Even young Valkyrie were ferocious.

Our plan wouldn't work. Not against these odds. Even leaving this floor required a voice recognition lock. Even *if* I could form my vocal cords to approximate the voice of another, I wouldn't be able to fool the voice reader. I have to get the tone *exactly* right, and we didn't have that kind of time. I looked at Nixie and gave her a nod. She gave me a huge smile and nodded back.

I shifted my ears shut so I couldn't hear. Nixie opened her mouth. Not only could sirens enchant others with their song, but with the right motivation, they could burst a person's eardrums.

Nixie screeched. The Valkyrie pressed her hands against her ears. Even so, the sound penetrated, causing her to drop to the floor, and the cheetahs followed. Nixie stopped as soon as they did. The only one that remained standing was the stone giant. It looked down at the Valkyrie, a dumb look on its face, not really understanding what was happening. I'd never met a stone giant before, but from what I'd been told, they weren't too bright.

I released my hold on Elijah and immediately began to shift into the form of a stone giant. The giant's reflexes, though, were sharper than its mind. The giant must have seen the beginning of my transformation before I could complete the change. He threw out his gnarled arm, knocking me in the gut. That single blow propelled me backwards into the wall. I hit hard, but wasted no time struggling back to my feet. I pushed my cells to change, expanding and reforming.

Elijah was already fighting with the stone giant. It was strange seeing him in action, but it always was where wraiths were concerned. Elijah punched the giant, and then changed his attacks by opening his hand flat, slapping hard against pressure points. The motion was unnatural. The movements were too fluid. The strikes too violent, too vicious. Elijah blinked out of existence then reappeared. His movements were quick and unpredictable. The giant swung out his thick solid arms trying to bat Elijah away same as he did me, but when he swung, Elijah was already gone. Stone was beginning to break free from the creature's carapace. That's when my cells finally set in place.

Nixie still had the cheetahs in hand, but the Valkyrie had regained her footing and was mid-rush at Nixie. Blood trickled from the Valkyrie's ears, a murderous glower on her face. She sprung forward, using her fist as her only weapons. Nixie backed up a few steps, trying to put ground between her and the Valkyrie. The Valkyrie wasted no time, striking without mercy.

Nixie moved with the swiftness of someone trained to fight from a very young age. In my stone giant skin, I lumbered over to the Valkyrie. Not matter how skilled a fighter she was, there would be little she could do against my new craggy skin and bulk—not without a weapon, at least. I crashed into her and her head whipped back as she knocked into the wall. She slumped to the floor, leaving a red smear. Part of me wanted to lumber over and finish off the threat, but I turned my bulk in the direction we needed to go. We had bigger issues.

The stone giant had collapsed to the floor under Elijah's rain of blows. Its skin now chipped and cracked in various places from Elijah's physical barrage. Elijah crouched on its chest. His hands pressed against the giant's head. The veins in his arms bulged with the pressure he exerted on the giant's head. Elijah barely looked strained, but he slowly, intentionally, began to lift with his legs. I knew what he planned. He was going to rip the giant's head from his shoulders. Unable to speak in my new body, I released a gravelly roar. He stopped, watching me. It took a moment before I could resume my own form.

"Don't kill it."

My voice was still gruff like a dwarf's. I reshaped my vocal folds and cleared my throat.

"Don't kill it, Elijah," I yelled again when he didn't relent.

"Why not?"

Elijah's black eyes were focused on me. His strange hands hovered over the giant's chest, ready to perform his species' dark ritual. Ready to penetrate that hard skin and reach inside.

"You know damn well why not. It's an endangered species."

Really, all paranormals were endangered, in a manner of speaking. But some of us were less abundant than others.

"Do a binding spell, and put him with the others."

Elijah didn't move for a while. I ached at the thought of him killing such a rare and beautiful creature. Like Audrey. In the end, he stood, grabbed the giant's arm, and pulled the creature into the first cell. Nixie sang the cheetahs into the cell next to the giant, and I moved the Valkyrie in with the cheetahs, afterwards resuming my normal form.

The doors to the elevators remained open. We entered together, and Elijah pushed the button. A wraith's ability to sense other paranormals could be valuable at times. We had made use of it in the past while on missions. I confess, until this point, I had assumed that he knew where Audrey was. But now, with the adrenaline in my system making me edgy and impatient, I started to pace. Nixie watched me, her eyes following my back and forth circuit.

I stopped abruptly.

"What?" I snapped at her.

"You just seem a bit more edgy than you usually are after a fight. Usually you are about as stoic as Elijah."

When I glared at her, she gave me a dirty look.

"It's adrenaline and all that shit," I muttered, continuing to pace the small room.

"We'll find her. We will." Nixie's eyes stayed fixed on the door now. Her hands were clenched in tight fists.

I tried to remain still, but my skin crawled with anticipation. My body was preparing itself for a change. It wasn't just that though. Nixie was right. I had to calm down before I did something stupid and killed us all.

Finally, the freight elevator doors opened. Nixie had positioned herself against the left wall, and I stood on the right. The elevator was large, metal, and didn't seem to have any security cameras. Elijah stood in the middle, creepily bereft of emotion, stepping forward out of the elevator like it was a Sunday afternoon back home. No sooner had he passed out of view that I heard the unmistakable crack of a neck. I stepped out myself.

"Do not worry, it was only a vampire. Easy enough to replace," Elijah said.

I didn't feel sorry for the vampire at all. Honestly, I would have done the same thing. But I stood by my decision to spare the stone giant. While the York and Braden Clan might fight each other, there was still some sense of honor between us. There were unspoken rules about harming certain species. None of us wanted to be responsible for causing the extinction of another paranormal race.

Nixie looked a little sick when she glanced down at the vampire. His head was twisted unnaturally, and the once aligned vertebrae popped out disjointedly. She didn't usually go on kill missions. Had no stomach for them. But we needed her to get Audrey back. I wasn't concerned with consequences at this point. I only wanted Audrey safe.

We moved silently through the building. Elijah took point, but I did my fair share as well. Nixie helped, but only by knocking a few wounded stragglers unconscious. Nixie had trained with weapons and hand on hand combat. With quick, efficient upper-cuts, she laid out the few that Elijah and I left in our wake. It was faster our way, and safer. Her song was magical and would alert the whole compound if we weren't careful. Deep inside, I felt an impulse that led us to the center of the complex— nameless, unknown. I had no explanation for it, though I knew it would lead me to her.

The twists and turns of the building were made to confuse trespassers. But I had trained in places like these. We waited tensely for the next set of guards. Finally, we stopped.

"She's here. Somewhere," Nixie whispered.

Nixie closed her eyes as if she was going to go off of feeling alone. I agreed with her, Audrey was near, but suddenly there was nothing. The sensation that had led me, led us here was suddenly gone. Vanished. And its absence was driving me insane. I started to pace, a growl forming in the back of my throat.

"There is a hidden door."

Elijah stepped up to the wall and pushed on a blank white segment. I waited for something to happen, but nothing did. Elijah stepped back and kicked his leg out unexpectedly. Nixie yelped as the sound of wood splintering resounded in the air. Inside was a small office. Bookshelves lined the wall and two elegant chairs sat before a large mahogany desk. I couldn't focus on the furniture though. My eyes instantly fixated on Audrey's terrified face.

A tall, dark haired man held onto her arm. His eyes matched Audrey's. She must not have realized that she had stepped closer to me because she looked surprised when he pulled her back. He bared his teeth at me in a snarl, baring long, sharp canines much different from any I'd ever seen. Like a serpent's teeth, only bigger. He was imposing, but so was the gargoyle behind him.

"Stone," my name escaped her lips, the man holding her heard it. He turned his eyes down to her.

"Who is this?" he snarled at her.

Audrey tried to shake her arm free from the hold the man had on it. She cowered backwards from his firm hold on her.

I stepped toward her even as the man pushed her behind his back. Then I heard the gargoyle hiss in the most unnerving way. Elijah moved to intercept, and before long they were exchanging blows. Elijah darted quick, powerful punches at his ribs. The gargoyle evaded while swinging his own fist in at Elijah's head. The red haired man lashed out at me. It was an easily anticipated strike that I dodged.

The man holding Audrey kept his eyes locked on mine. He held Audrey behind him. I crept forward, looking for an opening. Out of the corner of my eye I saw Nixie making her way around Elijah and the gargoyle. She, too, seemed be focused on getting to Audrey. Nixie made her way around Elijah, avoiding the flap of the gargoyle's wings, but the gargoyle's agile tail snaked around Nixie's neck.

"Stop!"

It was the first time I had heard Audrey's voice so strong.

"Stop, Drake."

I hadn't realized the other paranormal had moved. He was inches from me. My lips pulled back in a snarl. I bulked up my muscles, widening my shoulders and giving myself a few more inches so that I was better matched.

"So you've escaped your cells and, I am assuming, left a trail of bodies behind you. All for the sake of Audrey. Done like true members of the Braden Clan. I know how much Cain would enjoy completely eradicating us from the face of this earth," the gargoyle snarled at us. His hold on Nixie tightened slightly and her eyes bulged as her breath wheezed to a stop.

Audrey stumbled forward, her eyes wide as she touched her own neck. Could she feel Nixie's pain?

"Stop! Stop choking her!" I roared.

"And why the hell should I?" he retorted.

"You're killing them both. The siren and the girl share a bond," Elijah stated.

Drake, the paranormal who had been close to attacking me, stopped to watch Audrey. His muscles tensed. His gaze kept shifting from the gargoyle to Audrey.

"Xavier," Drake called out. There was a plea to his voice, but also a demand.

The gargoyle released his hold on Nixie.

Chapter 33

AUDREY

I was so scared seeing Nixie like that, but then I felt this tightening around the throat and a pain filled my heart. I gasped and backed away, clutching at my chest. A loss of breath. Blood pounded in my ears as my eyes bulged. All because of me. All because …

Xavier loosened his hold on her, and she slumped to the ground. His eyes met mine as I continued to gasp for air. A subtle hint of guilt flashed across his eyes as he watched me, but he focused his attention back to where Nixie had slumped to the floor. Xavier lifted the unconscious Nixie in his arms and gently placed her in his chair. My father held my arm as I tried to twist it from his grip so I could go to Nixie.

"What did you do to Audrey?" my father growled, watching Stone. He pulled me behind him, keeping a hand on my arm.

Stone. How was he here? But he *was*—he was here! Even if he was taller and bigger than the Stone I was used to, I knew him immediately. I stepped forward around my father to go to him. My father tightened his hold on my arm and stepped between us. Stone's eyes flashed a dangerous red color. The murderous glint there shook me to my core.

"I didn't do anything to her. She was only safe because of us."

The fear and pain that had overwhelmed me moments before was slowly beginning to thaw. The realization that Stone had come for us—for me—elated me for a moment.

He had come for me. He was here.

"You did a miserable job, if it was so easy for us to capture you. Now she will really be safe."

Stone's eyes changed to a pitiless black. His body quaked, his muscles enlarged, becoming more dangerous.

There was a loud crash, and I flinched. Stone rushed forward, pressing his thick forearm against my father's neck and forcing him backwards. His lips were pulled back baring his teeth, his jaw was clenched tight. Stone's face twisted into something animalistic.

Xavier moved with more grace and speed than Stone. He dug his claws in between Stone and my father to pry Stone away, but Stone merely swatted him aside. With stumbling steps, and the assistance of a chair back, I made my way back to the fighting duo. Xavier stood opposite me, watching my movements, his lips pressed shut, making no efforts to stop me. I stood next to Stone, his anger a palatable thing.

"Stone?" I touched the arm pinning my father to the wall.

Stone didn't take his eyes off my father, but relaxed under my touch.

"Please don't hurt him."

My breath was trapped in my lungs. The muscles rolling under my hand stilled.

"Stone …"

His head cocked in my direction. My voice tugged at him. Slowly those rage black eyes met mine. Everything was quiet aside from his ragged breathing. The black bled out to a deep red before finally returning to a muddy brown. There were flecks on his remaining anger, but he was in control.

Slowly Stone released his arm from my father's neck. My hand never left his as he dropped it to his side. Once I did pull my arm back, the red started to bleed back into his eyes again. Gently Stone brushed my cheek. I released a shaky breath. The absolute anger, at least, had melted away. His brow furrowed and his temple throbbed.

He dropped his arm, eyes shining with determination.

"We're leaving. Now."

Stone looked at Elijah, who nodded and went to pick up the still unconscious Nixie from the chair.

"Not with my daughter you're not," my father roared.

"Drake."

Xavier guided my father's gaze to his own. Quietly they spoke. I couldn't pull my attention away from them. My father's labored breaths eased, the severe line in his brows loosened. I had never seen anyone calm my father down like that. But my father's slit eyes slowly returned to his normal human blue.

"He is *not* going to take her away," my father rumbled quietly to Xavier.

"That's right. I'm afraid none of you will be leaving."

Fear snaked its way down my spine.

"You can't keep us here," Stone said. His hands gripped my hips, directing me to stand protected behind him. He pushed me backwards toward Elijah, who stood next to the entrance of the office with Nixie dangling in his arms.

"Stupid faceless one. You think I will allow that? I will *not* allow the Bradens to destroy her."

Stone's muscles trembled with silent rage beneath my hands. His grip on my hip tightened. His free hand tightened into a fist, the skin over the knuckles turned white. Brushing my fingers against the strained veins in his arm, he loosened his grip. Stone took a step forward.

"I'd never see her harmed, but what about you, *warrior*?" he spat the word with disdain at Xavier. "We *saw* what your friends the Vedenins did to her. I won't allow you to send her back."

"Send her back? I am York, head of this clan, and no friend to the Vedenins or the Bradens. Your clan seeks to use her."

"So you have her best interest at heart?" he gave a sharp laugh. "You would use her just like they did."

Stone again began pushing me backwards.

"We would never do that her. We've been trying to save her!" my father said, trying to push past Xavier again. Xavier's tail had wrapped its way around my father's calf and one hand rested on his chest holding him in place.

"You expect us to believe that? It's common knowledge that you work with the Vedenin Clan," Stone replied, still shielding me.

Nixie moaned quietly, twisting her head, her eyes squeezed tight as if the sound of our conversation hurt her head.

"We have no alliance with the Vedenin Clan. Your information is wrong."

My father moved forward, his eyes shifting to those of his dragon. The beast bled through the façade of the man. Whatever hold he had over that part of himself wavered. Xavier had released his hold on my father's chest, but his tail still had his tight grip.

"Enough, Drake."

My father took a minimal step backwards, pulling in a breath. His nostrils flared and his eyes blinked back to his human eyes for the second time in the span of a few short minutes.

"You have been kept in the dark about a lot of things. But I'm surprised you would go along with this façade of Cain's, wraith." His voice was stern, but there was a hint of pity directed at Stone.

"Elijah, what is he talking about?" Stone said.

"Jacobs lied. He was planning on destroying her. He was from the beginning," Elijah said, his black eyes on me, watching my reaction. He had known all along what my fate would be. I was to be destroyed.

There was a shrill crack. A jolt of surprise shot through me making me jump. Nixie, who was now fully awake and wriggling her way out of Elijah's arms, drew our attention.

"You asshole! Put me down now before I burst your damn eardrums!" Nixie's lips had twisted, her eyes raged, her cheek flushed red.

Elijah's blank face gave no warning as he dropped her. Nixie landed heavily on her backside, her hair falling forward to cover her flushed face. She shook back her hair and stood up. Once standing, she straightened her back and gauged the room.

"Here is what I've caught, guppies: you're Audrey's daddio," pointing at my father she turned her finger to Xavier, "and *you* are not only claiming that what we've been led to believe for, I don't know, years now is wrong. That you aren't in league with the Vedenins. And, to top it all off, our clan, the Bradens, are the bad guys?"

The room was painfully silent.

"That's a tall order. I think we need more of an explanation."

"Cain wants to kill off the returning paranormals," my father growled. His voice morphing into something unrecognizable. His anger was quick to take over him.

"Sorry, I couldn't understand that through the growling. What?" Nixie asked looking curiously, but cautiously, at Xavier.

"Paranormals that were thought to be extinct are resurfacing. We've been calling it The Rebirth. But Cain has other plans. He and the Bradens want to kill them off, and the Vedenin Clan wants to control them. So if you leave and take her back to your clan, you are ensuring her death," Xavier announced. My heart hammered in my chest.

This was all too much. My vision swam, blurring. The fear seeped bone deep. I was losing myself to it. Stone didn't say anything, but his muscles remained tense. His eyes were a rusty brown-red, his bitter anger shining through. I could feel it pouring off him.

The lines around Nixie's eyes, almost always crinkled by a perpetual smile, were gone. Her smile nonexistent. They filled with infinite sadness. She couldn't have known. She would never try to harm me.

"The only reason you're all not dead right now is because of her." Xavier watched me, indicating what he said in a gesture. "I'm aware of the damage you have done to my clan. I won't forgive you outright, but if you are willing to stay and listen, if you are willing to try and help undo the evil you have done working for Cain and the Braden Clan, perhaps you can earn my trust back. But I cannot allow you to take Audrey back. She was in more in danger with the Bradens than she ever was with the Vedenins. We care about her here. We want to protect her. It's your choice. Decide."

Stone, Nixie, Elijah, and I formed a semi-circle. None of us spoke for what seemed like forever.

"I don't trust them." Nixie's eyes slid over to Xavier and my father. My father was watching us, his hands loosening and tightening. Xavier was collected and calm, his back straight, wings tight against his back.

"Our best option is to play our hand." Stone spoke slowly and with purpose. There was more to his words, but whatever he was hinting at, it was beyond me.

"Agreed," Elijah said, speaking for the first time in quite a while.

Each of them spoke quietly. Peeking over to my father and Xavier, they seemed engaged in a conversation of their own. Xavier's lips pinched as he spoke, his nostrils flaring. My father dropped his head a little, his eyes remaining stubborn, but slowly he nodded, agreeing to whatever Xavier had told him.

Stone took the lead and agreed to Xavier's terms. After that, things moved quickly.

Xavier showed us to our rooms. I walked next to Stone. The halls were painted white, the color never varying. The maze-like layout of the building had my already addled mind warped.

Xavier presented the first room to Nixie, and started to usher her inside. Nixie went pale and took a step backwards.

"Do not *ever* touch me, York. Not *ever*," she hissed. She stepped around him keeping as much space from him as she could. She entered her room and slammed the door loudly behind her.

My father walked behind us as we arrived at my room, and he gathered me into a hug. It felt … normal to have his arms around me again. He was a part of my past that I longed for. A mixture of anger and sadness swept over me. Anger at those who took me away and sadness for myself at the horror I had lived through. I would never get that lost time back. Gabriel was silent, his eyes calculating, his gaze flickering between Nixie's room and Xavier. Perhaps he was trying to gauge how safe we would be.

My door was next door to Nixie's. The knowledge she would be close by made me release a slow breath of relief. Then Xavier and Drake led Elijah and Stone to their rooms. I waited until they disappeared down the hallway before I settled into my own.

Inside there was a small nightstand of a simple design. It had a single drawer and a small door closing off its bottom half. The frame of the bed was metal. The footboard was an oval shape with metal bars. The bed itself was made up with starched white sheets tucked beneath a plain blue quilt.

Four-hundred seventy-one. The stitching of the blanket was course under my fingertips. The numbers thrummed in my head. *Four-hundred seventy-seven.* Taking over. Releasing me.

Knock. A muscle under my eye twitched.

One. Two. Three. *Go away. Go away. Away.* Four-five-six. Seven.

"Audrey?" a familiar voice called distantly.

I went back to counting the quilt. I was desperate to hold onto my slipping sanity. This room was too familiar. *Four-hundred seventy-eight.*

"Audrey?"

The voice was so close now. So, so, close.

Something moved me away from the quilt. My eyes had been open, but my vacant gaze had seen nothing.

And then a face swam into focus before me. The green eyes spoke of volumes of worry. That is what I saw in his eyes. A kind of empathy tinged with worry. He had been captured as well, taken and attacked by my father.

"Hey, you're safe. I will never let anyone hurt you. I promised, didn't I?" Stone whispered in my ear as he pulled me closer. I could feel his breath on the crook of my neck. The slow inhale and exhale.

"My father promised the same thing, once upon a time. But he has. So many times," I whispered. I was scared. Insecurities about my father's failures were heavy on my mind. How many times had my father promised to protect me? Glimpses of past memories of when I was taken, to when his beast side took over. Even in the face of the things he had said, I was terrified Stone might do the same. Take me back to his clan. Back to his *family*. Pick them over me. Somehow the thought had rooted in my mind.

"What do you mean he hurt you?" Stone asked quietly. His lips touched the side of my head. My eyes closed involuntarily.

"I deserved some of these scars. But ..."

My father had made rules to protect me, to protect us. I was the one who had broken them. Some of them though. My hand went instinctively to touch the one on my face, but Stone's hand was already there, touching unflinchingly the puckered, revolting scars.

"No, you didn't deserve any of these scars. Especially these."

He leaned down and kissed each scar along its length.

I closed my eyes against the sweet touch. He laid me down now, his body lightly touching mine, never pressing against me too hard. He braced himself so I wouldn't feel trapped. And when I opened my eyes, his were a deep purple looking back at me. Desire, mingled with an emotion that was buried deep enough it was hard to decipher.

"You are the most stunning woman I have ever met."

He kissed my lips this time. I lifted my head slightly when it felt like he was going to pull away.

My hands moved through his hair. I now understood why his hands had always sought out my own. At the cabin, which felt like ages ago now, he hands would mindlessly find their way to my hair. Once, while we took in the night air on the deck, his fingers twined in it, seductive and enchanting. Lightly coiling the strands, making my head light with such a small delight. My eyelids had grown heavy. It was a simple pleasure I had never experienced. Now touching his hair, feeling how it slipped through my fingers, leaving a strange, tingling trail. I couldn't stop.

Stone groaned and his body pushed lightly onto mine. His lips left me, and when I tried to follow, he nuzzled my head back into place and kissed my scars again. He touched the damaged part of my lips, and I felt his tongue lightly trace every ridge. I shivered violently.

I turned my head to face him. I didn't want to stop kissing him, and he didn't resist. He allowed me to control it at my own speed. With a feather-light touch, the tip of my tongue timidly traced his lips before his mouth opened with another groan. I sighed as the taste of him permeated me. I was light headed. I was hungry for more. But, as much as I needed him, I also needed air.

I pulled away, trying to catch a breath.

"Gods, I don't ever want to stop kissing you."

Stone's hand drifted from my waist moving upward. My heart pounded in my chest. A sweet fear, a mixture of inexperience and nerves plagued me. A war raged inside me between what my body craved and what my mind couldn't let go.

"Gabriel," I whispered his real name. He paused, his hand frozen on my lower ribs. He looked at me. The purple desire was swirled with a vortex of rosy flecks, like chips of rose quartz, that hinted at ... love? Or deep affection. But the instant soon passed and the pink became lost in the whorls of purple that revealed his desire.

"Say it again," he whispered, his forehead touching mine.

"Gabriel."

He shut his eyes. For once, I was cut off from the stream of emotions that flickered in his eyes. Uncertainty filled me. But then I felt his hand delve deep into my tresses. His nails lightly raked my scalp, the feeling electrifying me with the pleasure and reassurance. The uncertainty fled, and in its wake came safety and security. His other hand wandered up to grasp the hem of my shirt. He fidgeted with the edge until my breathing evened out. His every touch left a trail of fire in its wake.

Stone's hand on my skin was close to the scar on my ribs. I didn't move. My breath halted in my lungs and I squeezed my eyes tight. When he touched it, his fingers splayed, seeking to map its contours. I felt my lungs expand under his open hand. His fingers moved with the motion of my breathing. Time passed slowly as he traced my scars. His torso hovered above mine, his face in clear view, his knees were pressed into the bed to either side of me. His eyebrows pinched together, like he was trying to figure out how this happened to me, why it happened.

"Why'd he do this?" His voice was strained, like it hurt to ask. "Please," he pleaded. His voice was so desperate, he could have asked anything in that moment and I wouldn't have denied him.

Without even realizing it, I had already started talking.

Chapter 34

STONE

"He marked me as a sign to everyone that I was his daughter. His to protect. *His*. My mother died bringing me into the world. I would never have known her without him, but the way that he spoke of her, it was like she was his entire world. The hopelessness in his voice whenever he told stories about her ... I honestly think he was terrified of losing me. Especially because, in his eyes, I was fragile."

She looked down as if she were ashamed to tell me this. I lifted her chin to meet my eyes, so she could see the sympathy there. Not pity, and not judgement. It was something new, something I hadn't felt before, wasn't ready to acknowledge, but still wanted her to see with her special sight. I couldn't believe myself. How could anyone feel love at a time like this?

"You are not to blame for the death of your mother. If she were able to speak to you now, I'm certain she would say the same. A mother, any true mother, would give her life for her child, no matter the circumstances. You did nothing wrong. How could you? You didn't ask to be brought into this world. It was simply her time, as it was your time to be born, and the only thing you can do now is accept your life and live—as she would have wanted you to."

Audrey's eyes remained unfocused, but she nodded as if she were still listening to me. She swallowed hard. Her gaze returned to mine. I could see the tears glistening there.

"How could she ever forgive me? How could I ever forgive myself?" she asked quietly.

"She wouldn't expect you to ask for forgiveness. There's nothing to forgive. The feelings you hold against yourself are something only you can deal with. One day you will be able to let go. One day you'll lay that pain to rest. And then you'll know, it's okay to live."

I touched her hair again and watched her eyes, hoping she would hear the advice I offered her. She took a breath. There was no real acceptance there, but there was a new determination in her eyes. Audrey moved to my side, her muscles relaxing, and she let out a small sigh. She closed her eyes and I wrapped my arm around her holding her close.

In my mind I replayed Xavier York's words over and over in my head. I had heard things. Whisperings. Hints. I had known the head of the York family had to be someone powerful. But a gargoyle? Their thick skin and inhuman reflexes had earned them a dangerous reputation. None dared cross a gargoyle until their greatest kept secret was revealed. Their human form. They were vulnerable then, which made them easy enough to kill. Some gargoyles even chose to live in their weakened human state, which made them targets. Why they would ever choose to do so was beyond me.

How did this gargoyle come to be the head of this family? Gargoyles had lost their status in the paranormal world. They were rare and often subdued. And what if what he told us was true? Would Jacobs betray us? Weren't Elijah, Nixie, and I rare anomalies ourselves? I had too many questions and not enough time, nor trust in those who could give us answers. There was only one person that could tell me the cold hard facts, but for tonight I couldn't leave Audrey. Her world had been rocked once again. Talking to Elijah would have to wait until tomorrow. Today had been exhausting for all of us. For now, all I wanted to do was sleep with Audrey in my arms.

I stroked her hair for a long time before sleep started to take me. My thoughts still raced even in my sleep.

***

When I woke, Audrey's hair pooled in silken puddles around her face. Both my arms were wrapped around her shoulders, snugly. My right leg was tucked over both of hers, I couldn't stand to be separated from her touch. I leaned my head down and inhaled deeply. She smelled like lavender and smoke.

I closed my eyes again, puzzling again over this emotion building in my chest. She had shared something with me last night, something painful from her past. While I knew she still struggled, every day I could see she was getting better. Each step she bravely took forward was a step toward healing.

This feeling went beyond simple sympathy. I knew exactly how she felt. But these were things I couldn't say to her while she was awake. I could never burden her like that. But while she slept was a different story.

I whispered the words, barely louder than the hush that filled the room.

"My mother was beautiful. She was just an animal shifter, nothing special. But my father fell head over heels for her. Which was strange, considering how he was always something of an elitist. And mom, well, she had an affinity for tigers. That's why I rarely shift to that form now. When she was alive, I remember thinking, *I want to be like her.* She would go off for a run, and I would go with her. She would be a tiger, and I would be her cub. She would always laugh and tell me that I was the cutest little cub she had ever seen. She told me I had great control to be able to shift already to such a powerful form. I was only six years old.

"I'll never forget the last time we went out as tigers. We weren't living with a clan at the time. My father was away talking to the Braden Clan, trying to find just which clan had the most of our kind. My mother took me out because I kept complaining about how my skin felt itchy, which is natural for our young. They can't control their bodies too well, and shifting brings relief. Sometimes we just need to shift. Not doing so can leave our skin feeling constricted and our muscles tight.

"I could have just changed my human form, but I wanted to run with my mom. I wanted to play, to hear her say what a good cub I was. But I was too young to know the significance of a full moon that night. Werewolves were out. We didn't know they were in our forest. And going out as tigers … well, there was an attack.

"My mother protected me the best she could. But there were too many. I watched as they tore her to pieces. It didn't matter that our kind regenerates and heals faster. They were swift. And I was small and powerless. I tried to help. But even the young wolf I fought was too much for me. Bastard bit me bad in my leg. I lost a lot of blood. Things became hazy and I panicked. I couldn't think straight. And my blood was everywhere, so while she was fighting, I ran. I shifted into a small bird and flew up into the trees. I didn't make it far. Once they left, I flew back to her. But there was nothing I could do.

"My father found us the next morning. She in her human form, and I curled in her arms as a baby tiger.

"The look on his face that morning, it was as if the world had ended. All the love and warmth I knew before drained out of him, leaving only a cold shell. His mouth was perpetually turned down into a scowl. I think he was terrified I was dead that day, when he saw me curled in her arms. So when he found I was alive … well, the rest of his life, he couldn't stop pushing me. He forced me to be better than the rest. He wanted me to be able to protect myself. He demanded that I be more. I became a killer. You unfortunately, my beautiful girl, are making me feel things I haven't felt in a very long time. Things that I chose not to feel."

I sighed and pressed my face to the top of her head. I held her tight. It wasn't just that I was helping her; she was healing me as well. I understood this, but it was hard not being scared. There was so much I could lose, especially if … especially if I eventually had to let her go.

"You make me so much more than I am."

I had fallen asleep stroking her hair, and the memories faded into the nothingness of my slumber. I woke sometime later to a weight on my chest. I blinked a couple times. Was I seeing things right? Audrey smiled, her lips pulled tightly across her face, her scars bunching together, her chin on my chest. Her clear eye sparkled in the light of the room.

"Beautiful," I whispered, my eyes searching her face closely. She shyly hid her face in my chest. Tender giggles shook her body.

"What? What is it?" I asked. I wanted to laugh along with her. I wanted to share every good thing with her.

"Nothing."

She peeked up at me, her voice muffled as she spoke into my shirt. What I wouldn't have given to be bare-chested in that moment. I wanted to feel the silky touch of her lips on my skin. But I pushed that thought away. Now was not the time. I reached out and touched her face. I couldn't help myself; I found myself touching her all the time.

A comfortable, reflective quiet reigned between us. Audrey laid her head down, her eyelids falling heavier with each blink. Her breathing deepened. I wondered why she had kept the secret she had shared for so long. Why should she endure all that she did alone?

"Did you always know you were a dragon?"

I focused my eyes on the hand I ran through her locks. The glossy strands slipped between my fingers. I kept combing and watching.

"I'm nothing special. I never have been."

"Why do you say that?" I asked.

"I could never be what he wanted me to be."

It was sudden, the emotion that choked and strangled her voice. A faint glimmer of light came from the tears collecting in her eyes.

"You are more than I could have ever hoped for."

The words slipped out, without warning, without hesitation. She removed her hand from its position over my heart. I wondered if she could feel how hard it was beating. She made no indication that she did, though.

Her slim, long leg nudged mine. My breathing grew heavy. Being with her like this, I wasn't sure how I was controlling myself. There were certain things, though, that I *couldn't* control. I knew that I had to be careful. She was still so fragile. I never wanted to push her beyond what she was ready for. But her long hair fanned like a curtain around us. We were in our own little world. Nothing could harm her. Nothing could harm me.

"You're extraordinary. I could live for a thousand years and never understand how you could possibly look at me like that."

With openness and love I don't deserve, I added silently. She leaned down, her whole body pushing against mine. I loved feeling her against me, loved feeling her pressing close.

"I've never felt strong before you," she whispered as she pulled away.

I smiled sheepishly at that.

"I should go. I wouldn't want your father to find me in here."

I wanted to stay. I wanted to stay with her forever. And I wanted her father to know that I had been here, had spent the night with her.

That she was *mine.*

***

An hour later there was a knock at my door. I opened the door to find the Valkyrie we had thrown into the cell. Her lips were pressed in a tight line, her eyes pinched in annoyance. She nodded to me, an indication of begrudging respect. She would be my escort to our meeting with Xavier.

Upon entering the room, I made a mental sweep of the layout and people present. At least two possible exits, but we were sorely outnumbered. The Valkyrie stood near the door, allowing me to pass by and enter the room. It wasn't exactly spacious, but all York's men made it feel claustrophobic. The large conference table was crowded with both York's people and our small crew. Audrey sat sandwiched between York and Drake on the far side of the table. Audrey's hair was brushed over her shoulders, covering a majority of her face. The sight of this sent a pang of anger through me. That was how she hid from the world, and she seemed submissive and sad. At the cabin she had kept it pulled back. Seeing her revert back to her old habits caused my gut to tighten and my skin to itch.

York sat tall and proud to her left. He was, after all, the one who called the meeting. He didn't take his eyes off of me as I continued to stand in the doorway, carefully debating where I should sit. Drake sat closer to Audrey, his body turned toward her, but still keeping a watchful eye on the room.

Nixie looked far too comfortable, leaning back in her seat, one hand draped over the armrest. She sat on the opposite side of the table of Audrey, closer to me. She had a wicked gleam in her eye, and when she looked up at me, her smile widened.

She lifted her hand to wave, bringing up an attached arm. Shining on her wrist was a handcuff attached to one of the were-cheetah twins. The same ones from at the cabin that we had also locked into cells.

The were-cheetah's lips were twisted, and his eyes were sour. Perhaps his punishment was to babysit Nixie because of his mishap earlier? While Nixie appeared relaxed on the surface, her legs weren't crossed like usual. They were tucked under her chair as if at any moment she was ready to jump up and run. Seeing that we were hopelessly outnumbered and divided, I chose to take the seat next to Nixie.

Nixie slouched back into her seat as I settled into place. She had a special hatred for the York Clan. I didn't know the full history. I only knew that she always worked extra hard on cases that would hurt the Yorks.

I looked to Audrey, whose eyes had a hardened a little. There was something more in the set of her shoulders, in the tilt her chin. A new defiance was growing inside of her.

The door clicked open again. Elijah entered the room, taking it in with disinterest as the male Zana followed in after him.

"Good, now that we are all here, I think it is time to get down to business."

York's voice boomed through the small space and I saw Audrey flinch. Her eyes sought out mine. Though I wore a blank mask, seeing her look for me for support made me sit just a little taller.

Elijah took his time finding a seat, and York watched him carefully. I thought back to what he said. I internally scoffed at the idea. Paranormals coming back from extinction was impossible, wasn't it? But … my gaze wandered to Drake. Then to the other oddities of the room. This clan itself was run by a gargoyle.

"A few centuries back, when the Council still ruled, there was a coup to overthrow the Elder Races. The massacre that occurred was started by the ruling clans. Now they are trying to kill off any other rare paranormal they consider a threat. My clan has known for a long time about the

240

surviving paranormals. Recently we have doubled our efforts in trying to locate them. To save them from Cain Braden or Abram Vedenin. Cain would see them destroyed, and Abram wants to control them."

"And what do you gain from all this?" I asked cautiously looking to Audrey. Would she be in danger in his care?

"Nothing. You should know that even my race isn't as abundant as we once were. Most have only been able to survive as a part of our clan. It is my birthright, as a member of a nearly extinct race, to take care of the other dying races. Other clans only want to destroy them or to control them."

"And where is your proof?" Nixie asked, her voice steel. She was eying him with suspicion. It only made sense. He was, after all, accusing our clan of something horrific.

"Here is proof enough, siren."

A file slapped on the table and slid toward us.

"If paper documents aren't enough for you, you could always ask your wraith friend right there."

York's purple eyes met Elijah's. My jaw tightened as I turned to Elijah.

"What the fin is he talking about, Elijah?" Nixie demanded.

"Cain had ordered Jacobs to eliminate Audrey. It would both weaken the Vedenin Clan and expunge her kind from this world." Elijah was watching Audrey as he said this, her skin had taken an ashy pale color. Her throat visibly constricted. I wanted to go to her, but I remained in my seat. I turned back to Elijah.

"You knew about this?"

"Of course. Jacobs wasn't planning on killing her right away, since she never showed any promise while captive with Abram. Jacobs was ordered by Cain to have our team gain her trust to find out where her father was hiding. We were behind the Vedenin Clan all these years. The only reason they had Audrey and not us was because we failed to extract Audrey before they did."

Slowly, Elijah's black gaze met Drake's. Elijah's head cocked slightly to the side.

"Her father was waiting for us and destroyed half the team. Then, the Vedenins arrived and took Audrey away."

"My father died on that trip," Nixie whispered, looking up at Drake. There was no sympathy for her in his eyes. Tears shined openly in hers.

"When Cain found out where they were keeping Audrey, he had Jacobs go find her. The real mission was always to retrieve Audrey. It's only coincidence that you and Dallas found her first and decided to take her. When Jacobs realized that gaining her trust through you and Nixie wasn't going to work, he decided to raise the bar a little.

"The next step was torture."

The room fell deadly silent. Audrey wasn't looking at anyone, anymore. Instead she had retreated into the far-away place in her mind that I had seen in her before. She sat a little farther from the table now, her hands twisted in her lap.

Without speaking or looking at anyone, she rose from her seat. Nixie was sitting on the edge of her seat.

"I swear, I had no idea ..." Nixie spoke quietly.

Audrey shook her head and left the room.

I stood as the door shut, considering my options. Stay here and listen to more of what York had to say, or reassure Audrey that the information we had learned was new to us? York was watching me, his jaw set. And when he looked away? That was all the permission I needed to go after her.

Chapter 35

AUDREY

Elijah's words echoed through my head. *Their* clan had planned on using me all along. Their *family*. I wanted to trust Nixie and Gabriel. I wanted to believe with all my heart that they didn't know, but hadn't Gabriel told me that he was a bad man? Was this another trick? A new form of torture? It was impossible to let go the fears that had burrowed so deeply into my heart. They had become part of who I was.

"Audrey!" Stone's voice was gruffer than usual.

I didn't stop. I kept walking away, not sure where I was going, but I knew that seeing him would unravel me. I was in shock after finding out that his clan had worked so hard and so long to kill my father and me just because of what we were. Because of something we couldn't control.

When he told me the story about his mother without realizing I had been awake, I had thought something new was beginning between us. I had pretended to be asleep, but I was sure he would tell his story again to my face when he was ready. Which was something I could completely understand. Trusting someone was difficult. To give them a piece of your heart in such a way was dangerous.

Thing was, I already had.

"Audrey, please!"

He caught up to me, his hand wrapped gently around my arm.

"Audrey, you know I was telling the truth. Tell me I wasn't. You can't, can you? Tell me that I'm lying to you when I say we had no idea, and I'll go away, I promise. But you know that isn't true. I would never have done that to you."

I looked up into his stormy grey eyes and saw regret, hatred, and disappointment. I hadn't meant to hurt him. But I felt overwhelmed. Drowning in uncertainty. My lungs burned for more air than I could give them. I felt terrible, even if I couldn't be sure if his disappointment was directed at me or his clan.

"You promised you would never hurt me," I whispered, looking away.

Slowly he moved his body closer to mine, herding me into an alcove in the wall. He grabbed my chin gently and forced my eyes back to his.

"And I meant that."

His voice was strong with conviction.

"Tell me how I can and I will make it right."

His eyes, turned a murky brown color. Total disgust.

"To your clan, your family, I'm nothing more than a monster among beasts."

"No. Not to me. You're good, Audrey. You have a light inside of you, one that I let dim years ago."

He pressed his forehead against mine and squeezed his eyes shut as he shook his head back and forth.

"I don't deserve you. You're too good for me. I could never see you that way. Gods, how could I? You, who survived so much and somehow kept your compassion." His hand was on my heart, his eyes clouded with teal tenderness. "If I regret anything in my life, it was losing my humanity for this long."

I didn't know what to say to him. What could I say? It was clear now. He seemed to be lost and as scared as I was.

A spark of courage ignited within me. I gripped the back of his head and pressed my lips against his. It was fierce. It was a kind of kiss that there was no returning from. How could there be anything better than this? He took control. I felt his hands at my hips. They slid gently around my body and under my backside, lifting me up. My legs naturally slipped around his waist. My hands ran through his hair. I couldn't get enough. His

244

tongue invaded my mouth while his hips ... Gods, his hips moved with a hungry kind of instinct. My body responded without a thought.

Gabriel pulled me away from the wall, walking blindly. Neither of us cared much where we ended up. We clung together, hungry, our lips seeking desperately. Lips, cheek, neck—it didn't matter. As long as I could touch him, feel him, everything else was forgotten. He fumbled for a doorknob with me still in his arms. I laughed lightly against his neck as I kissed it. A weightless sensation filled my heart. I had never felt so free before.

The door opened to what I now recognized as my room. He shut the door with his foot and laid me on the bed. My body hummed with a whole new feeling. I was floating, but Gabriel's weight kept me anchored.

My heart couldn't race any faster. His lips never left mine, slowly his weight pressed softly against me. He gently pushed my legs apart, settling between them. With a renewed ferocity, he kissed me again. I breathed him in.

These new emotions were overwhelming. I felt a tension building in a new and exciting way. His hand skimmed the edge of my shirt. He was waiting for permission. Waiting to make sure everything was okay. Covering his hand with mine, I pulled it against my skin, no longer frightened to inaction by the memories. He groaned once more and I sighed. The heat of his skin burned into mine. I never realized how cold my skin was until he touched me.

As his hand moved up, I squirmed. He was coming close to more scars, scars he didn't know about. He lightly touched their puckered edges.

He didn't pull away or look at me with disgust. Instead, his hand kept moving, touching the ugliest parts softly. To me the scars were revolting, but he drew away from my lips to bend down and kiss each of them. He tasted the skin there, letting his tongue run along the edges and ridges.

I was breathing hard, trying to process all the new sensations. His other hand had moved to my breast. My body tingled with excitement, yet at the same time, some dark remnant of my past made me unnerved having his hand there. Slowly, breath filled my lungs, causing my breast to move deeper into his hold. His hand cupped me gently. He brushed his thumb over my erect, sensitive nub. My body jerked.

"Wh-what are you doing to me?" I stuttered. My entire body was humming. The warmth from his hands tingled through me in lusty tremors. Sparking newfound feelings inside me. My voice came out breathy. Barely even there. I felt his chest rumble with laughter, and he placed my hand over his heart. It was beating in time with my own.

"More like what are you doing to me?" he whispered, trailing kisses across bare skin and shirt alike, reaching my face, again. "I don't want you to feel like we have to go any farther right now. I hope you know that. I want to take things slow with you."

His eyes were full of understanding.

While I didn't tell him exactly what had happened in the stone room, the one I had been tortured in, he knew of it. He had managed to coax many things out of me during our time at the cabin. I still hadn't learned much about his past, but he'd told me some of his stories.

I bit my lip looking away for a moment, my mind racing. The weight of his body wasn't the same as those guards. They didn't want me like Stone did. He wouldn't hurt me. He wouldn't pin me down, or force himself on me. He was tender. Coaxing.

"I ... I'm okay," I whispered. Stone watched me with eyes the deep purple of desire. I was hoping to see a different color. A color I was certain was in my own.

"Audrey, I want this." He looked at me when saying this. "More than anything. But I think that we should wait. There are still things that need to be discussed."

It was almost as if there was something else he wanted to say. Instead, he placed a lingering kiss on my lips. Before I knew it, my hands were tearing his shirt upward, pulling it off without a thought. My cheeks burned hot, and I turned my head a little, feeling shy. His fingertips brushed against my jaw, bringing me back to him.

"No, no. We don't have to. It's okay. When this happens, it will be beautiful. It will be passionate. And I promise when we take that step, I'll make you feel like you never have before."

I twisted my legs self-consciously.

"I want to make love to you. I want you to forget the scars of your past forever. I want you to only think of me."

He placed a small kiss on my lips and pulled away, putting on his Stone face. The moments we had alone, the moments he made me feel like nothing else mattered, like I was beautiful, in these moments he was Gabriel. Open and loving. Other times, like now, he was Stone. Unmoving and unfeeling. Even when he joked around, he kept a distance between him and the others. He was so unlike Nixie, who openly and willingly let people into her life with her easy smile and warm heart.

Stone grabbed my hand, and we headed back to the conference room. I was surprised how easily he found it. I was lost as soon as we left my room.

When we returned to the meeting, Nixie was yelling from her seat at Elijah who sat unflinching. Xavier was sitting watching them, but his eyes flashed over to Stone and me. I could see the displeasure in his eyes as well as the flux of colors: the red of his anger and slate grey of his disapproval. My father was nowhere to be seen.

"Good, you're back. Your father went looking for you," Xavier said. I felt Stone's hand tighten around mine. I don't think he realized he did it, but being reminded of him there beside me gave me the extra courage I needed. I moved to sit with him instead of in the seat I had before. The seat I was *expected* to take.

Nixie sat a little straighter, her eyes were still heated with anger, but there was pride in her eyes when they alighted upon me. The guard that had been handcuffed to her remained unyielding. Nixie's ability to act as if she was in charge was admirable, but also made me worry for her. So far, all Xavier had done was attempt to be reasonable and diplomatic. I feared the reason he kept Nixie handcuffed. Could it be because of her bond with me?

"Oh, my little guppy! I was so worried about you!"

She kissed my cheek. She pulled away and her coral eyes were shining brightly. At the same time, I heard Stone settle into his chair and start flipping through the file York had pushed across the table to us before we left.

"One of your team members, Cole, was sent on a mission to find a rumored rebirthed paranormal. Whichever elder race it was, I'm not entirely sure. But from the intel that my inside operative gave me, it seems that Cain was, and still is, willing to follow up any sort of lead."

Looking up from the file, Stone raised a brow at Xavier. It was unusual for a clan to give information away so freely.

"I keep a close eye on my enemy. I figured you didn't know the real reason for the separation of your team after you found Audrey."

"What would they gain by killing these rebirthed paranormals off?" Stone asked.

"Power. What else?" Xavier said with a derisive snort. "Right now our clan is revered even among the most influential families. Sure, the Braden Clan and Long Clan are at our heels. But the Longs keep to their Asian countries and roots. The Braden Clan, on the other hand, seems be getting restless. They want to expand their territory here in the states. And they have consistently taken in the most ... prejudiced of people. We, on the other hand, do not discriminate."

"No. That can't be true. That's a lie—it must be! My father was a good man. A kind man. And he was respected by Jacobs. There's no way he'd be a part of something like that." Nixie's voice was dangerous in its quietness. Like the calm before the storm. I doubt she even saw me. Her eyes bored holes into York with a deadly fire.

"No, siren. I was saying there is a higher chance of this happening within the Braden Clan. Narrow minded and scared paranormals fear the return of older, more powerful ones. Isn't it sad? How *human* our kind acts sometimes," York said those words as an afterthought, but Nixie took it to heart. She was obviously insulted.

Nixie ran her tongue between her teeth. Her hands pressed down upon the table and pushed herself into a standing position.

"You know what? I think it's time for me to leave."

"Nixie, sit down. If there is some concrete evidence here, we need to at least hear him out. What if Cain is getting out of hand? You know how proud he is."

I could tell right away he wasn't going to win this argument with Nixie.

"You don't get a say in this, shape-shifter," Nixie's jaw tightened. She reached between her and her guard and snapped the metal on her wrist in half. Xavier stood, his tail twitching, his gaze darting between the broken metal and her dark, fierce eyes.

"No need, York. I will escort myself out, thank you."

Nixie walked out of the room. Xavier simply nodded to the guard. He rose silently and followed her out of the room.

"Wait."

Xavier looked at me, small flecks of rust-red, displaying his anger growing. The vein in his neck pulsed and his nostrils flared.

"Let me talk to her," I said.

He paused a moment, considering.

"Fine."

I chased after her, but Nixie was already turning a corner when I finally got out of the door.

"Nixie!" I called. It was strange that I was the one doing the chasing now. But she didn't even turn to respond.

"You will never understand, my little guppy, so don't even try. And if you want me to go back into that room with that clam-headed asshole, there's not a chance."

She kept walking away as she spoke, her flip-flops clacking loudly every time her foot stomped down onto the ground. I had seen her angry before, but never this angry.

"Please … you're … you're my best friend," I said. She stopped. I could see her fists tighten and her back stiffen.

"Oh, guppy … why did you have to go and say that? Why? Why? Why?" she muttered as she turned on her heel. Nixie walked back to me and pulled me into a hug. "Fine. I won't leave you. But I *am* letting that blowhole know that I'm only coming back for you."

The dark rage that had colored her coral eyes didn't dim, but I guess her loyalty to me ran deeper. I couldn't help but feel a little bad for doubting her earlier. There was a deep pain in her eyes. It was the color of a fresh bruise. I knew better than to ask. A past pain wasn't something you forced out of someone. Like ripping off a Band-Aid that wasn't ready, it pulled on your skin, brought unnecessary tears to your eyes, and made it all the more painful to feel.

We entered the conference room again. Xavier wore his irritation like a sneer. Nixie and I took our seats next to Stone.

"How did you do that?" Xavier asked, looking sidelong at the half handcuff that still dangled from Nixie's wrist. Nixie shifted in her seat, and instead of answering, she leaned her elbow onto the table and put her chin into the upturned cup of her hand. Breathing loudly through his nose, Xavier accepted he wasn't getting answers from her now.

"Elijah."

Xavier put his hand out to indicate for Elijah to continue. Stone sat rigidly. I tried to find his hand with my own under the table, but when I did, it was balled up in a fist. Finding no response to my touch at his hand, I placed my hand on his thigh instead. He seemed to relax a little at last, which brought a small smile to my face.

"After that incident—" Nixie straightened like she was about to say something, but Elijah turned his cold glare on her and she shut her mouth without a word being said. I heard her mumble under her breath that he was a blowhole.

"Cain dedicated a whole team to finding and destroying these rare paranormals, but when rumors surfaced about old paranormal races returning, he decided to take things to the next level. To do that he needed to find Audrey and find out what she knew."

Elijah was leaving a lot out. I knew because he had come into contact with my memories when he pushed the other wraith from my head. No one had mentioned this so far, so maybe that might not be common knowledge? I didn't want to bring it up.

"So there you have it. Straight from one of your own clan. Will you stay or will you go?" Xavier turned his eyes onto Nixie and Stone.

"You know what you are asking us, right? You want us to turn our backs on our clan? To betray the people who have been like family to us for our entire lives?" Nixie asked, the blood draining from her face as she said this. Stone's jaw had started to twitch.

"Maybe they could have some time to think about it," I offered, looking at Xavier. It was strange, but his eyes softened when they looked at me. A small smile formed on his lips.

"Yes, they can think about it." He turned his attention to my friends. "You have a week to decide to stay or leave."

Chapter 36

STONE

A week wasn't a very long time to decide whether or not to betray the people who had raised me. What I had done, leaving with Audrey, was punishable. But in time they would forgive. When I had left, I had every intention of returning. I just needed time to think. Or perhaps, deep down, I already knew there was no going back. Not anymore.

After the meeting, I went with Audrey back to her room where she curled up next to me and fell asleep. I knew that these shocks were taking their toll on her. She wasn't used to all this excitement. Five years in isolation didn't allow for a lot of action. Just thinking about that made me grind my teeth together.

Things were crashing down around me. The loyal choice was to take her from here and back to my family, back to my clan. But how could I do that in light of the evidence York showed me? I thought about earlier today when we were in this very room. I still remembered that heat of desire. It was more than lust though.

Unconsciously, she wrapped her legs around my waist and instinct took over. My hips met her. I couldn't control myself. I was hungry for anything I could have from her. When she realized, she let out a gasp I don't think she intended. Not that I cared. I finally allowed myself to succumb to my tunnel vision. I wanted her. Gods, her skin was so smooth, and when I touched her scars, the scars that Nixie had warned me about, I felt the passion mix with a kind of rage.

It was a kind of anger that desired nothing more than to rip the person apart who had done this to her. A desire to protect. Those scars reminded me of our time together at the cabin. Where she had told me some about the *dark room* as she called it. But I could tell what she wasn't telling me.

A year of being abused in the worst ways. I almost stopped at that thought, but my body wouldn't have it. Not only was I painfully hard, but touching her skin was as relieving as jumping into the cool ocean on a hot summer's day.

Even though I wanted to destroy whoever had marred her skin, I didn't think any less of her. She was beautiful, inside and out, in my eyes. And I had to taste that, to taste *her*. I kissed every inch I could. Soon I'd lose all control. I looked down at her, her lips parted, her chest heaving. Audrey's eyes were half-lidded, half asleep, but even so, they were full of intelligence. As I watched her, I realized I wanted more than her body. I wouldn't accept anything less than all of her.

Audrey was curled on the right side of me. I looked over at her. I should have been asleep hours ago, but it was impossible to sleep. She brought me an odd sense of belonging, my heart always racing at the sight of her. She made me want to be more than who I'd become. She made me want to be better.

I couldn't help but think of my years before her. The endless victims of my past. Faceless, nameless people that all pleaded with me to stop. And they always did. They always *begged* me, because my kind had a skill other paranormals lacked. True, we all had our strengths, but a shifter could use a person's greatest fear against them. They would shriek. They would call for help. They would promise anything, as long as you gave them peace from their living nightmare.

Nothing was safe from me. That past was a part of me. Audrey's words from our first few days together hung in my mind. It was hard to believe how much had transpired and how little time had passed since I met her.

She asked me if those people had been innocent. The ones I tortured. They were punished for being from a different clan. In some cases, they knew things that they shouldn't. But I was removed from all that. I was a tool, one that was exceptionally useful. I was what my father had made me, a perfect weapon. Were he alive, I would have made him proud.

I had become untouchable. Nothing could break me. That's why the other shape-shifters had nicknamed me Stone. Nicknames were common among my kind. It was a way we prevented fey from controlling us with our names. My nickname reflected how, even under the most drastic of circumstances, I remained calm.

At first I had thought the nickname referred to the amount of torture I had endured myself. Just like stone, I was unbreakable. But in hindsight, I bet they had meant something else. Maybe those glances weren't in admiration. Maybe they were because I was a monster among beasts. A soulless creature created by Jacobs and my father.

I pulled Audrey closer. She made me better. She made me want to be good. She reminded me that even though people weren't always innocent, that there were lines to be drawn. Lines that shouldn't ever be crossed. What gave Cain the right to want to torture her for information about her only living family?

Isn't that what I had to be debating all along? Whether or not I wanted to stay with the people I considered my family. Or if I should I remain here with this magnificent creature in my arms.

She was already back asleep. A little moan escaped her lips and she twisted. Gods, I wanted to take her nightmares away. But instead of a pained look on her face or a tear falling from her closed eyes, I saw a small smile take form. She wasn't having a nightmare. No, for once she appeared to be having a good dream. Something she deserved.

I was singing to her before I even realized it. It was the same lullaby my mother used to sing to me as a child.

***

The next day was less eventful, but Elijah had come by Audrey's room to speak with her privately elsewhere. I needed to have a talk with

Nixie. So I left Audrey's room before they came back. I didn't know how long they would be gone, but I figured Audrey would find the note I left telling her I went to get some air. On my way to find Nixie I found old memories resurfacing. Things I hadn't thought about in a long time. Things I'd rather forget.

My father treated me like nothing more than a trophy. I was the thing he paraded around, so proud to call me son. He had lost any real love or affection for me when I was only seven years old. I think it would have hurt less if I didn't know he could care, but I remembered from before. My mother, he, and I always had a pleasant life. Those days had come to an end early. After that, in his eyes, I could always be better. I could be one step faster. I could be a little stronger. He had demanded perfection, and that is what I gave him. Nothing less. If there was more, he would have demanded that of me as well, and I would have gladly striven for it.

But I didn't push myself to my limits for him or myself. I had done it for her. Always for her. My mother.

She was the only person I couldn't save. After losing her, it was an easy decision if it meant choosing between hurting others and saving those close to me. If there had been a question between the two, I would do it. At my worst, my black heart didn't feel anything. Nothing except for physical sensations. Nothing except the oily warmth of blood as it spattered onto me. I would wipe it off and move on. I had no remorse for anything I had done.

Only what I had not done. Could not do. Her. It always came back to her.

My mother often sang to me. I remembered the song well. It was a sweet tune, but also a little sad in the way lullabies usually are. She would sing it to me when she gave me a bath or tucked me in at night. At times, I could hear her singing it when she thought she was alone. She had wanted another child, but there were complications with my birth. I would be her only one. That was another thing that I took away from her.

I found myself singing that song in my head whenever my father was showing me off. The proudest day of my father's life was when I was admitted into the Braden Clan's protective services and Jacobs' special ops team.

That night I had been dragged around by my father. He would slap me on the back and tell everyone how proud he was. How proud my mother would be if she were still alive. He still called me his "survivor." I hated when he called me that. It made my teeth grind and my whole body tense. But long ago I had realized that whenever I sang her song in my head, I was calmed.

I had become a person who could only take. I could never give.

The memory was clear for only a moment before it evaporated before my eyes. Nixie was nowhere to be found, not that I had any idea where to look for her. She wasn't in her room, but as I searched I was lucky enough to run into the Zeke. I asked if he had seen Nixie. I assumed she was still free from her were-cheetah chaperone after her display with the handcuffs. I doubt Xavier would want to piss her off any more than she already was. Zeke told me he saw her head out on the north-wing courtyard, so I headed that way hoping to find her still there.

I found her outside, not far from the building. The figure pacing the fringes of the yard had to be her. The courtyard was lush with greenery, but a subtle shimmer spanned its perimeter. It was warded. But were they keeping us in or keeping others out? The wind blew softly, coaxing me from those thoughts. As I approached her, I was surprised by the look of peace in her coral eyes, even if they did shine with moisture. They were the eyes of someone reflecting on something far, far away.

"Have you decided?" I asked, moving next to her, crossing my arms.

"So many reasons to stay, so many to leave."

Nixie straightened her back. Titling her jaw up, she breathed in. Silence reigned between us for what seemed like a long time. The weight of our decision was heavy upon both of us.

"You're different with her," Nixie paused. "Better. You look happy."

"Are you trying to tell me I should stay?"

Nixie let out a delicate snort.

"You weren't ever planning on leaving. It was obvious the moment you met her. Where she goes, you go."

My jaw tightened, my teeth pressing against each other. My frustration at myself was starting to wear on me. I had prided myself on being so unmovable. But that façade was beginning to crumble now. Everyone was starting to see me more clearly. It was an uncomfortable thing for a shape-shifter to feel. Being *known* wasn't something my kind cared for. At the same time, I had no desire to be the man I once was. He had all but dimmed in my memory, until he was nothing more than a shameful shadow.

"And you?"

"I don't know, guppy. Let's see where the tides take me."

* * *

Audrey and I were headed toward the kitchen. We had our own tail in the form of Zeke. And then Drake appeared. I felt Audrey twitch reflexively, and I could tell she wanted to hide behind me, behind anything, really. But she stayed where she was. My thoughts of Drake had been few and far between in light of our current situation. Seeing him stomp toward his daughter now, I couldn't help wondering at what supposedly extinct creature he was ... and what Audrey was.

"We start your training in the morning," Drake said. His eyes flicked between us, showing obvious displeasure at our physical contact. Regarding me, he stated as though commenting on the weather, "If it wasn't for Xavier, I would kill you for touching her."

I seethed at that.

"She's not your possession." I ground the words out between gritted teeth. I wouldn't cower before him. Imposing as he was, I stood my ground. Stood tall.

"Careful what you say, boy."

With a final glance at Audrey, who still stood her ground, he pushed roughly by.

"You shouldn't have said that," came Audrey's tiny voice.

"Why? It's true. He isn't your keeper. You're not his."

"You don't understand what he's like. You just ... don't understand." She sounded so defeated. Her right hand began to quest out, searching blindly for ridges or threads or something to count.

"You can tell me," I whispered back. I took the hand in mine, putting an end to its nervous crawling. I placed a kiss on her knuckles to hopefully settle those nerves.

"I ... well ... I don't know how to say this but ..."

This was difficult for her. She swallowed hard. Her desire for escape was keen in her eyes. I tightened my hold on her hand.

"We're dragon-shifters."

She looked up at me. Fear shined naked in her eyes.

Quietly I nodded. I masked my emotions with a carefully contrived expression. I wiped any traces of emotion from my face. My lips were lax, but not smiling. My eyes interested, but not greedy for more information. Inside, the shock of her words spiraled through me. Drake's possessiveness suddenly made more sense. Not that I condoned it, but his actions fit for the kind of paranormal he was. But delicate Audrey?

We continued on our way to the kitchen. I couldn't help but reevaluate Audrey again in my mind. From what I knew of dragon-shifters they were usually tall, their men built much like Drake. But even dragon women were tall, much taller than Audrey, not that she was short by any means.

"What did your father mean by 'training'?" I asked, still processing the fact that she was a dragon. Could it really be? I mean, it made sense in retrospect. That was why Abram had kept her locked up so tightly.

"I've never been able to shift." She looked away. "I gave up believing that I had a dragon form."

I held her hand. Dragon-shifters weren't the same as other *weres*—which could be said about all the Elder Races, really. In particular, dragon-shifters lived in a kind of unity with their animal spirit. They were never entirely human in their human form, and yet not entirely dragon in their dragon form either. The animal traits of were-creatures normally crossed over into their other half, creating a blended self even in their human and bestial form alike.

From what I remembered from fairy tales and childhood stories that involved the elder races, each held a special relationship with their paranormal spirit. Even were-creatures couldn't quite understand. Looking at her now, I realized how much deeper her pain must be than I had previously thought. She didn't even have the support that most paranormals received from being connected to their primal side. I pulled her close and she buried her face into my chest.

"What do you know about dragons, Audrey?"

"Only that they're hoarders. That their possessions are sacred. That stealing from them is almost certain death. My father never talked about our heritage, seeing how I might never be able to shift …" She trailed off, nuzzling a little deeper.

"I know a story about the first dragon-shifter. I heard it a long time ago. Would you like to hear it?"

I felt her nod into the crook of my neck.

"He was a dragon, black skinned and as the unforgiving night sky. Just as cruel, too, so the story goes. He would protect his horde fiercer than any other dragon, and even killed other dragons when they got too close. He attacked human villages that trespassed too close. One human village, desperate to prevent this fate, decided that maybe if they sent a virgin offering, he would leave them alone."

We continued walking through the cafeteria toward the kitchen. Audrey settled on a barstool that stood at the island in the large kitchen. It was a much smaller affair than the one back home. Or, rather, at the Braden Clan's home. And as I told her this story, I found myself on auto-pilot, preparing food for the both of us. Zeke sat on the other side of the room, giving us room, but making it obvious he was supposed to keep us in sight.

"Though this great, black dragon was known for killing humans without blinking an eye, he did *not* kill the woman who was sent to him as an offering. He had instantly fallen in love with her, with her long blonde locks and her pale brown eyes. She had pleaded with the dragon not to harm her family or village, even though they had sent her as a sacrifice. This made her even more beautiful in the eyes of the dragon, who had never seen such selflessness. He promised her home would be safe. After all, he had never seen someone so beautiful. He decided to keep her as he would a gem or any other precious jewels. But, unlike jewels, a woman can get sad. And she was sad—and broken, too.

"Over time, the dragon started to feel the same way, but he couldn't understand why. He thought that someone had stolen something from him. And so he went out and searched for a jewel he had convinced himself was missing. He destroyed towns and killed livestock. He murdered any man who resisted him. He only thought of his missing possession. He only cared for his missing jewel.

"While he was out, the woman, who had all but become a part of his collection, left his horde. She returned home only to find that it had been destroyed. Hurt by the dragon's betrayal of his promise to not hurt her family, she sought out the dragon. When she finally found him, he looked down at her and instantly realized he had found his missing jewel. That she had become his most precious thing. But she was brokenhearted and told him that she never wanted to see him again. He felt his heart break at these words. He couldn't understand a love that was different from his treasures. But seeing her tears, he let her go and flew back to his cave.

"For years, he mourned the loss of his most precious possession. He pleaded with the gods day and night to let him talk to her, human to human. And eventually, the gods took pity on him and granted him the gift of shifting. He flew down from his caves, leaving his jewels unprotected and forgotten, and went wholeheartedly after his love. When he found her, she had aged considerably, but he didn't care.

"He confessed to her that she was his most precious jewel, and that she would always be the rarest gem in his eyes. He began to explain that he hadn't attacked her family, but it came to pass that she had already forgiven him. She had heard from a local farmer that it had been a red dragon that had attacked her old home. She had missed her dragon, who she had come to love herself. She had missed him every day since she left.

"They lived many years together. He never aged, but she continued to grow older every day. Even so, he told her how beautiful she was, and she always believed him because it was true. But then the day came when it was time for her to leave this world. He didn't want to give her up. Couldn't bear the thought of living without her. And so he shifted into his dragon form and did something that was meant to be secret among dragons only. He plunged his claw into his chest, ripped out half his heart, and he offered it to his beloved. Years melted away. Soon she was the same age she had been the day they met.

And they lived happily ever after."

I looked over to where she was sitting and could see tears in her eyes.

"What's the matter?" I asked. It was hard not rushing over to her when I saw her like that, but I could tell she wasn't feeling the kind of pain she needed me for. I wouldn't do her any favors by coddling her. I continued my search for ingredients on my side of the counter.

"It's a beautiful story," she whispered. "I wonder …"

She twisted her hands together, her brows pushed together in thought. The cafeteria had a few bay windows, and the natural light diffused through the room from them. The angle of the setting sun sent an errant ray to shine on her. She shifted in her seat. I didn't want to have to coax the words out of her. She needed to be able to feel comfortable speaking her mind in front of me.

"I wonder if my father felt the same way about my mother."

Her lashes lifted, revealing eyes shining with hope.

I couldn't help myself this time. I went around and took her hands in mine and brought them to my lips. She blinked away her tears, and with it, the sadness there. Her expression softened into something closer to affection.

"I'm positive your father loved her more than anything," I whispered, pulling her head into my chest and stroking the back of her head. I hoped that my words were true. And if they weren't, I hoped she never found out.

She was quiet for a long while after that. I rubbed her back, trailing my fingertips comfortingly across its surface. As she relaxed in my arms, I gave her a peck and then returned to my duties at the stove.

"I never asked him about her … does that make me a bad daughter?" Audrey asked. Empathy filled me. How many times had I thought that same thing? Audrey nervously ran her fingers across the veins of the countertop.

"No."

I had the urge to tell her about my mother's death. For the first time in my life, I wanted to tell someone about parts of me—parts that I thought I'd never share. But that was a story for another time. There was a better one for this moment.

"When I was about five years old, my mother would tell me that the best way to a girl's heart was to make her a special dinner. That very night," I looked up at her, she was smiling, leaning forward, excited to see what I had to say, "I made her a peanut butter and jelly sandwich. With the crust cut off, just the way I liked it."

I continued to stir the sauce I had been preparing.

"That's all? How did she react?"

Though her voice was light and free, there was a hint of annoyance. I smiled inwardly; she was obviously just as eager to learn about me as I her. Her eyes were bright, she sat close to the edge of her seat, wearing an eager smile.

"She looked down at me, smiled, and she pulled me onto her lap. Then she explained that I had done a selfless and wonderful thing. The problem was that I had made the sandwich the way I liked it. I should have thought of what she would have liked. She assured me that girls would always appreciate the effort, but going that extra mile, doing that extra little thing for them, for their sake, that's what would make my special someone fall in love with me."

I swallowed, wishing I had listened to my mother more. But wishing for the past was useless. There was no point in it.

"So I ran back to where I had left the crust and picked it up, offering it to her. She laughed and laughed. I miss hearing it—her laugh. It was the kind of laugh that made you want to join in."

I kept my attention trained on the sauce in front of me, but never really saw it. Instead, through the eyes of a child, I saw my mother.

Small hands moved around my waist. I recognized the lightly tanned skin. Her cheeks had been so hollow before. I was pleased with how her new diet was filling in the hollowness there. Her thin wrists looked healthier now. There was a glow about her skin. She no longer looked drawn and ashen pale. She was practically a new woman, and it all started at the cabin. Which reminded me of her conversation with Elijah. I was curious about what had been said. What had made the wraith act so out of character around her?

Tendrils of fear and jealousy started to take root deep in my gut. It was completely irrational for me to believe that Elijah would ever feel something romantic toward Audrey, that wasn't how wraiths worked. But … there was something there that made me uncomfortable. Wraiths didn't go out of their way to help someone without a price being paid.

Picking up the spoon from the sauce, I cupped my hand underneath it to catch any drips and held it out to Audrey. Her eyes darted between the spoon and me, her eyebrows rising.

"Open up."

And her beautiful lips parted. I wondered if, even after all these years, it still hurt to move the scarred part. If it did, if even the slightest pain remained, I wanted to kiss it away. Every time she had to move her lips, I wanted to kiss the pain away.

Her eyes were closed, thank the gods, because I knew my eyes were a dangerous mixture of desire and something warmer. Something I was hesitant to label. Something that scared me more than any mission or assignment. Love? I watched as she licked the sauce from her lips. A sweet smile tugged at their corners.

I tossed the spoon back into the sauce and leaned forward to capture her lips with mine. The sauce was still on her tongue, tangy and robust, and I shifted my torso a little to pull at her hips with my hands.

When she finally pulled back for air, I moved my lips from hers to the corner of her mouth. To the scarred part. I kissed there and moved down to her neck. She allowed me free range over the sensitive skin there. She panted heavy and tasted sweet. Lightly, she spoke to me.

"I really liked the sauce," she said with a laugh.

My lips met her smooth skin as a laugh of my own rumbled its way through my chest. The way she gripped my muscles as we kissed said more than her words possibly could. We had this effect on each other. I could barely contain myself as her lashes lowered over the tops of her rosy cheeks.

"I am glad you like it," I whispered, nuzzling her cheek, my own brushing against her smooth skin. She shuddered. I stepped back. If I kept touching her, or even if I thought too much about that memory I had shared, I would not be able to let her go.

"So what did you and Elijah talk about?" I asked keeping my attention on the food that I was preparing. Out of the corner of my eye Audrey's back straightened.

Chapter 37

AUDREY

What could I say? Earlier in the day Elijah had asked to speak with me. Stone's lips had pressed into a thin line at the request, but that didn't stop me from going to talk with Elijah.

Elijah and I walked through the hallways of Xavier's home. Each hallway was a carbon-copy of the one before. The place was strangely empty. Rarely did we pass anyone else, but that might have been Elijah's doing. He steered me one way or another down the labyrinth of identical corridors. He hadn't mentioned what he had wanted, and while I grew braver in the presence of Stone and Nixie, Elijah was completely different. Even my father, who I knew not to cross, I understood somewhat. But Elijah was cold, hard, and completely unfeeling. He was different, and I knew instinctively not to push him.

"I've decided to stay."

Elijah walked with hands tucked behind him. He never gave an indication that he was watching me, but the hairs on the back of my neck rose. Without a doubt he was watching me. Gauging my reactions.

I swallowed. Did he want me to say something? I had to admit, I was curious at his involvement in all this. If he had been there all those years ago when I was first taken, he had known Jacobs plan the entire time. What had changed? Why was he helping me now?

"You can ask me," Elijah stated. He kept his pace steady while I started to lag behind, distracted as I was by my racing thoughts.

"I don't understand ..." I picked up my pace so that I walked next to him. Before I finished the statement he actually sighed.

"There is something about you."

His words, the way his body tensed ever so slightly, it almost seemed like he was ... frustrated?

"I find you completely aggravating. I can't quite decide whether I should kill you for making me ..." He clipped the thought short without pausing in his stride. "Suffice to say, I found being in your mind enlightening."

Elijah stopped abruptly, twisting around so that he was facing me. My eyebrows raised in a question even as my heart skipped a beat in fear. With a single nod he strode away without another word. What was so "enlightening" about me? His dismissal didn't exactly invite further inquiry, so I headed back toward my room.

Stone cleared his throat, pulling me back to the present. He was standing on the other side of the counter in the kitchen, worry evident the irises of his eyes. They were a blue-grey color.

I told him about the whole encounter. Toward the end of my story, I noticed that his hand had tightened around his fork so much the skin there was white. I wished I could explain my encounter with Elijah in a way that made sense. But I had no idea what the wraith was trying to say. Our conversation left me more confused than ever.

"I'll leave with you, you know, if that is what you want," I whispered to him. I focused my attention on the green digits of the stove-clock. So steady and regular. Their soft glow comforted me. Their color steadied me.

My stomach tightened nervously as soon as I felt his soft touch. Would this be it? The thought was a horrid reflex I couldn't seem to stop in myself. Would now be the moment he told me he was done with me? How could he not? The fear stricken girl etched in scars, the one he had rescued—why would he pick me, a virtual stranger over his family? Dragging my bottom lip between my teeth, I bit down hard. How could I be allowed to keep a beautiful creature such as him?

"Audrey, all I want is you."

My heart hammered in my chest at his words. I couldn't breathe right. That rosy color, pearlescent in its smooth honesty tingled with streaks of cloud-white and blush-red, the color in his eyes that meant love, truly and without any hesitation; that meant more to me than anything else the world. It was the color I had longed to see. It didn't linger long, but it was impossible to miss. My heart stopped. It gave my body the feeling of being suspended, buoyant, expectant—like I was about to plunge into something new and wonderful.

Stone pushed away from the counter and came around to where I stood. I couldn't keep my eyes off of him. His gait was controlled. He was obviously holding himself back. He towered over me, him standing, me sitting. A fluttering weightlessness consumed me, and yet I felt grounded, small, and delicate. His hand caressed the scarred side of my face, tucking loose hair behind my ear. I leaned into the warmth of his hand, loving his touch as though it were something precious. And to me, it was.

"I wish you wouldn't hide."

I had closed my eyes, luxuriating at his touch, but then I flickered my lashes open. He watched me, steady and unmoving. I searched desperately for a confirmation of his feelings toward me. His eyes had changed to a stormy color, bruised purple that crested with deep and yearning maroon. Desire mixed with love. He leaned his head a little closer and placed a small kiss on my lips.

"I want you more than I have ever wanted anything else in my life."

My arms moved with a mind of their own. They pulled his lips to mine so hard that they bruised together. The kiss was frantic, passionate. It conveyed the story of his words more purely, more truly. Told a better story than his hands, which were already at my legs. His huge hands wrapped under my thighs and lifted me up. Before he had responded on instinct, thrusting his hips in response. But he cradled me against his body this time. I felt safe. I felt cherished.

"Gods, help me, Audrey. I love you."

We were moving, now. Swiftly and without trip, without incident, we made it back to my room, still locked in our embrace. Feather light kisses found their intended places, here and there. He scattered his across my face, and I trailed mine up the muscles in his arms. This was more than simple desire. And when he closed the door, no sound could have been sweeter than the lock clicking into place. Closing the door closed us off from the world. Nothing would disturb us.

He set me down gently on the bed. He was always so gentle with me. His hands were at the edge of my shirt, encouraging it off. I was giddy with excitement. His hands explored every exposed piece of skin as his eyes drank me in. But I knew by the heat in his eyes it wouldn't remain on for much longer.

His right hand trailed along the edges of my scars, along their cliffs and the shallow valleys they formed. Stone stood in front of me as I sat on the bed, waiting for him to come close again, to bring his heat. How was it fair that such a beautiful man would lie with me?

Stone bent at the waist, his arms creating a cage around me. The veins bugled and every muscle strained against his skin. He pressed his lips against mine, drawing me upwards to deepen the kiss. Following his upward motion, I arched my neck after him. The heat of his body was scintillating against my skin, my hands itched with the need to touch him.

Slipping my fingers under the edge of his shirt, the muscles there contracted and flinched at the sudden cold of my hands. I grew bold as my fingers warmed upon his heated skin. First my fingertips brushed against the smooth flesh under his shirt. Slowly I spread my fingers there. As I continued to lift myself off the bed to meet him, his shirt bunched against my wrist.

My bashful stare met his in a silent request for permission to take his shirt off. His breath came heavy as I helped him tug the shirt over his head. My hands traced the contours of his body, wonderfully sculpted, perfect in every way. It brought tears to my eyes. Why couldn't I be as unblemished as he?

Pulling away from the softness of my neck, he looked me right in the eye.

"You okay?" his voice was breathless, gruff.

Desire tremored through my body with a force I had never felt. But old insecurities stuck like glue. Fierce as my lust burned, I couldn't let go of the thought that he might not want me. I shook my head to try and shake it away.

"What? What is it?" he said, brushing his lips against mine as he spoke.

"I'm so ... damaged. And you're ..."

"But not irreparable," he breathed, pressing a kiss of even greater intensity upon my lips. His body pressed closer.

"You have grown so much since the first time we met. You wouldn't even look me in the eyes then. You would shudder in fear whenever someone got too close. But you are so much more than you realize."

My arms wrapped around his wide shoulders. I needed to feel his skin against mine. It gave me strength. I took in a shaky breath.

"But you are perfect," I whispered. It took all my courage just to utter these words, and he grunted.

"No one is perfect, dear one. Especially not me." He nibbled on my earlobe as he said this.

I relished the sharp, hard, tickling sensation of his teeth on my ear. His lips trailed from there back to my lips and I kissed him back. All the while my body tingled, our heat intermingled, our breath interwove together in gasps and pants, and our desire amplified everything. Yet my mind still wandered. A small part of me doubted. He saw it before I had to say anything, though.

"Even though your skin is marred, even though it's been branded violently by another, believe me when I say that you are the most exquisite being I have ever laid my eyes on."

I pulled his body forcefully down to join me on the bed, his weight atop me. Our limbs interwoven. My hands fumbled with the top button of his jeans while he continued his caress my skin with his lips and delicate lashes of his tongue.

"Gabriel ... I think ..." My voice was breathless and staggering. Desperately I clutched at the sheets beneath me, trying to get a grip on something, anything, so long as it kept me grounded. His warm breath prickled goosebumps to the surface of my chilled skin and his warm lips soon followed, pressing a curled smile there and sealing it with another kiss.

A sunrise streaked with maroon bloomed in his irises, flecked with pearl, smooth pink trickling back. Warmth filled me from the inside. It diffused into my blood in a different kind of heat. One that lingered, adding warmth and comfort.

"I love you."

The color in his eyes changed dramatically. The maroon gave away to the iridescent pale pink. The color seemed to glow from the inside out, brightening his entire face.

"I love you, Audrey."

A desperate happiness swept through me. Love replaced it, warming my insides. His words, the change in the color of his eyes, these signs reinforced the feeling within me.

"Can we stay like this for just a second?"

I needed to live in this moment for as long as I could. The fear that anything I loved could be snatched away had been the only constant in my life for so long. The terror of it briefly gripped at me in those last few seconds.

"There is something I want to show you." He turned his head away from me, the base of his neck becoming flushed. A deep, blue upheaval that swirled in his irises signifying turmoil, followed by an ugly veil of green that flitted across the turmoil revealing disgust.

I bit the inside of my cheek. What was he going to show me?

Taking a deep breath his body started to shimmer and melt away. My astonishment grew and with it came a small flicker of panic. But it dissipated back to nothing as his transformation finished.

He hadn't shrunk too much in size. It was hard to tell. Maybe he was a little less broad in the shoulders, now, and perhaps a *little* shorter than before. His black hair was lighter, more tinged with brown. His eyes hadn't changed at all.

My hand reached out to touch his skin, but the emotions that raged through me caused me to tremble. For a moment I felt a companionship with him I hadn't thought I could feel with anyone. But this was soon swallowed by the deep sorrow I felt at seeing his new skin.

A moment before it had been tan and smooth. Now it was riddled with scars beyond number. Small ones that could be the result of knife wounds, bullet shaped ones, longer deadlier ones that looked like claws. Like my own scars. The skin in front of me was soft and smooth

270

everywhere I touched, even where his skin puckered much like my own. Alike, yet different. Mine were unique to my father's claws.

"Does it hurt?" I asked. I knew from experience that sometimes even though the pain was gone, the memories lingered. What was gone from the body can still exist in the mind.

"Not anymore."

His voice was a little rougher in this form. I looked up at him, the sadness in his eyes blended into the murky yellow of shame. I searched for more, hoping he would see my own acceptance. He looked down at his maimed skin.

"This is the real me. Completely and utterly. Shifters—animal, human—we all have one solid form. The real us. This is the form that we can't stop from aging. This is the form that reveals the wounds that have healed.

"Us shape-shifters have the power to control the cells in our bodies to form new ones, to heal faster, or in some cases at a normal rate, if we so choose. But it takes a toll on our bodies. When severe enough, wounds still leave marks on our real skin. But we keep our true self hidden, even among our kind. Shifters don't show their true form to others. You are the only exception I've heard of. We are a private people. We have long kept this secret. Even the head paranormal families don't know. There are some secrets that aren't meant to be shared."

His eyes were a steel grey color. A guarded color. His gaze flicked over the scars on his arms, the marked skin darkening the color in his eyes. Gabriel's worry was starting to overwhelm him.

"You must think ..."

"You're beautiful," I said before he could finish his statement.

The scars on his skin showed an intricate map of his life. I couldn't stop staring. He reached up to touch my face and I leaned into his hand, loving the raspy feel of it. His eyes were full of emotions, each shifting and glimmering as they danced with such honesty that I had to turn away.

I pressed a feather light kiss to the palm of his hand atop a small but deep scar. The heat flared through my core, spreading out into my limbs as his hand grazed across my scars, reminding me that he and I were similar. I would never wish these scars on him, but he understood pain, all sorts of pain. We were closer in a way others would never understand. His lips captured mine and his sweet taste radiated through me.

Stone had moved to lay beside me, but now he propped himself on his elbow while his free hand continued its exploration. The only sound was of our joined breathing and the rustling of the sheets. He brought his leg between mine, settling it there. Then he brought his other to join the first. I finally managed to unbutton his jeans. Stone pulled his lips away from me, trailing their softness against the skin of my neck and then continuing his course farther down. He kissed my breasts, releasing throaty sounds of ecstasy from me. Breathy groans thick with lust. My body tensed with anticipation. His hands moved to my jeans and he slid them down. I was finally ready. Even so, I couldn't help swallowing hard as his skin touched the sides of my bare hips.

I bit my lip in an attempt to hold in the sounds of pleasure begging to be let out. Whispers of embarrassment still clinging to me would not be silenced. Not with his hands slowly stroking my leg, from hip to the tip of my toes and back up again.

Stone was on his knees between my legs, with me lying before him. His hands tickled the sensitive skin on the inside of my thighs, causing another wave of gooseflesh to ripple through my body. My panties were off in an instant. He ripped the seams and threw them to the side of the room.

Restlessness twitched in my muscles. Slowly, I licked my bottom lip as I waited for him to make his move. He was frozen for an instant, drinking in the sight of me, crawling his hungry gaze over my body, setting my skin on fire with his need, making my stomach twist with desperate butterflies of desire. Any inkling of fear had been wiped away. The past was, for once, distant. I had never dreamed that even with him this could be something beautiful. But a driving need to be one with him surged through me.

This was my first time. I had never made love. While imprisoned, I had been violated. Been forced to do things that filled me with shame and disgust. There had been a product of violence and rage. It had never been like this.

Stone's hand brushed against my hip, slowly inching farther down. I shivered and tilted my head back. My whole body tingled with an uncontrollable delight. It shook my muscles, made my joints ache for more. I throbbed with the need for him, to be one with him …

We didn't speak as he pressed his body against mine, placing kisses against my skin as he moved back up to my lips. I was completely open to him, and he to me. My hands grasped for him, touching wherever they could reach. My tongue was insatiable for the taste of his skin. And then his eyes locked onto mine, his lips hovering right above mine.

"I promise …" he started.

I leaned up and captured his promise with a kiss. Bravely I wrapped my legs around his hips. I could feel him there, pressing against me. Needy. Hard with passion. And I needed him as much as he needed me.

Slowly I let out a breath and pushed forward. And so did he. He clutched my hand, the muscles in his neck flexing. Gabriel's eyes met mine.

"I would never hurt you."

My body relaxed. His hips bucked gently forward. I closed my eyes, suddenly feeling complete. Full, and most importantly, it felt right. He moved and I moved with him, tingles of pleasure arcing through me.

I no longer knew who was who or who did what. My hands, his legs, our motions melded together in a sweet kind of confusion. He held me close, kissing my shoulders, neck, and lips.

A whole new sensation spread within me, taut and lusty and begging for release. And, like a knot untying, I felt it come loose within me, sending wave after wave of pleasure through me. I came apart in his arms and I screamed his name into his neck. As I did, I felt him shudder and throb. I had fulfilled him as much as he had me.

He stroked my hair as we caught our breath and told me he would never let me break again.

***

In the morning, I woke up to delicate kisses all across my face, down my neck and exposed shoulders. I didn't want to open my eyes. I felt like if I did his kisses might stop.

That night was seared into my mind. It truly was my first time. Deep in my soul I felt the love I had for him, and it filled my heart. But I couldn't be sure I would be able to keep him.

These thoughts caused a streak of irritation to spasm through me. How could I think such things and ruin this perfect moment? I took a breath. No, I wouldn't waste our time together with old doubts. I pushed those down to a place they wouldn't bother us. I opened my eyes to see Gabriel still adoring my skin with light kisses.

"Good morning, beautiful."

Our bodies were still entwined, he leaned over to press his forehead against mine. I didn't want to leave his arms ever, but we had to get moving so my father wouldn't find us like this. Slowly I started to untangle our limbs, rediscovering who was who. The more space between Gabriel and me, the more my mind wondered. He made his decision, and Elijah had made his, but Nixie hadn't.

I still hadn't been able to talk to Nixie alone about our situation, but I hoped to soon. I would do it just as soon as my father finished our shifting training.

His eyes didn't leave me as we got ready. I felt self-conscious even though we had spent the night together, but I was trying to be bolder for him so I fought the urge to hide. I met his deep purple eyes and smiled coyly. I pulled on a dress from the clothes Xavier had provided. For once in my life I felt … sexy.

He circled me, his callused hands trailing over fabric and skin, grazing the scar on my back. I shivered, intoxicated by the touch of his real skin on mine. His lips dragged against my back, his teeth lightly brushing the skin there. I leaned my neck to the side to let him nuzzle me, relishing the feeling of his scarred skin against my own. I closed my eyes again.

"Gods, I love you, Audrey. I don't think I'll ever get enough of you."

His hands splayed across my stomach, slipping over the fabric of the dress.

"I will never let you break again."

"Gabriel …"

"I love when you say my name."

274

Brushing my body against his, I twisted in his hold. My fingers ran through his hair. I slipped my arms around his shoulders.

"Say it again," he demanded.

"Gabriel ..."

"Again," he growled, moving his hand under the hem of my dress to touch my thigh. I shivered and pressed my body closer. I needed his touch.

"Gabriel ..."

He languidly danced his fingers up and down my thigh in the lightest caress. My lashes fluttered, and I pressed my hand to his chest. Flirtatiously I peeked up at him, nibbling on my bottom lip.

"Say it again," he teased.

I smiled and began to say "Gabriel" before being interrupted. There was a sudden knock at the door. I jumped a little in his arms, clearing my throat.

Nixie walked in, apparently taking that as a sign to enter, still looking down at something in her hands.

"Hey, my little guppy girl, I was wondering if ..." Nixie finally lifted her head to see Stone and me both standing there. Thankfully his hand was on my hip, over my clothes this time. His hair was still ruffled from where I had been running my fingers through it.

"I had no idea you had company. Hello there, Stone-y-boy."

Gabriel's skin had returned to its flawless state, reminding me of last night and what had been shared between us. It was for us and us only. A warmth filled me at that thought. It was a selfish thought, but at the moment I didn't care.

"Nixie."

Stone nodded to her.

"What were you wondering, Nixie?" As I asked a light blush stole into my cheeks.

Chapter 38

STONE

In the morning, I remembered how her slim legs had wrapped around mine. How she'd called out my name. My real name. I never thought I'd be able to share that with anyone. I wanted to laugh and play with her, to forget the world and continue to kiss her—maybe this time somewhere entirely different. I managed, though, to keep myself in check. I didn't want to push her too far, too soon.

But when she said my name, it stirred something in me. All thoughts of leaving our room fled as I watched her perfect lips form each syllable of my name. It was unsettling how much the knock at the door surprised me. I hadn't noticed at all before someone knocked and then the door suddenly swung inward. I guess I should have been happy that it was Nixie and not someone else.

The girls talked while I tried to calm my body down. Audrey was close, so very close, and I *wanted* her. I excused myself to the bathroom. The disheveled hair in the mirror revealed the paths Audrey's fingers had traveled. I had to get the image of her out my head so that I could get ahold of myself. I decided to head back out, and when I did, both women appeared happy.

Nixie was standing with Audrey, looking her over. Leaning against the doorframe, I wondered what she planned to do, leave or stay. She still blamed her father's death on York, and I wasn't sure she would be able to stay because of him even if she decided not to return to Braden. But watching how she interacted with Audrey, I hoped Nixie would consider it.

"Oh, Guppy, you are beautiful in that dress!" Nixie announced.

She was right. Audrey's skin, now lightly tanned from our time at the cabin, looked healthier than ever. Her eyes shined brightly. Her hair, on the other hand, was still slightly unkempt. I couldn't help smiling at that. It was usual for her, but still cute. Briefly a thought flashed through my mind; her as a shining, scaled dragon. But just as suddenly, the image fled.

She may never be able to access that side of herself with all the trauma she'd suffered. It felt like a betrayal thinking about her in that way, as something she may never achieve. I was okay with it, if that turned out to be the case. It didn't matter to me if she could shift into her paranormally endowed form. As long as she was with me, I didn't care. I told her the truth last night. I loved her. But only now was the truth of that statement sinking in.

"What do you think, Stone?" Nixie asked, her head still turned toward Audrey.

"I think it looks perfect on her," I answered, my eyes never leaving Audrey, a light blush spreading across her cheeks. I remembered that blush from before. Last night. Gods, I wanted her even now.

"Yeah, well duh, clam-head! What I meant was, what do you think about her training in it? It will totally ruin the dress. No, no, we can't have that. I have been dying to see what you look like as a dragon! I was doing some snooping around, and what I really mean by that is I was eavesdropping and found out what your dad is … of course then my good friend the were-cheetah found me …" Nixie trailed off.

I walked over to Audrey. She was trying to keep the sadness in her heart inside, but I could see it reflected in her eyes. She took a hesitant breath, appearing mostly calm, but I knew her inability to shift hurt her deep down. She wanted to be able to feel that other side of her, the part that was missing, the part that even I could not heal. I ran my fingers along the edge of her hairline.

"You will never be any less than perfect for me," I whispered, kissing her forehead.

"How can you say that? I'm not perfect."

"Perfectly imperfect." I only paused to wrap my arms around her, binding her in an unbreakable hug. "Perfect for me in every way."

"Ah, excuse me? Sorry to interrupt this lovely moment you two are having, but your father is probably wondering where you are, Audrey. I wouldn't want you to get in trouble with him."

She gave Audrey a pointed look. Audrey nodded in agreement. She went back into the bedroom where new clothes had been folded and neatly placed in the drawers. Then she went to the bathroom and shut the door with a quiet click.

"Have you given it anymore thought? About staying?" I asked the green-haired siren. Her coral eyes flashed in annoyance.

"You make it sound like such a simple decision. If it were easy, I'd have given you an answer already. You aren't the only one who cares about her. I know … I know that if I leave it will hurt her. But this isn't just about her anymore, Stone. She going to need to learn to stand on her own two feet. We all have tough decisions that need to be made. Even being here makes me uncomfortable. Do you think I *like* sitting in the same room as my father's murderer? It broke my heart when I found out that murderous bastard Drake was related to her." She laughed bitterly. "Of course he's related to the one person I would call my best friend. Have you thought about any of this, or have you just been thinking about yourself and her? I'm not angry, and I'm glad she has you looking out for her, but you better think long and hard the next time you consider asking me *that* question."

With a happy-go-lucky smile plastered on her face, Nixie turned back to the bathroom door as it opened. Nixie was a fantastic actress, her smile and attitude changing immediately for our new audience.

"Come on, my little guppy!" Nixie skipped over to Audrey and hooked her arm around her friend. I followed behind.

Nixie had been on the team for as long as I could remember. We had never exactly grown close. Not that I was ever close with anyone on the team. My father made it clear that the only paranormals I should spend time with were our kind. I had lived by those rules for a very long time.

Old habits die hard, and all that. And yet, somehow Audrey had worked her way into my heart faster than anyone before.

Audrey led us to a room I recognized from the outside. How could I forget the doors etched with those arcane designs and small details? The domed room. I took at the crystalline ceiling, noting the dazzling jags of reflected light. The ceiling stretched on forever, curving gently as it rose to meet the blue sky. Pillars made of dark stone contrasted the light shining through the glass at regularly spaced intervals around the periphery of the room. The floor was similarly glossy with deep veins of black running through it. The rim of the room was covered with a high ceiling. On the far side of the room it looked like there was bed along with some other furniture. Before I could examine it too closely, the two men in the middle of the room stole my attention.

York waited patiently as Drake yelled at him. York's tail wrapped around Drake's arm, his hand touching Drake lightly. How could I have missed this before? After everything we had learned, how could I let this small but vital information slip by me? Gargoyles weren't intimate creatures by nature. Their kind used touch as a way of showing how much they cared. Drake and York stood close to each other. Closer than friends. It was obvious now. The way Drake's eyes softened upon looking at York, no wonder Audrey was so important to him.

York and Drake, it would seem, were a couple. That relationship worried me. For Audrey's sake.

I hoped she wouldn't notice. I didn't think she was ready for this kind of revelation. Not right now. Not so soon after she found the courage to admit her feelings about her mother. But her reactions and expression remained untroubled by the touching happening right before her eyes. There was still so much she didn't know about our world.

"Drake, we can talk about this later," York was already looking pointedly in our direction. Drake hadn't realized we had walked in, but he followed York's line of sight, pivoting until he was now facing us. Drake's gaze zeroed in onto Audrey, he stopped mid-sentence and snapped his mouth shut.

"Xavier." He twisted his neck to the right, his lips mouthing a silent plea. York's mouth had been set in a firm line, his eyes pinched, but he nodded to Drake. Audrey released her hold around Nixie's arm and came to stand between us, her curious stare on the two men.

"Could you two come with me, please? Drake requested we allow him time alone with his daughter."

I was uncomfortable with the idea of leaving Audrey alone with her father, to say the least. But the fact remained, York had been very lenient with us since we arrived here.

"I promise he won't harm her," he said to me as he walked past.

Audrey's eyes flickered to me, but she stood tall, chin tilted upwards. Her hands had bunched at her sides. Otherwise, she seemed to accept the conditions of her training. In that moment, I was damn proud of her. She was so brave.

Nixie huffed, but followed York out of the room. I, too, went out after them.

"York!" I called after him. Though Audrey had stood her own ground in there, from the stories she told me of her past, I couldn't help feeling the tension in my back. York strode forward until we had almost reached the end of the hallway.

"Look, I understand the reason why you're nervous leaving her alone with him, but there are things you don't understand. Things have changed," York said sharply.

"What are you talking about?"

York's eyes widened in surprise.

"You don't know?"

He sounded a little like he was talking to himself.

"Know what?"

Xavier shook his head, as if snapping himself out of whatever thought had seized him a moment before.

"Losing Coy, Audrey's mother, in child-birth. After ten years together, the grief was too much. His dragon side has always been a bit overbearing, but that day Drake lost part of himself to the beast within. He became obsessed with keeping his tiny little jewel, the final treasure given from his wife to him to protect, safe from anything or anyone. In that state, he viewed Audrey as his possession. Not just his daughter. He wasn't in his right mind, and that's why... he branded her."

Drake might not have been in his right mind, but that didn't change the fact she was his daughter. My father was a heartless man after we lost my mother, and he had done damage to me in his own way, but Drake had harmed his daughter and treated her like some *thing*. A thing to control and own. The deep set anger that I had bottled up for years surged forth. He had *branded* her. He had *scarred* her for life.

My nostrils flared. I strode back toward the doorway we had just left. How could he? My body screamed for vengeance.

"Wait … Stone, you don't understand!"

What didn't I understand? Drake had scarred his daughter, forced her into a life of solitude, even before she had been taken by Cain. I burst through the doors, my eyes turning to pinpoints as a wall of light slammed into me. My eyes darted about, looking for that monster. I would make him regret what he had done. I would have to be big to stand a chance against him. A minotaur might do. I had never attempted the form of a minotaur, but I was the best shape-shifter in the Braden Clan.

My mate would be avenged.

My cells began their work, stretching to their limits, taking on the form of this deadly beast. Audrey and Drake were both staring at me now. Her eyes were wide. Drake, though, had moved in front of Audrey, crouching down as if ready to fight me off.

Now he would protect her? I cracked my neck, consumed by a fog of pure rage. I charged forward.

"Stone, no!" a voice screamed out.

I hit Drake, but he was ready for me. Still, he flew backwards a few feet at the force of my blow. My roar shook the panes of glass above us. Drake got to his feet, his teeth growing to a dangerous size. I was already backing up so I could gain more momentum in my second charge at him. That's when he roared.

Drake's body shook, his skin peeling away to reveal large, strong looking scales. The room echoed with the sound of his bones and joints popping and reshaping. New appendages grew, first wings burst from his back, followed by a spiked, deadly looking tail. His huge head swung toward me, sharp, dagger-length teeth gleamed in the light.

"Fuck, Stone, move!" York screamed, his wings beating heavily to reach us. But the dragon had already taken form.

Drake stood before me, a giant monster. I couldn't hope to beat him, and I knew it. Not even with the form of a minotaur. Even the shifters in the legends of my kind couldn't take the form of the Elder Races. But my rage was not yet spent. I itched to fight.

Drake roared again, his eyes on me and nowhere else.

Chapter 39

AUDREY

Seeing my father transform and go after Stone made something in me snap. I don't know what it was. I just broke free.

My body began to burn, forcing something. I didn't understand. I was terrified. For me, for Stone, for what was about to happen. My skin felt tight, like my bones were growing too large. The pain was unbearable, but when my eyes fell on Stone again, the thought of losing him hurt more. My body shook, then exploded.

One second I was too far away, the next I was in front of my father, in front of Stone shielding him. When I tried to get words out, only growls came. I tried to scream, but it echoed around the room like a roar.

My father stepped back as if in shock, his long talons clicking on the beautiful stone floor. I tried to scream again, and again all that came out was a deafening roar. When I tried to move back, my body wasn't moving normally. I hadn't realized before that my arms were touching the ground. Moments before all I was concerned about was protecting Stone. Now looking down, I realized what had shocked my father.

I looked down and saw deep purple-maroon scales, shiny, new and beautiful, covering legs about six feet long. I tested one. It moved when I tried to move my arm. Connected to those were claws like my father's. I turned my neck some more looking at the curve of my spine, which extended into a long, delicate tail. My father's tail had spikes; I had none. But I had a tail.

A presence started to fill my mind, a piece of me that I thought could never exist. She had been what controlled our body at first. She had acted on instinct. I felt a cool hand touch my leg. I turned to see Stone staring at me in awe. I tried not to bite my lip as I would normally. In this form, I would only hurt myself.

"Audrey," Stone whispered, coming around to my front.

I asked the growing presence in my awareness if she would allow us to lie down, but she didn't really want to. After eyeing my father for a moment, she moved our legs. Stone moved close and I moved my long neck to bring my enormous head to meet him. I made small noises trying to get his attention, but he kept smoothing his hand over my scales. It felt like heaven, even though his form was small compared to mine, having his hand on me had a calming effect. A deep rumble built in my throat.

"You're gorgeous," he whispered. I wanted to smile, but my body began to shake. My vision blurred. I thought I heard a scream of warning, but the multi-colored world around me was turning black.

***

The first thing I noticed was a hand holding mine. A tight callused grip that brought memories of those hands moving on my body. I smiled, but it quickly faded as I remembered my dream of being a dragon. My heart cried out mourning the loss of something I never had.

"Audrey, if you can hear me, please wake up."

Gabriel's voice was so close. Maybe my time with him was a dream too.

"I know you are scared. But it was real, Audrey. It was real." Awe filled his voice.

I opened my eyes and looked at him. My throat choked with tears and my eyes burned at their buildup.

"I transformed?" The words were broken and quiet.

"Yes. You are the most stunning dragon I have ever seen." His eyes were light and I could see yellow flecks. He was happy.

"The only other dragon you have ever seen is my father." Then I realized what I said. I felt a smile jump on my face followed by a choked laugh. "I transformed!" It was still sinking in.

Now that I was awake, I could feel the subtle essence of the dragon spirit I had thought forever lost to me. Then the memories from after I had transformed flooded my mind.

"What happened?" I searched Stone looking for any damage, but I knew there wouldn't be any on this skin.

"I'm fine. The transformation was too much for your system all at once, so you passed out. Your father calmed down and I calmed down." Though I could still see that he wasn't. His fists were tight and his jaw clenched. "Why didn't you ever tell me it was your father? I mean, I suspected something, but until York confirmed it ..." He trailed off his eyes looking sad.

"It is in his nature," I whispered.

How was I supposed to tell him that even after all that he did to me, I still forgave him? That I never once blamed him?

"Before you came in he was telling me about my mother," I added looking up at him.

He sighed and pushed me over a little so that he could fit on the narrow bed with me.

"Where are we?" I asked quietly.

He wrapped his arms around me.

"The hospital wing." His voice was muffled as he pressed his face into my hair. "Tell me what he said."

I turned around and Gabriel kept his face in my neck. He didn't kiss me, but just laid there while I ran my fingers through his hair.

"She was a were-chameleon. He told me that she was small, much like I am. He fell for her big attitude. He said that she was the most beautiful woman he had ever seen. They were together for over ten years. He wanted to save her the night that I was born, but there were complications." My voice caught in my throat, and Stone placed a small delicate kiss on my neck. "The choice was to save me or to save her. They hadn't had time to get a doctor. He saw the cord wrapped around my neck. While he was freeing me, she was bleeding out. If he had stopped to save her, to give her half his heart, I would have died."

I cried. Stone switched our positions so my face was buried in his neck, and he brushed his fingers through my hair. We stayed that way for a long time. He told me about his mother. It wasn't as detailed as the first time he told it, but I felt honored that he finally decided he could tell me.

We fell asleep like that, curled in each other's embrace.

***

When we woke up a little later, it was to two voices arguing outside the room. I listened closer. I could hear Xavier and my father. I looked at Stone, who was also listening, but he didn't seem to be having a problem understanding them. His lips were pressed tight and a line creased between his brows. I wanted to smooth it away.

"Drake, she isn't a possession, you know this. Try to understand that he does care for her. And she obviously cares for him." I heard Xavier tell my father. My father growled something, but it was distorted so I couldn't understand what he was saying. Stone climbed off the bed giving me one last kiss. When my father and Xavier walked in, I noticed how Xavier's tail was wrapped around my father's leg.

"How are you feeling, Audrey?" Xavier asked, his eyes softening when they swept over me.

"Fine."

"That's good! We were worried about you. That was an amazing transformation you did. We were wondering if ..." Xavier paused looking at my father.

"We were wondering if you could still feel her," my father said, watching me closely.

I looked at Stone, hoping that he would give me the courage to speak openly to my father about this. I knew it was what he wanted for me for such a very long time, but at the same time, if I was truly a dragon shifter ... I looked at Stone. If that was true, I could never leave. My father wouldn't let me go, and it would be dangerous to leave, besides.

"I can." I wished I couldn't, though. I didn't think I would be able to survive without Stone. I knew he had to be missing his clan. How could I ever ask someone I loved to forget all that? To forget his family? Wouldn't that make me just a different kind of torturer?

"Wonderful! That is wonderful, Audrey!" Xavier exclaimed, moving away from my father to embrace me.

It was strange how caring he was toward me. It instantly put me on edge. I tried to take a hold of Stone's hand, but I couldn't reach it. I touched the blanket, counted the ripples. Xavier let go. My father stood unmoving watching how Xavier and I interacted. I wanted to ask why, but thought better of it.

"If you are feeling up to it, we will all sit down and have dinner tonight. In, say, about three hours?" Xavier didn't make it seem like a request, so I just nodded my head.

Stone watched the two leave, but no expression crossed his face. His eyes were a steely grey color though. I wanted to ask what was bothering him, but before I could, he stood, kissed my forehead, then walked out the door. I was left alone.

The thought of Stone leaving led to the thought of Nixie. I hadn't been able to see a whole lot of her. I knew I needed to give her space to decide what was best for her, just like Stone.

I wanted to find Nixie immediately to make things right, but how does one apologize for their father's sins? Truthfully, I had been avoiding Nixie as much as I had been trying to give her space. Usually Nixie kept our talks light and fun. We didn't talk about anything too heavy. Would she even accept my apology? I had to find out. I left the room and went in search of her. I knew her room was close to mine, so I headed in that direction. I raised my hand to knock on the door when it opened.

"I know you have been standing out there for a while, so I thought I would just let you in myself." Nixie offered a bright smile. Her coral eyes were tinted orange, meaning she was annoyed. I bent my head feeling bad for that. I hadn't wanted that.

"I literally hate this show! It's a total misrepresentation of ocean life! I mean, come on, talking sponges! Ridiculous! Plus, I know for a fact that starfish are very intelligent beings," Nixie complained as I sat down next to her. On the TV was an animated show that I had never seen.

"Are there sirens?" I asked. I wondered if she was homesick for her own kind, perhaps annoyed she was stuck here, in this building, not annoyed with me. I hoped, at least, that was the case. I hoped things hadn't changed completely between us.

"No, this show is worthless. What brings you, guppy?"

"I wanted to tell you ... I'm sorry," I whispered.

"Well, it is not like you forced him to do it. And I mean, you had to grow up with the clown-fish, not me."

Nixie was still trying to sound light, but looking into her eyes I could see the flecks of a deep blue. We watched the colorful images on the television for a few moments.

"I'm sorry, that was a bit rude of me. But there is something you need to understand, Audrey." She paused for a long time, looking down at her hands.

"I understand you couldn't possibly want to be friends with me anymore." I moved to get up, but she grabbed my arm and pulled me back down.

"No, that's not what I was going to say. Look, this is not going to be easy for me, so please don't look at me with your bright blue eye all sad and stuff." She seemed to be psyching herself up because she sat a little straighter and cleared her throat. "I have decided that I cannot go back to the Bradens, partially because I do care for you. You're probably the closest thing I've had to a best friend in many years. But mostly I think what they are doing is wrong. I will not be part of a clan that wants to destroy dying races. I have some other reasons, but that's beside the point."

I was about to tell her how happy I was that she decided to stay, but she put up her hand. She still wasn't looking at me. But I saw how hard she was swallowing, and I knew that she still had more to tell. The easy part was done. Now it was time for the hard part.

"Unfortunately, I don't think that I would be able to stay here either. I understand that I should let the past go, that your father was in the right to defend himself against the people attacking him, but your father killed

288

the only real family I had left. I can't just forgive that. I can't just live in the same place as that man." She looked at me, her eyes filled with shimmering tears. "I think the best decision is for me to go back to the sea. I will talk to York, tell him if he demands that I claim my loyalty to his family, so be it, but I will never be a York. And I don't think I would ever be able to live with Drake." Nixie's words caught when she said my father's name.

I nodded accepting her answer.

"I never wanted to hurt you, Audrey. I never wanted to do that," she whispered, grabbing my hand. I bit my lip to stop it from trembling.

We continued to watch the show, laughing at the right points and joking frequently. She never let go of my hand, and by the end of the third episode, she stopped trying to hold back her tears and let them fall. I hoped that we weren't saying goodbye forever, but I knew that I had to respect that this was not easy for her. Could I blame her for wanting to leave for the same exact reason I thought Stone should leave me? I couldn't find it in my heart to be angry with her. I kissed her cheek as I stood to leave.

"Thank you for everything, Nixie."

"This isn't goodbye, little guppy. For right now, it's see ya later."

I nodded, tightening my lips.

Chapter 40

STONE

I had to know for sure. York and Drake had to come clean with Audrey about what was going on between them. York was way too comfortable around Audrey, and it was making her uncomfortable. She still wasn't used to strangers touching her, hugging her. And now more than ever, the need to protect her was strong.

"York!"

He stopped, he twisted around so that he was facing me. Drake kept his back to me, probably assuming I would have a quick work with York then be on my way.

"What *exactly* is going on between the two of you? And when the hell are you planning on telling Audrey?"

Drake's shoulders tensed, bunching around his neck. Slowly he turned to face us. His top lip was pulled back in a dangerous snarl and his eyes flashed a bright blue color. York must have sensed Drake's response, even though Drake was still standing behind him. York reached out to touch Drake's arm in a calming gesture.

"Maybe this is something we should discuss in private," York said, taking the lead. I followed him and Drake as we walked quietly through the halls of the compound, our footsteps echoing eerily. My thoughts returned to Audrey. I wished I hadn't had to leave her alone in the hospital wing. Physically she was fine. I wondered if she would venture out to find her guest room.

In a series of twists and turns, York led us out of the hospital wing, through his maze of a building. It wasn't long before he ushered us into a small conference room.

"Drake, you should ..."

Drake gave York a dirty look and York's stone jaw twitched, but he didn't say anything else. They made their way around the table, seating themselves across from where I stood. I pulled out a chair for myself and sat down. Finally, Xavier went on.

"Well, everyone in our clan already knows. It's sort of strange explaining it. As I told you before, when Drake lost his ..." York turned his head to Drake for some sort of answer or support.

"Chosen mate."

And that's when it clicked. Chosen mates were the product of a *decision* to spend one's life with another. This was not, however, the case for true mates. True mates were rare. Many paranormals spent their entire lives looking for theirs. True mates were destined by the elemental gods to be a perfect match, but ever since the Great Conflict, when the Elder Races began to wane, they had become much rarer.

"Coy was ..." York started, but Drake cut him off.

"I loved her."

Drake stared at me hard as he said this.

"I loved her with all my heart, and if I could have saved her, I would have. But I had to choose." Drake's voice was deep and rumbling.

He spoke of Audrey's mother with great respect and love. His eyes clouded at what I could only imagine was the memory of the decision he had to make. His mate or his daughter. York patted his hand and leaned over to speak quietly to Drake.

"It's okay. You don't have to say any more. Let me finish."

Somehow it was heartwarming. How York offered Drake his support in telling such an obviously painful story.

Drake nodded in response and gave him a tight-lipped smile.

"All those years ago, I had been searching for him. For Drake. And when I found him finally, I warned him about the plans of the Bradens and

Vedenins. That they were coming for him and his child. But he had left Audrey at home when he came to meet me, so he went back for her while I called in transportation. That's when the attack occurred."

His voice was venomous.

"Vedenins. They knew just how to exploit a dragon's weaknesses, so there really wasn't any other option. Stay and die, or run and try to save his daughter later. He made the second most difficult decision of his life that day. He left, returning to me, demanding we save her. I gave my word we would get her back." York paused. There was something I still didn't understand.

"Why didn't you just grab Audrey and leave? Why'd you go back then, Drake?"

"She wanted that damn stuffed dragon I bought her, that's why! If I had let her grab it, we would have both been safe. But there was too much going on. The clans were attacking, and I had to fight them off and then Audrey ..."

Drake turned his head away in shame. Xavier took his hand and stepped alongside Drake.

"I got there too late. Drake was already severely wounded and his dragon had completely taken over. Bloodrage, they call it. Very dangerous. I couldn't find Audrey anywhere when I flew down to the house. Cain had his people torch the place ..." York took Drake's hand under the table and looked at him once again.

"Drake was still fighting when I flew back to him. Even as injured as he was, he would have destroyed everyone on that team. But I had evidence that not all team members were privy to the details before the attack. Several had no idea it was on a member of the Elder Races. It seems their true motives were limited to a discreet few. And we had been trying to recruit some people to our side. Most paranormals are quite uncomfortable at the prospect of causing the destruction of another race. We even had some agents working undercover. Unfortunately, Kai, Nixie's father, was one of ours. But I got there too late. I couldn't save him. Drake had lost all control. His sanity, itself, had slipped. The dragon ruled. The only way to save anyone at all was ..." York paused.

"To give Xavier part of my heart," Drake finished.

292

I observed them in a new light. What they spoke of was no easy feat. A dragon giving up their heart tied them to another for life. There was no going back. I didn't know the particulars, but I did know that a dragonheart bond was psychological as well as physical.

"By giving him half of my heart it tamed my dragon. I was losing myself to it, had been since Coy was taken from me. Not only that but Xavier and I found out many years ago that we were indeed true mates. I … I wasn't ready to accept it then."

Drake glanced over at Xavier sheepishly. Xavier sat strong and tall. He wasn't ashamed of who he was, of who his true mate was. True mates, rare as they were, were always treated with respect in the paranormal world. I had heard stories of some paranormals recognizing their true mate at first sight, but with others it could be more complicated. Still, the bond was undeniable. Eventually, instinct took over when one found their true mate.

Drake slumped a little. The story had obviously taken a lot for him to share.

"A dragon spirit is naturally soothed in the presence of its true mate. I knew that I couldn't always be around Xavier since I had to find my …" he paused looking again at his mate, "our daughter."

"He made his decision, but we hadn't realized until afterwards that our hearts wouldn't be able to separate for more than a couple of months at a time. A dragon hasn't bonded his heart to another in a very long time. We're still learning things about it."

"Which made looking for Audrey difficult."

We were silent for a while.

"When are you planning on telling her?"

I didn't know how to feel in the face of all this. My anger still burned at the man who scarred and abandoned his daughter, but the story wasn't quite so simple. The shame at what he had done when under the influence of his dragon was evident. He wasn't proud of the pain he had caused.

"Tonight. We had hoped we could let her get used to me. She still seems uncomfortable."

Xavier watched me with dark eyes.

"Do you know what happened to her these past five years?" Drake asked, his voice sounding strained and broken.

"Yes," I answered flatly.

"Could ... could you tell us?" Drake asked again, a note of caution in his voice. Seeing this overbearing dragon act so tame and nervous put me ill at ease.

"No," I answered, turning my own cold eyes on Drake. "She can tell you when she is ready. If ever."

***

After I left, I returned along the same route York had brought us. Audrey wasn't in the room I had left her, but I hadn't expected her to remain there for long. Without any real clue where she might have headed, I made my way back to her room. It was empty aside from the small metal frame of the bed, the nightstand, and small dresser. I figured the best I could do was wait for her here.

The door clicked open awhile later pulling me from my thoughts. I couldn't stop thinking about what Drake and York had told me. If Audrey's childhood home was burned down, had they thought for the past five years she was dead? If so, it made sense why she had been left to rot in a Vedenin cell.

Audrey stepped in. She pushed her hair behind her ear, exposing a red-tipped nose and bloodshot eyes. I stood, inner anger already beginning to boil. She collapsed into my arms, her hands clinging to my shirt. I held her close and steered us toward the bed. She sat down, still holding me tight, her quiet sobs pressing into my shirt.

"Shhh ..." I tried to soothe her. Eventually her shoulders stopped shaking.

"What happened?"

"I went to talk to Nixie. She said she isn't going to go back to the Braden Clan, but she doesn't think she can stay here either," she said through sniffles.

"Audrey ... I'll go tell your father and York. We can hold off on dinner for tonight."

I kissed her forehead and went to go find Drake and York. I needed to tell Nixie what York had told me. That Nixie's father had been a spy for him. It might change how she felt about York, but I didn't think she would ever forgive or accept Drake for killing him.

As I left the room, my body felt tight and uncomfortable. I didn't know why. I could only assume it was because I hadn't shifted into an animal form in a while. That and stress.

On my way to the kitchen it felt like there were pins in my neck. It was so bad that I tried to rub them away. And the building itself seemed eerily quiet, but also emptier than when we first arrived. Most likely York's doing. He would want to keep our knowledge limited until we gave him a definite answer whether we would stay or go. If we went with the Braden Clan, the witch who had attacked Elijah that night at the cabin would likely erase our memories of this place. But the less we knew, the easier it would be for the witch to erase.

While I contemplated these thoughts, I lost track of how far I had gone. I was headed for the kitchen, which was on the other side of the building from the rooms. It was a minor inconvenience, but I figured this was because our rooms were in the guest wing. Glorified prison rooms really. Not that I could complain too much. It was better than being in some dungeon far away from Audrey.

I thought back to our night together, and it was hard to believe the short time in between those sweet moments and these bitter ones now. I could still feel her skin, taste her lips, and unfortunately, my body couldn't help responding. My blood beat a little faster, my skin radiated heat. An expectant tightness filled my groin. I needed to get back to her as soon as possible. Not that she'd be up for anything tonight. Her encounter with Nixie seemed to leave her pretty exhausted.

I'd almost reached the kitchen when, without warning, lights started to flash and a piercing shriek rent the air.

I immediately went into combat mode. My muscles strained against my skin, my body already shifting into a more lethal form. My eyes darted around the exposed hallway, trying to locate the danger.

These were warning alarms. If they were going off, that meant someone was trying to get *in*. The kitchen door slammed open. Drake stood there, his chest heaving.

"Audrey."

I turned and ran as fast as I could, my skin melting away into the form of a cheetah. I heard Drake running behind me, but I was losing him fast. I didn't care. I needed to get to her.

The door was already kicked in by the time I arrived. She wasn't there. The stench of fear clouded the air. Her fear.

I ran.

I ran until I thought my heart was going to beat its way out of my chest. I ran at top speed through the halls, rounding corners roughly until the smell led me to Drake's room, the one with the glass ceiling. Inside I heard a roaring commotion. I crashed through the doors just in time to see a black clad figure holding an unconscious Audrey over its shoulder. A cord was also in his hand. A cord connecting them to a helicopter hovering above a broken section of the glass dome. They were already half way up, hanging midair. All I could see, all I could think of was the fact that Audrey was being taken from me. I shifted forms again.

I turned into a massive eagle and took flight. That's when something struck me in the neck. I fell back to the ground, twisting my wing beneath me in the process, breaking it. I shifted again into my human form, forcing my cells to repair my broken arm. But everything felt so slow. My cells wouldn't listen. My commands to my body fell on deaf ears. My last sight was of my Audrey disappearing into the night sky.

Becca Vincenza

Chapter 41

Audrey

After Stone left I stretched out on the bed and stared at the door. I was desperate to go after him. Not because I felt like I couldn't be without him, but because I was weirdly restless. I rolled over and closed my eyes, listening to the light taps of his retreating footsteps. Then, something else. I couldn't put my finger on it. No matter how hard I concentrated I couldn't figure out what it was.

Until it was already too late. That's when the door crashed in.

I tried to scream for Stone, but a black-clad figure was running full speed at me and knocked me down with his weight. I grunted as I tried to push the body off, but I couldn't get enough leverage. He was too heavy for me to lift. He started to pull something from his pocket.

My eyes locked on to the glinting edge of a syringe.

"Help! Stone! El—"

A hard slap across my face cut off my cries. My teeth clacked together loudly washing my mouth with pain. Hot tears flooded my eyes, adding a burning sting to my irritated skin.

"Oh my fucking Gods! Eli—" Nixie's voice rent the air. My eyes went wide, and I twisted my body to see her better. Where was she?

The man was still straddling me but was momentarily distracted by Nixie. I took the distraction to try throw him off. I jostled him and kept

297

wriggling underneath him. Still, he wouldn't budge. Then my skin registered a sharp, prickling sensation, and the world went fuzzy.

"Nix ..."

But the world was already black. I had never been so afraid of the darkness before.

***

My wrists were cold. Not only that, but my whole body shivered. My eyes slowly peeled open. The room was grey. Roughhewn rock was on the side closest to me. Another dungeon. Another cage. Another prison. My whimpers echoed off the walls. I tried to pull my arms close. This only caused chains to rattle loudly, echoing off the walls back to my ears. My pulse throbbed in the veins of my neck. My eyes stared wide, my breath came in sharp gasps. The fear was so cold it iced the blood in my veins.

Jagged rocks pressed into my back. I pulled at my arms, the tendons straining, taunt. The muscles already ached, which told me I had been in this position for a while. One thought ruled all others: I needed to withdraw. To pull into myself. To make myself small. I *needed* it. If I could only get small enough, maybe they'd miss me. Maybe I wouldn't be hit. Tortured. The memory of pain forced my body to more urgent movements. The metal bit into my wrists, but the pain barely registered. My desperate cries echoed around the room.

Small. Small. Small.

There. Some slight salvation. In the wall, barely visible in the weak light—cracks.

I began to count.

One. Two. Three. Four. There was a sound. What was it? *No, I* thought, shaking my head to myself. *Don't stop.* Ten. Eleven. It grew closer. And accompanying it, the sound of metal on metal. A sharp noise. Twenty-four. My mind kept counting, but that didn't stop the frantic thoughts. *Please make it stop. Please make it stop.* My eyes lost their place. Start over. The noise drew even closer. Don't look. Please, please, please don't look.

But I couldn't help myself. I looked.

Standing in the doorway was a beautiful blond man. His hair fell in his eyes, partly hiding his face. He was large. Much bigger than me. Fear electrified my body. As the door clicked behind him, he looked up.

Horrible, yet somehow beautiful, eyes stared back at me. Such a strange hazel color. Rings of light brown, green, and grey. They were freckled with the black of cold-blooded hatred. I cringed against the wall. I wanted to crawl inside it. I wanted to get away. His footsteps echoed around the room as he approached.

He smiled cruelly.

"Right where you belong."

His smooth, inviting voice terrified me. It held a beautiful, cruel promise. I swallowed.

My skin crawled under his stare. It reminded me of before. *Eyes watching everything. Drinking me in.* Deep seated fear rose again. He was standing in front of me now, his breath muggy against my skin. My instincts told me to turn away, but a defiance, a kind of self-belief I had learned from my new friends, encouraged me to keep eye contact.

His arm snatched out quick as a snake, gripping my neck between his fingers and pressing lightly. He tilted his head to the right a little and watched my reaction. I forced my face blank. Blank like Stone's. Even though on the inside the fear was already making my blood sour in my veins.

Stone. I would think of him and find strength. I had to. A burst of courage began to spread throughout me from a point deep in my gut. I had to remain strong so I could return home. Not broken. Not damaged.

"I'd rather it if you were dead." His lips curled around the words in a snarl.

"And yet, I breathe."

Did I just say that? My voice didn't even waver. His hand tightened around my neck. Each finger pressed into my skin a little more tightly.

"Yes, but only because I ordered it so. If I had ordered you be killed, nothing would have saved you. You would be dead. But I was curious. I couldn't help wondering one small thing. You see, I can't figure out why three of my best agents are abandoning their clan for you. But there are always new opportunities. And you, my little treasure, are going to bring something even better my way. I will be the one who destroys the dragons. And when I do, it will be once and for all."

"You're Cain."

The Braden Clan leader. He` confirmed my suspicions with a smile. He shifted a little closer, and I pressed my back against the unforgiving stone behind me. He dipped his head beside mine.

"You will be dead soon. No matter if you know my name. Now, tell me, Audrey, how did you sway the wraith on your side? That is what I am *most* curious about."

He pressed his mouth to my ear. He touched me like my lover, and nausea crawled up my throat. I maneuvered my legs tightly together and angled them away from him. He gripped my neck tighter. I couldn't breathe.

"Do you actually believe that I could ever want you? Laughable. I was only wondering if you had tempted him with this." He cupped my breast. I gasped in shock, pain, and disgust. "Or did he feed? I think he would have feasted quite nicely. You reek of fear."

His words bit into me. Spots filtered into my vision, my lungs burned desperate for air, struggling to get even a bit of air. I gasped burning to taste it. For the first time in a very long time, I felt a desire to survive. But Cain was no novice when it came to torture. He released as soon as the darkness started to crawl in from the edges of my vision.

I greedily pulled air into my lungs.

"If you won't talk, you will simply be destroyed. I have no patience for your *kind*."

Cain turned so that his back was to me and strode out of the room. The door remained open. Someone else stepped in. Someone I recognized. A werewolf.

Jacobs looked a little older since I had last seen him. It had only been weeks ago, but he'd obviously been punished for losing his prized prisoner. His gaze held a glint of madness. His lips pulled back into a wolfish grin that promised pain to come. If only I had passed out from lack of air.

Now the real torture would begin.

Time slowed. Minutes stretched on for years. Each second dragged against my skin like a jagged knife.

The dim light flickered from the bare bulb overhead, clearly displaying the only tools of torture Jacobs would need. Those black tipped claws of his, which glittered darkly in the light. A whimper caught in my throat.

The first cut tore at my battered soul. The baggy shirt that I had been wearing tore open, leaving me completely exposed. But his gaze wasn't hungry for my flesh; it was hungry for my blood.

He was entranced by the old scars scattered across my body. His eyes glazed over in sadistic delight. His lips quirked to one side. Quick and fast he shot his left arm backwards and underneath my ribs.

My scream echoed around the room, seeming to go around and around and around. Unending. The pain overwhelmed my mind. I thought that I would lose consciousness. But my body remembered the pain. Remembered how torture missed was revisited. The moments of darkness were the most dangerous.

And this was just the beginning. Keeping his shorter claws piercing my side, he traced the pads of his fingers over old scars. He touched the claw marks my father had made years ago. The scar tissue still puckered and ultra-sensitive.

Lightly at first he dragged his claw against it. Teasing me with what was to come next. I shook my head, mouthing hoarsely, pleading with him not to do it. From one tip of the scar to the other he dug in, reopening it, reopening the skin that never quite healed right. I thought my first scream had torn my voice from me, but I found myself screaming again.

Blood ran in rivulets down my skin, painting grotesque artwork in reds against my pale skin. My head was growing light from blood loss. Pain burned a steady fire deep in my veins. My vision blurred.

Jacobs released the claws digging between my ribs and I slumped forward. The taste of blood was fresh in my mouth, making me gag.

"Don't get to comfortable, we've only just begun ..."

His knuckles curled tightly, he slammed them against my ribs. The force threw my back into the wall, grinding the vertebrae of my spine into the stone. My ribs burned while my back spasmed, and all I saw was white. The pain had blinded my mind of anything else. I was only brought back to my senses by an instant of release followed by something new.

And then my mind drifted back into a peaceful darkness. He wasn't doing this for any purpose. It wasn't for information. It wasn't for anything more than his own pleasure.

And then it began again. And again. And again.

He didn't speak. Not yet. Later, he might make a cursory interrogation. But this was meant to be revenge. Was meant to show me who was in charge. He was the Alpha here. I was nothing compared to those claws. Jacobs had lost status by losing me, or at least in his eyes he had. He was reasserting his place on top. I had been that catalyst for the mutiny in his special ops team. Now here I was, to be tortured for his pleasure.

So much blood. It puddled and formed a river that moved around his feet and soaked his expensive shoes. I hoped it soaked his socks, too. A delirious laugh fogged through my mind. The pain had consumed my body, but my mind retreated, searching for an escape.

When he finished, he left satisfied with his work. My head lolled forward. I could finally rest. Darkness was a comfort once more.

How I had missed it.

***

Time lost all meaning. I fell asleep and woke up so many times I wasn't sure if it was the same day, month, or if only minutes had passed. Nightmares haunted me even in the waking world. My throat was raw. I had no voice left to scream with. I feared those moments. When the screams stopped. When even the blood dripping from my wounds went silent.

I was barely holding on.

My eyes glanced downward to view his work. My poor skin. New angry lines, slimmer and shorter, joined the long thick scars I already wore. But the new wounds were healing quickly. Much quicker than they had ever before. My dragon, now awakened, was lending me her strength.

I could feel her. She stirred when I first woke, but now, blood loss, exhaustion, and fear caused her to retreat deep inside my mind. Curling around herself, she became a ghost in my mind. There but unreachable.

Together we were stronger than I could be by myself. If only I could find a way to tap into her power. But it was all so new. So foreign, still.

I gasped as my body worked to repair itself, inside and out. My torn skin started to knit back together, only to be ripped apart again. My insides pinched and stung as muscles and nicked organs worked to become whole again.

I fell asleep again. Or fell into something *like* sleep. My hands were numb when I woke. My body had slumped forward, putting even more pressure on my wrists. Lack of circulation numbed my hands and fingers. When I tried to move them, the pins and needles made me hiss. My legs were weak from standing this entire time and could barely hold me up. I was too weak to think. I cast my eyes in the direction of my numb hands, but all I could do was hold still and hope the fog in my mind cleared. But as it did, it started to take me places I did not dare visit.

I remembered a scream. Nixie's. Had they taken her as well? Was she safe because of her connection with the Braden Clan, or was she being tortured and beaten as well? I couldn't bear to think of her going through the same pain I was.

From there my mind wandered to Stone. To his eyes as they shifted to the pink color, the proof of his love for me. To his beautiful, scar-mapped skin and to the feel of callused hands as they touched my face. I leaned forward, delirious for the phantom of him in my memory, wishing I could have felt his touch one last time.

Something brushed down my cheek. My mind fluttered with a single thought: Stone? And for a moment, they were Stone's fingers. Wiping away the grime, dried sweat, and speckles of blood covering my face. My heavy lids lifted, but I was alone. Then it came again. I wept in response. What was happening to me? And how was it possible that I had tears left?

After a period of suffocating silence, a new sound emerged from the silence. I had become so accustomed to noise after being freed from the white room, I hadn't realized how precious the sound of everyday life had become. Especially the small noises Stone made in his sleep. The creak of the bed, walls, and floors. The symphony of small and innocuous sounds you never notice till they're gone.

But this new sound did not bring comfort. Footsteps. They proceeded in a measured fashion until they came to a stop outside my door.

I hoped futilely they would move on.

"Oh, wee lass."

I lifted my head up. Marcus stood there. His shocking red hair and strange yellow eyes seemed so unnatural in this dark, dirty place. He entered the room, footsteps lightly treading against the ground. I tried to flinch away from him, but my body could barely move.

"Lass, I would ne'er hurt ye."

His words soothed me and spread over my skin like a balm. I shouldn't believe him. He was one of them. But I wanted to so badly. I just wanted to be safe from violent hands.

"Can ye lift yer head for me, Audrey?"

I lifted my head as much as I could. His hands offered gentle support as he poured small amounts of water into my mouth. It soothed for a second before it, too, became a torture of its own. I coughed up the lukewarm water as it burned down my hoarse throat. It felt like it coursed over sandpaper. My body slumped. It was easier to give up. And I wanted to, but Marcus wouldn't have it.

"Nae, lass, stay with me. We will have ye out of here soon. Waitin' for reinforcements," he said.

I didn't understand. I tried to tell him. To ask him to explain. He only gave me a reassuring smile.

"Th' less ye know, th' better."

Marcus tried to feed me some more water. He did this a couple more times until my throat began to feel less raw. It took patience, but eventually I was able to get the water down without coughing it back up.

He left, promising to be back soon. I craved sleep, but my stomach clenched painfully, too hungry to release me to sleep. The water absorbed quickly into my dehydrated system, but I needed food. I tried to think of anything else, the pain, my friends, my family—anything to keep my mind off of the gnawing hunger. But the pain only grew worse.

Hunger mingled with the pain of torture until it started to weigh heavy on my mind. A mindless, primal need. For sustenance. For survival.

Old desires, those I had learned well before I had met Stone, before Nixie, before being reunited with my father. I started to rise.

I hung on by a thread, waiting for my sanity to snap.

Sometime later, a noise roused me from sleep. The rhythm of fear entered my heart again, a rapid, painful pulse. I shook my head weakly side to side. No, I couldn't handle another round of torture. Straining my neck backwards to glance around the room, I didn't see anyone. My eyelids fell heavily against my cheeks. The healing of my body was taking its toll. A headache pounded loudly in my skull. There was something there though. Something hidden in a dark corner. The hairs on the back of my neck prickled.

I opened my eyes and still there was no one to be seen. And then there was a stirring. From somewhere deep in my mind. An immense presence. My dragon. She was waking.

She stretched slowly through my mind, testing the boundaries where she ended and I began. Her presence was warm and comforting, but I feared it wouldn't be enough. She pushed at my mind insistently, as though trying to send a message. As though asking me to give her control. I had no strength to stop her, but I didn't have the strength to shift. Too much pain. My body couldn't give any more. Still, she pushed again. I let go and the darkness claimed me.

Slowly I came back to consciousness. My wrists still hurt, but the pain was bearable. I could feel my hands. The numb feeling had left, and they were under ... my head. My legs were curled underneath me, while my bare stomach touched the rocky floor. I opened my eyes and I couldn't see my arms, I panicked. The noises that came from me were rough, animalistic. Had Cain done this?

Footsteps again sounded outside the door. My eyes widened and my head snapped in its direction. From where I sat now, I had to look up at it, as opposed to before when I had been roughly eye level. I swallowed, curling my limbs close to my torso.

The door slammed open, and I flinched backwards. Jacobs filled the doorway, but his pleased smile soon melted from his face.

"Where the hell is she?" Jacobs roared as he stepped farther into the room.

His voice echoed in my ears so loudly I recoiled. Even though he was looking right at me, he didn't appear to see me. Following him into the roughhewn torture room, Dallas looked intently around the room, his mouth open in a silent question. Marcus came in last, his eyes immediately found mine. He blinked hard at me. His eyes held so many questions. Curiosity was there as well, and a glimmer of awe. But his features soon were unreadable, and he too *searched* the room.

"Dallas, go inform the guards. Marcus, check the rest of the prison and see if she is hiding somewhere. And get me the damned guard from last night!" Jacobs continued yelling as he moved through the dungeon. I didn't dare move until Marcus came back to the cell I was being kept in.

"Wow, lass. Ye look like a wee-dragon. I knew yer father was a dragon, but I was under th' impression ye couldn't shift."

Marcus moved closer to me. I backed away, confused by what he was saying. How did he know my father? How did he know what we were? But his words still rung through my head, a little-dragon? What did he mean?

"Ah, they did nae tell ye yet, did they? You're lookin' at their greatest kept secret. A York family spy."

Marcus winked at me and gave a bright smile.

"No, lass, we have tae get ye out of here. Stay just as ye are though, I am nae quite sure what is goin' on, but ye are invisible tae everyone else. Weel, everyone but fey. But we've got glamours in our blood, it's no surprise I can see through them. Come along lass."

I watched him closely. I wasn't sure if I could trust him. Was it another trick? Another lie? That's when I remembered what Stone and Nixie had told me about fey. They couldn't lie, though they could twist their words enough to make things sound as they desired, but he *told* me that he was going to help me get out of here.

He told me not to shift, but I didn't even know what I had shifted into. My body felt so similar to how my dragon form had felt, just smaller. My dragon pressed forward, offering her instincts and knowledge, allowing me to move this new body fluidly.

Marcus looked back at me a couple of times.

"Amazin'. In all my years ..."

I looked up at him, not understanding what he was so amazed about. In this form I couldn't speak. I would have to wait. But I was going to be free.

Chapter 42

Stone

The drugs left my system, but I remained groggy as I started to come too. There was a moment of complete confusion, but as I sat up and shook my head, it all rushed back. Audrey being lifted out of here by the Braden Clan.

A murderous rage surged through my blood. I needed to stand, move, burn off the fiery energy that begged to be let free. It wasn't long before I dashed off to find York and Drake. I recalled them following me as I raced to the domed room. The hallways were awash with people. It was the busiest I had seen the compound since I arrived. Different paranormals rushed about, with only a few sparing me a glance.

I quickly lost what little patience I had. In moments like this, I had to keep my head. But with Audrey abducted, it was difficult. I grabbed a witch passing by and demanded she tell me where York was. The witch led me to his office before scurrying off again, probably too scared to speak.

Drake and York were already in the office, which was packed with other officers of the York Clan. York's office was the opposite of Jacobs', who held meetings in a large spacious room, relishing the trappings of his title. York's office was cramped with bookshelves which lined the walls. Ancient, wicked looking weapons were also perched here and there among the tomes. York sat behind a large mahogany desk that was dwarfed by his size. Papers were scattered across it, files opened. Drake paced to the left of York's desk.

Drake saw me first, his eyes flashed, and his pupils changed to reptilian silts. He rushed forward, a snarl twisting across his lips. I brought up my arms defensively, but the drug was still affecting me and I was too slow. He slammed me against the bookshelves. The wood pressing into my spine.

"You did this," his voice was deeper, gritty. Less Drake and more a mix of him and the dragon that was never far from the surface.

My anger flared, I knocked his arms back and pushed him backwards. My cells reforming to give me the strength I needed to check his rage.

"No. I didn't," I spat through gritted teeth.

Drake started to growl, his thighs flexing as if he was getting ready to throw himself at me again. I bent my knees getting ready for the attack.

"Stop! Now," York demanded from his desk, now standing with his wings outspread. "Drake control yourself."

Drake slowly straightened his back, his eyes never regaining their human roundness in the pupils. His movements were stiff, muscles still ready to attack at any given moment. My own were strained, ready to fight again. Adrenaline pumped through my veins, demanding I take some sort of actions. I curbed the frantic need by reminding myself what was at stake. I wouldn't be able to rescue Audrey by myself.

The thought of her alone again burned my blood. In the hands of the clan I had once worked for, the clan I had once called *family*. I had spilled blood in their name. These thoughts almost brought me to my knees. She was undoubtedly scared out of her mind. Gods, help me if I started to think about what they would do to her. If I started down that path, I'd probably shift into an animal and fly after her alone, as foolish and stupid as that would be. At least I would be with her.

Goddammit. I needed to go. She needed me.

"What are we waiting for?" I asked, trying to focus on the task ahead of us. Logically I knew we had to come up with a plan. We needed more information. But logic became secondary when Audrey was in danger. Every fiber of my being demanded action.

"I'm waiting to hear from my contact. For now, you need to get yourself prepared if you are planning to fight with us."

York's eyes met mine in a steely determination. I felt hatred and respect for him in equal parts. He was using Audrey's abduction to test my loyalties. To test my restraint.

"Where can I get combat gear? And where the hell have they taken her?"

York sat back a little, he was still as tense as the rest of us. His wings fanned out, still and daunting. The muscles in his arms were taut and ready for action.

"I'll have Drake take you to the armory. If you see Elijah on your way, tell him to come see me."

Drake glared at York with a scowl, but York didn't even acknowledge it. Drake pushed off from the wall he was leaning against and brushed past me. Taking one last look at York, I followed Audrey's father hoping we would get the answers we needed sooner than later.

"Does York have any leads on where they took her?"

"Don't you?" Drake growled from ahead, his shoulders tense. I kept my mouth shut. I knew that if I answered Drake, it would only escalate things between us. He and I would eventually trade blows when we needed to stay focused. Drake led me through the building with ease, fewer paranormals passing us than before, but when they did they gave Drake wide berth.

Drake led us back to the dome room. Around the edges of the room were scattered pillars behind which a door had been hidden. Drake unlocked it with a code from a small keypad beside it. Inside was a storage room filled with combat gear, non-perishable foods, and other necessities for battle.

"Was anyone else taken?" I asked, Nixie on my mind. She and Audrey had been talking not long before Audrey had been abducted.

"No. Just Audrey."

"Can I get Nixie some gear too, then? We were in the same unit. I know what she'll want."

Drake agreed with a nod, and I pulled out clothing I knew would suit her. When Drake left the room, I changed quickly. Then I followed him out, carrying a bundle of clothing tucked under an arm for Nixie. Now I only had to find her.

"Do you know where Nixie is?" I asked as I emerged from the room. Drake's back was pressed against the pillar.

"Here, guppy!" Nixie strode forward, her eyes shone with determination. "Those for me?"

Nixie grabbed the extra combat fatigues from my hands and headed right into the room like she owned the place. She came out a few minutes later, all dressed in black, like Drake and I. Her hair was pulled back into a tight ponytail. Now we could do little more than wait until York gathered more information.

In the logical part of my mind, I knew that we were waiting to hear word from York's man on the inside while we chose a best course of action. But I couldn't think past the black suited man that had taken her. He had worn the same tactical gear I had worn as a member of Braden family's spec ops team. I had thought myself justified. Everything that I stole, every person I "liberated," I had thought it was for the best.

I slammed my hand against the wall. Audrey might have never looked at me like a monster, but dammit if I didn't prove her wrong. My past weighed heavily on my mind. Whatever was happening to her now, I would always blame myself for it.

"Time to head out," York announced from the doorway. He looked almost as angry as Drake. He was filling his position as Audrey's new parental figure well, and I respected his decision to treat her like kin. But she was mine.

I wanted to brush past him. I wanted to *show* that she was mine. I restrained myself. He was my only way to her. I would play nice. For now.

***

I twitched in my seat as the helicopter shuddered in the wind. Nixie sat next to me. Her skin was a little greener than usual, and her eyes were shut tight. Her lips moved in silent mutters. She hated the sky. Across from Nixie and me sat the Valkyrie, Elijah, and the witch Imogen all together. Elijah kept giving Imogen a brutally cold look, even for him. She,

311

on the other hand, parried with a smile. It made me wonder if she had a screw loose in her head. She was looking death in the face and smiling. The Valkyrie kept watching the skies around us.

Drake had shifted into his dragon form the moment York gave the command to move out. He and York both flew close to the two helicopters that carried the rest of us.

The forest beneath us was never ending. The distance we had already traveled small and insignificant. Something was calling me further and further into the direction we were headed. My leg bounced with my impatience. The Eurocopter EC155, a military model, couldn't go fast enough. I didn't even want to think how York had got his hands on this deadly machine.

My skin felt tight with my anxiety as if I needed to change forms. I straightened my back, instead, and tried to get more comfortable. Nothing would calm me until I knew Audrey was safe.

Normally, I was cheered when Nixie and I had to fly together. I always got a kick out of her hatred for the sky. But even that familiar memory didn't break the steady stream of dark thoughts now passing through my mind. I used to be one of the torturers. I knew what they would be doing to her. I could feel it on my skin as if it was happening to me. How could I have let them take her? I would never forgive myself. I had promised I would protect her. And I had failed.

I kept shifting in my seat. It had only been a day since she went missing. But a lot could happen in a day. From what Drake had told me, I knew she was alive. Before we left he had mentioned that Marcus the fey was their last, and best, undercover agent in Braden Clan. The others had all been killed in combat or found out and punished accordingly. This was more than a rescue mission for Audrey, it was also an extraction mission to save him as well. I nodded absently, I prayed to the gods he could help her in some way.

We were getting closer. The pilot was informing us of our location. The ground flew past as I watched. Though I'd grown distant from my past life, it still felt like I was returning home in some ways. But it would never be my home again. The past didn't matter anymore. My home was with Audrey.

The helicopter started to slow its pace and we began our descent to the ground. The Valkyrie scooted to the edge of her seat, gripping the bar above her and leaping to the ground. I followed suit on the other side. The area was mostly clear of trees, but the forest thickened at the edges of the clearing. I had no idea where we were—not exactly. Judging by the geography I had seen, I would have put us about thirty miles out from the Braden compound.

York darted down from the sky, while Drake followed slower and more powerfully. The Valkyrie nodded for the others to exit the craft.

I paced restlessly as Drake, who had chosen to stay in his dragon form, descended. York walked over to him, a grim look on his face. His tail twitched and wings fluttered. His apprehension seeped into me. His fists were clenched tight.

"We haven't heard from Marcus. He should have contacted us the moment Audrey stepped into that building. Drake wants to attack. I don't know how long I can hold him off. And gods dammit, Stone, would you stop that infuriating pacing?" York snarled at me.

"Do not tell me how to act when *my mate* is in there." I had charged him, my body shifting instinctually to match his height, my gaze slipping beyond his shoulder to glare at Drake.

"What if it was Drake?"

I kept my voice low out of respect for their bond. If Elijah and Nixie didn't know, that was his and Drake's business. Though I wouldn't be surprised if Elijah knew already.

"You're not the only one that has something at stake here. Remember that."

I growled, my anger still bright and hot. But I understood. We were all on edge. We all wanted to get her back. I started to pace again, the feeling that something was wrong unrelenting. I had to move, I had to do something, *anything*. Drake blew a bit of smoke toward York as he headed over to exchange words with his own mate. Drake seemed to be showing his affection, but it also betrayed his anxiety.

Twilight started to descend. The sky deepened from a light blue to a purple hue. My anxiety intensified with nightfall. It felt like my skin would snap and give way at any moment. My thoughts never strayed far from

313

Audrey. Every moment we waited, she would endure worse torture. Deep and ugly memories wormed their way from deep inside me, morphing in such a way that those I had harmed were now replaced with images of Audrey. Like I had done this to her. But, having let them take her, I guess I had.

I knew the types of torture and the way it would be implemented. I had perfected the art while in Clan Braden. We didn't take prisoners to let them live. It was our policy to extract information in a way that left it untainted by deception or lies. And this could only be accomplished by taking control of every fiber of a prisoner's being.

Out of the corner of my eye I saw Drake's head pop up as if he heard something in the distance. I watched him closely. His nostrils flared and his slit, reptilian eyes narrowed.

I expanded my senses as much as I could. I closed my eyes and focused on the scents and sounds around me. And there it was, a scent that filled me with hope, *her* scent—smoke and lavender. My eyes snapped open.

I ran through the familiar trees toward her scent. I dodged around underbrush fluidly, in the way only a shifter can. Nothing would get in my way. My heart pounded in my chest. The sole thought that dominated my existence in that moment was the simple fact that she was close.

"Turn th' other way. They are right behin' us." Marcus's voice was urgent, and he spoke quickly.

Marcus moved gracefully, but for a fey in his natural element, that was expected. His kind could bend nature to their will, as he did now to clear the way for him. Audrey was nowhere to be seen, but her unique scent was so close. Had he left her behind? My breathing was ragged. My head spinning. I could smell her, but *where*? Had she not made it?!

"Where is she?" I roared rushing Marcus, pinning him to a tree.

"Pal, she's right behin' me," he said pointing to an open space where there were only plants. Nothing. Did he think me stupid? A bloody rage clouded my mind, tinging my vision red. Everything else fell away. There was only Marcus and my anger. And my anger demanded blood.

I punched him ruthlessly in the face.

"Where is she?"

I was desperate. After thinking she was so close only to find nothing. My lungs came in trembling, erratic puffs of rage. My ribs felt tight. I was out of control, desolate with fury.

"Gabriel!" her voice soothed me instantly.

I turned and Audrey was there, naked as though she had just shifted. New scars covered her body, along with dried blood. I pulled off my shirt it as quickly as I could. I wrapped it around her, pleased that it extended past her thighs.

"Audrey …"

I ran my hands through her hair, cupped the back of her head, and pulled her in for a kiss. I touched her lips and I felt my whole body sigh. She was safe. I pulled her closer.

"Stone, come 'en. We have tae go, pal."

Only then did I realize the woods were full of noise. Heavy footsteps, the crack of branches, shouted commands. A witch spotted us between the trees and hurled attack spells. A barrage of fireballs sizzled through the air, exploding against tree trunks only for crackling lightning to follow.

I pushed Audrey down to protect her from a spell that had come dangerously close. The woods were tactically better for us. We had more cover for protection. But while the witch had long-ranged attacks, Audrey and I were limited to close-combat. We needed to keep moving.

Our reunion would have to wait. I pulled Audrey along. A bolt of lightning seared through the air by our heads, splashing the warmth of magical energy upon us as it crackled into a tree. If that had hit us … well, we likely wouldn't be moving. We were approaching the clearing now, but Audrey was barely keeping up. I knew she was tired. I knew she was in pain. Hope grew in my heart when I saw Drake's tail in the clearing. He was already fighting on the other side of the helicopter where he had drawn most of them away from us.

Nixie hugged Marcus briefly before she shoved him into the helicopter. It was already whirling back to life. The noise was deafening. I shoved Audrey ahead of me hoping she would get to the safety of the helicopter. The witch behind us was relentless. She continued throwing deadly bolts of energy. I snuck a peek behind me just as she emerged into the clearing, determination written all over her face. Her eyes locked with mine. There was no other choice. I had to protect my mate. I knew who she was aiming for. The next bolt would surely kill.

I protected Audrey. I wrapped her in my arms as I shielded her back with my own. I couldn't know if this would be the end for us. But I did know that if I let that bolt hit her she wouldn't survive. She was too weak.

Time slowed as she twisted in my arms to look back at me. To make sure I was there. With her. Like we were meant to be. And then her eyes widened. Her mouth contorted in a scream.

I felt it surge through my entire body. Somehow I stayed on my feet, blocking Audrey from all harm. The energy continued, flowing through me with destructive power. A million slivers of pain raced through my body. My organs spasmed and crawled with electric fire. My skin felt raw. I tried to hold onto my form, but the blast was too much. It all happened so slowly. I could almost feel each cell as it reverted, seeking a familiar shape.

My original form. I couldn't breathe as I toppled.

Chapter 43

AUDREY

A phantom shock went through me when the first bolt hit. My nerves tingled, yet I felt no pain. The witch used her magic to conjure sizzling lightning that arced through the air, straight toward us. When the second bolt hit Stone, I felt its strike right over my heart, like an echo of his pain. The shock electrified me, a kind of heat that spread through my blood. Tears sprung to my eyes. Pain radiated through my limbs as the electric shock made my entire body shudder to a stop. I stumbled, my breath lost.

A scream ripped from my throat. Gabriel lay sprawled on the ground in his true form. I couldn't leave him. The helicopter blades beat incessantly behind me. Everything was distant. I fell to my knees beside to him. I didn't know what to do. I was desperate for something. Anything. Sobs quaked through me and my hot tears dropped from my chin to his scarred chest. A hole gaped below his ribs on the right side. His chest heaved, the breath coming in labored gasps. I felt his pain in my own heart.

"No. You promised … Gabriel!"

My heart tore itself into a million pieces. Sorrow stung my veins, pricked my eyes with tears, fed my heart with the shattered glass of loss which then filtered into my entire body. My lungs choked at my attempts to breath. The lump in my throat only allowed ragged gasps. His pain-glazed eyes looked up into the sky. Blood poured from his wound. I could do nothing but hope he could somehow repair himself.

Someone shouted something somewhere. Hands pulled at me, gentle and insistent, but I jerked away. Everything blurred. The images were vague. Blended. Who was it? I growled loudly. I became his shield, as he had been mine. I was oblivious to the chaos surrounding us. My hands counted the stitches in his clothes.

My full attention was on Stone. My lips found his, now cold and clammy from blood loss and the chill of the early evening. Dark stubble dusted his cheeks and chin. His real form was more beautiful than any other shape he had taken. My hands grasped at him. His scruff scraped against the skin on the tips of my fingers. I couldn't let him go. I wouldn't. Tears filled my eyes as I shook my head.

Without thinking, I could feel myself moving. My form shook and broke apart, the bonds of my human shape expanding, twisting, *changing* into that of a full dragon. My dragon spirit guided the actions. I felt a claw—my claw—slip beneath my scales. My dragon side innately knew how to open the way to my heart. As I reached inside to a piece of it, a deafening roar filled my ears. Was that my voice? The pain was unimaginable, far beyond the pain of torture I had suffered. But the pain of losing Gabriel after I had only just found him was too great.

I held a bloody, beating piece of my own heart in my dark talons. Like all normal hearts, mine was bound to me by the passions and experiences that had accumulated in it. Dragon hearts, I now understood, were the core of our mystic power. And this precious, intimate thing would soon join us together. Now that half my heart was missing, the other half fluttered in my chest at a faster pace. It stuttered at first, painfully. I laid the piece in my hands over his heart and whispered to him.

"*I love you.*"

He looked at me then, his eyes still clouded with pain, and smiled. He brought his hand up to touch my scales and I leaned in. I knew my words were lost in the noise, but I hoped he understood. As quickly and painlessly as I could, I used the tip of my claw to cut an incision above his heart. I pushed the piece of my heart into his chest, watching as it wove together. His eyes widened as my heart sunk into his chest. It seemed to

318

come alive as it touched his blood, insinuating itself into his body. I swallowed hard. Part of me was scared it wouldn't work. Scared I would lose him. But it strengthened his slowing heart, morphing as it did, absorbing into him just as my dragon knew that it would.

When our hearts were fully conjoined, the sensation was like sinking and twisting into something new. In that instant, a bridge formed to connect us. And then the pain ended and I was filled with something else. A kind of peace. I had never felt as peaceful as I did in that moment. Then came the pain. It overtook the previous peace I had found. The battle still raged around us. Spells glanced off my scales, painful yet distant. None of that mattered, though. Stone was safe.

I pulled away, my focus becoming loose. The corners of my vision swam. My already weak body could do no more. An inward ripple reverted me to my normal form. I lay next to him. The transfer of half my heart had drained my last reserves.

Gabriel was already passed out from the pain. He had lost consciousness during the binding. Still, he held my hand. My tired eyes lovingly took in the sight of him, bringing my free hand to touch his cheek. I smiled as tears spilled from my eyes. I couldn't focus.

I was ready to say goodbye to him. He would live with my heart beating strong inside of him. I could bear no more. I could die peacefully knowing I had saved him. There was no way my body could survive. I was too weak from the torture. This would surely kill me. I couldn't save anyone else. Only him. But that was enough. At least I had saved my love.

"I am so sorry," I whispered. "I just wanted you forever."

Chapter 44

STONE

I wish that I could have answered her that day. I wish I could have told her I was hers as she was mine. That I didn't ever plan on letting her go. I was barely conscious when she pressed her heart into mine, everything else was lost in the pain. Her words came to me from a great distance. I wanted to reassure her. To tell her I was hers. I was hers the moment I saw her wedged in the crevice formed by the wall and floor of her cell. I would always be hers.

I reached to pull her close, but she was no longer there. My eyes shot open. She was nowhere to be found. Bare walls surrounded me on all sides. To my side, medical equipment beeped softly in time with my pulse. A plain t-shirt and scrubs replaced my combat fatigues. My head pounded explosively. The pain in my head was only intensified by my shock.

"Easy there, warrior," York's voice came from the opposite side of the room. When I twisted my body to face him, I winced at the pain in my muscles.

"We had to separate you two. She needed to recover, and you were delirious. Weak as you were, you kept trying to keep people away from her."

I released the breath I had been holding. She was safe.

"And you needed to recover as well after being struck with that bolt. What do you remember?"

My heartbeat felt strange, like there were two tempos fighting for dominance. I touched my chest. There was fresh scar tissue there. My eyes met York's.

"Everyone has conveniently forgotten about your skin being so … marked. Marcus did the decent thing and put a glamour around you as soon as he could. I'm sorry to have violated your privacy, even inadvertently. Nixie, Drake, and I were all too close—we saw what lies beneath. With their permission, I had Nixie's and Drake's minds wiped. I know enough of your people to know how sacred you hold your true form. I will have Imogen wipe mine as well as soon as we finish our conversation here, should you desire it. I've already had her take care of the preliminaries. She knows where the memory is located, but I made sure she doesn't know what it is. She never will. I promise you that."

I stared at the leader of one of the most powerful clans, confused at what he was saying. The secret of our true form had stayed hidden until now. He was giving up valuable information. Cain Braden would never do that.

"I respect all paranormals. I also respect that each race has its own secrets. I will not use that against them." He stared distantly out the window as he said this.

I knew right then and there that I respected him. I also knew that he spoke from experience. Too many people knew the secrets of the gargoyles. It was likely why so few of them were left.

"It isn't easy," he sighed heavily. "Being their mates, I mean. Having a piece of them in your heart. The wildness of it. The depths and heights of their passions. The power."

"Things being easy aren't as important as being with her." My words came out low and intense. I wasn't angry. I wasn't trying to challenge. I was simply telling him the truth.

"You don't understand. Not yet. To have a piece of their heart is to have part of their strength, their power, and their emotions, too. She is now as much as piece of you as you are of her. Her heart is literally yours to protect now."

And with that, he left. I still didn't completely trust the man. While I was grateful to him for offering to erase his memories, magic wasn't always a guarantee. Power was a tempting thing for any person, but to a gargoyle who ruled a very powerful clan? Gargoyles had been one of the first paranormal races to turn on the Council. And he had a lot of power now that two dragons had joined his clan. I couldn't shake my suspicions of him. But all that could be saved for later.

For now, I only wanted to find Audrey.

Turns out, finding her was the easy part. Drake stood guard outside her door, refusing to allow anyone in. When I arrived, I waited for him to move. He stared down at me. I had kept a form a little taller than usual, but I had taken a liking to it. Maybe this would become my new normal.

"Thank you, for saving her. There's no turning back, now. You carry a heavy burden."

I nodded. He stepped out of the way and headed down the hallway, his gait slow as though he wasn't quite ready to leave his post.

I closed my eyes as her scent enveloped me. There was the subtle creak of a door opening. Before I could open my eyes, I felt a light touch on my lips and a small giggle. It was a beautiful sound. A sound I cherished.

I took her hips in my hands. I didn't even open my eyes. On instinct alone I sought her out and kissed her hard. We had almost lost each other. The door clicked locked behind us under my hand. I fully intended on making full use of our time alone together.

I pressed my hips against her, pulling her body flush to mine. Blinking my eyes open to watch her reaction. She gasped slightly, not expecting the sudden movement. I would never again let her go.

"You said you wanted to keep me forever," I whispered, pulling away from her lips. She stood before me, her hair brushed straight, glossy, and clean. Her skin was pale under the harsh lighting. She had been placed in a room similar to my own. It wasn't the same as the medical bay, where beds had been separated by curtains. She nuzzled her cheek against mine. She nodded against my cheek, bristling the stubble there.

I remembered her touching it before. She knew how much I liked it. She brought her hand up to run her fingers against it again. Such delicate hands. This stopped me short. Her lips moved their way up my neck.

"Audrey ..." My voice was unrecognizable.

"Hmm ..."

"Did …" Gods, I couldn't even get it out, even if I had to know. "Did anyone …"

She stopped me with a word.

"No," she said. Her voice wavered, though not, I think, because she was ashamed. After all we had been through, it was probably hard to believe we had made it. She feared that speaking it out loud would somehow change her answer. And then I couldn't stop myself. I had to touch her skin. I had to know that she belonged to me as much as I belonged to her.

My hands slid under her thighs, lifting her so she could wrap her legs around my waist. I could feel heat radiating from her. She clawed off my shirt as I kissed every part of her I could reach. This time was different from our first, gentle coupling. This was a desperate, unquenchable thirst for each other.

I helped her remove my shirt the rest of the way. I wanted to do just the same. I couldn't wait—wouldn't. I ripped the plain white t-shirt down the middle. I bent my head to her breast kissing the soft, supple skin. Her body leaned into me, tilting her neck upward as she arched her back. Her chest pushed forward. I moaned. It was all becoming too much. I was consumed with my need for her.

I lowered her to the floor, her legs disengaging reluctantly. We backed to the bed. She fell, with her pant-clad legs slightly spread, an invitation for me to rip them from her body. Desperate to take her clothes off, I tugged at the soft material that covered her legs.

Her legs kicked the last of the fabric away. Her panties needed to go. Lust had driven me to this point; I was enamored with her body. Audrey sat up, beginning to fumble with the draw-strings of my pants, pulling them loose. Her eyes peeked up at me, her tongue darting out to touch her bottom lip.

I released my hold on the shape I used around others, wanting to be in my real form with her. Where the bolt had gone through me, the skin was leathery and raised. Compared to other scars, it looked especially brutal. But there wasn't even the slightest hint of disgust on her face. She brought her head closer to it and brushed her lips there. My senses withdrew almost completely, save the point she touched with her lips. Her hands moved over my back, stroking old scars and making me shiver.

Slowly pushing her backwards, pressing my chest against hers, I laid her flat on the mattress. Our lips danced together, in a rhythm we both knew. I was greedy with my need to kiss her. I wanted to taste her *everywhere*. My lips drew away from hers and I pressed a small kiss to her chin before dragging my lips down the column of her neck. Her fingers scraped against my skull, sending a hot jolt to my straining groin.

Her bare legs wrapped around my waist, her hips pressed upwards against mine. I hissed against her collar bone when my tip touched her. She whispered my name, saying it as a plea. I nibbled gently as I positioned myself. Her head was thrown back, eyes closed, a sweet smile on her face. She was absolutely stunning.

A lusty moan escaped her lips, and unable to resist her any longer, I pushed inside. She shuddered, her smile transforming from a quiet moan back into that sweet, satisfied smile. We moved together. Our bodies responded on a basic, primal level.

***

I didn't wake up this time fearful, not knowing where she was. She was in my arms. I hugged her tighter and buried my nose in her hair. I never wanted to leave. I was perfectly happy here with her in this place. When I kissed the top of her head, I felt her stir. I looked down and saw her open her eyes. Her fingers traced my heart. Our heart.

"Do you regret it?" I hoped that my fear didn't shine through. This was a sacred thing. Not something to take lightly or impulsively, as part of me feared Audrey had done.

"I could never regret it."

She bit her lip. She had more to say, so I waited for her to speak.

"That day that you showed up in the white room, remember how I told you to go? How it sounded like I was trying to save you? That was a lie."

I recalled it. I thought she had been trying to warn me and Dallas. To get out before the guards came. Thinking about it warmed me even now. I tried to catch her eye, but she averted her gaze.

"What do you mean it was a lie?" I drew lazy designs on her skin with my fingers.

"I had hoped you would take me with you. But I couldn't say 'save me' without saying 'Save yourself, too.' And you did, Gabriel. You saved me."

Her words rang in my head, loud and clear. I saved her? That was far from the truth, really. She had saved me. I wouldn't the man I was now if it hadn't been for the way she had looked at me with her big, beautiful eyes that day we first met. She may have thought she was a monster then, and maybe even now, at times. But in truth, she was the loveliest of us all.

"I love you, Audrey."

But she had already fallen asleep in my arms once again.

Chapter 45

Audrey

A few weeks had passed and with no word or further incursions from the Braden Clan or the Vedenins. I couldn't believe they would just give up, but at least for now we had a little time to rest and come up with a plan. My father was trying hard to accept Stone as a part of my life. Xavier was there every step of the way. I appreciated his help. He had a calming effect on my father.

It was only a week after they rescued me before I was fully healed. Then we finally had our dinner together, Xavier, my father, Stone, and me. That's when they told me they were true mates. Xavier himself held a piece of my father's heart in his own body. That night, Stone embraced me tighter than he had any night before. He knew how their story affected me. I was upset about the loss of my mother, but also happy that my father had found love somewhere in his time of need. I didn't doubt my father when he told me he truly loved my mother. That he would have saved her if he could.

My father continued to tell me more about my mother, from whom I'd inherited some abilities. Marcus and I had discovered this that night at the Braden's headquarters. Dragons generally stuck with their own kind. Apparently, I was the first, and maybe only, dragon-were combination.

I continued to work on gaining control of my other form, which was like a memento from the mother I would never meet. What's more, through the heart-bond we shared, Stone could somehow *feel* how to shift into dragon form, a feat no other shape-shifter had ever accomplished.

When he shifted for the first time, he was a midnight black dragon. It didn't come naturally to him, like it did to me. It was actually funny, seeing him try to fly. Flying as a dragon wasn't quite like any other animal. I, on the other hand, caught on fairly quickly.

***

"Audrey, could I have a word with you?"

My father stood tall, looking slightly annoyed for some reason. He was still getting used to having to ask permission to see me. But Stone and I had to stay close. Our heart-bond, so fresh and new, required time spent together before it could strengthen.

Our hearts were still getting accustomed to being combined. It was both an amazing and an uncomfortable experience. His heart, which was now part of mine, and mine as a part of his, worked together rather than separately. Being closer to him felt most natural.

"Okay," I answered quietly, pulling away from Stone. But he reached out and snagged me back, his hand tightening around mine. Apprehension freckled his eyes in the form of tiny green specks.

"It's okay, Stone."

I touched his cheek, bringing his attention back to me. His eyes softened to a lively swirl of the pale pink and white of his love. I smiled.

"Come back soon," he said with a kiss, letting me go.

I felt his eyes on us the entire time we walked away. I wanted to stay with him, but I was curious what my father had to say. We hadn't talked much since I had returned to the York facility. We headed toward the dome room, which had already been repaired.

"I have something for you. Wait here."

With that, he left me at the edge of the living area and disappeared behind one of the columns. The dome room was meant as a safe place for air paranormals who wanted to take flight. Since my father still had

327

problems controlling his dragon, even after all these years, it was easier for him and Xavier to train inside the dome room.

My hands fidgeted in front of me, my heart beating a little faster. It was difficult to stand still when I felt my heart being drawn back to its other half. I stared hard at nothing really, getting lost in the invisible pull that tugged me back in the direction of my love.

"Audrey." Xavier was suddenly standing in front of me and touched my shoulder lightly.

I backed away from his touch. I still wasn't comfortable with him. I hadn't really been comfortable with anyone's touch except Stone's since I had been rescued.

"I ... I was ... waiting for—"

My father came out with his hands behind his back. He gave Xavier a loving glance.

"I have something for you, Audrey."

Xavier smiled at my father as if he knew what was about to happen. When my father stood in front of me my stomached knotted.

"It's a little later than I was hoping, but ..."

From behind his back my father pulled a black, raggedy looking stuffed dragon. Aiden. Still missing the same eye, and some new scratches on his face, but unmistakable.

My fingers brushed the soft fabric as the distance between me and my childhood toy fell away. I looked up at my father with tears in my eyes.

"You ..." the words out came out, but difficultly, "you saved him."

"Of course I did. I'd do anything for you."

My father pulled me close and kissed my forehead as he pressed my old friend into my hands. The door behind us opened, and I turned to see Stone standing there with a worried frown on his face. Our bond drew him to me, and me to him. Did he feel the change my emotions? On my side the bond wasn't quite that strong yet.

"Stone, he saved Aiden," I whispered. Stone pulled me into his chest, the only thing blocking me from the beating of his heart was Aiden. My favorite toy snuggled between us.

"Thank you, Drake," Stone said.

He pulled me away a little later and took us back to our room. I never let my grip of Aiden loosen. The toy meant even more to me now. It was a symbol that after all those years in hell, my father hadn't given up on me. One day, I would get the full story of what happened during our time apart. But for now, I had all the proof of his love I needed.

***

After the rescue mission, Elijah remained as distant as usual, but worked closely with Xavier. Their partnership seemed odd to me, but Elijah was a mystery I still didn't understand. Probably never would. Xavier, though, seemed stressed by whatever it was they were working on. Whenever it came up, his wings twitched.

I spent most of my days with Stone and Nixie learning about the world that I was now a part of, but also separate and shielded from. Nixie was still uncomfortable within the walls of the compound, but she had told me she was adjusting. She was different after we arrived back from the rescue mission. Maybe her loyalties had shifted that day, after seeing the cruelty of the Braden Clan.

After learning about what the Braden and Vedenin clans were up to, we couldn't just hide here, safe. We had to try and protect other Elder Races. When I told Stone that I wanted to stay and help, he nodded and kissed my forehead. He told me he understood. Stone had called us true mates. I didn't care about the label. The only thing I knew to be true was that I loved him.

We were sitting outside, my head on his shoulder, his hand entwined in my own. His song, the one his mother sang to him, emerged almost indistinctly from between his lips. He crooned the tones, much like a bird might sing the lullaby. This time, I allowed myself to drift on the lilting cadences of the song. I didn't fight to stay awake. I was content. For now, all was right in my world.

For once, I felt completely free.

Epilogue

ELIJAH

I watched from the edge of the forest. They never noticed me. She never noticed me. I did not know what interested me in her, but I couldn't stop thinking about her. She would be my downfall. It had been a foolish mistake to wander in her mind for so long. I had become attached to certain memories. Granted, those were memories she would be better without. Yet, instead of feeding on them and taking them away from her, I watched them. I lived them with her. I enjoyed every dark moment of her mind and delighted in her agony. At times, when she relived the terror of those memories, she may have even noticed my spirit form lingering there, in her memory.

Audrey had clung to me at times, using me as a security blanket. The darkness I emitted had brought her a warped sense of comfort. It was an odd feeling. One I cannot say that I enjoyed.

I couldn't get rid of the feeling of her nails biting into this body I possessed. The feeling was trapped in my mind. I would stare and remember every part of my body her slight frame touched. How I wanted to curl around her and offer her something to stop the shivering. I could not warm her. I did not radiate warmth. But the fear. The fear had been *marvelous*. It had slid against my entire body, with every touch. It was the most pleasurable experience.

And yet when I watched her trying to learn how to shift with her shape-shifter mate, I couldn't help but wish that her eyes wouldn't sparkle quite so brightly. I was entranced by this damaged woman. The one I watched now, while not unscathed, was no longer the same. She would not shiver in my arms as she once did. Still I couldn't tear myself away from the scene.

What was wrong with me?

"I knew I would find you here."

"You have been staring for a while yourself, Xavier," I stated, my eyes still trained on Audrey and her shape-shifter. I knew that his reasons for watching were much different from my own.

"Yes, but I am still intrigued to find out how Audrey could have possibly captured the interest of a wraith."

Xavier stepped a little closer, watching me with narrowed eyes. His protective suspicion was unnecessary. His wings were folded tightly to his back which was tense, his fists and jaw were clenched; his tension could only have been captured in volumes.

"You disapprove?" I asked, watching Audrey and Stone.

"No, he is a good match for her. But I do disapprove of the way you watch her. You look as if you want to steal her and break her all over again."

I was silent for a moment, allowing him to draw his own conclusions. I had no qualms about who and what I was.

"You came here for a reason. What is it?"

"Yes. I have a mission for you. Far from here." His voice was even harsher than it had been moments before. He was resisting his instincts to attack me.

"She is not yours," I said looking back at Audrey.

"No. But she's not yours either."

He spoke the truth. Though I didn't seek to possess Audrey. Just to quench my thirst of these unnatural *feelings*.

"The task. Will you do it?"

"I will."

End of Book One

Appendix

CLANS:

Vedenin: Russian family that had captured Audrey—the clan that wants more power and to control new emerging paranormals.

York Clan: One of the most powerful families trying to protect the new paranormals and wants to eventually reform the paranormal world so it's not so divided.

Braden: Stone's family—the clan that is trying to destroy the emerging paranormals in order to make the shift of balance of power in the paranormal world in favor of the *were* clans.

Long Clan: Primarily Asian clan—one of the top families ranking next to Braden, but still beneath York

PARANORMAL RACES:

Dawon: A fancier term for a were-tiger—originally from Hindu mythology—they are slightly bigger than other were-tigers and from different lineages. (earth)

Djinn: Also known as genies. They have incredible power, unless they are captured, and the line "Memberikan saya tiga" is said, then they become servants to their "master" until the three wishes are used up. (spirit)

Dryad: Wood creatures who live in trees and protect the forest. They can manipulate the element of earth, but rarely do. These creatures are nonviolent. (earth)

Dwarf: Short sturdy creatures that once lived in mountains. They tend to be hairy and silent. (earth)

Nepilim: Half angel-half human or half-demon-half human. They are stronger more agile than a human, longer lived, and have wings that either are feathered or bat-like depending on their origin. (air)

Gargoyles: Grey-toned skin creatures, wings, and fierce warriors. Once were the guards to the council. (air/earth)

Mermaids: Water creatures that cannot leave the water, with strange toned hair colors—usually ranges from dark blues to coral like colors. (water)

Sirens: Water creatures that use their siren song to persuade people. They can live on land for extended periods of time but must go back to the water in order to regain their strength—usually their hair color ranges from dark blues to blondes (green is rare). They have both a human form and a water form. Their skin turns scaly, fins grow from their feet, their hands become webbed and clawed. Eyes get bigger and gills grow. (water)

Shifters: There are three categories. (earth)

Human-shifter: They can change into any type of human form.

Animal-shifter: They have one human form and can change into any animal.

Shape-shifter: They can change into any human or animal form.

Stone Giant: A-senee-ki-wakw—a race of stone giants, the first people Gluskab, the god that brought all giants into existence, created but then were destroyed because they crushed other animals and injured the earth with their great size. From Eastern Canada: Torngat Mountains. Legends from Abenaki. (earth)

Valkyries: Norse god warriors who are fierce human-like warriors. They can come up with complex strategies in seconds flat (earth).

Werecreatures: Contains all different kinds of animals. Werewolves, werecats, etc. These are humans with animal spirits entwined with their human side. They have more animal like instincts and characteristics. (earth)

Witches/Wizards/Warlocks: Witches are female magic users—witches have the power to summon or force wraiths from their bodies. Males who can use magic are wizards, though they do not have power over wraiths. Warlocks are similar to wizards, but like witches have the power over wraiths. Warlocks are very rare. (earth)

Wraiths: Demonic spirits that can take over a human body. Their human forms have pitch black eyes and spiked teeth. They are heartless, emotionless. Rare and very dangerous—full powers unknown. (spirit)

Zanas: Zana are characters in fairy-tales that are basically fairies that protect children who are in the woods and other good people that need help. They are also known for being able to impart gifts, like dancing, kindness, beauty, and luck to babies still in the womb. (earth)

REBIRTH CREATURES:

Dragon-shifters: A human and a dragon spirit separate from each other, don't tend to influence each other. Thought to be extinct. (earth, fire, air)

Water Nymphs: have the powers of both a mermaid and siren and can control water—only water nymphs can do this, and partial shift. (water)

Phoenixes: They don't have a bird form, but instead have feathers that extend down their necks to their back. If someone were to take a feather from a full grown Phoenix, they would be able to survive any type of death, once. Life = one feather. It takes five years for a new feather to grow. This is extremely painful for a Phoenix if the feather is not given willingly – also they could feel the pain of the death of the person holding their feather. (fire)

Unicorn-shifters: When in their unicorn form, they can escape any trap, nothing can lock them in. While they are in human form they can be trapped. They can heal anything while in their human form. If someone were to take the blood of a unicorn while in that form, they would become immortal. (spirit, earth)

Griffins-shifters: They are the kings of all beasts—in other words they can control most were-creatures and animals. Extremely powerful in their human forms, and even more powerful in their beast form. (spirit, earth)

About the Author

Becca Vincenza lives in wonderful Michigan. She has an obsession with candy, her animals and of course books. When she's not wearing her author hat, she's working to pay off her student loans for her acquired English degree.

Stalker Links:

Facebook: https://www.facebook.com/beccavincenza

Website: https://beccavincenzaauthor.wordpress.com/

Newsletter: http://eepurl.com/Z2vwP

Made in the USA
Middletown, DE
23 May 2019